The Root of All Evil

A Murder Mystery

The Root of All Evil

A Murder Mystery

B.K. De Paolis

Merano Writers Ink

Los Angeles

Cover Design by
John Davis
and
Chris Askew

ISBN 978-0615880426
ISBN 0615880428

Printed in the United States of America

The Root of All Evil

ONE

Pin shafts of light sliced through the blinds of the otherwise dark bedroom. Outside, a battering Southern California downpour muffled a loud pop. A silhouette passed across the window. Then all was still as the storm, like some unwilling accomplice, slackened and moved on.

LOS ANGELES 2007

As May West turned the key and opened the door to Sybil Hansen's condo, recurring waves of regret flooded over her like a woman caught in the throes of a doomed love affair. She always thought: why Sybil and not me? They had known each other off and on since childhood.

She once believed her life had promise. After all, her mother had given her a name that she thought would bring her "high yella" daughter attention. Well, another of her mother's many miscalculations. May wanted to dance, but over the years she had lost her ambition to the bottle, the needle, and the street. Her color hadn't helped her one bit, and too many empty promises had done nothing but tarnish her name and her dreams. She'd done a lot of dirty work for a lot of dirty people, but now her dirtiest jobs were cleaning up for Sybil and her girls.

Moving into the condo, May carefully balanced a styrofoam cup of coffee, her purse, umbrella, and coat. You just didn't drop stuff in Sybil's place. She managed to put the coffee on the floor without spilling it and hung her coat in the entry closet. Placing her handbag on the 18th Century French commode and kicking off her shoes, she padded barefoot across deep, plush white carpet.

As she headed to the kitchen, May caught a glimpse of herself in the hall mirror. Not bad. She was happy the hard times and hard work had not diminished her looks. Even without heavy make-up she still looked only thirty-five or maybe thirty-eight, but no more than forty.

There were guys where she danced who told her she didn't look a day over twenty-nine. She knew they were lying, but she listened to their rasping whispers anyway, laughing as she tossed her shoulder-length chestnut brown hair and swung around to a hot salsa beat.

She could still get away with keeping her make-up light, but it was her green eyes that drew all the attention. She enhanced them by adding long, thick artificial lashes and sparkly emerald green eyeshadow even when she was out during the day.

Men liked to look into beautiful, seductive eyes making promises that could only be kept when she was drunk or high. Still, while her face showed no signs of aging, her legs were not holding up as well. Thank God for leg make-up. She had noticed the beginnings of purple threads snaking down her thighs to her knees and remembered her mother's horrible varicose veins, stripped over and over only to leave unsightly scars and unbearable pain. May's worst nightmare was dancing in agony, her legs encased in hideous elastic stockings.

She turned back to the work at hand. Sybil had been good to May, even giving her a job after rehab and her release from CIW in Corona until she started working and found an apartment in Altadena.

Despite her complaints about the way Sybil wanted things, May enjoyed working in her kitchen most. It gleamed with white imported Italian designer cabinets and Miele appliances. Sometimes she wondered why Sybil even bothered having her in. Nothing got dirty, and nothing was ever out of place.

May took a CD from her pocket and stuck it in the Bose player on the counter. Hot Latin rhythms exploded into the kitchen, animating her steps.

She danced every Saturday night frequenting places that would never see an agent or talent scout even though she was one of the hottest salsa dancers in the area. She still had the moves, but the dream of a professional career had died long ago. If she wanted to eat, she had to work. As she moved around wiping the counter tops, she was surprised to find a cup and saucer in the usually immaculate sink. She quickly washed and dried them while keeping the beat with her movements and sipping her lukewarm coffee.

When she opened a cupboard above the sink, there was another surprise. An expensive, multifaceted crystal wine goblet stood like a sparkling diamond in front of plain juice and water glasses.

"Shit, who the hell put this here?" There was no one to hear her, but she voiced her irritation anyway.

She did a quick cha-cha step, grabbed her half-empty styrofoam cup in one hand, the goblet in the other, and carried the fragile beauty to the antique mahogany hutch in the dining area. May thought, as she opened the ornately carved doors, how she could have had such expensive things if she hadn't gotten mixed up with drugs.

"Well, those were the breaks," May muttered and did a quick spin over to the floor-to-ceiling windows, opened the patterned vertical blinds, and looked out. The sky had turned a leaden gray. It had started to rain harder, and her hip began to ache.

"God, will it ever stop?" It had been raining off and on for two weeks.

White roses in a large crystal vase gave off a faintly sweet fragrance. Some stems had begun to drop their petals onto the highly polished table top.

"Maybe she'll get some fresh ones this morning. If not, I'll just change the water. They'll last another couple of days." May spoke to the empty room. Sybil would be at her office by now. Ms. Workaholic never slept in. "Damn it, I wish I could stay in bed. Let someone clean for me."

In Sybil's bedroom, May started to open the blinds but a sudden uneasiness crept over her; some strange compulsion seemed to guide her hand as she slowly pulled the cord, bathing the room in a muted, eerie light. When she turned toward the disheveled bed, a gasp stuck in her throat -- the scream followed.

May stood in shock, wanting to touch, to shake, to awaken the limp form before her. Sybil's body was slumped towards the wall side of the bed; her right hand rested by her side, a gun mere inches away. The .45 round through the head splayed bloody bones and tissue over otherwise perfectly patterned pink silk wallpaper.

TWO

LAPD Detective Stas Nowak worked Robbery-Homicide out of Parker Center. He finished a file and slipped the closed folder into the bottom drawer of his desk. He then took the murder book and placed it on his partner's, Sid Edwards, desk.

The division secretary stuck her head into the squad room and looked up to the wall clock. "You still here? I thought you started your vacation."

"Yeah, I'm just finishing some stuff for Sid, then meeting someone in Santa Monica."

"Hot date?" She smiled as he slipped into his suit jacket.

"Working on it. Taking it kinda slow."

"Well, you looking good. I'd give you a shot at it."

He made a guttural noise of agreement, not sure what the "it" was, and returned to wipe off his desk and computer monitor. Stas was turning forty in a few days and had to take some vacation rather than lose the days. Some time off was welcome, but he didn't feel like celebrating his entrance into a new decade without company. Well, he hoped to remedy that tonight.

He seemed poured into his new charcoal grey suit from Nordstrom's Rack, but the secret of the fit was to have the jacket meticulously tailored so as not to suggest the presence of a shoulder holster with his Glock. In the locker room, he changed into a clean white shirt, buttoned its collar, and knotted a stylish blue and silver striped silk tie. His image in the mirror reflected a full head of dark brown hair that he kept a tad too long and grey eyes that missed very little. Nodding his satisfaction, he patted his face with a subtle hint of aftershave. All of this in pursuit of Liz from Dispatch.

A month ago, she had popped up on his radar as they stood in line at their credit union. Stas was able to check her out from behind: an attractive woman in her mid-thirties, with long shapely legs, a well-toned body, and brown hair that curled softly on her shoulders. And when she turned, she flashed a warm, engaging smile. Liz dropped a packet of traveler's checks, and he bent to retrieve them, handing them back.

"Thanks." She looked at him over her shoulder. "I took these to Poland, but the banks wouldn't cash them."

He smiled. "You've been to Poland?"

"My sister married this guy from there. We all went to visit his family last month. Do you know Poland?"

"I'm first generation Polish-American." He held out his hand. "Stas Nowak. I don't run into many people who've visited there. The most people know about Poland is either sausage or bad jokes."

"Liz Beemer." The smile broadened.

"Where'd you go?" He asked, feeling a connection. People rarely talked in line, but he sensed she was a talker.

"Just Warsaw and Krakow. There were lots of family and heavy food but not much sightseeing."

"Then you'll have to go back. It's a beautiful country with a rich history."

The credit union conversation led to coffee afterwards, then a couple of evenings with jazz and drinks. She liked the music but not one of his favorite foods, Chinese. So tonight he was planning to reintroduce her to Polish cuisine. They were meeting at the Warsaw Restaurant in Santa Monica for drinks, dinner, and a proposition he hoped she couldn't refuse, a week-end trip in Santa Barbara to check-out a new jazz club on State Street.

When he entered the Warsaw, he saw the head waiter, Mariusz, who pointed to his watch then to the rear. Stas knew the drill. He was early, so he headed to the back, took a seat at the bar, and ordered a Chopin on the rocks. The icy vodka warmed him and gave him that extra courage to frame his proposal, keep it from sounding like a typical cop come-on. He wanted this transition with Liz to grow into something special. There was no rush.

Stas chewed ice as he sipped his drink, wondering what Liz thought of him. Over the years he had dated a couple of women from Dispatch, a few from Records, but avoided female cops from LAPD and the Sheriffs.

He caught sight of Liz through the mirror behind the bar. Wow! She looked great -- a new hair cut with light brown highlights that brightened her complexion. Things were looking up. He went to join her just inside the entrance. She planted a soft kiss on his cheek as he ushered her to an empty table. He caught a scent of something sweet, a new fragrance. That was a good sign.

"Sorry I'm late. I got a little lost."

"No problem, I just got here myself." He looked at his watch. "We're early. What are you drinking?"

Liz looked around, letting him take her jacket, putting her purse down. "Something light. Chablis," easing into the chair he held for her.

Stas went back to the bar, ordered for Liz, then returned with his drink. "You look fantastic. I like what you did with your hair."

She brushed a long curl behind her ear. "I'm not sure if the highlights are too much, but what the hell, they'll grow out or back," she giggled, "whatever hair does."

The bar man brought Liz's wine. She took a sip and nodded her approval, then leaned in towards Stas. "So what have you been working on?"

"Just cleared my desk. Taking some time off. What do you have planned for the next few days?"

"Nothing special, work and the usual weekend stuff. Why?"

"There's a new jazz club just opened in Santa Barbara, thought I'd run up, check it out." He took a sip of his drink. "How about joining me?"

She looked up. "For the day or ...."

"The day would be nice, the weekend would be better."

Liz reached over and put her hand on his. "Stas, I'd love to, but ...."

"You're busy this weekend?" He paused. "We can do it another time."

"That's not it. I turned in my resignation today. I'm only working up here for two more weeks."

He leaned back, drawing his hand away to lift his drink to his lips. "Is everything okay?"

"Yes, everything's fine. I just wanted you to hear it from me. And I wanted you to know how much I've enjoyed hanging out with you." She touched her hair again. "I've been the envy of Dispatch. The gals don't say much, but I know what they're thinking. Me, seeing someone, you know, with a fantastic car, a great dresser. You don't even seem like a cop. You look more like a stock broker."

"I hope an honest one. So what's going on?"

She paused, then nervously fingered the stem of her wine glass. "I think I'm going to take the plunge."

"The plunge?" Stas shifted in his chair.

Liz blushed. "I'm getting engaged. He asked me to move to San Diego."

"He? I didn't know you were seeing anyone."

"It's been on the QT until his divorce was final."

"What does he do?" Stas could feel a coldness kick in.

"He's a cop, works vice for San Diego P.D."

Stas straightened. "You're planning to marry a divorced vice cop?" He hoped she hadn't heard the disappointment in his tone.

"Yeah, I know." She grinned and sipped her wine. "You think I would know better."

On their first date, she had confessed to him that she had been married to a K-9 cop from Glendale. "My ex cared more about his damn dog than me. When he started ordering me around in German, I knew it was over. I wasn't about to wait around for the doggie treats."

Stas smiled dryly and drained his glass, dreading making small talk over an expensive dinner.

"Didn't you work Vice?" she asked. "It can't be that bad, just gambling and street walkers."

"Vice has its own hazards."

"Well, it's good to know that I have such a fantastic friend if I need one at LAPD." Liz picked up her purse. "I don't think I'll be able to stay, but I'll put this place on my 'to try' list when we come up to LA." She rose.

"I'll walk you to your car." He stood, held her jacket for her, then followed her to the front entrance as Mariusz approached to seat them for dinner. Stas pressed some folded bills into his palm. "We can't stay."

Mariusz looked in his hand and smiled.

"I'll catch you later," Stas added.

Liz and Stas walked in silence to the parking lot. When they reached her car, she turned to plant another kiss, but he extended his hand in an indifferent shake.

"Good luck in San Diego."

She opened the car door and slid under the wheel. "If you're ever in San Diego, look us up. I'm sure my cell will be the same, at least for a while."

"You got it." He shut her door and watched her pull out of the lot, then returned to the bar for a couple of double vodkas, no ice.

Stas remembered driving home but didn't recall the route. Several times he was tempted to make a call, thought of the lateness and short notice, and continued to Glendale. As he opened the front door to his complex, a numbness was taking hold, and he almost missed the small package at the foot of the door of his rented condo. An attached Post-it told him it had been delivered in error to his neighbor. He ripped the brown wrapping before opening his door and read the note taped to the plastic CD cover:

"Hey, man, I moved to warmer climes, Phoenix, and found this in an old shoe box. Made some copies. Enjoy. Hope you still practice. See you soon. Riley. P.S. You ever think about the widow?"

Riley Bridges was an old army buddy who had put together a jazz combo when Stas was pulling the last two years of his Army tour at Fort Leonard Wood, Missouri. They had both played sax and switched off between alto and tenor, though Riley was the more accomplished musician. He had gone on to make a name for himself in jazz circles and had made several acclaimed CDs.

Stas unlocked his door, hung-up his jacket, then went straight to his CD player to insert the disc. He eased into his leather recliner, pushed play, and closed his eyes. The music engulfed him, helping him repress the encounter with Liz and flooding his senses with pleasant memories from the past. He recognized the first cut, "Bella Donna," a raunchy blues piece written by Riley. Stas nodded off, waking on the final cut, "Widow's Peak." Yes, he remembered the young widow and how the band's music, along with several of its members, had eased her grieving. The song had echoed the widow's final release; that high shrill note left nothing to the imagination. *Damn, Liz!* And hearing the sensuousness of that saxophone duet only intensified his unmet needs. He made a mental note to make that call the next day.

Early Saturday morning Stas trod in his bare feet to check his mailbox. Nothing! Proof that no one else remembered his birthday. There had been no calls, no cards, no gifts, and no invitations for dinner. He would have even settled for going out for a drink. Not that he really expected anything, but to be totally forgotten even by family was a bummer. There had to be more to this passage into mid-life.

Saturday evening he worked out at the gym, came home, showered, and dressed. He had phoned Honey Malone that morning, inquired about her health and that of her fiancé. They had been engaged for over ten years, together even longer. He guessed they would never marry since both were well into their seventies. By the end of their chat, Honey had set him up that night with Alicia, a third year law student who was anxious to graduate from law school and, as soon as she passed the bar, from Honey. Alicia had been a disappointment. She lacked that professional touch, but if nothing else she had eased his desire for Liz.

The next morning found Stas relaxed and dressed for a run. After five miles, he picked up bagels, cream cheese, and the Sunday L.A. *Times*. He made coffee, ate and carefully dissected the paper. An article about a London madam caught his attention. She was awaiting trial. He had read about her months earlier, working her high priced call girls between London and Paris. He had a fleeting glimpse of Alicia, yet had already forgotten the color of her eyes. But he remembered Honey's eyes--large and brown behind silver rimmed glasses. The same eyes, only large and angry when he and his partner first met her. They were working vice at the time. Honey was enraged when one of her girls kept money, a lot of money, from her. Stas and his partner had helped recover her funds without any direct police action. Honey was from Nashville, Tennessee, where she had been a high-class madam who gave it all up to follow her man, a retired Nashville P. D. deputy chief, to California. But even in L.A. Honey had not completely given up work. She still ran a few beautiful young women, most of them working their way through graduate school. However, one had gotten greedy and could have paid with more than just returning the money. And Stas and his former partner were rewarded from time to time for their past assistance. But Stas wanted more. He'd even given some thought to a serious relationship, to maybe even settling down, and had been hopeful that something might have happened with Liz.

As he started to pack, even the idea of a vacation sent him to the bedroom closet for the dull black case. He took it to the living room, removed the sax, put in Riley's CD, and played along on several of the cuts.

"Damn!" His fingers were stiff, his mouth dry. *Guess I do need practice.*

Monday morning he awoke to a drizzling rain. Another excuse not to get on the road, then he thought about an insignificant file he wanted to leave for his partner and went back to Parker Center Monday evening.

After leaving the squad room, he stopped for a quick one, anything to lift him out of his funk. It wasn't too often that he sought companionship, but even at his age, birthdays and rejection seemed to cry out for company. So he decided to warm a familiar bar stool for a few hours before beginning a trip that now held more dread than anticipation.

The evening was gray and dreary. Those lone drinkers at the Second Set Bar and Grill halfheartedly watched the Clippers playing a road game on the new 50 inch plasma TV over the bar. Since the Lakers had the night off and the Staples Center was hosting a hockey game there wasn't much interest on what was going on overhead. Stas's quickie turned into a couple of vodkas neat. He looked at his watch and pushed the empty glass toward the bartender for a refill, then turned on his stool to scrutinize the patrons when two young women entered shaking their damp locks as they looked for an empty booth. They were not regulars and seemed out of their element, moving in unison like two synchronized swimmers out of water.

"Pickin' always kinda lean on a Monday night, especially with the rain," Troy drawled. He was half of a matched pair, but his identical twin Roy smiled more, talked less, and made better martinis. Somehow the customers, especially the women, never knew who was on duty on any particular night until the first sip of their cocktails. When the brothers worked together on the weekend, putting on their light and liquor show, everybody was happy.

Stas and Troy watched the two women settle at a table and look towards the bar.

"I bet they're looking for company." Troy smiled.

"Wanna-be badge bunnies." Stas turned back to his drink. "I'm not interested." He sighed and looked at his empty glass. "Just not ready to go home. And I sure as hell don't want to take on two."

"You think they come together?"

"I'd make book on it."

After placing another drink in front of the detective, Troy went back to arranging bottles; a dreamy smile lit his face as he wiped the counter. The Second Set Bar and Grill was a watering hole for the LAPD detectives who liked their booze in a quiet place, their jazz cool, and their women classy. Here, cops didn't have to deal with the usual groupies, either young or old, who hung out at some of the other bars catering to the uniformed, vice, and motorcycle cops.

Even though there was no love lost between cops and reporters, what was left of the more seasoned press corps also called The Second Set home. And occasionally a high class, long-legged, four-figures-a-night lady of the evening could be glimpsed in a back booth, sipping an apple martini while she waited for her well-heeled client.

Stas looked at his reflection in the mirror behind the bar and tried to remember when he first started coming to The Second Set. Was it after his divorce when he needed a place of quiet solace, or after his promotion to detective when he wanted a place to celebrate? He'd been coming ever since. One thing was certain; he loved being a cop, taking the motto, "To Serve and Protect," personally.

He sipped his drink and thought again about Liz. Had he missed something, been a little too anxious to have a normal relationship? Most women usually found him attractive in a rakish, sensual way. Some even considered him a good catch, but with the exception of Liz, he shied away from any kind of commitment after his disastrous marriage. At times his dispassionate detachment turned many women off who might have been interested. One or two dates usually cooled the ardor of any woman who dreamed of more than dinner, drinks, music, and bed. He was pleasant company, even funny with his wry humor, and he was more than adequate as a transient lover, yet no one had breached his inner sanctum. Still, he would sometimes catch himself checking out what he considered the all-American woman and wondering about family life, complete with remodeled suburban ranch, kids, and a dog or two. But most importantly, she would have to be someone who saw value in his work and respected him for doing it. With Liz, he couldn't understand why they hadn't connected. He ran his hand through his hair, then drained his glass.

One of the girls moved toward the bar. They hadn't been served. Nancy, the bar maid, was probably having a smoke in the back, resting her aching feet on a case of Coors, something she often did on slow nights.

Stas watched the young woman's movements in the mirror that backed the bar. She slowly shed her jacket, revealing a torso that had been poured into a low cut knit sweater, but the swelling breasts and inviting cleavage did nothing for him. He eased up off his stool and turned to get a better look at her legs. The skirt was too tight and too short for the fat knees that he knew led to even fatter thighs.

She had reached the bar and leaned over to get Troy's attention. "Can we get a couple of drinks?"

"What would you like?" Troy wiped in circles and grinned as he moved towards her.

She brushed against Stas.

"I'm sorry." She held out her hand, "I'm Sam," and drew it back when he didn't offer his. "That's short for Samantha."

"I think Troy's ready for your order."

She wedged herself between an empty bar stool and his while still maintaining contact with his arm.

"Is this place always so quiet?" she asked.

"Most of the time, unless there's a raid." Stas smiled.

"A raid?" Panic touched her eyes.

He gave her an icy stare. "The cops are always in and out. They've been keeping this place under surveillance. A lot of unsavory types hang here." Stas turned back to the bar.

Sam edged away, leaving Troy holding back a quiet laugh that wrinkled his nose.

"That was cold." Troy wiped the spot of bar where Sam had leaned.

"She's out of her element," Stas said.

As he lifted his hand to order another vodka, Ralph Townsend slid onto the next bar stool. "Can I buy you a drink?" He coughed to clear his throat.

Stas was suspicious. "Man, I got nothing for you," he said as he looked into his empty glass. "But I will take you up on the offer."

Townsend, in his mid-forties, was a streetwise reporter who had spent at least fifteen years working the LA crime scene. His good looks and glib tongue complemented his uncanny knack of getting the jump on a story, then working it for every bit of information he could garner, yet Ralph could be just as generous with leads if he liked you. Theirs was a love-hate relationship, but it worked.

Overly conscious of his six feet, four inches, he tended to stoop when he walked and to bend down to shorter speakers to listen, and he was a damn good listener. His signature tan corduroy jacket hung open over a faded blue polyester shirt. With darkly stained fingers, Ralph nervously rubbed his natural tonsure, an affectation he subconsciously demonstrated when he needed a cigarette. Since he couldn't smoke in the bar, the next best thing was a drink, so he leaned over to get Troy's attention. "Give me a Scotch on the rocks and Stas another of whatever he's having." He patted his jacket pocket for his cigarettes as he waited for the drink. "What brought you out tonight?"

"Just started my vacation."

Troy poured and placed the drink on the bar.

Townsend raised his glass in a mock toast. "Where ya going?"

"Up the coast, maybe do a little fishing," Stas replied.

"In this weather? You don't strike me as an angling man," Townsend retorted.

"My old man used to take me."

"So now you takin' him?"

"I don't do much with him anymore." Stas stared coolly ahead, lost for a second, before taking a sip from his refill.

The Monday night basketball commentary went dead when Troy hit the MUTE button on the remote. No one seemed to notice. The DJ had returned from his break and started playing some jazz, leaving the basketball players rebounding to a soft, sensuous tenor sax.

"Damn, I forgot how dead this place is the first of the week. Where are the chicks?" Townsend took a quick look over his shoulder. "I stopped at the Brass Bull. For a rainy Monday night, it was crawling with short skirts, bare bellies, big boobs, but LAPD's finest were in short supply. Things got so desperate that a couple of near-naked groupies tried to take on two motorcycle cops."

"A fight?" asked Stas, smiling.

"Ouch, you have been coming here too long," roared Townsend. "But it sure wasn't like the good old days."

"I paid my dues there a long time ago. I don't need that kind of action anymore, plus the department's trying to shed that image."

"God, you sound ancient. What you need is one of those hot little outdoor types snuggled down in your sleeping bag." As he turned to take a second look around, Townsend added, "On second thought you'd better watch it, sitting here all alone." Ralph spied the two young ladies slipping into their jackets. "I don't see a soul in here you could take home to warm your bed tonight unless...." He nodded toward Sam and her companion moving towards the door.

"Not my type. If I needed my bed warmed tonight, I'd get a hot water bottle. Anyway they're a little too young for me. I like a little more experience handling my equipment."

"Man, relax! You don't have to take them home to mama, just have some fun." Ralph sipped his Scotch, coughed. "You know, you're wound too tight. That's not good for a cop. I'd say you need somebody and soon."

Troy edged closer nodding toward the door. "He scared them when he showed his badge."

Townsend looked the young women over again before taking out a new pack of Camels and laying it on the bar. Troy frowned watching the reporter anxiously drum his fingers on the cellophane wrapped box.

"You need to quit," Stas admonished. "I did ten months ago."

"Well, if you still countin', you still got the urge. I see you edging closer to my jacket just to get a whiff of that awesome smoke and nicotine. You never can quit. Anyway, every man needs a few vices." Townsend coughed, pulled the thin red tab, and opened the package. He half saluted the departing Sam and her friend with a cigarette. He held it to his nose, inhaled, then put it behind his ear when Troy turned back to the bar.

Stas looked at the pack, then Townsend. "Look at you -- holes in your jacket, and your fingers -- they're beyond yellow -- they're charcoal, and that hacking cough." He turned back to his drink. "Man, stop worrying about me. You need to find yourself a woman to take care of you, and not one from the Brass Bull or...." He waved at the table recently vacated by Sam and friend.

Townsend looked at his fingers and wiped them on his trouser leg as if that action could cleanse away years of built-up tar stains. "No, offense, but you're just a little..." he paused. "too anal."

Stas turned defensively on his stool. "So you're telling me that if a man has his shit together there's something wrong with him?" He picked up his glass and drank half of its contents. "Why are we even having this conversation? Look at you! Slob!"

Townsend looked down. "Yeah, and what organ do I have to sell on Craig's List to look like you?" He patted himself down. "I got all my shit, and the ladies love it. Who cares about clothes when the lights are out? No wonder you don't have a woman, you spend all your damn money on your threads and that car...."

The talk about women hit a nerve. "Fuck off!" At that moment, Stas's cell phone vibrated giving off a faint buzz. He opened it on his belt and strained to read the display without responding.

"You're not going to answer?"

The detective pushed a button, a vague pang of excitement as he recognized the last four digits of the number.

"Something going down?" Townsend asked.

Stas's gray eyes twinkled. "If I didn't know better, I'd swear you had a police scanner implanted in your head. I think it's someone I helped out of jam a while back, so rein in your antennae."

Townsend smiled. "So now it's pay back time? You gonna call her?"

"Her? I didn't say..." Stas tossed off his vodka and slid from his stool. "Thanks for the drink."

"Anytime!" Townsend raised his half-empty glass. "And here's to filling your sleeping bag."

Stas looked at the last four digits, 6000. Goode, Dina Goode. The recollection warmed him.

THREE

Stas walked to the lot and deactivated the alarm on his black Mercedes 500 SL. Once inside, he opened his cell phone and punched in the number from his call list. It was busy. Driving home, he thought of the caller, Dina Goode. It had been almost two years since he'd seen her, but even with their brief encounter, he hadn't forgotten her.

That night he had used a handful of linen napkins and pressure to stem the flow of blood from her slit throat. Blood was everywhere. She had held onto him, her eyes fluttering, her breath shallow, until the paramedics arrived. He walked along side the gurney as they wheeled her to the ambulance. When they opened the doors, she still clung to him, so Stas, his own hand sore and bloody, rode with her, holding her, talking to her, trying to ward off shock until they arrived at the hospital.

In the ER, the medics, nurses, and doctors had left him alone once he showed his ID. They probably assumed he wanted to question her once she was stabilized, but he'd left her when they sent him to X-ray. It was early morning when they finished with him.

The attending physician, looking bone-tired, leaned against a gurney and gave Stas the news. "Nothing's broken, but your hand's going to be sore for a while. You might want to ice it when you get home." He tossed Stas a packet of pills. "Take these for pain."

"Thanks. I guess we both could use some sleep."

"I have another six hours on my shift." The doctor forced a smile and waved before trudging down the empty hall.

Before leaving the hospital, Stas stopped at the information counter on the first floor to get Dina's room number, then took the elevator to the third floor where he found a perky Filipino nurse in bright blue scrubs manning the station, her attention focused on several charts. He waited. She finally looked up as he fumbled for his ID.

"Dina Goode?" he inquired.

"Ms. Goode is resting, and I think that's what you should be doing. Question her tomorrow. She's not going anywhere."

"I brought her in. I just wanted to check if..."

The nurse didn't let him finish but pointed toward the room. "Three ten. One minute and don't disturb her." She turned back to her charts.

He needed to see her again. He eased into the room. She must have been heavily sedated. Her thick lashes lay on pale cheeks, but one tanned arm resting on the white thermal blanket, reflected her true color. An IV drip-fed her medication in the other arm. She looked like a survivor, reminding him of a gentle yet wild thing held in captivity. *Better back off.* Then he left. As he struggled to get into the car, he tried to tuck her into the folds of his memory for future reference.

Before starting the car, Stas managed to free a couple of pills from the packet and popped them into his mouth, swallowing them dry. There was still the report to fill out. He needed to remember all the details: his meeting with Mack from Vice, an evening of camaraderie and drinks, Dina's screams, the pressure on the assailant's hand until the bastard dropped the knife. Stas knew his ass would be ground to dog meat if his report wasn't perfect, or the department was later sued, so instead of going home and falling into bed, he returned to the squad room and filed his report.

When he awoke the next morning, his hand still in pain, the young woman hadn't stayed tucked away. The image of her drew him back to the hospital, not to ask questions, but to take her a gift, a stuffed baby panda that he had seen late that night in the window of the closed hospital's florist shop. What could be more wild yet vulnerable than a panda? When he walked into her room, he found her propped up on several pillows, her neck swathed in white bandages, all color drained from her face.

"I'm Detective Stas Nowak."

It was awkward trying to show his ID and offer the panda with an injured hand that still throbbed with pain.

Dina straightened up, ignored the ID, and reached for the panda with childlike enthusiasm. "You brought me in last night?" Her smile was weak, but her hazel eyes, fanned by long lashes, were intelligent and curious.

Stas nodded. Her paleness belied the fact that she was of mixed heritage, but he couldn't tell what. She looked to be in her late twenties. He hadn't seen her chart. She wasn't one of those classic beauties, but a beauty, wild and exotic, nonetheless, like some endangered species, one that hinted of hidden peril. For the moment, he ignored the inner warning: proceed at your own risk. Instead, he imagined a lovely, inviting body and long shapely legs concealed beneath those sterile hospital covers. His mind drifted for a second. Her question drew him back.

"Do you work vice?"

"No, Robbery/Homicide. I used...." He paused. "Listen, I have to go. I just wanted to check if...." When he handed her his card with the gold and blue shield of LAPD embossed in the center, he sensed a brief hesitance on her part. He turned the card over, placed it on the table, and wrote another number. "This is my cell. Call if you ever need anything."

"I don't have a card, but..." With an effort, she reached over to the metal bedside stand for the little note pad and pencil, then scribbled. "Here are my numbers."

Their fingers touched briefly as he took the paper.

"How can I ever thank you?"

"Don't worry about it. It's all in the line of duty."

"You hurt your hand."

"It'll be okay." He looked at the paper, noticing that the last four digits of the first number ended in 6000. It reminded him of her last name, Goode.

After he had gone, Dina leaned back on the piled high pillows, feeling a flush and an accelerated heartbeat. At first she thought it was the medication, but she knew better. It was the man. She could still smell his lingering scent, like bergamot and vanilla. It had mingled with the sterile hospital odors and would later creep into her dreams. She knew instinctively that there was nothing sterile about this man. She touched the bandage at her neck and closed her eyes wondering if she would ever see him again.

So now, after two years, 6000 - Miss Dina Goode was back in his life. When Stas got home, he hung his jacket in the hall closet, flicked on the light, and opened the top desk drawer in his dining area office. It took a few seconds to find the neatly folded slip of paper Dina had given him in the hospital.

The first number was the same as the one on his cell. He went to his land line and dialed. Still busy! *Who in the hell was she talking to at this hour? Was the phone off the hook? What did she need? Was she in trouble?* Not knowing, made him anxious, a feeling he didn't like. But then, he remembered her line of work. This was *her* hour.

Taking the cordless and the numbers, he moved to the black leather recliner that faced his entertainment center. The apartment was modest, ordered, and, except for the latest audio/visual toys and the flat screen TV, quite Spartan. Before punching REDAIL, he picked up the remote, switched on the TV. *The Charlie Rose Show* was on. Stas then made a trip to an efficient and immaculate kitchen where he got a glass from the cabinet and took a bottle of Chopin Vodka from the freezer. He poured the water tumbler half full, then drank part of it off before returning to the living room with his drink and bottle. He tried Dina again, got another busy signal.

"What the hell!" He looked at Charlie.

But Rose only smiled and continued his interview.

Stas turned off the TV and carried his bottle and glass to the bedroom. As he undressed, he thought about Liz and this forced vacation. It all seemed like his life was falling into a boring routine, but like a blind man, he put shoetrees in his shoes and dirty clothes in the hamper.

In the bathroom, he examined his naked torso. His body was still lean and taut. He worked out his six foot, one hundred and eighty-five pound frame with regular visits to the gym, games of handball, and, if time allowed, keeping up with his martial arts. It had been an eighteen-year routine, yet had he reached his prime? As he picked-up his glass and took a drink, he pinched his midsection to measure the body fat, then looked at the glass and thought he'd better slow down on the vodka if he wanted the same body at fifty. In a mock toast, he raised his glass to the image in the mirror and the invisible guests who crowded the bathroom. "Happy Birthday!"

The next morning brought a feeling of foreboding. *Was Dina in serious trouble?* After showering and dressing, he made coffee and pressed the redial on the phone while he drank from his LAPD mug. Her phone was still busy. He dialed the second number on the slip of paper. A woman at her service answered. He asked for Dina. No one had heard from her for several days. He left a message and tried her first number one last time. Busy. *Damn!*

Well, if she were on the phone, she would keep until he found an address to go with her phone number. He went to his office area, turned on his computer, typed in recollection, and input Dina's number. He was in luck. It was a landline. Not only was the address given but also a map pinpointing the location of her residence.

Stas went out, picked up a sandwich at the Whole Foods' Deli, then returned home. He ate standing in his kitchen, then changed into pressed jeans, a white dress shirt, purple tie, and a dark sports jacket. If he was going to have to lie his way past a manager or two to get into Dina's apartment, he needed to look like he was working on a case: not an LAPD case but a television cop case. They had much lower sartorial standards.

FOUR

Dina Goode lived at the Florentine Arms, a well-maintained, nondescript apartment complex that resembled so many others in the Mid-Wilshire district. He parked near the corner and walked back to the building.

While the area wasn't Beverly Hills or Westwood, Stas was sure the rent set her back a pretty penny. *Business must be good!* The front entranceway was awash with reds, oranges, and magentas of the neatly trimmed azaleas planted along the walk. He wondered why all the bright flowers? What was wrong with just plain mowed grass and trimmed bushes? He was greeted at the entrance by even more flowers, fleur-de-lis etched into the glass doors. He dialed 87; the number that came up on the display for "D. Goode," got a busy signal, then dialed the manager. The lock on the front doors disengaged with a loud buzz. After entering the bright foyer, Stas expected to find a plaster of Paris statue of David with or without fig leaf nestled in more foliage but found shiny silk plants instead.

When he pushed through the second set of glass doors decorated with six golden balls arranged on a coat of arms outlined boldly in black, a large red finger on a white sign pointed to the manager's apartment to his left.

At the door he knocked, reached for his ID, but dropped his keys. He stooped to retrieve them and saw perfection: long legs, shapely and energetically poised in high heels. But as his gaze rose he encountered the legs' owner. Although he had no first hand experience, he imagined her literally lifted from another clichéd Hollywood era, a fifty-ish bottled blonde who stood posed in her doorway wearing a garishly flowered dress. Stas presented his shield. She looked at it, striking a dancer's pose. He mentally noted the overly made-up face and hair that seemed to be from another time when the showgirls and their legs were the mainstay of most Hollywood movie lots. He doubted she had ever been in a studio stable, but who looked beyond the legs.

Her smile cracked, bleeding into the wrinkles around her bright red mouth. Her upper cheeks were dotted with flecks of dried, black mascara. She reached out to shake Stas's hand and pull him into her lair.

"I'm Ms. Todd, the manager. You need something?"

"I'm Detective Nowak. I'm trying to locate an errant witness. He gave this address, apartment 316." He flashed his most winning smile. "I really appreciate your cooperation."

"Did you ring him?"

"Sometimes it's better to just knock on the door." He smiled. "Flight risk."

She relaxed her stance and fluttered heavy eye lashes as Stas told his story. Ms. Todd seemed more impressed with his shield, his attire, his attitude, his engaging smile. He'd seen her type before. She probably would have let him into the building under any pretense, even let him have the run of her apartment as she coquettishly sucked on one of her very long, very red fingernails. He could almost hear her wheels spinning, trying to figure out how to detain a prime piece of LAPD's finest. To many women, a blue and gold shield wielded by a police officer was, for starters, an effective, seductive tool.

"Do you need me to go with you?"

"That's okay. No need to bother you."

"It would never be a bother. Shouldn't you leave me your card, just in case...?" she trailed off.

He suspected, given time, that she could manufacture some felonious distraction for him to investigate but handed her his card. He nodded his good-bye and headed for the elevators. Ms. Todd watched until the elevator door closed behind him. *Well, she bought it.*

Entrance into Dina Goode's apartment was much too easy and just as illegal. A thin metal plate the size of a credit card disengaged the lock. He would have to talk to her about better security. Once inside, he was met with a chilled silence.

Despite the cold, the apartment was open and airy, laid out with expensive pieces of contemporary furniture and accessories that made the mauve and gray decor of the living room inviting. He paused; a delicate essence took him back two years. The scent that had been tucked away in his subconscious roared to life, counterbalanced with warnings that he rarely felt except on the street.

In the bedroom, faint light seeped around the edges of the closed drapes. Stas pulled the cords and flooded the room with the morning's brightness. The crumpled figure on the bed stirred and flung a hand over her eyes, shielding them from the glare. Stas expected a scream as Dina pulled the covers to her throat. But she only stared, trying to focus on the figure silhouetted in her window.

He moved closer. "It's me. Detective Nowak, Stas. Are you okay?"

She closed her eyes for a second. "I didn't think you'd come. I wasn't sure you'd remember."

"How could I forget."? He smiled. "You cost me a very expensive jacket."

"How did you get in?" she whispered.

"We always have ways."

"Do you have a key?" she asked, puzzled.

"I don't need one." He looked for a place to sit. The nearest chair was draped with clothes.

"I've been calling you since yesterday. Your line's still busy. You need to hang it up." He watched her try to rouse herself. "I even called your service. No one's heard from you for three days. Did you even get my message?"

"I haven't called in."

"What's going on? You look like you lost your best friend."

"My boss." The effort brought moisture to her already reddened eyes, but she held back a flow of tears. "Sybil is dead."

Stas didn't react but looked around to grab something for her to slip into so she could get up, and they could talk. Finding nothing at hand, he changed tactics. "Have you eaten recently?

"No."

"Get up, take a shower," he ordered and turned toward the door.

"Are you leaving?"

He sensed panic in her tone and hoped he wasn't dealing with a psycho.

"No, I'm going to make you some breakfast." He looked at his watch. "Or brunch." Then left to find the kitchen.

Even with Stas there to motivate her, it took a major effort to drag herself out of bed. There was nothing at the foot to cover her nakedness. *Suppose he comes back to check on me?* With a groan, she padded to the bathroom.

Dina avoided looking in the mirror, afraid of seeing what he had seen. When she stepped into the shower, the first spray of cold water shocked her system awake, then warm water enveloped her like a protective cocoon. She lathered her body trying to wash away the lethargy, the loss, the pain. After stepping out of the water, she felt better as she wrapped herself in her terry robe.

Wiping a swath of steam from the mirror, she stared into a puffy face and red-rimmed eyes. There had been too many tears. She fingered a slightly keloid scar across her neck, a stark reminder of past pain, pain that bound her to this detective. She managed to tie up her hair but trying to apply lipstick was just too much effort. The tube dropped to the counter.

At any other time she would have welcomed this man into her life and her bedroom. For two years Detective Stas Nowak had been an ongoing fantasy. Now, here he was in the flesh, looking better than she had remembered or even imagined, and she was a mess.

Oh, what the hell, he's seen me looking worse.

In Dina's efficient kitchen, Stas found what he needed to make an omelet and a pot of coffee. He was impressed with her neatness and organization. Donning an apron from a hook near the stove, he found a bowl, eggs, skillet, butter and got to work.

When he turned on the radio, jazz broke the kitchen silence, warming him to his task. *Maybe this won't be a total waste after all.* He started to set a place at the bistro table for Dina but first moved a crystal vase of dead flowers to the sink. He was tempted to trash them but left them on the counter instead. It wasn't his call, so he poured himself a cup of coffee and waited, hoping the omelet wouldn't get cold or rubbery.

Five minutes later, a freshly scrubbed Dina slumped into her chair. Stas turned the omelet onto a plate, pulled up another bistro chair, and joined her with his coffee.

At first, giving in to her hunger, she ate greedily. They sat in awkward silence. When she did look up, he was watching her.

"What?" she asked nervously.

"You want to tell me about it?"

Dina hesitated. "I can't believe Sybil's gone." She moved the last of the omelet around on her plate like a little girl afraid of being scolded for not finishing her food.

"Was she sick?"

"No! And she wasn't depressed either. Things were great." Dina took a deep breath. "Why would she shoot herself?"

"She shot herself?"

Dina nodded and pushed her plate aside.

"And I take it, you don't believe it was suicide?"

"No!" Tears fell. Embarrassed, Dina tried to wipe them away with the heel of her hand.

He'd forgotten napkins and looked over to the counter. He grabbed what looked like a clean dishtowel and handed it to her. "Maybe you're just in denial, Dina. People do a lot of strange things if they're pushed hard enough."

She wiped her eyes. "You didn't know her."

Stas's jaw tensed, but he said nothing.

She continued, "She was, ... she was ..."

He interrupted, anxious to get to the reason for the call. "... like a mother?"

"No, my mother was the queen bitch." She looked at him to see if he understood, then went on. "Sybil was more than a boss. She was a good friend, especially since...." She fingered the scar at her neck. "I could never repay her or you after the attack."

He stood and refilled his coffee. "Just doing what I'm paid to do."

"Riding in the ambulance, coming to the hospital--I don't think that was in your job description." Dina's gaze dropped to her plate. "You never called."

"I never promised."

"But you said, if I needed...," she added tearfully.

"And I'm here." Yet he made no move to comfort her.

She stiffened, trying to compose herself.

"Tell you what, I'll take a look at the file. We'll see." He ran water in his cup at the sink and put it on the drain. "Now that you're up, what are you going to do the rest of the day?"

Dina slowly rose, using the back of the chair for support. "I'm going back to bed. I'm so tired."

"I'll let myself out. Where's the bathroom?"

She pointed as she trudged down the short hall to her bedroom. "There." She stopped and turned to face him. "When will you know something?"

"Give me a day or two." He closed and locked the bathroom door, then locked the door leading to Dina's bedroom. He flushed the toilet and turned on the faucets full force while checking in the medicine cabinet. No bags of drugs, but he hit pay dirt in the top drawer of the cabinet: one large orange vial of pills, prescribed to LISA BANE. Stas recognized the medication: one of the strongest sleeping meds on the market. There was no time to count them, so he dumped all but six in his jacket pocket and put the vial back. She couldn't do much harm with what was left except have a prolonged rest.

So Detective Stas Nowak's quiet vacation would be postponed for a while. As he took the elevator down, he wondered, who the hell was Lisa Bane, and what was she doing giving Dina enough pills to kill a horse? At his car, he decided to check on her later that night.

Got to get a key. Stas used the credit card trick again after calling a random number and getting buzzed in. The bedside clock read 12:36 AM. Dina was out like a light and sweating profusely. He managed to get her out of the heavy robe and into a nightgown that he found hanging on the bathroom door. After getting her settled in bed, he had warmed with the effort or the temptation. He didn't want to think about her. *Just get my ass out.* But one thing for sure, he knew how to guarantee her a good night's sleep. *Leave it alone, Nowak, just leave it alone.*

FIVE

The next morning Stas made a few calls that left him with even more questions unanswered. There were problems locating Sybil Hansen's file. He made a quick stop at Parker Center where he picked up the faxed copy of the initial report from Hollywood Station. It took fifteen minutes to drive to the Los Angeles County Department of Coroners on North Mission Road, then another ten to wait for a space to free up in the parking lot. His patience was wearing thin when a petite woman took her own sweet time getting into a gigantic SUV and slowly relinquishing her space as if by giving it up, she was losing her maidenhood to the virile Benz and its driver.

He waited at the foot of the ramp as an attendant pushed a gurney to the entrance of the reception area. As he walked over to the sign-in sheet, the large doors to the Crypt slid open ready to receive a new occupant. He glanced in, always fascinated by the bodies stacked on their metal racks that seemed to go on forever. The cadavers that he could see were swathed in some type of plastic wrap. From a quick glance, he could make out the tops of heads and shoulders. The doors closed, and Stas turned back to sign in, then moved into the hallway passing to his left the remains of a young man whose head, shoulders, and upper torso looked intact. He had yet to be bagged or wrapped, but as the detective took a step closer to the gurney, the attendant stood in his path to block his vision.

"You don't want to see him. Got hit by a train. There's only the top half."

Stas turned back and continued down the hall to the elevator, peering in at Chuck Reyes, "fingers." It was a marvel that someone could spend days reconstituting severed fingers: dried, shrunken, mummified fingers. All removed by killers hoping that the dead could not be identified. But Reyes worked his miracle, and victims were named, family was found, and sometimes, justice was served.

Stas took the elevator to the floor housing the offices of the MEs to see Dave Holliday, M.D. a pathologist who always seemed oblivious to any of the imperfections of his occupation. He had worked as a Medical Examiner and professor of forensics for so long that his sallow complexion had taken on the pallor of his oldest and dearest teaching cadavers at USC.

The detective knocked at 116.

"Come on in," a husky voice called through the closed door.

The detective entered to find the ME sitting in an old beat-up leather chair, hunched over a sugar donut and coffee. Upon seeing Stas, he gestured him to a small chair over flowing with files and loose papers. "Just put that stuff on the floor."

Stas looked for an empty space and seeing nothing added the contents of the seat to an overflowing box near the bookcase and sat down.

Holliday was a veteran from the old "choir boy" days. Back then, MEs were known for their hard drinking, womanizing, and mishandling of evidence with their sloppy techniques. Some of them and their stories had become legends. Now there were new, stricter guidelines because of adverse publicity brought to the Coroner's Office over a number of incompetent autopsies that resulted in lost criminal cases and hefty lawsuits filed against the county.

"It's been a long time, Stas. What brings you to our circle of the damned?"

"Just taking another look at a suicide and wanted to know what you thought."

"I don't give opinions anymore. Just holding on, trying to keep the bodies from spilling out into the street and enraging the public."

"You can't do many cuts munching on sugar donuts," Stas observed.

"I did one this morning. It was kinda messy. Activated my sweet tooth. Holliday brushed off his lab coat before reaching for a powdered twist. "I'm not cutting much these days. We finally got some help other than techs and media freaks who only do celebs that might get them million-dollar book deals."

"I thought you'd still be up to your old antics. I can't imagine you letting these rookies off so easy. It's not your style." Stas smiled.

"Yeah, I still remember your first post." Crumbs dropped from Holliday's full mouth as he tried to talk.

Stas's smile faded. "Damn, I'd seen corpses before, but I'd never seen bodies stacked like those in the Crypt. And the number of them."

"That's why I took you to the Bull afterwards. You got so drunk you threw up all over some cute little dispatcher from Hollywood Division who was trying to get you in her pants."

"Funny, I don't remember that."

"Hank Wood dumped you in the storeroom. The next morning when we came to get you, you were still drunk. Must've gotten into some more booze during the night. I had to take you home, throw you in the shower, and try to explain the situation to your wife. She couldn't understand the drill." Holliday shoved the rest of the twist into his mouth. "No more sweet young techs on the gurneys at night, no more body part jokes, no more Jack Daniels assisting." He swallowed hard and took a swig of coffee, dribbling some down his front, further staining his lab coat. "Good old Jack. But then you're not down here, dressed like that, to discuss the good old days."

Stas handed over the copy of the report. "This one might make for a good book deal if you could name the right people."

Holliday put the cup down, wiped his fingers on his sleeve, then opened the folder. He stopped abruptly without reading past the first few lines. "I didn't do it. One of the new MEs did the cut."

"Why would someone new do the post on this suicide?"

Adjusting his glasses, Holliday looked back over the report. His levity had vanished. "Did you know Sybil Hansen?"

Stas didn't answer.

Holliday continued, "I mean in the biblical sense."

"I busted her once."

"Before or after your stint in Vice?" Holliday held up his hand. "No matter, wrong move."

"I found that out too late. She had friends in high places, and I didn't."

"Then you were stupid. You knew the routine. She had a reputation to uphold. She needed to maintain her business and keep the money flowing. Make everybody happy. They all got laid free: cops, lawyers, judges, prosecutors, newspaper editors...."

Stas interrupted, "and MEs?"

"Yeah, a few of us got lucky, too. Some of the best tail in town. Everyone respected Sybil. Hers wasn't the only game in town, but it was probably the classiest." Holliday pointed to Stas. "You were just a sorry little prick and didn't know any better. I guess that can be forgiven. Why the interest? You know what she was."

Stas leaned into the littered desk. "Yeah, but she's dead. So if her death wasn't a suicide, then it was homicide. And I don't give a damn what she was. If she was murdered, then I'm interested."

"Well, the body was on the table when a call came down from on high." Holliday looked heavenwards. "Said we had a routine suicide and leave it at that. I wasn't about to do or say anything stupid to jeopardize my pension. That morning I got sick. Another ME passed on it. I don't remember why, so she was given to the new guy. Go see Dr. Wu." Holliday turned back to his cold coffee and another sugary twist.

Stas took his file, rose, nearly tripping over a pair of Birkenstocks next to the chair and left the office. He found Dr. Steven Wu sitting at his desk in a small office at the end of the hall. In passing, the space could have easily been mistaken for a broom closet, except for the small white plate, 116, attached to the door.

Stas could see why the door was half open. He tapped on the doorframe to get Wu's attention. When he looked up, Stas was surprised at his appearance. He was young, almost boyish, the sort of professional Chinese mothers wanted their daughters to marry, a fine young man to bring honor to the family. Wu sported a stock of unruly black hair and horn-rimmed glasses that he looked over as Stas waited. Wu beckoned him into the cluttered room. His only chair was also overflowing with books, papers, and a dirty lab coat draped over the back. Stas wondered if this disorder was endemic to MEs: order for the dead, chaos among the living. Wu came around the desk, put everything on the floor, and offered the detective a seat.

Before sitting Stas presented his ID. "I'm Detective Nowak."

"Steven Wu. Sorry for the mess. I never seem to get caught up, and this room is like a closet. That's why I have to leave the door open." He returned to his chair. "How can I help you?"

Stas gave him the file. "Holliday tells me you did the post on this woman."

Wu adjusted his glasses and quickly looked over the first page. "Was this your case?"

Stas hesitated, hoping the ME would divulge a tit-bit or two before the truth was known, but Wu waited patiently for a response. "No, not really. I'm just looking into it for a fellow officer. There have been some questions, and they might reopen the case. If they do, it might come to us at Robbery-Homicide Division."

Wu pushed his microscope aside and leaned into his computer monitor, his nimble fingers magically touching the keys as if playing a piano requiem. Stas could hear the screen jump to life but could see nothing.

"Yeah, I remember her. She must have been beautiful. Had an awesome body." He cleared his throat, then returned to the screen. "The blood spray pattern, perfect." He moved his pen as if connecting the dots, dots that Stas could not see. "Yes, everything was perfect, like graphics from a text."

Stas waited, hoping Wu would let him take a look at the perfection.

The invitation didn't come as the ME pushed away from the screen. "I certainly didn't expect to see anything like this in real crime scene photos, especially in a female suicide. She seemed posed. From the pictures taken by the coroner's investigator, the whole thing looked orchestrated."

Stas steeled his jaw. "Yeah, except she's dead, and women don't usually take that way out." Even though he could not see them, he could not imagine the grisly pictures of Sybil Hansen in death. Just the thought of her blowing her brains out blotted the mental image of the beautiful woman he remembered. "They're too vain, and they don't like mess even if they wouldn't have to clean it up."

"Yes, she was in her prime."

"Did you find anything unusual in her system that would suggest that she was unconscious or semiconscious so that someone could position her to make her death look like a suicide?"

Wu nodded at the folder in Stas's hand. "Did your detective friend send over the autopsy report?"

Stas fumbled through the file. "He faxed these to me. The report may be back at the squad room. I was in a rush. Wanted to get here before you guys took off." He tidied his folder and started to rise but leaned into the desk, sensing that he wasn't going to get anything else, he tried one more tactic. "Off the record, if the suicide looked staged, why the verdict? Don't you guys discuss questionable deaths?"

"We do on some cases, but I think someone concluded it was self-inflicted before we even got the body."

"Who? The field investigator?"

"I don't know. I submitted my verdict. The team that reviewed my work felt I was clutching at straws, that I was too influenced by textbook theories. In the end, what I thought didn't count." Wu rose to escort the detective out.

Stas turned back again. "I'm curious. If you had a theory based on your textbook, who could have executed something like this?"

Wu took a few seconds. "I don't know ... a film director." He looked uneasily at Stas, then added, "or a cop."

"Thanks a lot." Stas headed for the door, then turned back. "Did you run a urine test?"

"I can't divulge that detective." Wu winked slyly. "But did you see the note?"

"What note?" He started to open the file but the top fell back into place. "Did you see it? Who has it?"

Wu shook his head. "See the investigators. They usually give it to the next of kin when they claim the body.... unless it's a minor."

As Stas took the elevator down to the ground floor, there was another question to ask Dina. "Did Sybil have a child?" Back in his car, he made a note on the outside of the file folder. Got nothing! But she didn't kill herself!

SIX

As Stas pushed open the entrance door to Dina's apartment complex, he realized he had made a grave mistake. He hadn't looked first.

"Oh, shit!" he muttered under his breath.

Ms. Todd was in the hallway spraying a substance on the leaves of the artificial ficus.

She eyed the key in his hand. "You find your witness?"

"No, but there's a guy here I know, well it's really his girl friend. She's trying to get on the force, as a favor, they loaned me a key so I can keep an eye out," he lied.

Ms. Todd smiled, not questioning further. She had on her stage makeup, wore a very short, very red-patterned muumuu, and very high heels. He wondered how she maneuvered, but she did so with an easy grace, her movements fluid like a cat in the wild, tracking its prey.

"Sweetheart, I could have given you a key if you needed a stakeout. You could've even used my place. I see everything."

"That's all right," Stas retorted. "It's under control. Thanks anyway."

He could feel her steady gaze, boring into his back, giving him an uneasy feeling as he headed for the elevator. He imagined her with x-ray vision slowly peeling his clothes away and, for the moment, her eyes caressing his retreating backside.

"Officer!" She called after him.

He turned, retracing his steps.

"Could you do me a small favor?" She batted her spider-like lashes.

"That depends." He wanted to refuse but smiled instead. "I can't fix tickets."

"Oh, nothing like that. I just need to hang a picture. It'll only take a minute."

"I'm not very handy."

"But you're tall. Come on, I won't bite."

Somehow Stas thought that a little nibble was the least of his worries as he followed her into the apartment. Why did he feel that he was stepping into a predator's lair?

The apartment was bright, too bright: bright colors and bright lights that played off each other. All the lamps had been turned on throughout the living-dining room, their main function, to illuminate the many photos of Ms. Todd hanging on all the walls. He paused and looked at them. There were shots of her as a child posing in black tap shoes and a red costume trimmed in gold braid. Other pictures chronicled her from preteen hoofer to chorus girl to show girl. Fascinated, he followed them around the room. She posed, her hand on her hip and watched him. As each photo progressed along the wall, the heels got higher, the costumes skimpier, and the makeup heavier.

When he stopped, she pointed to a picture on the coffee table. "I just got this back from the framers. I have hundreds, but I got to wait for coupons. You can't imagine how much *this* cost." She picked up her latest photo and crooked her finger at him. "I have the perfect spot."

Stas followed her into a short hallway just off her bedroom, the door was ajar, but he kept his eyes focused on the hallway. A five-foot ladder leaned against the wall; a hammer and nail were close at hand, and X marked the spot. He removed his jacket and looked around, her outstretched hand relieved him of it.

"Looks like you might run out of wall space, Ms. Todd."

"Don't be so formal. Call me Livia."

"Short for Olivia?"

"No, Livia was my stage name. She was an empress, you know, during Roman times." She moved closer, embracing his jacket.

This was starting to look like a setup. He wondered how often she used the picture-hanging ploy.

Livia continued. "I get dizzy when I climb up on a ladder. I fell out of a swing once, broke my leg."

"A swing?"

She laughed showing good teeth. "In a show in Reno, I was the girl in the velvet swing."

He could just imagine Ms.Todd, Livia, swinging half naked and out of reach above a bunch of drunken, excited men craning their necks and spilling their drinks as they strained to get the best view when she passed overhead. Stas climbed the ladder and, standing next to him, she held up hammer and nail. She had been right; it only took a minute to affix another of Livia's moments into place.

Stepping down from the ladder, he turned to her for his jacket. "Did you ever get back on your swing?"

"No, I had to stop dancing. My break didn't heal right. One leg is just a tad shorter than the other." She raised her short skirt even higher to reveal strong, shapely thighs.

He checked the still beautiful legs and wondered just where the break had occurred and which leg was a 'tad' shorter.

As if reading his mind, she added. "You can't see it, but it throws me off balance when I dance."

Stas loved long, shapely legs, but he wasn't going to let Livia seduce him with hers. He handed her back the hammer, closed the ladder, and leaned it against the wall, ready for its next victim.

"Can I get you something to drink: coffee, tea, something stronger if you ain't on duty?"

"Got to go, Ms. Todd." He was at the door.

"Livia, call me Livia."

As he pressed the UP button at the elevator, he could still feel her eyes on him, feel the short hairs on the back of his neck bristle, and then he smiled. It was a wicked smile, one that he was glad no one could see or understand because he was thinking about

Livia and her legs catching some guy in their vise. Then the elevator door opened, and an elderly man stepped out. He looked up at Stas and returned the smile as if he understood its universal significance.

On the ride up, Stas again envisioned those legs and imagined what Detective Chris Marlowe, a single member of the squad, would say about an encounter with Livia. "Bag her head, man, and keep on humping. Let her squeeze the fucking life out of you." The door opened on Dina's floor, and the image of Livia's legs vanished, but others took their place.

He took off his shoes and went to the bedroom. Dina was still asleep. He retraced his steps. Nothing seemed to have been disturbed in the living room or the kitchen. He took a small flask from his pocket, found an old-fashioned glass in the kitchen cabinet and poured a drink. While slowly sipping, he left the kitchen, moved into the dining area, then ended up on the sofa. He placed the folder on the coffee table, looked at a couple of pages, then closed the file, and stretched out. His mind wandered, questions formulated, images of Sybil then Dina flooded his subconscious, and finally sleep came.

Dina slowly opened her eyes. The bright winter sun filtering through an opening in the drapes lifted her, for the moment, out of her depression. Her mouth was dry and sweet as if it had been eating cotton candy. She wore a long silk nightgown that she didn't remember putting on. It wasn't something she would have slipped into to sleep alone.

Though she was awake, her mind was foggy. Then she vaguely remembered a visit from Stas and turned to see if the other side of the bed was occupied. It was empty and undisturbed. She must have dreamed, a dream so vivid that she could still feel his lips, his hands, his ..., but she knew nothing had happened. Yet, there was that trace scent of Stas's cologne. Well, this was a first, she'd never been seduced by a man's aftershave before.

Her feet touched satin slippers that weren't normally beside the bed. In the bathroom, she ran a glass of water and drank. *Why am I so thirsty?* Peering into the mirror, she was surprised to see the puffiness gone from her face, and her eyes were clear. Something was working. *Be patient.*

An abdominal rumble caught her by surprise when she exchanged her silk gown for her terry cloth robe, and she realized she was starving. Heading for the kitchen, Dina stopped short as she noticed a pair of highly polished men's shoes beneath her mahogany coffee table. A gray wool polo sweater was neatly folded on a side chair, a jacket hung on its back.

Stas's lean frame, covered by a light blanket, was stretched out on the mauve sofa. A folded rose chenille throw served as a pillow. Dina laughed to herself at the sight of his feet dangling off the edge. She opened the drapes, bathing the room in bright sunlight. *Give him some of his own medicine.*

The sudden light jerked him into wakefulness as he caught himself to keep from falling off the sofa.

"How long have you been there?" Dina asked. "What day is it?"

Before responding, Stas sat up, grabbed his sweater and pulled it on. "You've been asleep for about ..." he looked at his watch, "... maybe thirty-two hours."

"Did you give me something?"

Ignoring her question, he reached for his shoes, loosened the laces, and slipped them on. "How do you feel?"

She wasn't sure. He made her nervous, uneasy, like a school girl on her first date with a guy she had had a crush on for ages. She wasn't comfortable with the feeling. Stas slowly tied his shoes, then turned his attention back to her.

"Is this a police trick, me sleeping so long?" she asked.

"No, no tricks, I promise." He rose. "I'll even tell you what I found out about the case over a cup of coffee." He hadn't been able to tell her anything the evening before because she'd been unable to keep her eyes open as they tried to talk in her bedroom.

In the kitchen, Dina made coffee from freshly ground beans, carried the carafe from the counter to the table, where he sat in silence, and poured two coffees. *Well, so much for small talk.* Still feeling anxious sitting opposite him, she watched him warm his hands around his mug and inhale the heady aroma before taking a sip.

"Well, what did they say?" She nursed her coffee.

"They didn't say anything. To them, it all seemed pretty routine. Her death was ruled a suicide, but ..." he paused and drank, "if the police had had some reason to think otherwise, they would have investigated; there might have been more questions. Plus, they couldn't tell me anything since it wasn't my case."

"So you didn't learn anything?" She bit her lip.

"Hold on, babe. Did anyone give the police any reason to believe the cause of death wasn't self-inflicted?" He waited for a response. "If not, end of discussion."

"Well, if that's the end of it, then what?"

"But, there *is* more."

She tried to read something beyond police jargon into his cold gray eyes.

"The death was too pat, like it was staged." He refilled his mug and looked across the table to make sure Dina was following. "Sybil was a beautiful woman, right?"

Dina nodded.

"Most good-looking women don't blow their brains out, mar the beauty even in death. They're too vain. They'd take some pills or cut their wrist or both, but ..."

They fell silent for a moment.

"Who made the biggest fuss at her death?"

"I guess I did."

"Why?" he asked.

"Sybil had everything going for her: money, looks, success."

"Yeah, but in her business that could be short-lived."

"I know, and she knew. That's why she was looking for someone to take over. I think she was getting out, but there was only one person who showed any interest. She had even gone to

Honey Malone, but she's retired. So I went back to why should she kill herself? But everyone seemed too ready to accept the fact. I kept asking questions. They kept trying to shut me up. I guess I lost it at the funeral. Someone had to give me something."

"Who?"

"Who what?"

"Who gave you something?"

"Lisa."

"Who's she?"

"Lisa Bane, one of the girls. She also helps with the books."

"Is she legit?"

"What do you mean?"

"Is she an accountant or an escort?"

"She's both. She couldn't pass the CPA exam, said she made more money escorting then doing taxes, and since one was sometimes just as illegal as the other, she chose to have more fun and pocket her money."

"Do you have any idea what she gave you?"

"Something to calm my nerves and make me sleep."

"She had pills at the funeral?"

"She gave me two there, then brought me some later, here."

"How many did you take?"

"I don't know, a couple." Her eyes pleaded for his understanding. "I was desperate to sleep."

"Back to the person of interest."

Dina looked puzzled.

"The person who was interested in the business," he added.

The phone rang. Dina reached over for the wall-mounted phone between them. He caught sight of firm, tan breasts as the top of her robe fell open. She clutched its top. He closed his eyes for a split second as her scent engaged his senses.

"Hello? Yes ... I'm better." She rose and moved toward the counter. "Hold on for a minute while I change phones." She looked at Stas as he pushed his chair back. "Can you hang this up when I get the other phone?"

He nodded. She placed the receiver on the counter. Stas gave her a few minutes after she hurried out before he picked up the phone. Hearing her voice, he hung up.

He sat and finished his coffee, remembering that rare fragrance from the past, now even more pronounced in the kitchen. When Dina returned, she replenished the carafe and refilled both mugs.

"What time is it?" she asked.

Stas glanced at his watch, then looked back at Dina. "Going somewhere?"

"That was Lisa at the agency. I have an engagement this evening." Dina nervously ran her fingers over the rim of her mug before sitting. She glanced toward the small, curtained kitchen window in an effort to avoid his hard stare.

"I love the euphemism you girls use." His jaw tightened. "You ready to go back to work? You need money?"

Dina rose and took the carafe to the counter, mumbling her reply. "It's not a date. It's just dinner with an out-of-town client who needs a companion. I know him. It's okay."

He took his mug and joined her at the sink. "You didn't answer my question. You need money?"

"And you didn't tell me the time, but no, I don't need money."

"Then why are you ..." He broke off.

"I need to get back into circulation. Lisa said ...."

She tentatively touched the back of his hand. He drew away, turning to go. His signals were strangely mixed. She didn't know how to gauge him. Had he been there all night? Had he undressed her, put her to bed?

"Anyway, we have a major problem. Something happened to Sybil's computer. Lisa said it crashed."

"What do you mean 'crashed'"? He looked back at her.

She shrugged her shoulders. "I don't know much about computers."

"What did she say exactly?"

"Just that the hard drive crashed."

"What about backup?"

"I don't know. I ... I told her you were here. I want you to go in with me."

"I can't do that."

"Yes, you can. It's just an office, nothing shady."

He hesitated. "I know computers, but I'm no expert. Sybil couldn't have been a very good business woman if all her shit was so easy to get to."

"That's just it. She always said everything was secure. You can't imagine the sensitive information she had. Some people would kill ..." Dina put her hand to her mouth.

"Maybe somebody did. We need to have a talk about Sybil."

Later that evening, after Stas had gone, Dina dressed for her date with an old client, Mr. Walter Sage from Denver. Not only was he an old client, he was older, eighty-five if he was a day. His only interest these days was to have a beautiful woman on his arm as he attended an annual social/business event in Los Angeles with gentlemen in the same age group. Dina enjoyed his company, and that was all he ever wanted. He was a perfect gentleman, always tipping exceedingly well and bringing her an expensive gift. This was one engagement she didn't want to miss.

After pushing the DOWN call button for the elevator, she glimpsed her reflection in the shiny metal door. Dressed in a shimmering green silk dress, matching jacket, and four inch sandals, Dina nervously fingered a four-strand pearl choker that covered the scar at her neck. At her green Saab, she pushed a button on her key pad to deactivate the car door locks and alarm system. As she paused to get in the car, a figure eased from the shadows and reached for her neck, only to grab a hand full of beads, ripping the necklace from her throat.

"Fuck!" His effort wheeled Dina around as the broken strands rained pearls to the floor.

She kicked out aiming for his groin but missed her mark, the spiked heel striking like a stiletto, puncturing the trouser fabric, and stabbing his calf, drawing blood. Groaning, he fell back in pain, his hand slipping from the silk fabric of the jacket to grab his leg.

Dina fell to one knee in the angle of the car door and the driver's seat. With the brief respite she clung to the bottom of the steering wheel. The assailant reached for her again, filling his bloody hand with the jacket's hem. In a split second she slid an arm from the jacket, leaving most of it in his grasp as she struggled to slip free.

Breathless, she shook her other arm loose and hefted herself into the car. He reached for her dress again. Releasing the wheel and turning, Dina raked her long crimson fingernails across his face drawing more blood. His grip loosened as he felt the fresh welts burn and swell. "Fuckin' bitch!" His breath came, short and ragged. "I'll kill ..." he tried to suck in air as he was hit in his gut by a figure who had materialized from the shadows to slam hard with another powerful blow that dropped the assailant to the ground.

Stas knelt in his back. Grabbing a handful of thick hair, he pounded the attacker's head into the concrete. The nose cracked on contact, a guttural groan was half muffled by the hard surface. The detective half raised and slammed the attacker down again until he felt him go limp.

Satisfied that the assailant was no longer a threat, Stas turned his attention to Dina who was still slumped over the wheel, but as he reached for her, the garage gate slowly cranked upwards, an engine roared to life. Stas, caught off guard, could not reach the assailant as he struggled to his feet and somehow managed to throw himself into a dark sedan that slowed to retrieve him. The car, its passenger door hanging open, the assailant's feet dragging on the concrete, peeled out of the garage, and into the silent street.

Within seconds there was an explosion, an impact of metal on metal. And just as quickly, Stas reached for Dina's garage remote from the driver's side visor and pushed the button. The heavy gate came cranking down. He then eased Dina out of the car.

"We got to get out of here."

"That...that bastard, he tried to kill me." She trembled and balled her hand into an angry fist.

Stas didn't respond, but walked her to the passenger side of the Saab, opened the door, and helped her inside. At the driver's side he swept away loose pearls by the car with his foot, then stooped to pick up her beaded bag and tossed it to her as he settled under the wheel. She eagerly reached inside for her cell phone. He slapped the purse away.

"No! We have about five minutes for a response, maybe less." He backed the car out of its space, grabbed her jacket, got out and swept more loose pearls to other areas of the garage. In determined silence, he threw the jacket to the back, got back in the car, and raised the gate again. He looked at the clock and muttered, "Two minutes', then pulled out of the garage, and made a right turn, away from where he suspected the loud impact had occurred. People were starting to gather on the sidewalk, but Stas didn't slow or stop until he found a quiet side street about three blocks away. He parked, took a deep breath, then got out of the car.

"Don't move! Keep the doors locked. If someone, say a cop, asks. Tell'em you're waiting for your husband."

"But I need to go back to my place."

"Not tonight. No, that's not a good idea. We don't want to be involved."

"Where are you going?" Her voice almost bordered on hysteria. "I thought you were in a hurry!"

"I am, but I want to know what went down." He glanced back through the window, touched the glass, and mouthed, "You'll be okay."

She nodded.

He walked back towards Dina's apartment complex and heard the wailing sirens of the first responders approaching the scene.

About a third of a block ahead, he saw the flashing light bars of two LAPD cruisers on the opposite side of the street where a dark, sedan had slammed into a light standard. Uniformed officers and EMTs were gathered around the car, its headlights still on, illuminating the empty sidewalk as steam hissed from the radiator, puddling fluid beneath the car before running into the street. Traffic was being diverted at the corner by one cop, while two others moved around the wreck to stretch yellow crime scene tape.

As he crossed the street, Stas got a glimpse of Livia wrapped in a fiery red cape and carrying a walking stick. She looked like a middle-aged Red Riding Hood ready to take on the urban wolves and vanquish them with her own ax. He hoped she wouldn't spy him, but she paused next to an elderly woman and pointed to the wreckage. He breathed a sigh of relief, having slipped, for the moment, beneath her radar.

He was torn between the accident scene and going back to Dina, but his detective instincts kicked in. Approaching the wrecked car, he flashed his ID to the uniformed officer who was about to wave him away. The cop didn't bother to look closer, and there was no sign-in sheet. As far as he was concerned, Stas was just another looky-loo, only one with a shield.

"What happened?" Stas asked.

"Looked like an accident at first, but the passenger's been shot. No sign of a driver."

Stas stepped closer to get a better look at the body wedged in the half-opened passenger door. He was almost positive it was the garage assailant, but he backed off, now even more certain he didn't want to get involved, to be questioned. "Who's the DI?"

"Hasn't arrived yet. We called it in as a possible homicide when we saw the blood and a clean entry wound to the head. So we're just waiting and keeping away the looky-loos." He pointed to the small group that had gathered near Livia.

Stas looked around. "Any witnesses?"

"Not a living soul. When we arrived, the street was as empty as a graveyard. Someone heard the crash and phoned 911. This is what we found."

Still hopeful that the investigation would not involve them, Stas reversed his steps but stayed on the side of the street of the accident. He didn't want to be recognized by Livia, but he noticed that she had abandoned her companion and edged into the street where she engaged a young uniform in deep conversation. She just missed seeing Stas.

He walked back to Dina and tapped on the window for her to unlock the door.

"I'm pretty sure that's the guy from the garage, and he's been shot," Stas said as he settled into the driver's seat.

Dina put her hand to her mouth and turned to look back. It took her a few seconds to respond. "Did you tell them what happened?"

"No!"

"Why?" She continued to look over her shoulder, but on the side street, there was nothing to see.

"I said I think it's the guy. I couldn't say for sure. And someone was probably waiting for the dead guy to bring you out. If he'd been successful, there would have been two bodies at the crime scene." He paused to let that aborted scenario from her garage sink in. "Anyway, we don't want to get mixed-up in a homicide investigation. Too many questions and not enough answers." His tone was cold, all business. He started the car and made a U-turn when he pulled into the street.

Finally, Dina spoke. "Where are we going?"

"To my place."

He drove back to the corner, slowed, and looked down the street. There were still people on the sidewalk. Portable lights were being set-up. He caught a brief glimpse of red moving back to the apartment building. Livia seemed to have been undeterred by the police tape. He briefly remembered other crime scenes. There was always the proverbial bystander in every crowd who could insinuate himself or, in this case, herself into the midst of an investigation.

His sigh of relief was short-lived as he pulled behind his car in the next block and realized that maybe his problems were just beginning. Dina seemed lost in her own thoughts and had said nothing until he turned off the ignition, handing her the keys. He opened the door, activating the dome light and revealing her short skirt that had ridden up to mid-thighs.

He looked over at her for a second. "Just follow me. I don't want you going back to your place tonight. If whoever came after you can get into your garage, they can just as easily get into your apartment. Your lock is a joke. We're going to Glendale."

"But you said he was dead." Apprehension returning to her tone.

"There were two inside, and there's no sign of the driver, probably just walked away." He helped her out of the car, back into her driver's side, but waited until she was buckled in before going to his car.

Traffic was light, and Dina easily followed the Mercedes. His condo complex was on a street east of Brand. Once in the underground parking structure, he directed her to a space next to his.

"Is this some kind of LAPD safe house?" She asked.

"No! I told you we're going to my place."

In silence, they took the elevator to the second floor. When the doors opened, he jingled keys and walked down the quiet hall. Dina slipped off her heels to keep up with his long strides. A dog barked at one apartment door, but Stas walked on, unlocking the door two units away.

Once inside, he switched on lights that did little to soften the Spartan appearance of his place. There was a black leather sofa that matched his recliner. A cocktail table and two end tables of the same dark wood of the entertainment center completed the furnishings. Several excellent sepia-toned photos of scenes from a mountain range were the only wall decorations. Off to the right of the entrance, a small office with desk, computer, printer, and fax machine occupied what had once been the dining area.

Dina draped her jacket over the desk chair, then nervously ran her fingers over the edge of his desk.

"I dust." He reached for her jacket, eased out of his, and hung them in the hall closet.

"Oh, I wasn't..." she looked at the tips of her fingers. They were spotless. Dina trailed over to a large window flanked by two floor-to-ceiling bookcases neatly filled with books. She took one off a shelf and read the spine. "You've read all of these?"

"Most."

She put the book down on the coffee table and sat on the edge of the sofa, waiting. Stas returned the book to the bookcase.

"When am I going home?" Dina asked.

"Maybe tomorrow." He turned on the sound system, flooding the room in soft music.

Dina looked around. "Then where am I sleeping?"

"You take the bedroom. It's not the Biltmore, but at least you don't have to worry about getting assaulted again."

She smiled weakly. "Where are you sleeping?"

Stas pointed to the sofa. "It's comfortable enough, but it doesn't matter where I sack out. Can I get you something to drink?"

"Coffee?" She paused, shook her head. "No, I don't want to stay awake. Do you have juice?"

He nodded. "You want something in it?"

"I guess. What do you think?"

In the kitchen he poured her a glass of orange juice and took the Chopin from the freezer. He poured four fingers of vodka in a tumbler and tossed a shot's worth in her glass. When he returned, she had eased into the corner of the sofa. He handed her the glass that she drank down. Stas doubted she even noticed the alcohol.

"I'm exhausted." Dina rose, still clutching the empty glass and went toward the dining area.

He took the glass and laughed. "No, you're heading to the kitchen. Here, I'll show you."

The bedroom was just as Spartan as the living room. There was a neatly made queen-sized bed, two nightstands, a chest of drawers, and an empty straight-backed chair. Two color photos, one was of a young man in an army uniform, the other of a policeman in LAPD blues were the only decorations.

"Is that you in the army?"

"Yeah."

She moved the pictures closer to the edge of the dresser for a better look. "When was this taken?" pointing to the one in police uniform.

"Graduation from the Academy. I was much younger."

Dina looked from the photos to Stas and back as she moved the double frame to its original position but made no further comment. She then put her clutch on the nightstand holding a simple lamp and a clock radio. The other nightstand held the phone, a notepad, and pen along with a twin of the other lamp.

Stas brought sheets, towels, and an oversized Vice Squad T-shirt. "I think you'll find everything you need in the bathroom." He removed the comforter, putting it on the chair and stripped the linens off the bed.

"Here, let me help." She put clean cases on the pillows.

They remade the bed. After replacing the comforter, Stas took a pillow and a blanket from the top shelf of the closet, and left Dina sitting on the edge of the chair while he went into the bathroom. When he came out, he had changed into worn black sweat pants.

"I left a new toothbrush for you on the counter. Sleep well." With bedding in his arms, he gently closed the door.

After Stas left, Dina still sat. At first events had moved in fast-forward, now she seemed to be pulled along in slow motion. Well, at least things had begun to register. Here she was in Stas's apartment, about to sleep in his bed. She finally rose and looked towards the closed door, as if expecting an intrusion. There was no lock, and she could hear him moving about in the other room. After undressing, she folded her clothes and placed them on the lone chair, then took the t-shirt and towels to the bathroom.

It, too, was devoid of decoration. He had left a packaged toothbrush, compliments of Wm. Rossi, DDS, on one side of the counter. His electric toothbrush, toothpaste, recharging electric razor, cup, and cologne stood on the other side of the spotless sink.

Dina picked up the Chanel Egoiste and sprayed it into the air, fanning the fine mist, inhaling the lingering citrus scent that triggered memories from two years before. It also triggered her curiosity.

There was nothing in the bathroom that gave any indication of who the man was other than the brands he used. Feeling nosy, she looked into the medicine cabinet. The nearly bare shelves gave up no secrets. They contained floss, some first aid items, a container of aspirin, a box of Band Aids, and little else. The cabinet drawers held several combs, a stiff bristle brush, nail clippers, sharp scissors, small candles, and matches. The gray towels all matched and were hung with military precision.

Dina looked into the oversized shower stall before turning on the taps and stepping in. She needed to purge the pain of yet another assault, allowing the cascading water to envelop her in its warm refuge.

She squeezed water from her eyes and looked for shower gel, but found only bar soap giving off a clean, masculine smell. She adjusted the spray, letting the needles massage the muscles of her back. Before getting out, she thought of Stas and touched her breasts, feeling the nipples harden.

After drying off, Dina pulled on the oversized T-shirt and looked at herself in the steamy mirror. She shook her head, having a hard time believing that after two years they were, at least, in the same space. She made an effort to hang her towels on the empty bar like the others before flipping off the lights. As she climbed into bed, she wondered what the next few days would bring. Her thoughts were blurred with images of Sybil. She mustn't forget why she had sought out the detective. Could they really discover if Sybil had been murdered? Could they find the killer? After the incident in her garage, she was positive he was still out there, and she was now a target. But why? She didn't know anything. Dina punched, then kneaded his pillow, releasing an essence of lemon and bergamot. Within seconds she had drifted into a deep but troubling sleep.

Stas threw the blanket back. He swung his feet to the floor and sat there, debating whether to make coffee or go for a run. He rose and headed for the bedroom, slowly opening the door. He cursed the owner for "remodeling," taking out the other entrance to the bathroom so guest could use it without going through the bedroom. *Well, how often do I have "company"*?

The early morning light seeped through the bedroom's partially opened blinds. Dina had kicked off part of the comforter revealing a long, shapely leg and thrown her arm across her eyes as if shielding herself from another nightmarish attack. He stood at the side of the bed and smiled, wondering how long he could resist her in such close quarters. Not returning to the hospital or calling her two years ago may not work this time.

He managed to get his running shoes and a sweatshirt from the closet without waking her. Before going to the kitchen, he opened the blinds in the living room. The view revealed the city shrouded in a smoky haze. It was a typical winter morning. The fog would burn off later, but the city would still be overcast and dreary.

Stas took coffee to his desk where he examined his watch that he had broken fighting with the assailant. He looked up when the bedroom door opened, and Dina emerged looking rested despite the ordeal of the previous night.

"Thanks for the toothbrush and shirt."

"How about coffee?" He headed back to the kitchen.

"Sure, black, please." Dina tugged at the oversized T-shirt and curled her bare feet under her as she settled on the sofa.

With Stas in the kitchen, she took the time to take in the room in daylight. A black upholstered, low backed easy chair fit into the angle made by one of the bookcases and the wall. A brass floor lamp completed the compact reading area.

She next turned her attention to the entertainment center. It was closed and silent, yet she remembered the rich, almost sensuous music from the previous night.

He put down one of the coffees when he passed his desk and swept the remains of the watch into the wastebasket. Picking up his mug, he walked over to the sofa and handed a coffee to Dina.

She looked towards his desk. "What was that?"

"What's left of my watch. I busted it last night."

"Can't you get it fixed?"

"It's not worth it. One of these days I'll get a good one. It was a knockoff. I've got more in the drawer. If you don't get too close, you never notice the difference."

"What, no pulsating secondhand?" Dina slowly sipped her steaming coffee and looked around. "Am I under house arrest?"

He just glanced at her for a second.

"What am I suppose to do for clothes," Dina continued, "since none of your girlfriends left anything for me to wear?"

Her sarcasm was not lost on him. "I don't bring women here. And you don't seem like someone who'd want another woman's leavings." He looked her over. "That t-shirt looks much better on you than it ever did on me. We'll go to your place later, but I don't want you there by yourself. If I can get in, so can they."

"You do believe me then?"

"That something's going on? Yeah." He nodded slightly.

"Why were you there last night?"

"Just a gut feeling that your date wasn't real." Stas went over to his desk and brought a file back to the sofa, spreading its contents on the coffee table.

"It wasn't a real date. I told you, it was for dinner, nothing else." She leaned towards him. "I don't understand."

"Who've you been talking to besides me?"

"Lisa, some of the other girls, Sybil's lawyer. I was upset. I don't remember."

"Maybe you're talking too much, asking too many questions." He caught the scent of her hair and reached for his coffee. "Anyway, here's a perfect suicide committed with a surplus gun the CHP sold somewhere up north. How'd she get it?"

Dina hunched her shoulders. "I don't know." She raised the cup to her lips, then put it back down. "Probably from Matt."

"Who's Matt?"

"Matt Brown, he did Sybil's security. He's an ex-cop."

"Being a cop doesn't necessarily make him legit. Maybe that's why he's an ex-cop."

Dina seemed to weigh his comment before she continued. "He also runs a limo service and does security for industry people. You know, rent-a-cop for films, music, visiting VIPs."

"Hmm, some of the same circles."

She didn't look up. "I don't trust him."

"Why?"

"He wanted into the business, wanted Sybil to make him a partner, but she wouldn't with him. I know she was looking to make a change, maybe even sell. Running that kind of business isn't easy. You just can't call up any security company and tell'em you want protection for your operation, your girls, and you sure as hell can't call the local real estate agency and ask them to list your brothel. She was stuck."

"Did you ever see the gun?"

"Once, in her desk with a box of shells."

"Did you recognize the caliber?"

"I don't know anything about guns. I don't like them." She drank down the last of the lukewarm coffee and frowned.

"Could anyone in her office have access to the gun?"

"I guess. It was in the bottom drawer. I don't know if she kept the desk locked."

"Tell me about Brown?"

"I heard he had issues as a cop. That he used excessive violence, and was forced to resign."

"Where did he come from?"

"I'm not sure, San Jose or Fresno. I'd have to ask around. Is it important?"

"Could be."

Dina frowned. "But now there's another problem. Lisa wants me to come in. It's about the computer. Everybody's in a panic. Lisa needs money for operating, and Raven's with some of the girls in Europe."

"Who are these people?"

"Lisa does the books, and Raven takes care of the money."

"Next, you'll tell me Sybil had a tax accountant."

"She did have some legitimate businesses. We had a boutique next to the office. After all, we were a modeling agency."

"Yeah, sure." He closed the folder. "You have access to money?"

"Raven and I have a safe de..." She broke off.

"Don't tell me anymore. I'm a cop, remember?"

"Things are happening so fast. Please come with me. See for yourself."

"Just how do you plan to disguise me to get me in?"

"You don't look like a cop, and you certainly don't act like any I've known."

Stas leaned back and thought a minute about her suggestion. "Who else did you tell about me?"

"Just Lisa. I trust her."

"Then I guess we should go see Lisa." He stood. "So how should I dress, like a computer techie or a pimp?"

"You worked vice. You understand." Dina looked down at her t-shirt. "But I can't go like this."

SEVEN

After folding his covers and stacking them on the end of the sofa, Stas made another pot of coffee and brought it to the living room while he waited for Dina to finish in the bathroom.

"You want cream or sugar?" he asked placing a mug on the coffee table in front of Dina."

"Black's good." She came from the bedroom, settled on the sofa, and sipped her coffee.

"I won't be long." In the bedroom Stas stood in black boxer briefs, taking his time picking out what to wear. His suit had to reflect money: be a cut above a street hustling pimp but decidedly below a Wall Street stockbroker.

He selected a charcoal gray wool and silk pinstripe he'd had made a year ago by his LA tailor's Hong Kong cousin. The suit had cost a mint, but he hadn't found any occasion to wear it after Marlowe, a fellow detective, asked where he got his "pimp" suit. After that put-down, Stas had thought about donating it to the Salvation Army but laughed at the image of some down and out vagrant wearing it to look through skid-row dumpsters. So the suit went back into the closet hanging in its individual garment bag advertising in large gold letters the sartorial expertise of JIMMY WONG, HONG KONG TAILOR.

He put on a light gray Egyptian cotton shirt, a gray and gold silk striped tie, black socks, and black Italian lace-up shoes. He had made his point: the look proclaimed that some chick had spent a lot of time on her back to put these threads on his.

Dina smiled broadly when Stas joined her. She caught a whiff of his cologne, which added to the overall effect. "You look good and..." she paused, "and smell even better." To keep his scent in her presence, she had sprayed some of his Chanel Egoiste on a tissue and tucked it in her handbag.

"You ready?" He grabbed the mugs and took them to the kitchen.

She rose and waited for him at the door.

They took the elevator to the garage. With all of the furor of the night before, Dina had paid little attention to his car. Now as they walked to the black Mercedes, it registered.

"Where did you get this?"

While she looked on, Stas busied himself wiping off the dust that had settled on the black finish. "Bought it at a DNA auction." He held the door open for her.

"Aren't you afraid?"

"Of what?" He went around and slid into the driver's seat.

"The old owner!"

"This car is the least of his worries. He'll be too old to drive when he gets out. He's doing twenty-five to life at Pelican Bay."

"Sounds like a resort."

"Yeah, and his life's a real picnic."

"I didn't know cops made enough money to afford..." she paused as if to calculate.

"We make enough. I could say the same for you and your Saab."

"It was a gift."

"See, now *that* I believe." He eased the car out of the garage and into traffic.

"Shouldn't I know something about you since you're an old friend?" Dina asked.

"The name is Polish, Vladeislaw, after my father. I guess I'm a junior. He's Vlade, so I got stuck with Staszek, my middle name. At work it got cut to Stas. Some people have trouble with the last name, Nowak. They keep mispronouncing it. In Polish, the W is pronounced like a V."

"Were you born in Poland?"

"My folks were. My mother came following my old man. Then she sent for her sister. They lived together in Chicago. The little trio split when I was born."

"In Chicago?"

"Nope, I'm a native Angelino."

"How long have you been a cop?"

"Ever since I got out of the Army. I guess twelve years."

"And your wife?"

"My ex, that's ancient history. Nothing to know there."

Dina smiled as she gazed out into the traffic.

The drive from Glendale to the Wilshire district took less than half an hour. Dina closed her eyes as a Chopin "Polonaise" lulled her into a light doze. She opened them when she felt the high-performance car downshift when it approached the driveway leading into the garage of her apartment building. Reaching into the evening bag on her lap, she took out the remote control and opened the gate.

Stas parked in a secluded space some distance from the elevator. "Give me your key and come up in five minutes. I want to check things out first." He got out of the car. "Let's hope I don't run into your manager."

"You know Livia?"

"Doesn't everybody?" He grinned. "She accosted me the first time I came by. Now I know what it feels like to dodge a process server. I got the impression that nothing or no one gets pass Livia, especially if he wears pants."

"Yeah, Livia has that special radar, usually activated by a strong presence of male testosterone."

Luckily, there was no sign of Livia on the ride up to Dina's floor. Her apartment was empty and showed no signs of intrusion.

Five minutes later Dina pushed the door open and peered in before entering. She was hesitant as she looked about her living room.

"Is everything okay?" she asked.

"When this is over, we need to change your locks. A blind ten year old could get past yours in less than a minute."

She ignored his comment and fingered the dusty leaves of a dying plant. "They need water."

He frowned. "Leave them 'til later."

"I guess I'd better get dressed." Dina headed to the bedroom.

Stas started to sit but walked to the bedroom door and called in. "Better bring some things for a couple of days."

She didn't respond. While waiting for her to finish dressing and packing, he took a closer look around the apartment. On the wall next to the sofa, a handsome antique table served as a desk. He flicked through a couple of unopened envelopes that looked like they contained bills. There didn't seem to be any personal mail. Several expensive looking prints mixed with a few original watercolors and two small oils decorated the walls. He was surprised at the reading material on the coffee table. There were two current news magazines, four copies of *The Guardian,* and one on natural health but none of those glossy women's magazines proclaiming 101 ways to satisfy a man in bed.

He looked out onto a small balcony off the living room. Stas checked the locks on the sliding glass doors, found them secure, but didn't go out. He could see a profusion of greenery spilling from ceramic pots in a corner protected by an overhang. The plants seemed healthy. When he turned back from the balcony, he noticed a large empty vase on a side table. She liked natural things, no plastic flowers like Livia's. That was good. Finally, he relaxed and wished for a vodka.

He did not wait long. Dina emerged from her bedroom wearing gray slacks and a long gray cashmere sweater that covered everything but accented the swell of her breasts, the flair of her hips. He liked her understated make-up, even her hair, pulled back into a ponytail. A whiff of something unfamiliar and exotic meant to mildly excite completed the picture. Now he wanted that drink even more. He rose to help her with her two bags.

"What's all this?"

"Just a few things." Dina tried to force a smile as she grabbed a jacket from the hall closet.

"C'mom, Livia doesn't need to see this." Stas held the door open, then checked that it was locked when it closed.

After a stop at Dina's bank, the drive to Sybil's agency took about twenty minutes. Her various enterprises were located on the fifth floor of a typical mid-Wilshire office building. Stas was unsure if the "Appointment Only" on the door of the boutique was the shop's name or the only method of conducting business. But he felt sure that it was a legitimate front that probably laundered some of the money from Sybil's other endeavors. The discreet, off the street, out of your face, location assured its clientele privacy and promised the ultimate discretion.

Dina and Stas entered through a door marked AGENCY about ten feet from the boutique's entrance. *Well, that says a lot,* Stas thought. The outer office was decorated with headshots of some of the most beautiful women he'd ever seen. Large silver letters on one wall announced "THE HANSEN AGENCY".

Sindy, a tall, well-endowed synthetic beauty who looked like one of Hitchcock's Hollywood blondes, acted as receptionist. She made a feeble attempt to adjust a very short skirt when she came from behind the counter.

"Lisa said you were coming, but she didn't say you were bringing a guest." She addressed Dina without taking her eyes off Stas.

"He's going to look at the computer," Dina offered as she made her way toward an unmarked interior door. "Wait here a minute."

Stas took a seat on a red camelback sofa opposite Sindy's desk. They exchanged smiles as he checked out the reading material: *Cosmopolitan, Vogue, U.S. News and World Report, Perfect*

Ten, and Playboy. Something for everybody, he thought. He wondered where they kept the *Penthouse* and *Hustler.*

Sindy watched him with her cornflower blue eyes, shaded by artificially long, thick eyelashes. Even Stas couldn't resist the eye candy. His gaze dropped for a second to the deep, full cleavage revealed by her low cut blouse. She definitely wasn't there to make appointments. She *was* an appointment. Stas picked up *Perfect Ten.*

"Can I get you something, something to drink?" she offered. His steel gray eyes gave her a slow, deliberate stare. "No, thanks, I'm okay."

Sindy returned to buffing her nails, disregarding any pretense of work. It was obvious she had lost interest.

Sybil's office was a large L-shaped space distinctly decorated and divided into three sections. A large ornately carved mahogany desk with several upholstered Queen Anne chairs occupied the short end of the "L". The long side of the "L" housed the computer, printer, fax machine, and several telephones connected to elaborate recording devices. A long mahogany conference table with eight matching chairs took up the rest of the area.

Wallpaper and window coverings of rich, muted pastels complimented plush oriental rugs scattered throughout the room on hard wood floors. Several original oil paintings graced the walls. The room could have been the office of the director of a Beverly Hills art gallery rather than that of a high class Hollywood madam.

Anyone entering for the first time would have been impressed by the expense expended to create such an atmosphere of affluence and luxury. If this room was a creation of Sybil Hansen, then it truly reflected her tastes, which no one would have expected from a woman who trafficked in the sensual and the carnal.

Lisa Banes was both an associate and the agency's accountant. Since the death of Sybil, Lisa had undertaken the day-to-day running of Sybil's enterprises: a modeling agency, a boutique that catered to the ladies of the evening, and an escort service, all of dubious legitimacy. In her late thirties she was a stunning natural red head with emerald green eyes that the manufacturer of colored contacts would have given a fortune, or made one, to duplicate.

She was on her hands and knees under the computer stand fooling with wires and cables when Dina walked in. "Thought I'd make sure there's nothing wrong with these. I still can't believe this shit. How can I do the books? I can't find back-up, nothing."

"Now do you believe me?" Dina asked.

"Don't even go there. The hard drive crashin' got nothing to do with Sybil's death." Rising, Lisa brushed off her hands. "Do you have it?"

Dina took a fat envelope from her shoulder bag and gave it to Lisa. "Stas came with me."

She looked back at Dina. "The cop? Are you giving him freebees?"

"No!"

"Then what's going on? Why are you over there?"

"He thought I'd be safer."

"Yeah, what? Safer from him? What's in it for him or for you?" She kicked some loose cables. "This the same guy from two years ago?"

"Yes, and there's nothing going on." Dina took a deep breath and bit her lip. "He's just been there for me."

"Nobody is 'just there for you.' They all want something." Lisa continued. "You know he busted Sybil?"

Dina was visibly surprised. "No, when?"

"When he was in Vice. You *do* know he worked vice?"

"He's a detective now and was two years ago."

"Don't be stupid. Why do you think they call each other 'brother' officers? They look out for each other. It's like a cult."

"So what happened to Sybil?"

"Nothing. She had people in higher places. The DA dropped the charges. Just watch it. He's still a cop in bed or out."

Lisa returned to the computer. "Well, since he's here, let him look. What harm can it do? Just be careful. Raven's not due back from Europe 'til tomorrow, and Matt's on the prowl. He thinks he's finally getting his dick in the door."

Dina walked back toward the outer office. "I'd better rescue Stas from Sindy."

Lisa laughed. "Yeah, she's always looking for fresh meat."

Dina opened the door and beckoned Stas in.

Lisa offered her hand as she looked him over. "You don't look like a computer nerd. Are you sure you can fix computers?"

"Not really. I'm more interested in the timing of your crash. Too much seems to be happening. I doubt it's all coincidence." Stas walked over and looked at the CPU unit. "Where did you keep the back-up?"

"In a lock-box in there." Lisa pointed to a closet. "And it's missing too."

He shook his head. "So much for security. Was there another back-up?"

"Sybil kept a set, but I haven't been able to find it." She walked over to the desk. "There's nothing else here. I guess it could still be at her condo."

Stas followed her to the desk. The locked drawers had been forced open. "Who did this?"

"Matt. We couldn't find the key," Lisa said.

"I'd like to have someone look at this." He touched the computer keyboard.

"Another cop?"

Stas smiled and shook his head. "This young felon knows more about computers than most departments can learn in a year. Sometimes we have to consult him. Trust me, if anyone can reconstruct your hard drive, he can. But I can't believe Sybil would leave sensitive data out here for anyone to access." He looked at Lisa, "Tell me it isn't so?"

Lisa hesitated. "Sybil had her own devices." She pointed to the phones and recorders. "I just do the books. I don't book the tricks." She looked from Dina to Stas.

As Dina, Lisa, and Stas talked by the computer, Matt Brown entered. He was about forty-five with a flawless chocolate complexion, making his exact age difficult to discern. His good looks were reminiscent of the male profiles found on ancient Nubian tombs, and his well-sculptured frame was poured into an expensively tailored suit.

Lisa turned first. "Did you hear about the computer?"

He didn't respond, but looked hard at Stas, who failed to flinch under Brown's scrutiny. Both men stood their ground like two fighting cocks, each taking the measure of the other before the fatal match.

"So what's your interest?" Brown finally spoke. "You fix computers?"

"I asked him to take a look," Dina chimed in.

"I didn't ask you." Brown's voice was cold, cutting.

Stas demeanor stiffened. His response equally as cold as Brown's. "Yes, I can fix computers, and if I can't, I'll find someone who can." With that, Stas ignored Brown and turned back to Lisa. "The guy's name is Stealth. If he can't help you, nobody can. You may want to put him on the payroll, especially if you continue to have problems." He wrote a number on a slip of paper, handed it to Lisa, then turned to Dina. "I'll wait for you." He nodded toward the door and brushed by Brown.

In the outer office, Stas returned to the *Perfect Ten* that was still open to the article he had been reading. As he sat back, he was joined on the sofa by a petite Asian beauty. He hadn't heard her enter, but he was aware of the pressure of a body, warm and fragrant, looking over his arm at the article.

When he turned to her, she smoothed her black leather miniskirt that covered very little but revealed a lot if one cared to venture a look. She flipped long, silken tresses over her shoulder and met his gaze with a mocking smile. "I'm Dar Ling."

Stas didn't introduce himself but was aware of a deep breath that swelled the upper part of her black satin blouse. It was evident she wore no bra, nor did she seem to need one. She slowly moistened her lips, then dropped her hand to Stas's upper thigh. Without looking down she edged it higher.

In one easy motion, he removed her hand from his crotch and dropped it back into her lap.

"So, you gay?" she asked, her laugh like tiny crystal bells.

He closed the magazine and stood. "You think so?"

"No, but I don't get to check out..." she looked in his lap "...the equipment." She rose and patted her hips. "Listen, I've forgotten more about pleasing a man than Dina and Lisa combined." She nodded towards the door to the inner office. "Remember that, when you want to experience the ultimate pleasure."

As Dina walked in, Dar Ling once again tossed her hair over her shoulder and mockingly blew Stas a kiss. "See you around, lover."

A surge of unspoken tension seemed to engulf the small reception area.

"What was that about?" Dina stared after Dar Ling as she left.

He was amused at Dina's concern. "I think she wanted my body or a certain part of it."

Dina angrily sailed through the outer door he held open. "Bitch."

EIGHT

It was late, and Lisa Banes had awakened feeling for Matt Brown next to her. His side of the bed was empty. She covered her nakedness with one of his shirts that she found draped over a chair and went to the den where Matt struggled on the computer.

"I take it you're not coming back to bed?" She rested her hand on her hip. "How about coffee?"

"Great." As his fingers punched the keys, he groaned at the monitor's display.

Lisa returned with two mugs of coffee and handed one to Matt. "Careful, it's hot." She stood behind him watching a spreadsheet fill the screen. "This is all my work. I could have told you she never kept her personal stuff on this computer. There has to be another one at her place."

"We need the keys again. Did you give them back to Raven?"

Setting her mug down, Lisa massaged Matt's shoulders. "I can always get the keys." She kneaded the well-defined muscles of his upper back. "Why don't you come back to bed, let me work this tightness out?"

He inserted another flash drive from a small black case. "I need the names. We're sitting on a gold mine, damn it, and I can't get the names."

Lisa returned to her coffee. "What good will it do us if you start blackmailing our clients?"

"I don't give a fuck about the business, especially if Raven's running it." Tension and frustration were building in his tone.

"Well, I care."

He turned and pulled her to him, running his hand under the shirt. "If I get those names, to hell with the business."

"How long is all this going to take?"

"Nine, ten months. It might mean relocating to DC. How would you like to work in Washington?"

Lisa smiled. "All those politicians."

"My boy's got to win first."

"Your boy?'

"Edward A. Lawson, Esquire, Congressman Lawson, Senator Lawson, President Lawson, nice ring, huh?"

"Well, he ain't won yet." Lisa pulled away from his roving hand.

"He will." Matt turned back to the computer.

She picked up her empty mug and started to leave, then paused. "How did you hook up with this guy?"

"We go way back, to Fresno P.D."

"He bust you?"

"Didn't you know I was a cop." There was a hard edge to his voice. "A damn good one, 'til..."

Lisa edged back to the computer. "What?"

"Not now."

She hunched her shoulders. "All right by me, but what do we do about Dina?"

"You two need to get together, do a party."

She laughed. "It may not be that easy. It's not like selling Tupperware."

Matt Brown drove his black Lexus down the Wilshire corridor to Fairfax. He slowed in front of a storefront where window signs announced the candidacy of Edward Lawson for United States Congress. Brown squeezed into a parking spot that was much too small, leaving the tail end of the vehicle extending into a loading zone. He disregarded the white curb as well as the flashing display on the parking meter indicating it had run out of time and needed to be fed.

Inside, the large front area of the campaign headquarters was equipped with several tables filled with political literature and colorful bumper stickers. The walls were festooned with red, white, and blue bunting; American flags covered the rest of the empty spaces. Photos of Lawson smiled down on a group of young, cookie-cutter blondes who manned telephones and stuffed envelopes. Their lithe, nubile figures, clear, healthy complexions, and, with a few exceptions, sparkling blue eyes made them the poster girls for a new moral generation.

Several girls near the entrance flashed their condescending smiles which Brown ignored as he headed for a door in the rear of the room. He opened it without knocking.

Edward Lawson and the Rev. Dr. Robert Aagard sat at a small conference table looking through a stack of official looking documents. Lawson, a man in his mid-forties, turned when Brown entered and mumbled something. Aagard didn't bother to look up but continued with the papers before him.

Brown walked over to a narrow table against the wall and poured himself a cup of coffee from a large, commercial coffee-maker. He grabbed several packets of sugar before sitting down at the table.

Aagard raised his deep blue eyes to question rather than greet Brown. "Has there been some change in schedule?"

Brown shook his head and stirred sugar into his coffee.

"Then why are you here?" asked Lawson.

"Because we have a problem." Brown offered.

This got Lawson's attention. "Problem? What kind of problem?"

Brown's hand shook, tipping his cup and slopping coffee onto the table. He moved his chair back, careful not to let the spill drip onto his expensive gray suit. "I think there's a cop in the mix."

Lawson arched his eyebrows. "A cop? Are you sure?"

"One of the girls brought him to the agency." Brown reached for a napkin and wiped around his cup.

"And you're sure he's a cop?" Aagard asked.

Brown stared defiantly at the minister.

"Something about him. The way he carried himself, the way he looked at me."

"You mean you couldn't intimidate him?" Aagard's voice was deep and resonant. "Somehow, I'm not surprised. Why was he there?"

"He was supposed to be a computer expert."

"And was he?"

Brown smiled. "He couldn't fix the hard drive. Nobody can. My computer died weeks ago, so I switched them."

"Just what do you hope to gain with this business?" Aagard asked.

"Some ammunition if I need it."

"Listen," Lawson added, "We don't need anyone asking questions, especially cops. I certainly don't want anyone going up North. You're supposed to be handling our security not messing around with cops and computers."

"Let them go wherever they want," interrupted Aagard. "There's nothing to be found, but maybe you need to stay away from Sybil's for a while. If the question ever came up, how could you explain your connection? We certainly don't want attention drawn to something that might implicate you or your business with anything illicit."

He tented his fingers and looked heavenward as if ready to launch into a sermon on some grave, moral issue.

Lawson stood and eased into his jacket. "I've got an appointment with the Mayor."

His navy suit was cut to perfection. His shirt collar caressed his neck; the sleeve lengths were perfect, showing just enough cuff. The blue and white striped tie complimented the clean, crisp look. A gold pin enameled with an American flag graced his lapel. Lawson's image was near perfection. He knew he was worthy of the people's confidence and, therefore, worthy of the people's vote.

"Listen, Matt, don't do anything foolish with whatever you find. Don't contact clients on her database. And don't make any promises to anyone. Just leave all that shit 'til later." Lawson patted his pockets for wallet and keys. "Don't fuck up."

Aagard stiffened at the expletive. Ever since he aligned himself with the neo-cons and the religious right, he had foresworn any semblance of vices, real or imagined.

Both men watched Lawson grab his briefcase and leave.

"Matt, you need to understand, that once we win the primary, there'll be time to make use of any data you find but not now. We must be discreet. You are being discreet, aren't you?"

Brown nodded but said nothing.

Aagard was right or at least convincing. He had been able to turn a mediocre legal practice into an enterprising business that marketed clients who advocated correct moral behavior. Marrying well had catapulted him into different social and financial strata. As a co-founder of the Consortium for Moral Standards, he saw himself as a modern Cromwell, ushering in an era of national righteousness supported by a new fundamentalism.

Brown had become one of his associates not out of any religious conviction but solely for the prospect of political and financial gain. It was always easy to get religion and scruples if the price was right.

The silence was finally shattered when Brown suddenly stood, letting his chair fall noisily to the floor. "You know, if I wanted the cold, silent treatment, I'd go find me a woman."

He had never been able to get a handle on Aagard's stony stoicism. They had known each other for years, met while working for Fresno PD, but even then, there had been tension. While Brown had busted his butt in a patrol car, Lawson and Aagard had gone to law school at night and, after passing the Bar, gotten jobs in the DA's office. Still, Aagard hadn't languished in the prosecutor's office trying to make a name for himself. He'd gone into private practice and had advanced his career through the bedroom instead of the courtroom by marrying into money and influence.

When Fresno's Internal Affairs investigated Brown for using excessive force on a civilian, it was Lawson who insisted that they use Aagard as his attorney instead of the police union's counsel. Aagard had gotten Brown's charges dropped, but to avoid a civil suit, Matt resigned and moved to Los Angeles, and Lawson, with some urging from his wife, Brown's former partner, made the connections for him in LA.

"I'm out of here. You have the schedule. If there are any changes on your end, call me."

Aagard had not flinched when the chair fell, and now, did not raise his head from his files.

Outside a taxi double-parked in front of the campaign headquarters just as Brown was about to get in his car. The cabbie made no effort to open the door for his passenger but idled and waited for the woman to pay him. Gwen Lawson backed out of the cab on the street side, amid blaring horns and inaudible but visible obscene hand gestures. She dragged a suitcase and tote bag after her. Her anger flushed her face when she flung several bills through the open passenger window.

Brown watched from the curb and laughed when she turned. He should have known that butt anywhere. "He doesn't know who he's messing with."

Gwen dropped her bag, just missing his toes and gave him a big hug. "Matt, am I glad to see a familiar face."

"Why didn't someone tell me you were coming? I would have sent a car for you. Hell, I'd have picked you up myself." He disentangled himself from her and held her at arm's length. "Still looking good even out of uniform."

"I took a few days off. I've got to get used to this campaigning." She mockingly bared beautiful teeth. "See, the perfect demeanor of a loving and dutiful wife."

"That's all he needs. A loving wife by any politician's side gets the votes every time, especially if she can bake cookies."

She gave him a gentle push. "Suppose I don't want to bake cookies. What about my needs, my career? I love my job. I don't want to quit. And I'm tired of this damn commuting."

"Somebody has to make the sacrifice. Take a leave. You can always go back if he doesn't win."

"I'm not supposed. to have those kinds of thoughts." Gwen rested her tote atop her suitcase. "I'm supposed to meet him for dinner?"

"Ed's not here."

"Robert?"

"The play-maker, spin-meister..." Brown's disdain was evident.

"I'm really not up for his pontificating."

"Well, better you than me. Let's get together soon for a drink."

She gave him a little salute and rolled her bags into the building.

When Gwen entered the back office, she found Aagard still poring over computer printouts. He looked up and flashed his most engaging smile, the one usually reserved for well-heeled matrons with fat investment portfolios, ready checkbooks, and a need to feel involved. He had a particular line and a warm touch designed to facilitate a quick signature on a generous donation. Whenever he was with female donors, Aagard was able to address their deeply rooted fears and anxieties. They would pour their hearts out to him, and he would promise with his eyes, his smile, and the light touch of his hand that stirred fires they thought long dead ages before. Yet once the check had cleared, the promises slowly turned to ashy embers awaiting the next outstretched hand of a willing patron.

Gwen had known Robert too long to succumb for his seductive smile and his glib tongue.

"Ed's not here," he offered.

"I know."

His eyebrows rose in mock surprise.

"I ran into Matt on the street. I just need to leave my things here since no one bothered to get me a key to our new place." She walked over to the wall table and poured herself a coffee.

"I'm about finished with this. I can give you a lift. I have a car and a driver at my disposal."

"And you have a key to our place as well?"

"Yes, I have an extra."

"Then I'll take it." She held out her hand. "I'll call Ed later, maybe he can meet me for dinner somewhere."

Robert rose and walked around to Gwen. He was poised to rest his hands on her shoulders, but she turned abruptly, leaving him standing awkwardly beside her.

"I thought you and Beth could get together. You know, do some girl things: shop, make-up, hair."

Gwen touched her chignon that had started to come undone. "What's wrong with my hair and make-up?"

"I was hoping you'd make a few changes, nothing major. Soften your look. You still look like a cop. You know, create something new, something more appropriate as the wife of a congressman. It's all about image, family values...."

"I didn't know there was a family-value hairdo or moral makeup." A splash of pink started to rise up her neck.

"Gwen, it's not just that, it's also attitude. You're a strong woman. You could be running for office in your own right, but Ed doesn't need a partner standing next to him, he needs a helpmate. People need to see that strong family bond."

"This is bullshit. You might have taken in Ed with this 'makeover', but I'm not falling for it. I'm warning you, Robert, be careful. My husband isn't as malleable as you think. For all we know, he may have his own agenda."

"Well, at least call Beth. She's been dying...." He walked back to his chair, fumbled in his pocket and pulled out a smartly designed gold key ring.

"I bet." She snatched the key, picked up her purse, and left.

NINE

Dina pushed a bowl with the remains of Chinese take-out to one side of the coffee table. Stas gathered up everything and took them to the kitchen, leaving the heady odor of ginger and garlic still lingering in the air.

"Don't you ever leave things just laying around, even for a few minutes?" she called after him.

Stas called back from the kitchen doorway. "Like what?"

"Dishes, books, papers, clothes, I don't know. You seem so compulsive."

He returned with two mugs and put them on the coffee table, then went back to his desk and brought over the file. "Don't put me under your microscope, babe."

"Well, do you have enough for an investigation?"

"No. The DA would laugh me back to the Academy," he said, tapping the file. "This would never fly."

"But the doctor said...."

Stas sat next to her and opened the file. "Do you know how hard it is to overturn a suicide verdict with no evidence and no body to exhume?"

"But the gun, the computer, the attack...."

"All barely circumstantial and weak at that. We don't know if any of this concerned Sybil. What I'd really like to see are those backup disks. How sensitive are they?"

Dina withdrew to the corner of the sofa and reached for her coffee. "Names, numbers, money. Wouldn't you guys love to get your hands on them?"

"The IRS more than us." He didn't want to press the issue but tried another tactic. "Tell me about Sybil."

"There's not much to tell. She was biracial, I think, beautiful and smart, a unique businesswoman who ran a very profitable but illegal enterprise. If it had been legal, she'd have been one of those top women execs you read about in *Money* or *Forbes*. She even tried to get us to save, invest, but we bought cars, clothes, got a nice apartment. If there was anything left, we put it away, maybe, bought a condo, maybe." She smiled. "There was always great money..." her smile faded, "... and the gifts."

"You okay?"

"Yeah, I'm fine. I know I can't do this forever."

"Then why do it at all?"

"Money. Getting all the things I always wanted or thought I needed and knew I couldn't afford without the right education, the right connections, or the right husband."

"Did you get them?"

"A few. Sybil made the contacts and took her cut. She said we were like pro-football players, that our backs would last about as long as their knees or maybe it was the other way 'round." Her laugh faded as she reminisced. "She ran a tight ship. She didn't take any shit...from..." The words trailed off.

"Interesting group of ladies. It's beyond me why you, why they do it, but..." Stas picked up his unopened fortune cookie, crushed it, and tossed it in the trash.

"We do it because you men want it and are willing to pay for it."

Stas sipped his coffee. "Was she still turning tricks?"

"She had one special client. He was like her boy friend. I don't even know if he knew. I heard he was a scientist." Dina cracked open her cookie and read the fortune without sharing its content. "She also had some very influential friends."

"Yeah, I know."

Dina waited for him to elaborate. "Did you ever sleep with her when she was working?"

"I was still married."

Dina laughed. "Who do you think are our best clients?"

"Well, even if I had the inclination, I didn't have the money." In the brief silence, Stas could feel painful memories surfacing. He didn't look at Dina when he spoke. "You're suppose to get it at home, but it's kinda hard having sex with someone who hates being married to a cop. I felt inadequate before I even dropped my briefs. We were two angry people living in the same house but too lazy to move out, to move on. There was no love, no sex, nothing."

"I can't believe you went without."

"I didn't say that."

"You should have let Sybil or one of her girls relieve some of that tension and anger."

"Anger? What anger?"

"Hell, I can feel it over here."

Stas ignored her comment and rose with his mug. "You want a drink?" Without waiting for a reply, he went to the kitchen and returned with a frosted fifth of vodka and two tumblers. "Did Sybil have kids?" he asked as he poured, filling his glass and giving Dina the equivalent of two fingers.

"What's this?"

"Vodka, mother's milk to Poles, drink up." He lifted his glass in a mock toast.

"So you do have vices to go along with your..."

"What? My rage? I didn't know it showed." Stas drank most of his vodka down and refilled his glass.

"I didn't say that."

"But were you thinking it?"

"No, I was going to say bitterness. But I'm not sure. You can feel it, sense it, like what do they call those blue things that surround your body?"

"An aura?" He laughed. "Do you see an aura?"

"No, but I feel something. Do you rage? Am I going to have to be careful not to antagonize you, drink my ration of vodka and go to bed like a good, little..." She drained her glass and coughed.

"We've gotten off track. Sybil, remember this is about Sybil. We don't want to get sidetracked." He watched her nod in agreement and smiled. "You haven't answered my question."

"What? Did she have a kid?" She hunched her shoulders. "There were rumors." Putting her glass down on the table, she looked up, "Do you have kids?"

Stas shot her a look. His gray eyes seemed a shade darker as the alcohol started to take effect.

"I'm sorry," Dina continued. "They say she fell hard for a cop. Later, she stopped working and just ran the business. If there was a kid, it was never in the picture, and I wouldn't know where to start looking."

"What about the scientist? Who is he?"

"I don't know."

"Well, someone does. I want his name." He took another drink and cleared his throat. "Who else would know about a kid?"

Dina looked puzzled by the urgency of his questions.

"I need to get into Sybil's apartment. Do you have a key?" Stas asked.

"I thought you didn't need keys." She flashed a cynical smile. "May should have one."

After first stopping at Peets for coffee, they drove to Pasadena in silence. Stas exited the 210 freeway at Lake Avenue and took it north towards the mountains. Altadena was one of those bedroom communities that had once been home to Easterners who wintered in their mini-mansions nestled in the foothills of the San Gabriel Mountains. Most of these winter transplants were not rich enough to afford to build the large mansions that once graced South Orange Grove in Pasadena, but they built large stately homes near the mountains, nonetheless.

The area still reflected some of the opulence of many of the old estates tucked among old, gnarled oaks and guarded by tall, skeletal palms, like silent sentinels from the past.

Following Dina's directions, Stas turned left off Lake onto a street that had neither the grandeur of the past nor the overindulgence of the present *nouveau riche*. The street looked more like an afterthought, a collection of small houses built on lots so deep that for extra income many owners had added rental apartments behind their homes.

"Okay, what's May's connection to Sybil?" Stas asked.

"She found the body. She cleans, cleaned for Sybil. She cleans for most of us. Anyway, they were old friends, and Sybil had helped her out along the way."

May lived in a small one bedroom in a complex of four apartments built behind a modest dwelling on west Alameda. The street was a mix of small homes with more citrus trees than patches of grass or beds of flowers. At least the residents didn't have to go far to make a fresh lemonade.

May's street had no curb or sidewalk, so Stas parked on an earthen rise that separated the street from the front yard. While he retrieved his maglight from the trunk, Dina tried to get out of the car alone but lost her balance trying to negotiate the awkward angle of the car perched on the hump.

He rushed around to help. "Babe, wait for me next time."

She refused his hand and followed Stas down the shadowy driveway, past the front house to the apartments in the back. "Oh, shit!" Dina touched the wall of the building for balance.

He flashed a beam onto the peeling siding. Up close, it looked like a leprous pox shedding flaky patches of dead skin. They climbed the steps to May's unit on the second floor. As they approached her door, they could hear loud salsa music coming through a partially opened window. The bell was taped over with a card with "Knock" printed in small, childlike letters. He gave the door a solid pound.

"Don't tear it down, I'm coming." A shrill voice shouted at them. "Who is it?"

"Dina."

May fumbled with several locks and a chain before the door slowly opened. She hesitated when she saw Stas.

Dina pushed by him into the tiny apartment. "It's okay."

May stepped back. Inside the air was stifling and close even with an open window. The apartment was clean but cluttered. Dina ushered Stas to a plastic covered love seat and joined him. May lowered the volume on the boom box and waited.

"This is Detective Nowak. He's with LAPD. I can't explain now, but we need the key to Sybil's place. You still have yours?"

May blinked surprise. "Key? I gave them to Lisa." She thought for a moment, then nervously looked at Stas, "But I think I got one." Her smile was weak. "I always keep a spare."

She went to a hutch and rifled through a beat-up blue tea caddy decorated with a picture of Princess Diana and Prince Charles commemorating their nuptials. Like magic she produced a large ring of keys that jingled as she sat on a straight chair next to the sofa and fumbled with her collection.

May scrutinized Stas. "Tell me something? What did you guys do about the glasses?"

Puzzled, he looked from May to Dina. "Glasses?"

"You know, she was so particular about everything. If something got a little stain or hole in it, she threw it away. I never seen such waste. You should see my closet."

He moved to the edge of the love seat wanting to snatch the ring from her. The more she fiddled, the more difficult it was to remove the key. She was nervous, and Stas felt it wasn't about the keys.

"Here, give it to me." He was on his feet, taking the ring from May and removing the desired key.

She grabbed the ring back and tugged loose another key. She held it steady between two fingers and handed it to Stas. "This one's for the front door."

He pocketed both keys. "Now, tell me about the glasses." His gray eyes narrowed.

"The day I found Sybil, there were these two glasses..."

"What kind?"

"Wine glasses, her expensive ones, Saint somebody from France. Couldn't ever put'em in the dishwasher. There was one on her nightstand. The cops took it, and I found one earlier in the kitchen cabinet. It didn't belong there." She turned to Dina. "You know how particular...."

Stas interrupted. "You think she had a visitor?"

"Well, somebody had been there, drinking, and who knows what else and didn't even know where the glass go. It wasn't in the kitchen the day before."

"Did Sybil often have visitors?"

"Just the doc or some of the girls." She threw a look at Dina.

"What doc? Had she been ill?" Stas asked.

May shook her head. "He ain't that kind. He was a science guy. And he wrote books. He even got some kind of award and sold something to some Germans. Made lots of money."

"Do you know who he is?" Stas asked.

"No, but I sure as hell know what they did. Who would think it, and he a cripple?"

Stas looked at Dina, then took her arm, ushering her toward the door.

May followed. "You want me to clean this week?"

"I'm staying somewhere else for a while. I'll call you when I need you."

He turned. "May, tell me something."

She stood at attention.

"Did you read the note Sybil left?"

"What note? I didn't touch no note. I didn't see no note. I watch cop shows on T.V. I know don't touch nothing."

Stas led Dina out of the apartment. "We'll see you later, May."

May frowned as she watched them carefully descend the stairs. She didn't want to see anybody, especially a cop.

Before they reached the car, Stas grabbed Dina's arm. "Does she clean for you?"

She turned towards him, almost twisting her foot on the uneven asphalt. "Yes, why?

"She has a key to your place, too?

"She has keys to all our places. I told you she cleans for most of us."

"I wonder why a goodlooker like her does housework?" He felt her arm muscles tense.

"Because we pay her well."

"Any other reason?"

"It's kinda hard to get decent references when you just got out of a women's prison and drug rehab."

"She still using?"

Dina jerked her arm free as they reached the car. "How the hell should I know? I don't." She paused to let him open the door for her. "I never have."

"Well, something's up, and it's not fancy wine glasses."

"Always the detective."

"That's why you called me, babe."

It was after midnight when Stas and Dina got into Sybil's condo. Although shrouded in darkness, the night lights of the city filtered through the open vertical blinds leaving ghostly tiger stripes on the carpet. The living room was freezing cold. What had once been a place full of life and energy was now still. Entering, Stas handed Dina a pair of latex gloves just as she was about to flick the light switch.

"No, light! Here, put these on."

Edging in closer to Stas, she whispered. "Is this breaking and entering?"

"No, babe," he said, injecting a little humor, "We got d'key." He moved to the windows and closed the blinds, then turned on his maglight.

The beam from his light picked up a beautiful cobalt blue Murano glass bowl with a scattering of cigarette butts.

Dina reacted. "Sybil must be rolling --"

Stas picked up a half-smoked butt and ran it under his nose. "Somebody's been here. These are recent. Where's the bedroom?"

She put her hand over his and directed the beam to a half closed door. He took her hand and led her to the other room. Vertical blinds, identical to those in the living room, were drawn back. Stas moved to close them, then swung the light over the stripped bed and stained wall. Almost simultaneously voices came from the living room. He turned off his light, grabbed Dina, roughly pulling her with him into a nearby closet still packed with clothes. He closed the doors just as the voices entered the bedroom.

Stas parted clothes in the back and pressed himself into the corner of the closet, bringing Dina into the fold of his arms. She could feel his muscles tense, smell his cologne mixed with the stale blend of perfumes from Sybil's clothing.

"I can't breathe," she whispered, her lips brushing his neck. "I'm going to faint."

"No, you're not. Put your arms around me."

She hugged his waist, nuzzling into his chest. He held her close, feeling her rapid heart beat in rhythm with his own.

Light seeped under the door, the silence broken at first by the opening and closing of drawers, then by a heavy female voice: "I'm not leaving this shit here."

"That's not what we came for," a male voice responded.

"Should we try the closets?"

"Been through everything but these handbags."

"Maybe she kept them in a safe deposit box."

"I don't think so. She'd want them where she could get her hands on them, update them."

"The car then. I think I saw her briefcase in the trunk."

The light went off, and the voices receded into the living room.

Stas waited until he heard the front door slam before opening the closet door. Dina emerged breathless and flushed. She eased onto the bed but quickly jumped up, losing her balance. He caught her and held her for a moment still feeling the staccato beat of her heart.

She tried to mask her arousal with an angry outburst as she pulled away. "Damn it! Are you always so controlled?"

"I didn't know this was a test."

He flicked on the nightstand lamp.

"Won't someone see the light?"

"It doesn't matter. People seem to come and go at will. Who's noticing?"

Stas quickly walked around the room, flashed his light under the bed, around the baseboard, then focused on the upper portion of the walls, stopping at a vent near the entrance of the bedroom. He retraced the beam back to another vent over the closet. Leaving Dina standing near the dresser, he left the bedroom. There was a click, then stale heat flowed through the vent by the door. He reentered and walked over to the closet, holding his hand up under the second vent.

"Hold this for me." He handed Dina the maglight and took a small packet from his jacket pocket.

She looked at the vent. "Why?"

"It's a fake." Removing a tiny screwdriver, he pulled a delicate antique chair over to the closet. "I hope this thing holds me. Steady the light on the vent." He unscrewed the vent cover and let it drop to the floor. Reaching inside, he retrieved a small, intricately hand-carved wooden box and a small black vinyl case. He handed Dina the box and slipped the case into his pocket, then screwed the vent cover back, and returned the chair to its place.

She started to open the box.

Stas grabbed her arm. "Not now, babe, let's get out of here."

Sybil's box and its contents had been neatly spread on Stas's coffee table. A bottle of Chopin stood on the floor, a half full glass sat within his easy reach on the table. As he picked up several pictures, Dina came in from the bedroom wearing a loosely tied, long silk robe. The effect of her change and freshly applied perfume was not lost on him as he sipped his drink.

"You didn't wait for me?"

He waved his hand over the display. "Everything awaits you now." His tone was warm, relaxed.

"What's all this?"

"If we had an investigation, this would be part of the evidence, but since there isn't a case, it's just some of Sybil's stuff." He handed one of the photos to Dina when she sat next to him. "Does this look like Sybil?"

Taking the picture, she turned it over and read the inscription first. "'Mimi and Sybil'. She's just a kid here. I guess it's her if it says so."

"Is this her mother?" He reached over and indicated the older woman.

"I don't know. When we met, she told me her mother was dead." She picked up a ring and fingered it, turning it until the light played on the little stone. "I wonder if this was hers?"

Stas unfolded the birth certificate and studied it before handing it to Dina. "This is hers. So is the passport."

He pushed aside a tiny plastic bag containing a ringlet of auburn hair and absentmindedly played with a key while Dina looked at the documents.

"What's that?" Dina pointed to an envelope in his hand.

"It's a letter from someone named Tony." He took it out and read aloud: "'Darling, I know it's rough, but whatever you decide, I need this to be over for you. I'll see you when I get back. I miss you. Tony' No way of knowing when it was written. The paper looks like it might be official stationary, but the top's torn off. The lab could..., but we can't use them." He held it up to look at the watermark, then dropped the letter back on the table. "You know anyone named Tony?"

Dina shook her head. "He may have been before my time."

"When was that?"

She had drawn closer while Stas read the letter. When he moved to put it back on the table, the lower part of her robe fell open, exposing long, shapely legs.

"Babe, it's late for a seduction scene, and I'm tired."

Hurt and confused, Dina pulled her robe closed as he started to put everything back into the carved box. "Well, you're not making any moves. You said you have needs. I know I do."

Stas's discomfort propelled him from his seat. He drained his glass and took it, with the bottle, back to the kitchen. When he returned, he took his leather jacket from the closet and turned back to the living room. "It's late and this isn't the time."

"What about the other stuff?"

He didn't answer. The front door closed softly behind him. The metallic click of the deadbolt accentuated the silence.

So leave me. No good-bye. No 'bitch kiss my fucking ass'. Nothing. Dina sat frozen on the sofa feeling angry, abandoned, rebuffed. She wanted to get up and check the door but didn't have the strength. *Shit, am I locked in?* She had never dealt with this kind of rejection before. Thinking about Stas, even dreaming about him when he had been a fleeting memory, had been easy to deal with. But how was she going to handle his presence and her increased longing for him. Her seductive ploys had always worked before, and now the man she most desired had just walked out on her.

Two conflicting emotions twisted her mind and her heart. She longed to go home, but also wanted to have the episode with Stas play out. At least there was one consolation; she felt safe with him.

Dina needed something. She went to the kitchen, found his chilled vodka in the freezer, and poured some in a coffee mug. Maybe a drink of, what had he called it, "mother's milk," would give her some comfort, but its cold fire burned her throat. She swallowed hard, coughed, and blamed the tears that filled her eyes on the alcohol.

Holding on to the counter, she tried to finish the drink wondering how he did it, how he drank it off like a glass of frigid Arctic water. Was that what he used to keep his feelings suppressed? Still, he had to let his defenses down sometime. After all, he had been married. She felt a sting of jealousy at the thought of Stas having a wife, sharing a bed with a woman who once had a legal claim to him, no matter how long ago that had been or that it had ended in divorce. Dina sighed and poured the rest of her vodka down the drain. Out of spite, she left the mug in the immaculate sink and returned the bottle to the freezer.

She needed to know more about him, find what made him tick. Besides his TV, books, and music, there wasn't much in the apartment that would give him comfort or pleasure.

Standing in the middle of the living room, she was drawn to his reading area. She flopped into his low easy chair and pulled herself closer to the neatly arranged books.

She opened a book on forensic investigations and immediately let it drop to the floor. Pictures of dead bodies and autopsy reports would not help her find his Achilles heel. Leaning over even farther, she picked out a thin mystery and settled down to see if what he read would unravel the enigma of Stas Nowak.

Reading wasn't working. Dina yawned and felt woozy. She would have to devise another strategy. *Oh, well, I have time.* The open book slid to the floor while she dozed.

A loud siren passed beneath the window and startled her awake. She looked around trying to get her bearings, then picked up her fallen mystery and carried it with her to the bathroom.

Her dry mouth tasted like silvery antiseptic. After brushing her teeth and drinking several glasses of water, Dina slipped on Stas's police T-shirt, sprayed some of his aftershave, and inhaled the falling mist. Dina held up the bottle. She'd have to get one, use if when she had a date with a married man. Well, if she couldn't take him to bed, she could, at least, conjure up his presence in her dreams.

She turned back the covers, but needing answers, curiosity tempted her to his closet. Perhaps his clothes would reveal more about him than his apartment's minimalist furnishings and decorations.

His shoes were neatly arranged on a double wooden rack on the closet's floor. Each shoe, even his black running shoes, was fitted with a cedar-scented tree. Suits were hung by color on thick wooden hangers. She removed one. It was an Armani. The cut was classic, expensive. She ran her fingers over the fine imported fabric and fondled the sleeve. As she put it back, there was that faint scent of bergamot and vanilla, the same scent she had sprayed. Dina closed her eyes for a second, then turned to his perfectly ironed shirts. Even his sweats were hung on hangers next to a black-watch plaid woolen robe.

Stas had made room for her at the end of the closet, but even with space given over to her few things, his clothes weren't crowded. The two top shelves held folded sweaters, and at the far end of the closet, bolted to the floor, was a large standing metal safe. She reached down and fingered the dial, hoping that the cold steel would release his aura, could be captured by her fingertips that moved to the scar on her neck. A large leather case that looked like one for a musical instrument rested on top of the safe. *So do you play a horn?* She thought of Chris Botti and his sexy stance fingering his sensuous trumpet. But the case was too long. A trombone? Somehow he didn't look like a trombone player. *A sax!* Without looking in the case, she knew he played a sax, a sexy sax.

Her proximity to his belongings rekindled the desire that she had spent her lonely evening trying to suppress. She closed the closet doors. Dina touched her erect nipples through the cotton fabric and willed them to relax. She climbed into bed wanting him there, holding her, loving her. The clock radio on the nightstand read 2:37 a.m. She tossed and turned, her longing and curiosity denying her sleep.

After turning the light back on, she looked into the nightstand drawer. There was a notepad and pencil but nothing else: no condoms, no K-Y jelly, and no girlie magazines. Maybe he hadn't lied about women coming to his place, yet she found little comfort that she was the first, especially if he treated her like some stray puppy he brought home before taking it to the pound.

The other nightstand drawer was empty except for several books of matches. Did he smoke? Had he given it up? She wondered where he was, who he was with, what he was doing?

Awake now. She picked up the book and tried reading again, but sleep finally came, and she never heard him return.

The next morning after showering and dressing, Stas had to shake Dina to wake her. She'd fallen asleep over one of his mysteries. He picked it up from the floor and put out the light. Sitting on the edge of the bed, he waited for her to open her eyes before handing her a glass of orange juice.

She looked at him, raising herself enough to take the juice. "Are you leaving again?"

His seemed anxious. "My father asked me to pick up my sister at LAX. Tonight's my parents' 50th anniversary. There's coffee made. I'll bring something to eat when I come back."

"About last night, I can leave if she's coming here."

The thought brought a lift to his stormy gray eyes. "Don't worry about it. She's staying with my folks." He rose and left.

Traffic to LAX was heavy for a Saturday morning, but then traffic seemed heavy all the time. He smoothly maneuvered his Mercedes around vans, buses, SUVs, and pulled to the curb when he saw Anne, who stepped to the car as he stopped and killed the engine.

Living in the Northwest had done nothing to improve his sister's sense of fashion; a drab, bulky woolen coat covered her thin frame. Observing her rigid movements, he doubted her disposition had improved since he'd last seen her several years earlier. It was hard to imagine she was only two years older. She looked at least fifty.

He went around to the passenger side of the car to assist her, but she jerked her arm away and dropped her bag on the pavement. After picking it up and throwing it in the trunk, he got back into the car, slammed the door, and waited for her to settle herself, arranging the unwieldy coat around her as if Stas was about to drive her into the eye of a Southern California snowstorm.

"You'd think at forty you'd get a sensible, affordable car."

"Don't worry about it. I drive what I like." He jerked the car in gear. "How was your flight?"

"Listen, we don't need to make small talk. It's wet in Seattle. My work is great. My love life is adequate. I'm here because I feel obligated. Just like you're here because you feel obligated. We're dutiful children. So don't take me being here as some kind sibling reunion. I'm not interested in your work or your love life. I just want to get this over with and go home. Now, I think I've covered all the bases." She turned from him to look out the window.

Still the fucking bitch. It's funny how some things never change.

After a few minutes of silence, Anne turned back from the monotony of the slow moving traffic on the 405 Freeway. "What brought this,... this celebration on?"

"Misery loving company. It got you down here to see him drinking in the garage and her bitching and moaning in the kitchen, didn't it? The guests'll come because they like to see other dysfunctional families on display, reassures them that they're not alone. Plus, there'll get plenty to eat and drink."

The rest of the ride was made in icy silence. There were no good-byes as Stas left her in front of his parents' drab California bungalow.

TEN

May fingered the black leather case in her pocket. The bus rides had taken almost two hours, but the time allowed her to cement a plan that she had formulated the night before. She needed to get rid of Sybil's case, even though she wasn't yet sure just what it was or what it did. The cop with Dina had frightened her. She smiled that he hadn't tried to see the duplicate keys. There was a drawer full of them, at least two to every place she had ever worked. Was she going to have to hide them too? Suppose he or others came back to her place searching for evidence, wanting to reopen the investigation into Sybil's death? And now a damned note. She didn't remember a fucking note.

She took the case from her pocket. May knew it was important. She'd seen Sybil fiddling with it, hiding it away in a tiny compartment in the Chinese hutch. Those Orientals had been sneaky devils, making clever secret niches for their opium. Well, she had no hiding place, and if someone came looking, she didn't want it found on her or discovered among her things.

Dina must be shacking with that cop. She knew the look, and Dina had it. Well, since Dina was playing "Fuck the Cop", May decided to hide it in Dina's apartment. If she ran into Livia, May would just tell the bitch she had changed her cleaning day.

But May didn't see Livia, and she didn't clean. Instead, she hid the case in one of Dina's lingerie drawers under mounds of shimmering underwear and wondered, as she fingered the silky thongs, touched expensive lace, how much one of those skimpy French bras set Dina back.

She fluffed everything over the little black case. If someone found it, well, it would be Dina's ass. May went back to the living room and stretched out on the sofa trying to think of her next move. Perhaps what she had was worth something, but who would want it? If Sybil had been murdered, what had she had that someone would pay big bucks to possess? She dozed but awoke with a start. The front door was opening.

"Hello! Hello? Dina?" Livia shouted stepping into the apartment.

May jumped up. *It was that nosey bitch. What did she want?*

Livia held out a key. "You left this in the door."

"Oh, shit!" May automatically felt in her pocket, then snatched the key from Livia. "I told Dina I would clean today."

Livia gave the living room a quick perusal. Dead flowers filled two vases. A woolen throw was folded like a pillow at the end of the sofa. May huffed as she stepped into her beat-up brown slip-ons.

"You need to be careful with your keys. I wouldn't want Dina to come back and find any of her stuff gone. I'd have to call my friend." She struck one of her poses accenting those long dancer's legs. "I have a friend who's a detective with the LAPD."

May put her hands on her hips. "Well, I'm sure Dina has lots of friends in the LAPD and sheriffs, too. Anyway, I was about to leave."

She followed Livia's gaze to one of the vases.

"I just need to empty these." She walked over and grabbed both vases. "I'll see you around."

On the long bus ride back to Pasadena, it hit May. She'd call Matt. She trusted him. He'd helped her score a few times, even slipped her a couple of twenties when she told him about Sybil's new lover. From time to time, she had even given him juicy tidbits of gossip on some of the other girls. Yeah, she'd call Matt. If he didn't want it, he'd sure as hell know what to do with it and probably get her some money for it, to boot. Satisfied, she closed her eyes and slept all the way to her transfer point at Lake and Colorado.

ELEVEN

Stas stopped at the Second Set after dropping off Anne. A little Chopin always sweetened his mood. It was early and the bar was almost empty. Troy had his drink on the bar when Stas slid onto the stool.

"You in kinda early." Troy continued polishing glasses.

"Just picked up my sister at the airport."

Troy nodded and placed a water back next to Stas's glass. "You want some orange juice, you know, make it like breakfast? They can cook you up something. That way you won't feel guilty."

"The Maestro never makes me feel guilty." Stas sat for a while before finishing off two drinks. He checked his watch, then laid several bills on the bar. Walking out to the parking lot, he felt a strange yet alien feeling: going home to a woman. Even the act of stopping for his favorite Chinese and remembering what she liked from the previous night seemed alien after going home so many times before Dina to eat alone.

After hanging his jacket in the closet, he saw that she had established herself in his reading chair by the bookcases. She looked relaxed. He wondered if she had resigned herself to the temporary living arrangement.

She looked up from her book. "And I missed you, too."

Stas ignored her sarcasm, started to walk over to her, but changed his mind and headed for the kitchen where he deposited a bag of Chinese take-out.

"There's food on the counter. I gotta get dressed." He disappeared into the bedroom.

She called after him. "How long will I be under *house arrest*?"

He shouted back. "Getting tired of my cooking?"

"But you haven't cooked, and I've already read two books. Why can't I go home or call a friend and go to a movie?" She flipped several pages. "Suppose I don't like Chinese?"

Stas returned to the doorway. His shirtless torso was lean and firm. "How do you know it's Chinese?"

"I can smell the ginger. It's okay. I just wanted to give you a hard time, and I'm bored."

He stood for a moment watching her. "I don't want you going home or going anywhere without me, have you forgotten -- someone tried to kill you?"

Dina looked at him and sighed. "Then what am I supposed to do while you party?"

"I'll think of something. Anyway, I may not be gone that long. This isn't an event I'm looking forward to."

"You make it sound like you're going to an execution."

He made a choking gesture with both hands around his neck and returned to the bedroom. Dina returned to her book.

When Stas finally emerged, he was elegantly dressed in a navy pinstriped suit with a white Egyptian cotton shirt and a navy, silver and gold chevron tie. He felt overdressed.

Dina looked up when she caught a whiff of that all too familiar scent. "Wow! You look like you're ready to strut your stuff on some fashion runway in Milan."

He ignored her comment. "A friend's coming over."

"Who, some Nazi matron from LAPD?"

"We don't have matrons. He's not a cop." He paused. "He's a reporter, so watch what you say to him."

Dina looked at him, puzzled.

"I'm serious. Do you know Ralph Townsend?"

"No, is he my baby sitter or my jailer?"

"Listen, Dina, Ralph is an old acquaintance. He's a good guy."

"But he's not one of your friends?"

"We have this love/hate relationship, like most cops and reporters."

"What am I suppose to do with him?"

"I told him to teach you Gin."

"To drink it or play it?"

"Dina, I don't have time for games."

"Maybe I don't want to play games -- with some reporter?"

"Then play whatever you want with him." There was a hint of mockery in his tone. "I just thought you might want to see someone different for a change."

"Why would you think that?"

He grabbed his keys off his desk. "I'm out of here."

Since Ralph Townsend hadn't arrived by the time Stas left, Dina had time to check her hair, freshen her make-up, and put on jeans and a sweatshirt. She was anxious to meet one of his friends since he had impressed her as a loner. She curled up on the sofa with her book and awaited her keeper.

Stas had left a bottle of Scotch and two glasses on his desk. She gathered that was Ralph's drink of choice.

The phone rang about forty minutes later. After buzzing him in, she waited, almost counting to see how long it would take him to reach the apartment. When the light tap came at the door, she opened it. She was surprised. He was not at all what she had expected; he was nothing like Stas. Townsend was taller, almost lanky, with a funny haircut. His eyes were a warm brown, and he gave her a broad, winning smile. Dina knew she was going to have to be on her toes. She had been taught to be leery of reporters. They were always looking for a story and could charm information from you if you weren't careful, but despite being a little fearful, Ralph seemed harmless.

He was dressed casually in jeans, button-down collared beige Oxford shirt, and brown corduroy jacket. She noticed the deeply stained fingers as he grasped her hand in a firm shake. If he wore cologne, it was overpowered by the stale cigarette smoke embedded in his clothes and perhaps in his very being. It was obvious he was a hardcore smoker, and in Dina's book that was a strike against him.

Ralph looked around the living room, then at Dina before taking a seat in Stas's recliner. "So you're the damsel in distress?"

"What?"

"I was with him when he got your call."

"Oh, -- you hang together?"

"Just the same bar and sometimes the same crime scene, but you know cops and reporters -- like oil and water." He noticed her disappointment. "I smoke too much, and he drinks too much, occupational hazards." He took out a new pack of cigarettes and a lighter.

Dina watched him nervously fiddle with the cellophane wrapping, and she instinctively realized he needed something to take his mind off a smoke. "Would you like a drink? Stas left some Scotch."

"Thanks, he knows what I like. Join me?"

"Maybe." She wanted to keep her mind clear. "How do you take it?'

"Neat, about four fingers."

Dina rose and went to the desk where she poured two old-fashioned glasses about a quarter full. She handed him his and sat back on the sofa where she slowly sipped hers.

Ralph took a deck of cards from his jacket pocket and pulled the recliner over to the coffee table. "Do you know how to play Gin?"

"No."

"What about strip poker?"

"We'll play Gin." She went to Stas's desk for pen and paper.

Much to Dina's surprise, the evening was not the total waste she had expected. Ralph was charming, could talk about anything under the sun, and taught her the rules of the card game so well that she beat him when they changed from Gin Rummy to Five Hundred Rummy.

"I like this better." She laid down a final spread, catching Ralph with a handful of face cards. She calculated the final tally. "We should've played for money."

"I need a smoke." Ralph walked over to the window and opened it before lighting up. A rush of cool air carrying the scent of eucalyptus faintly masked the smoke from his cigarette. He tried unsuccessfully to blow the smoke into the night air. He finished, closed the window, and called from the reading area.

"How long have you known Stas?

"About two years."

Dina tried to hold back a yawn when Ralph returned to the sofa.

"Listen, you're sleepy. Go to bed." He glanced towards the bedroom. "Tell Stas we just played cards."

"He wouldn't care."

"I always wondered what women find so attractive in him."

"I wouldn't know. We just reconnected..." she paused trying to think of the right phrase for her relationship with Stas, " ... as friends."

Townsend wasn't listening. "I don't know what it is, but they throw themselves at him, then he turns on those cool gray eyes, and poof." He waved the air like fanning away invisible smoke. "And he got'em, but he doesn't seem to keep'em. You tell me."

"Maybe it's the car," Dina said.

"You haven't had that experience, I take it?"

"What? Throwing myself at him, his eyes, or the car?" She smiled coyly. "No, I'm afraid I haven't succumbed to any of those yet. And what does he do with the ones he catches?"

"That's just it, I don't know. Well, maybe we can play again sometimes."

"I'd like that." But Dina's smile was non-committal.

Ralph finished his drink without returning to his chair. "Don't get up. I can let myself out."

When she heard the door close, Dina went to the hall closet and grabbed the pillow and blanket that Stas used in the living room. She turned out the light and curled up on the sofa. Tonight she didn't need to spray his cologne. She could feel his presence when she wrapped herself in the blanket and fell asleep.

TWELVE

Stas slowly cruised his parents' block looking for parking. Nothing. The clock on the car's dash read 6:17. He finally found a space a block away and walked back to the house. For appearances, he should have gone to Our Lady of the Mount Church, but he didn't want to sit through any mass, especially one in Polish. Why give religious credence to a marriage that was a farce? Even attending the celebration at the house made him feel like a hypocrite.

He could hear the loud accordion music as he crossed the yard to the porch. The front door was ajar, probably to allow some much needed ventilation if the house was as crowded as the cars on the street indicated, or if the vodka was flowing, heating up the guests.

The living room was immaculate, even though the crowd was well on its way to consuming a great deal of alcohol and that could get messy. Helene Nowak's bunko ladies had taken over the sofa and love seat. To join the group, one woman had dragged over Vlade's worn recliner, the only untidy piece of furniture allowed in the room.

Other women from bunko helped with the serving, moving from the kitchen to the dining room with platters and bowls of food. When they saw Stas, they smiled and waved their hellos.

He recognized Rose and Paula, squeezing themselves onto the love-seat with another woman he did not know.

"That's their son, Vladeislaw. They call him Stas. He's a cop," Rose said.

One of the ladies leaned in. "Nice. Is he married?"

When his mother's friends gathered, he was often the subject of their conversations, especially if they had young women of marrying age in their families. It always amazed Stas that these women, who knew little about him still saw him as a suitable spouse for a daughter or niece.

With a great deal of effort, Rose pulled her considerable bulk off the sofa and joined him near the drinks' table. There was enough vodka set out to keep guests happy until the next Polish celebration.

"You didn't go to the church?" she asked. She had one of those round puffy faces always flush with excitement. Her fine silver hair and watery blue eyes made her look like a geriatric cherub.

"I don't go to church, and I didn't see any reason to start now. I doubt if I was missed."

"I'd like you to meet my niece." Rose turned and looked over the crowd that had gravitated towards the dining room and kitchen where there was even more liquor.

He followed her gaze but saw no one who caught his interest.

When a sighting of the niece didn't materialize, Rose reluctantly moved on to the dining room table that had been pushed against the wall. The niece was momentarily forgotten while she piled pierogies from a platter onto her plate. "She must have gone outside. She'll be back." She waved her fork with a dumpling balanced on its tip towards the kitchen.

If the niece had gone out back towards Vlade's garage, Stas was sure he didn't want to meet her.

The guests of honor hadn't arrived yet, but the dining room buffet table was laden with every imaginable Polish delicacy.

"Hey, Stas, you coming from the church?" Someone shouted from the other end of the table.

Mariusz, the son of an old family friend, handed Stas a tumbler of vodka and looked over the guests. "Who the hell are all these people?"

"Who knows? I'd guess old friends from Poland, Chicago, guys from work, drinking buddies, Mom's bunko ladies." He followed Mariusz's eye to a couple of young women. They definitely were not from the Motherland or old drinking buddies, and the way they were dressed, he doubted if they were the daughters of his mother's friends.

Stas was about to take a drink, when a flashy young blonde, with her bosom straining to explode from her dress, brushed her abundance against his upper arm. She was tall, and her three-inch heels brought them eye level with each other. She smiled seductively and held her ground. Stas backed up, wondering if the friction on his jacket sleeve might trigger a mammary explosion or if this was Rose's niece just trying to get acquainted.

"Could you pour me a drink?" she purred.

Before Stas could reach for an empty glass, Mariusz placed a tumbler into her waiting hand. Ziggy played a series of loud chords on the accordion to announce the arrival of Helena and Vlade Nowak as they entered with Father Andrew, Anne, and the frozen chosen who never missed a chance to go to church, even to attend funerals of total strangers, especially if there was the hope of a bountiful repast afterwards. The guests applauded. The celebration was now officially underway.

An older woman, bent with arthritis, grabbed Helena's arm before she could clear the entrance. She pointed at Anne who had just stepped out of her reach.

"That's your Annie? Looks just like you. I'd know her anywhere."

"Yes, yes, she just came down from Seattle."

"Is she married?"

Helena shook her head, carefully pulled her arm free, and walked over to her daughter. Both women were slender with pale, pinched features. Helena, in a stark, high-necked black dress, looked her sixty-eight years; only the veil was missing. Her one strong feature was a full head of beautifully coifed platinum blonde hair piled high and stiff on her head. Her coloring made her light gray eyes look even paler behind oversized silver-rimmed bifocals.

She whispered in Anne's ear. "They always ask the same damn question, 'Is she married?' Like it's some kind of stain on the family."

"Do they ask that about Stas?" Anne looked for him across the room.

"Oh, yes, but it's different. They want to marry him off to some homely relative so the shame of having her unmarried won't be on their house."

Stas watched the scenario unfold and wondered what was so important to take his mother from her guests. Leaving Anne standing alone, Helena put on her best smile and followed her husband. Even though she was being honored, she was ill at ease being the center of any kind of attention.

It was evident that, no matter when or where they gathered, the life of the party was always Vlade, and most of the guests were there for him. It wouldn't take long for the senior Nowak to get the real celebration going. At sixty-nine he was still tall, handsome, virile, a man who was enjoying his prime and had no intention of giving it up anytime soon.

Just as Anne resembled her mother, Stas, while not quite as handsome, shared some of his father's physical features. They were both the same height, both had a full head of thick hair, both had those slate gray eyes that saw everything but gave away nothing, yet Vlade's promised just a hint of mystery and mischief, like a faint scent of a rare elixir in the wind that only a few were quick enough to catch and savor. When he threw off his jacket, the decibel level rose as the gathering shouted greetings in Polish and English.

Ziggy played a short polka to clear a spot in the dining room where people were suppose to dance. An elderly couple took a turn around the cramped space until Mariusz, cigarette dangling from his lips, bumped into them as he carried more bottles of vodka.

He turned to Ziggy. "I don't know how this is going to work. Maybe you should play out on the patio. There's more room."

Ziggy stopped playing for a moment. "You don't think it's too cold out there?

"That's why I brought in more antifreeze."

It took only a few seconds for the guests to turn their focus to Vlade. When he poured himself a drink and moved through the dining room, most of the guests, especially the men, moved with him. The living room was not in Vlade's sphere of interest.

Stas was always amused at his father's charisma, and even though he admired him, he never wished to emulate him. Vlade was a user, but people loved him.

Stas watched, unaware of Anne's presence until she lightly brushed his sleeve.

"I don't know why I wasted my time coming down here for this fiasco." She folded her arms across her chest. "I don't know why they bother! Look at her. She's not having any fun."

"For her, it's not meant to be fun. It's living another lie, see how much mileage you can get out of it. It's hard to let go, even after fifty years." Stas loosened his tie and removed his jacket, neatly putting it over the back of a nearby dining room chair that a man had just vacated to follow Vlade.

Before he could turn back to his drink and Anne, Helena emerged from nowhere to pick up the jacket and take it to the hall closet.

Anne watched the vignette unfold. "Doesn't she ever give it a rest? The two of you make me sick." She reached for a bottle of vodka on the nearby table and poured a drink into a plastic cup. Before replacing the bottle on the makeshift bar, she turned it around to look at the Belvedere label. "At least they buy the good stuff."

Stas didn't respond. He and his sister had never been able to communicate even as children. Now, in their forties, when they should have been enjoying a sibling relationship, there was nothing. When he eased away to find another bottle of vodka in the kitchen, Dina and Ralph crossed his mind. He looked at his watch and wondered what they were doing.

In the dining room Ziggy played a loud riff as Mike Klinski put his arm around Vlade and looked around. It was time to give the toast, cut the cake, and get on with the serious drinking.

"Where's Helena?" Mike looked over the room, catching sight of her in the wide archway between the living room and dining room. "C'mon Hel, get over here." His speech slurred. "Bring Annie with you."

One of the men pushed Anne to the table where someone held out a cake knife to cut the two-tiered white and yellow cake. The sugared roses were beginning to droop, and the faded bridal couple that topped the confection looked as strained and posed as the real celebrants.

"Where's that son of yours?" Mike looked over the room for Stas. "Where's LA's finest?"

Stas had retrieved his jacket from the hall closet and was slipping it on when Rose pulled him over to the table. Someone made an effort to pose the foursome while a photographer tried to get them in focus. Another person passed out little plastic glasses. Several women moved among the guests pouring champagne.

Mike whispered to Stas who shook his head before raising his glass to the anniversary couple. "Listen up everybody, here's to Vlade and Helena. May they have another fifty as good as these. *Na zdrowie.*"

Rose pushed Mike from the front of the table, raised her glass and nodded towards Vlade. "*Pierdykniem bo odwykniem.*"

Everyone who understood Polish laughed at her somewhat vulgar insinuation, knowing full well there would be no conjugal action by the anniversary couple when the guests departed.

Mike finally got everyone's attention. "Come on everybody, drink up."

Glasses were raised in unison, and those closest to the couple tentatively sipped their champagne. Two pieces of cake were cut and given to Helena and Vlade who took mincing bites but made no effort to feed each other. Still everyone clapped; a few cheered, and most found a place to abandon their plastic glasses and turn back to their vodka and newly lit cigarettes.

Vlade left Helena standing at the table as one of her friends started to cut more cake, and another put thin slices on plastic plates. The smell of faux lemon mixed with the scent of cheap champagne seemed to repulse the guests who knew that the Polish fare was far superior. Rose moved around the room trying to serve cake to reluctant eaters. Most plates were left untouched and quickly tucked under or behind a table or chair.

The buxom blonde came back to stand next to Stas. She refrained from rubbing any of her anatomy against him this time. Instead she basked in the magnetism of the elder Nowak.

She blew a minty breath at Stas. "He's your father?"

Stas nodded.

"You know, I've never done a father and son before."

He stood there speechless as she walked towards the kitchen. Vlade was there easing his way toward the open back door. Even in the evening chill, some of his buddies had taken the party to the patio along with a blue vapor trail of hazy smoke. The temperature and the bodies would soon heat up, especially when enough vodka had been consumed.

Ziggy, like a pied piper, had moved his music to the activity in the kitchen. The statuesque blonde and a few younger, more animated females had joined the raucous males. Like some giant, surreal pinball machine the livelier group tilted to the back of the house.

Stas was drawn in that direction, then looked towards the living room. The bunko women had returned with refilled plates of food to the comfort zone of the stiff sofas and bright lights to continue their usual gossip. His mother slowly moved in that direction, picking up soiled plates and flatware along the way.

"Hel, get in here!" Rose shouted.

But Helena turned her attention to the kitchen. She, too, felt compelled to focus on the activities in the back of the house.

Stas grabbed the trash from her hands. "Here, I'll take that. Rose wants you." He stepped into the kitchen.

The blonde playfully tussled Vlade's hair, pulling him towards her ample chest. He ushered her along with him towards the outside and gave her a caressing pat that lingered too long on her rear.

Stas watched the unraveling scene as he put the dirty plastic dishes in a trash can by the stove. Helena had not returned to the living room but stood behind him, transfixed by the unfolding tableau.

Her shriek in Polish was, at first, inaudible. Then silence fell like a pall over those closest to the kitchen. Helena continued to spew her venom. *"W moim domu? Czy znów mam chować twojego bękarta? Prędzej zobaczymy się w piekle!"*

Vlade turned, his tone, hard and cold like tempered steel cutting through the room, shouted. "You barren bitch. If I go to hell, you'll be the gatekeeper." He grabbed the blonde and pushed her through the back door.

All conversation ceased. Those left in the house rose, put plates and glasses down, gathered jackets and coats, and started to leave. The celebration in the house had come to an abrupt end, but the party with Vlade and his friends was just getting started in the back patio and garage. Within minutes Mike returned to the house to retrieve more bottles of vodka and eased out the back door as Ziggy launched into a lively polka.

THIRTEEN

For the first time in his life, Stas felt the effects of alcohol without feeling drunk. His senses were starkly awake, yet he didn't remember leaving his parents' house. He certainly didn't remember saying good-bye to anyone and walking to his car.

Even through light traffic, driving was oppressive. He tried to make sense of the words his parents had spewed at each other, and then there was the look on Anne's face as she stepped out of the shadows like some vulture ready to devour the carnage Helena had left. Anne had glared at him and then smiled. It was the first time in years that he could remember her smiling at him. He wanted to forget the cruel curl of her lips, that slow release of years of pent-up hatred.

As Stas opened the door of his apartment, he felt weighted down, yet he moved effortlessly through the darkness. Dina was apparently asleep; no light came from his bedroom, but he was vaguely aware of her presence, of that fruity, spicy scent that was uniquely hers.

He grabbed a glass and vodka from the freezer before returning to the living room and sitting on the edge of the sofa. With practiced adroitness, he poured a drink and set the bottle on the floor. He knew he had had enough, but he still sipped, trying to translate what his parents had said, then cursed himself for not taking seriously the Saturday morning Polish classes when he was a kid. Stas leaned back and closed his eyes but did not sleep. The words he had heard streamed like subtitles across his mind.

When he opened his eyes, he was aware of a subtle pressure on the cushions next to him. They sat in silence. Then he felt her weight shift as she angled her body toward his. He wanted to turn, take her in his arms, but he could not move. Dina lightly brushed his thigh as she rose. He watched her shadowy silhouette move toward the bedroom and closed his eyes again.

The next morning driving back to the Nowak home took both curiosity and iron will. It was the detective that kicked in rather than the son. Stas stopped at a liquor store and bought a fifth of Chopin Vodka. He had them put it in a brown paper bag, no gift-wrap for the old man.

As he drove, he wondered if Vlade was still at home or if his parents had actually left, despite the blowout, for their second honeymoon. He laughed at the thought. If they had gone away together, he doubted that there would have been a cozy week away for the vitriolic Nowaks. And sex, he shuttered at the image. Vlade, Stas felt, was still active, but Helena was repulsed even by the intimacy of a handshake.

In the late morning sunshine, the house looked dark and foreboding. He parked in the driveway and walked through a tall redwood gate to what had once been a two-car garage but had been converted into a workshop and getaway for the elder Nowak. Stas remembered fun times sequestered there with his father, building kites, repairing fishing gear, talking about soccer, and secretly drinking beer that his father had hidden in a little fridge under his workbench.

When had those fun times ended? He thought back to when his mother caught him with one of his old man's *Playboys*, or when she found him drunk from the vodka kept stashed away on a high garage shelf. At thirteen Stas had acquired a taste for vodka rather than the cheap beer Vlade drank. There had been violent arguments in Polish that he hadn't understood. After that, Helena took control, sending him to St. Benet's, an all male high school, and involving him in more church and school activities under the watchful eye of her friend, Father Marty.

Somewhere, in the back of her mind, she believed she had received divine inspiration. She conspired with the good Father to prepare Stas for the priesthood. Vlade vehemently objected but to no avail, so he retreated into the garage with his girlie magazines and booze, abandoning his son to Holy Mother Church and Helena.

Everyone's efforts seemed to pay off. Stas applied himself religiously but not for the seminary. He signed up for the Army ROTC, got his college education paid for by the United States government while earning a degree in four years at St. Regis College. From there, he did a six-year stint with Army Intelligence before joining LAPD.

Helena never forgave him for the deception, but then she never forgave him for a lot of things, offenses she had been reminding him of since his childhood. She had been a harsh disciplinarian. Compared to his mother, the discipline of ROTC and the Army had been a cakewalk.

The door to the garage was unlocked. Vlade was sitting on a high stool bent over his worktable slowly turning the pages of a *Penthouse.* Since Stas's teens, the old man had graduated to seamier stuff. He looked up when Stas sat the bottle on the bench.

"Happy anniversary." It was a cold, empty greeting.

Without responding, Vlade reached for two glasses at the back of the table, blew dust from them, and took the top off the bottle. "Your mother's not here." He poured two glasses full, handing one to Stas.

"She went alone?"

Vlade took a long, smooth drink and refilled his glass before answering. "She took your sister." He laughed and returned to his magazine.

Stas watched, annoyed. "You just don't give a damn, do you?"

"About what?"

"About a lot but especially last night. It's like nothing happened."

Vlade closed his magazine, took off his glasses, and turned.

Now that he had his father's undivided attention, Stas continued. "Do you want to tell me what that was all about?"

Vlade emptied his glass again. "Not really. Didn't you understand any of it?"

"She called someone a bastard. Why did I feel she was talking about me?"

"It's what she talks about all the time. You just never figured it out."

Stas started to feel warm in the confines of the workshop but ignored the perspiration beading on his forehead, dampening his underarms. "Maybe it's time to enlighten me. The last time I checked my birth certificate, she was still my mother and you, my father, unless she..." He left the rest unspoken and downed a quarter of his drink.

"She didn't do anything. She couldn't. She had a hysterectomy in Chicago a year before you were born."

Stas felt rivulets of water trailing down his spine, soaking into his shirt. He rubbed his eyes as if to clear his vision, needing to see as well as hear. "Then who -- who is my mother?"

"Don't you know? You never guessed?"

"No, god-dammit!"

Vlade's voice was barely audible. "Irina."

"Aunt Irina?"

"Yes." Vlade cleared his throat.

"You adopted me?" Stas tried to find some logic in this revelation. He felt a chill, felt his gut churn, swallowed hard.

"No."

Stas reached for his father. "What kinda fucking game are you playing. If I wasn't adopted..."

"Irina had you at the hospital and used Helena's name. She gave you to Helena."

"Then who's my father?" The anger and tension caught in his throat, giving his voice a deep tremor.

"I told you, We brought you home."

Stas then realized. He tensed; the veins pulsed in his neck. His throat and ears flushed as he pulled Vlade off his stool, bringing them eye to eye. "Talk to me you fu---." The word stuck in his throat. The muscles in his arms tightened as he tried to restrain himself from hitting his father.

"About what?"

"About me, damn it, about Irina."

Vlade sighed, taking a deep breath. "It's simple; Helena couldn't have any more kids. I wanted a son."

"So you got Irina pregnant? Anne knows. She understood. No wonder she hates me." Emotionally drained, Stas could barely speak. "Are you sure you wanted a son or did you just want to --, just wanted Irina, and I was just a by-product? So what was it?" He took a deep breath before continuing. "And Aunt Irina?"

"She died."

"I know that, damn it, before she died?"

"She did what a lot of beautiful women do."

Understanding the implication, Stas could only stare in pain.

Without looking at his son, Vlade continued. "She liked the good life, liked good things."

"A whore?"

Vlade didn't answer.

"And you kept screwing her?"

Vlade's shoulders dropped, weighted down with the oppressive secret. "Yeah, sometimes, until..."

"Until what?"

"Until she got involved with a black cop."

Vlade stared at his son, looking for that male understanding.

"Fuck you, Vlade." Stas turned. "You know, you're the bastard!" he shouted.

Resigned, Vlade returned to his magazine and his drink. "That's what your mother keeps telling me."

Outside, Stas blinked in the late morning sun. He wanted to hit somebody. Leaning against the car, he realized that Vlade's revelations would take time to absorb, but could he ever forgive what had happened to him at the hands of Helena? How long would it take before the pain turned to hatred, or had that feeling always been there almost dormant, repressed for years by the sheer strength of his will? Had Dina called it? Bitterness. But was there rage waiting to surface?

He backed the car out into the street, unable to deal with another unanswered question. He needed someplace to think. He needed another drink.

After driving randomly around the city, he ended up taking Western Avenue south. That route was almost automatic. He had been assigned to South Central after the Academy.

Pain blurred his vision. He paid little attention to the people going about their mundane routines. There was no connection. He could have been driving on Mars.

He finally pulled over and parked in the red in front of a run-down liquor store. Three winos had taken possession of the sidewalk underneath a window covered with a metal grill. There was a dusty display of a beautiful black woman pouring a suave looking black man a drink from a bottle of Black Velvet. The faded advertisement enshrined behind filthy glass had probably been there since "Super Fly" days judging from the couples' full afros.

The drunks were sober enough to edge away from the entrance as Stas approached. He felt that he looked more menacing now than he ever did in his days on patrol when he might have harassed them for just looking high. Now, he didn't give a damn what they drank or smoked.

A security gate partially covered the dirty glass doors that allowed only one person at a time to enter or exit. The lights inside were dimmed not from wattage, but from years of accumulated grime. The brightest spot was a large frame of uncovered florescent bulbs hanging over the clerk, voluntarily sequestered behind a counter with metal grillwork on the upper half. The whole setup seemed strange. The opening on the counter of the cashier's cage had just enough room to pass a six-pack through. Stas couldn't see how this would deter someone from sticking a gun through the opening or running off with a couple of fifths or a case of beer, yet the detective's every move was followed by beady black eyes. Stas scanned the store for a security camera and saw none. *I guess you're it.*

Still conscious of the clerk's watchful gaze, Stas walked to the shelves next to the makeshift security cage. The selection of hard liquor was slim and cheap. He took the first pint of vodka he saw. *Topper, never heard of it.*

He turned the bottle over and read the back label to himself. Bottled in San Jose, California. He passed it through to the young man.

"Three fifty-nine." The clerk grabbed the bottle.

Stas peeled off four ones from bills he took from his pocket and slid them over the counter, disregarding the change the young man eased back.

"No bag," Stas said.

The cashier grabbed a small brown paper sack from beneath his counter and dropped in the bottle, shoving them both through the opening.

Stas took the bottle out and wadded the bag into a tight ball and bowled it back through the opening. "Fuck the bag." Outside he leaned against the window, broke the seal on the bottle, and took a long swig, coughing as the fiery liquid burned his mouth and throat.

"You okay?" One drunk asked as he raised himself half off the plastic crate he was sitting on.

Stas didn't answer but waved the man off as he took another drink. He shuttered with its rawness, but no matter how cheap, the vodka could still deaden the senses and dull the pain. As he recapped the bottle, he caught the strong smell of urine. Grayish streaks snaked in tiny rivulets from the building to the curb. He took his time getting into the car. The three men gathered again, closing ranks like inebriated knights guarding their feudal fiefdom.

They bent in unison to peer into the car as he stashed the bottle under his seat. Here he was, an officer sworn to uphold the law, drinking in public. He could have written himself up for multiple violations.

Someone honked as Stas pulled out into traffic without a turn signal or a backward glance. *What the hell!*

He continued south on Western and finally ended up at White Point Beach. The day had turned cold and overcast by the time he found an isolated parking spot. Stas sat in the car and listened to the pounding surf juxtaposed by Kirk Whalum's plaintive sax. He took several more gulps, put the bottle back under the seat, and reclined.

His thoughts conjured up images of Irina that were so vivid that he raised his hand to stroke her ash blonde hair, then closed his eyes and imagined her gray-blue eyes sparkling with mischief or promise. He straightened, reached for the bottle, and drained it, then tried to picture the real Irina. Was there a difference?

She was one of those classic Northern European beauties. Real or in a dream, his memory of her was so vivid that he felt he could reach out and touch her, hear her whispered teasing.

By contrast there had never been an imagined relationship with Helena. She never held him, whispered to him. She never tucked him in at night or read bedtime stories. Helena had always been cold, calculating, and controlling for as long as he could remember.

As he grew older, he had seen less and less of Irina, but there were times when she would just show-up, breathless and beautiful, tousle his hair, look into his face for a long time, then kiss him on the forehead and disappear again for months, even years. But his most lasting memory of her wasn't an image at all but her scent, her essence that would linger with him long after she had gone. Was she why his olfactory senses were so sharp now, why a certain scent of a woman could get his attention and interest?

He had to get out of the car and stretch and wished for a cigarette. He threw the empty vodka bottle into a wire trash container and looked for a place to relieve himself. The nearest restroom was locked. "Shit!" He spied a bush and was glad he was male, glad no one was nearby to accuse him of exposing himself.

Not ready to make the drive back to Glendale or get in the car, he walked along a path that ran parallel to the shoreline. The smell of kelp was strong along that stretch of beach. Gray-green ropes of algae littered the sand as the tide washed in and out of the rising surf, its roar echoing the building tension in Stas.

He returned to the car as the sun began to set, its soft pink glow passing intermittently behind narrow bands of gray clouds. His thoughts turned to Dina, her warm softness, her fragrance seeping from his subconscious, and now that exotic, heady essence was slowing gathering him in like some siren song that he had avoided two years ago and even now tried to evade. Was that why he'd left her alone? Maybe she was right; she was his prisoner.

The craving for nicotine made him realize he hadn't eaten all day. Hopefully Dina had found something in the freezer. *Shake her off. Damn it, shake'em all off.*

The drive home took much longer than he had anticipated. The traffic was heavy, for the earlier clouds at the beach had turned into a full blown storm that dumped rain here and there along the freeway. Stas cursed and turned on the air. But the cold blowing in his face did nothing as he tried to ignore the knot starting to build in his stomach. What he really needed was another drink.

His apartment was dark and silent except for the heavy rain that now pounded the outside. Light seeped under his closed bedroom door. Dina must still be awake. He started to knock but Maestro Chopin summoned him to the kitchen instead. He returned with a glass and his bottle, turned on the desk lamp, and settled down in his recliner, but he didn't pour a drink. Earlier his mind and not his body had absorbed the alcohol, for he felt nothing. How long would it take to go numb?

Bright light from the bedroom roused him from his funk. Dina stood in the doorway toweling her hair, her untied terry robe hung loosely around her. She smelled of citrus, like she'd just bathed in lemons and dried in lemon grass.

"How long have you been back?" she asked.

Stas rose. "You need a drink?"

Dina stood her ground as he brushed by her. "You still don't know what I need?" Her voice was husky.

Stas stopped, drawn to her heat. He bent to take in her fragrance, to stroke her damp hair. But once he touched, he knew there would be no turning back, no withdrawing his hand from the fire.

He caught her roughly, pinning her arms behind her, pulling her to his midsection, letting her feel his arousal. He kissed her, long and hard, feeling her trying to catch her breath as his mouth smothered hers, but she didn't resist. When he released her she almost collapsed with his intensity and her need.

His hands reached into the open robe. "Is this what you want?" His voice was raw.

"Yes... yes!"

When Stas picked her up, the robe slipped from her shoulders exposing hard swollen breasts. In the bedroom, he dumped her to the bed and pulled off his sweater. She sat up to undo his belt and unzip his fly. Her urgency was matched by his own as he hurriedly peeled off shoes, socks, jeans, briefs.

Naked, he fell on her, pulling the bunched robe from under her and tossing it to the floor. His lips moved to her eyes, nose, chin, then lingered for a moment on the scar at her neck, his tongue tracing its raised ridge. When he continued to her erect nipples, she pulled him back to her lips while she hungrily opened to him.

His roughness as he entered her jolted her, but she met him stroke for stroke in a feverish coupling that bathed their bodies in a fine sheen of sweat. Then a rare and incredible convulsion swept through Dina, cramping her toes, straining her thighs as she clutched him to her. She felt overwhelmed trying to hold back, she screamed as she reached her peak. He continued, bringing her to another powerful release. She gasped and cried out again when a final wave brought them both to their completion.

They lay breathless for a moment. Then Stas rolled off and cradled her head in the crook of his arm as they rested.

Later, he raised up and strained to switch off the lamp, but Dina stirred. *Forgot the light!* He settled back under the down cover pulling it over their nakedness. But he couldn't sleep.

Looking at Dina as if seeing her for the first time: her tan skin, the dark curls, tangled and plastered to her temples in their dampness. He fingered the slightly raised keloid ridge on her neck that invited his touch. The scar, the only visual evidence of the assault, had brought them together two years ago, but Stas didn't believe in fate. He closed his eyes to shut out the growing feeling that he was being drawn into something that was beyond his control.

Dina turned her body, pressing her breasts into his ribcage, but she didn't awaken. She emitted a little snort that turned into a soft snore.

He didn't know how long she dozed or if he even slept, but his arm was getting numb. As he shifted her head from his shoulder, she opened her eyes. He had forgotten their color: hazel with flecks of gold.

Well, this was a night of firsts. Dina had breeched his inner sanctum

Their lovemaking was less urgent the second time. They moved together in that primordial rhythm. She didn't have to use her tricks or utter words of encouragement to enhance his performance. Again, she felt that new sensation building in her pelvis. She tensed then relaxed. Just let it happen again. But would it?

Dina had never experienced an orgasm with a man before Stas. And here it was again swelling and expanding inside of her. She gripped his hips with her thighs as the membrane of the balloon grew thinner and thinner until it exploded again. She squeezed her eyes shut and clutched Stas to her. Her heart raced on, propelling the sensations throughout her body.

She released his shoulders, dropped her hands to grab fistfuls of sheet and cried out, briefly aware of Stas tensing and then his pounding release. They collapsed, exhausted in each others arms, their bodies once again damp with perspiration. Dina cradled him as he slept. She stretched, content that it had happened again, then managed to reach the switch to turn off lamp.

The rain, light and steady, continued into the morning. Stas awoke and ran his hand over the surface of his abdomen. There was no evidence of anything physical, but he felt a heavy knot like a twenty pound tumor in his stomach. He didn't want to acknowledge the emotional pain. He had felt it before with his marriage. And it wasn't the same as work related stress: the final stages of wrapping a case, going after a perp, coming under fire. Now this was personal.

He heard Dina's soft breathing, like the purring of a contented cat and realized that she slept peacefully next to him. The events of the night briefly abated the pain of the previous day. It had been awhile, and he had almost forgotten just how good it could be. She was the first to share his bed and his personal space since his divorce.

As he swung his legs out of bed, he saw his clothes littering the floor. Automatically he reached to pick up his jeans but stopped. *Leave 'em.* He went to the bathroom, shaved, and took a cold shower. Wrapping a towel around his midsection, he returned to the bedroom.

Dina eyed him, half peering from the covers. "Are you up already?"

"I guess so." He tried to maneuver himself so that she could not see his growing arousal.

"You're a liar. You need to come back to bed." She swung the covers back, inviting him to the warmth of her body.

Stas let the towel drop and joined her. It was a morning of exploration. Dina was an artful lover, full of tricks and surprises that kept him going for what seemed like hours. When she finally fell back sated, her last cries leaving a smile on her lips, she slept the peaceful slumber of an infant.

He thought little of what had happened with his father. It felt good to have a woman next to him, warm and damp, his own scent mingled with hers. He covered her bare shoulder with the comforter and closed his eyes.

The display on the night-stand clock read 3:07 p.m.. They had spent the better part of the day in bed. He couldn't remember the last time that had happened. Finally, Stas got up and went to the kitchen. Although tempted to pour a drink, he made coffee instead. He carried the thick, black brew in two mugs to the bedroom. Dina slipped on his T-shirt when he sat on the edge of the bed and handed her a mug.

"You seem to go from one extreme to the other."

"What? Oh," he looked down at his nakedness. "They only do the sheet thing in the movies. You want me to cover it up now that you're through playing?" There was a hint of sarcasm in his tone. He laughed but made no effort to move or cover up.

Dina sipped her coffee. "So now you're going to talk dirty to me?"

"Is that what you like?"

"No, but you'd never believe what some of them say or do or even want you to do."

"You're forgetting what I do for a living, babe. I see it all, and most of it ain't pretty."

She needed to talk. "It's the rich ones who want to dress up in women's underwear and have me spank them or curse them. Or they want to crawl around scrubbing floors and cleaning the toilet while I..." she didn't finish.

"So get out."

"And do what, sell make-up at Macy's, share an apartment with three other women who look as good as me and sleep for nothing with guys they pick up at a club? They spend the rest of the time trying to make the rent because they gave it away. Or they wonder if the next guy's going to be adequate. I've seen enough pigglie-wigglies in my day."

"You took a chance with me."

"No, I didn't. I knew." She looked into the dredges of her mug. "I just knew, and I was right."

"Then let's leave the other guys out of our conversation. Focus on changing. Let me help." With that, Stas picket up the towel he had tossed on the floor and went to the bathroom where he showered and returned to his closet for sweats and running shoes, grabbed briefs from the chest, and dressed.

Stas didn't go for a run but returned to his parents' home to seek answers to the endless and sometimes mindless questions that ravaged his mind.

He phoned from the car. Helena was still away, and Vlade was going to his early evening poker game leaving the house empty long enough for a good search. It was funny. Stas thought going through Helena's things shouldn't take long. Crime techs would love her, for she was a compulsive organizer, saving select memorabilia: photos, letters, awards, diplomas, all put away in neat little boxes and plastic bags. Well, he planned to invade her private spaces, those dark recesses of her closet and the chest at the foot of her bed. But he didn't have a clue what he was looking for.

The knot in the pit of his stomach seemed to grow bigger and harder the closer he got to the house. Stas wiped away a fine sheen of perspiration from his forehead and wished for a drink or a smoke or both. Instead of parking in front of the house, he drove past, parked on a side street and walked back.

The house looked cold and isolated. The porch was devoid of any greenery. There were no beds of flowers or potted plants. The Nowak house stood in contrast to the neighboring homes that were alive with winter color. Blooming azaleas bordered the fronts of the houses on either side of theirs. Several large camellias in full bloom added splashes of pink, red and white to the other yards. Along the street, lawns were carpets of green from the winter rye and recent rains, but there was nothing that gave any sign of verdant life at the Nowak's.

He still had a key and opened the front door to a cold, dark living room. Two days after the party, everything was in order. Stas wondered how long it had taken Helena to erase the remnants of the celebration before she left on her trip. The furniture had been put back, dishes and glasses put away, the drapes drawn. Stas passed through as he had done all his life. The living room and dining room held no secrets.

Stas looked in Vlade's room first. His old man's life was an open book. The covers had been pulled up over the bed in haste. Several pairs of shoes and slippers played hide and seek from under the bed. Old work trousers were thrown over the back of his worn and faded recliner, which faced a big, screen TV sitting on a low wooden cabinet.

He didn't need to open the doors to know its contents. His father made no secret of his triple X-rated taste. There was a combo VCR/DVD player, a gift to the old man some years back plus his sex tapes and a few mindless action and violent videos thrown in. The smell of cheap aftershave lingered in the closed air. Stas smiled. He doubted Vlade had gone to a poker game.

Like an instant replay of his early teens, he remembered the fight. The police had come, called by neighbors because Helena had raged with a cleaver, threatening to "cut it off." Vlade had been caught with a young woman in the garage. The "whore" had escaped with her life but not her underwear. Helena had let the woman's panties and bra lay in a pool of black on the garage floor. She had forbid Stas to go to the garage to view the evidence of his father's infidelity. After his parents went to sleep, he sneaked out and touched the lacy undergarments that had been removed from the floor and put on Vlade's workbench.

That incident had been another that marked the beginning of the end of their father/ son relationship. There were no more soccer games or fishing trips. His father had moved out of his parents' bedroom and into the den. Vlade continued his whoring but did so away from the Nowak domicile, and Helena took on the rearing of Stas.

Sitting on the edge of the bed, he looked around wondering how his father had survived all those years on video sex, violence, and vodka. As he rose, the thought hit him. The life of a cop wasn't that different. He closed the door and moved down the hall to Helena's room.

Standing at the threshold, he paused. When he finally entered, he saw the bed neatly made. There were no shoes or clothes thrown about. The room was clean and free of clutter. The wooden surfaces had been polished to a high sheen probably just before she left, leaving the room devoid of any semblance of living or loving, as if she existed in a vacuum.

Stas started with the dresser. The top center drawer contained two small plastic boxes. He knew what was in the blue box when he raised the lid. There, wrapped in clear plastic, were all of his Boy Scout badges, but one had been separated out, the first and only badge he had earned as an Eagle Scout. Holding it brought a flood of memories.

When he moved up in scouting, he had changed location and scout leaders. The old leaders had gathered a diverse group of young boys and molded them into young men. When they had gathered in the dark, dank confines of the Methodist Church basement, it had been more the presence and example of the older men rather than any scouting manual that gave them a sense of what life would be as they entered adulthood.

Stas smiled, wondering if any of the boys had developed lung cancer from the second hand smoke produced by the leaders. In those days there had been no prohibition on smoking in the presence of developing young men. They all took chances; some, like himself, even acquired the habit. He started smoking after giving up scouting and Holy Mother Church.

He put the box back and picked up its companion that contained several art ribbons won by his sister. Unlike Stas, Anne had fought anything that resembled order. She had been the teenage rebel, her only interest being art, design, and escape. She managed to achieve all three by becoming a graphic artist and moving to Seattle.

The lower drawers were in meticulous order: panties, bras, pajamas, hose. There were a few pieces of nice jewelry, each in its own cloth pouch. Another drawer held blouses and sweaters in plastic bags. He examined under the bags and found only flowered drawer liners yellowed with age, its promised perfume no longer present.

As he turned from the dresser and looked about the room, its starkness reminded him of his own Spartan existence. Stas started to open the chest but was drawn to the closet. It was narrow and deep, containing two rods, one behind the other, of hanging clothes. A pocketed bag on the door held shoes, some in cloth sacks, some with shoetrees. Dresses, skirts, and jackets hung neatly on the first rod. These he parted revealing two garment bags hanging on the second rod. When his hand came to rest on a long dingy bag, a bag so out of character in this closet, he felt a cold sensation, as if someone had run a shard of ice down his spine. He paused before pulling down the zipper.

He parted the opening and ran his hand inside, touching something cool and silky. Stas pulled out what had once been a royal blue dress now cut into vertical strips, leaving only enough fabric at the neck to allow it to be pinned onto the wire hanger. As he looked further, he found two other dresses that had been similarly mutilated. It was the third dress that triggered long, forgotten memories. He held it to his face, inhaling. Nothing, nothing but musky dust, no perfumed residue to bring back the vision of the woman who had worn these garments.

The memory blinded him like a blast from a Glock at close range. It had been their secret when Irina had arrived in a limo at St. Benet's one day before his graduation. She'd come to take him out for an evening on the town. The other guys at school were blown away by her beauty, the sweep of her hair, her perfect make-up, the short dress, the long shapely legs, the four-inch heels.

She had taken him shopping, then dinner at a restaurant with a secluded table decorated with candles and flowers. He remembered that their fragrance seemed to overpower hers, so he had asked to have them removed. Stas couldn't remember their conversation, but he could still see her smile, hear her laughter. She seemed proud when he told her about college, but her smile faded when he told her about ROTC and the army once he graduated.

The later events of that night were etched in his mind and most certainly in his maturing body. He'd never told a soul about what really had transpired, where she'd taken him. He never saw her again after that night. He had sneaked into the house just before daybreak and slipped into bed without undressing after shoving the shopping bags under the bed to be dealt with later. The few hours of sleep that might have come didn't. He lay awake thinking about their secret, feeling sensations he'd never imagined existed. Then Helena had come in without knocking to tell him it was time for school, but there was no school. It was his last day.

The memories winched the knot tighter in his stomach, squeezing venom into his system. He stopped. He had to control himself before he destroyed everything in the room, everything in the house that belonged to Helena.

Breathing deeply, he paused before reaching into the bottom of the garment bag and retrieving two handbags. One was beautifully beaded in vibrant colors; the other looked as if it belonged to an ethnic costume. The first bag was empty, its silk lining worn and discolored with age. The second bag contained several photos that Stas took to the nightstand to see in a better light.

There was a black and white picture of two girls, one was obviously Helena, who even as a child had that pinched, unsmiling look. He guessed the other girl was Irina; her face had been x-ed out, scratched beyond recognition. There was another black and white photo that included a young man in an ill-fitting suit. It was Vlade with Helena and a mutilated Irina. The third photo, a family gathering, was in color. He recognized his mother's stance if not her mutilated face. It was Irina holding a toddler. Stas lovingly fingered her image. He sighed and put everything back as he had found it. It was time to leave.

The drive back to his apartment was slow and round about. Several drivers blew at him for not exceeding the speed limit.

When he parked the car in the underground garage, his stomach was returning to a semblance of normalcy. And now he was hungry. In the elevator, thoughts of Dina seemed to touch every sense, prod every appetite. Was there another hunger creeping into his system?

As he hung his jacket in the closet, he heard noises coming from the kitchen. Dina had wrapped his LAPD Chili Cookout apron around her sweats and stood at the stove stirring a pot that smelled vaguely of tomato, basil, and oregano.

"You're not cooking are you?"

She turned, a wooden spoon poised in midair. "You know, I can cook!"

He looked in the pot. "What's this?"

"I saw some tomato puree on the shelf, so..."

"So you're making pasta sauce..."

She nodded. "You hungry?"

"I'm ravenous." He smiled.

Dina turned back to her pot, giving it a stir and a taste. "I called Lisa. Sybil's lawyer is reading the will tomorrow."

"She knows you're here?" The levity was gone. Even though Dina had only phoned, he knew the situation was somehow compromised since Lisa now knew of Dina's whereabouts. He felt the other escort had somehow invaded his space, and he didn't like it.

Dina observed the change. "I like you better when you're hungry." She put the spoon on the stove. "I told her I'd be there. I have to go."

He reached in the cabinet to get a glass for a drink but put it back. For some reason, he didn't seem to need the vodka. "Then I'll take you, babe."

FOURTEEN

Stas took the better part of the morning trying to nail down Stealth. When they finally connected, there was a brief moment of silence on the other end while the young computer hack checked his lines. Stealth trusted no one and never talked long under any circumstances. He always suspected wiretaps or some type of government eavesdropping. If he was suspicious, he'd hang up, and Stas would have to try again or wait for the computer techno-felon to call him back.

"What's up?" The voice on the other end was nervous and high pitched.

Stas couldn't waste time. "I need to read a data strip about the size of a stick of gum."

"Is it new, old?"

"I'm not sure, but I think she's had it awhile."

"You need a PDA. If it's new, try Best Buy, but if it's old you may be looking at a Sony Clie."

"A what?"

"Clie, man, Sony Clie. Try E-Bay. Gotta go."

"Wait?"

There was no disconnect. Stealth was still on the line. "Hope you got the password." Then the line went dead.

"Fuck it." Stas stared at the receiver in his hand just as Dina emerged from the bedroom wearing a smart brown suit, brown suede slings, and carrying a matching clutch. She looked like the other half of a yuppie couple off to see their CPA about saving their tax shelter in their financial downturn. "Lookin' good, babe. What time is the reading?"

"Noon."

"Noon? What happened to those long lawyer lunches?"

"The girls ..."

"Yeah, I know, sleep in." He jingled his keys and held the door for her.

In the garage, Dina waited by the elevator for Stas to bring his car.

"Why do you live over here? Does anything happen in Glendale? The city's like a tomb."

"That's why I moved here. Cops don't like to live where they work. It's like taking a crap where you eat." He hoped he had cleaned up the expression. "Another cop owns the condo. I just rent, but he put a lot of work into it."

She looked back at the building as he pulled out of the underground garage into the empty street.

"It's things you can't see, babe, like the metal core in the door, longer dead bolts, extra security cameras in the entrance, garage, and elevator. I'm not the only cop living here. Don't worry, the building is very secure. We look out for each other, but we don't intrude."

When he glanced over at Dina, he sensed more burning questions.

"I moved here after the divorce. We bought a small house in Pasadena. I thought that might help. Hell, I was even willing to start a family. But it only made things worse. She was afraid someone I'd arrested would find out where we lived, break in, ... kill her."

"What about you? Didn't she worry about you?"

"You kidding? With her it was the money and the time I didn't spend with her. I worked overtime for a fatter pay check, but even with that, there was never enough. It was a losing proposition all round so I finally moved. She served me with papers, sold the house, and moved to San Francisco."

"You still in contact?"

"She and my sister are. If I hear anything, it's third hand, and as the judge would say, that's inadmissible. I don't want any contact."

"You seem... are you bitter?"

"Back to my rage. Am I bitter? With her? Yeah, I guess so, but I wasn't about to change my job to save a bad marriage. Anyway, I like what I do, and I'm damn good at it. Are there drawbacks? You bet. Paper work, no wife to come home to, no kids to play with. If you get married again, and you're still a cop, the wife may find someone else to give her attention, a good fuck now and then 'cause you don't have the time or the energy, then all the kids want is the money."

"It sounds a little selfish, especially on their part."

"I'm trying it the other way."

"So you stay single?"

"It's a pretty safe bet." He laughed. "Or you can always get shot."

Stas found the parking lot behind the Stewart Building full. Lots of girls doing business at lunch. He was glad Dina could not read his mind. He watched a man in sweats stroll towards a BMW. Stas eased in position near the car and effortlessly swung into the space when the other car pulled out.

"If I'm not here when you finish, wait for me." He nodded toward the back entrance.

Dina turned as she opened the door. "Where are you going?"

"To Best Buy."

She didn't wait for him to explain. She was out of the car and halfway to the building's rear entrance before he realized he was still sitting, staring out into the vast metal wasteland.

At the Best Buy on Wilshire, Stas asked for information from a young man in a yellow vest who looked more like a Caltrans' worker than a store greeter. With a wave of a hand he directed Stas to the computer-electronics department. And was waited on by a young black woman with perfect teeth and a smile to match.

"Can I help you?" She leaned over her side of the counter.

He took the plastic baggie from his pocket and handed over the strip. "I think I need a PDA, something to read this."

She motioned for him to move to the side of a display of several PDAs. "Which one?"

"I don't have a clue. I just need to read this."

She didn't take the strip but took out two devices. "These could do the trick, except there's the Palm 22 which is primarily an organizer." She flashed her pearly whites. "We don't carry that one any more."

"I need to read data not get organized."

"Well, there's the TIX and the Tungsten E2. They both have memory card slots."

"I don't want to buy it unless I can see if it works. Will it read this?" He tapped the baggie.

She smiled. "If you want to stick your strip in and read it, honey, you're buying it."

Stas wondered if there was a hint of sexual innuendo. "Why can't I try it here?"

"This isn't a library." The smiled flashed off like a neon sign at closing as she moved to put one package back. "You know dear, no milk unless you buy this cow."

"Look, I'm a cop." He started to reach for his ID but took out his credit card instead. "I'm working on a case."

One box was now suspended in midair. "And I'm an actress working on a big block buster with Denzel." She had slammed the door in his face.

"Okay, okay."

The smile flashed on again. She was once again open for business. "You have to take it to the cashier."

"Which one are you giving me?" He hesitated looking again at the box poised in front of him. "I don't need the most expensive one."

She took an appraising gaze, assessing his suit, tie, his overall manner. "You look like a man who wants the best." She had him again. "One's $314 with 32 MB. The other one has 120 MB."

"How much?"

"Three forty-nine."

"Now, you're sure it will read this?" He waved the strip once again.

"Well, it depends on the data strip, but I'm sure it will." She didn't want her sale slipping away. "I've never heard of one that didn't."

He reached for the proffered box and read her nametag.

"Thanks, Tyisha. That's a pretty name."

"That's what all the cops say." She rolled her eyes.

Stas laughed. "I really do have I.D."

"They say that, too. Next time, show it to me when you come in for strips."

She leaned over the counter as Stas stepped away. "You know, if you're reading someone else's strip, you'll need a password."

"That's what I've been told. Well, we'll see."

"You'd think the police would have their own device." She called after him.

Stas thought the same thing as he stood in line to pay, but he wasn't about to share Sybil's info with any one in his division or vice until he found out what was on it.

Finding another parking space at the Stewart Building seemed to take longer since Stas was anxious to check the device. He drove around the lot, then decided to wait for someone to pull out. He glanced at the brightly colored bag on the passenger seat and finally dumped out the boxed PDA. It was sealed tighter than Fort Knox.

He leaned over to retrieve a small tool kit from the glove department while still keeping an eye out for Dina or a space. He pried apart the fused plastic letting the box's contents fall in his lap.

The PDA looked like a rectangular cigarette case no larger than his palm. The tiny computer screen covered the face. He took the plastic bag from his jacket pocket and nervously slipped the strip into the slot. Nothing happened.

Realizing he didn't have a clue what he was doing, he decided to read the directions. As he resigned himself to learning about another new, expensive toy, he saw a car pulling out near the rear entrance of the building. Quickly dumping the contents from his lap onto the passenger seat, Stas swung into the vacated parking space.

Although the weak winter sun was not hot enough for shirt sleeves, he had to get out of the warm car. He removed his jacket, folded it on his seat, and stood by the door unfolding instructions to the PDA. He wanted a cigarette, looked up and saw a lone woman walk out of the building. It had been five, six years, but he would have recognized Raven Crawford anywhere. She should have been named Raven Brown. She had silky burnt chocolate coloring and almond shaped dark brown eyes fanned by long, dark lashes. Her mocha colored hair was worn short, accented with long dangling earrings. She had to be over six feet and towered over Stas by half a head. Bare foot or in heels, clothed or stripped, she was the embodiment of many men's fantasies. She truly personified the song, "Bubbling Brown Sugar," he had played once. Raven walked over and, as if reading his mind, pulled out a silver cigarette case, flicked it open, and held it out to him.

"You look like you could use a smoke." Her voice was sweet yet deep, like someone speaking through a veil of honey.

He paused. "I quit."

"Really?" Raven put two cigarettes between her burgundy lips and lit them with a silver lighter, then handed one to him.

There was no refusing Raven. He took a long, hard drag, the smoke filled his lungs, the nicotine slowly coursing through his veins. He closed his eyes for a second to savor the rush, then exhaled slowly, blowing the smoke skyward. *Damn, it felt good*!

"See, you needed that." She took a deep pull on her own cigarette and turned to blow the smoke away from Stas.

"So did you ladies divvy up Sybil's wealth?" he asked.

"It's no joke. She had plenty. I got controlling interest of the business, so I guess I'm the CFO, controlling the fucking outfit. Dina's next in line. She and Lisa got money; the kid got money, and her boyfriend got a big chunk of change to 'continue his research.'"

"You thinking about quitting the business?"

"Not likely. Anyway, I have a few options. I just got a very sweet offer from an old friend of yours."

"Old friend? And who's that?"

"Honey Malone. She asked me to help her out with her business."

"I thought she was retired."

"Semi. With Sybil gone, Honey may want to fill the void." Raven smiled. "But I'm sure you know all about this. She said you talked recently."

"Just a courtesy call, see how the old gal was doing."

"Yeah, I bet."

Stas coughed on smoke that went the wrong way. "You said Sybil had a kid?"

Raven nodded.

"So where is it."

"She lives up north somewhere, Marrs knows." When she turned to blow the smoke away again, she caught sight of Dina coming towards them. "How are you and Dina doing?" Raven stubbed out her cigarette and shifted her weight, settling it on one hip.

Dina looked from Stas to Raven and back to Stas as he dropped his butt and crushed it.

"I didn't know you two knew each other?"

Raven straightened. "Oh, Stas and I go way back." She turned to leave. "I'll see you around."

Stas reached into the car for his jacket. Before he could get around to the passenger door, Dina was getting in the car.

"C'mom, we're going back." He tried to take her arm, but she pulled away.

"Why?"

"I want to talk to Marrs about Sybil's kid."

"Raven told you?"

"Were you going to?" His voice was cool as he locked the car and waited for Dina to join him.

They walked in awkward silence until they reached the elevator. No one joined them on the ride to the sixth floor.

"I picked up the PDA."

"Did it work?" She asked.

"No, damn it. I need the password... and power." He paused. "And I'd better read the instructions. What's the boyfriend's name?"

"I don't know, didn't Raven tell you that, too?" She walked ahead of him to the double walnut doors of Marrs's office when they exited the elevator.

They found the attorney in the reception area, preparing to leave.

"Mr. Marrs?"

The attorney turned on a dime despite his bulk, glanced at Dina, then at Stas. "Who are you?"

"LAPD. Stas Nowak." Stas produced his ID. "I'm not here officially."

"Then why are you here at all?"

Stas's tone hardened, damn the prelims. "I know you just read the Hansen will. I need to know about Sybil Hansen's child. Raven told me the kid was left money."

Dina had taken a seat when Stas approached Marrs. He looked towards her, and she nodded her okay. "Come into my office, but I only have a moment." He held the door, waiting for Dina.

In the inner office Dina and Stas took chairs facing Marrs' desk.

Stas spoke first. "I don't want to involve you or anyone else in an investigation that doesn't exist. I'm just looking into some issues for Dina, and I would like to talk to the girl." No one commented, so he continued. "... see if she or her parents can shed some light on Sybil and why she would have taken her life. And if she didn't, then maybe we can figure out what did happen. If it wasn't suicide, then we may have an investigation. So… you know anything about the adoption?"

"I set it up, made the placement."

"Where?" Stas asked.

"Near King City, family named Atwood."

"Were the records sealed?"

"It was a private adoption. You won't find any thing on the original birth certificate. She listed the father as a John Doe." Marrs looked at his watch.

"Have you notified the Atwoods about Sybil and the money?"

Marrs tapped his fingers. "I hadn't planned to until after the reading of the will."

Dina moved to the edge of her chair but said nothing.

"Could you hold off a couple of days? I'd like to speak to them first." Stas rose.

Marrs also rose. "I don't see what's to be gained, but you have forty-eight hours.

Stas stood behind Dina's chair. "By the way, who was the father?"

Marrs smiled. "I'm not at liberty to say."

"But you do know."

Marrs was at the door, holding it open for Dina and Stas. "Good to see you again, Dina. .Good-bye, Detective Nowak."

At the car, Stas took the box and its packaging from the passenger seat and put it in the trunk.

"So what about Sybil's disk?" Dina asked.

"It's not a disk. Tyisha called it a 'memory stick'."

Dina shot him a cold look. "Who the hell is Tyisha?"

"She's the cutie who sold me the PDA at Best Buy."

"Cutie? I bet she was sixty if she was a day. She probably was a guy. How many women you know, even care that much about computers?"

"Sybil did. Even in death, she's still locking us out."

"Where are you going?" Dina questioned as Stas passed in front of her building looking for a parking space.

"How long will it take you to get some things together?"

"For what?"

"A little trip."

"Where?"

"King City."

"For how long?"

Stas maneuvered into a tight space and cut the engine. He smiled as he turned to Dina. "You work for the prosecutors?"

"I just wanted to know what to pack."

"You heard the man. He gave us forty-eight hours. Pack warm and light, babe."

FIFTEEN

The distinctive ring on the phone awakened Matt from a light doze. He had been watching the Lakers host Chicago. Without Michael Jordan, the long time rivalry was without its old excitement. He groped for the telephone receiver next to him and gruffly answered.

"Yeah?"

The voice on the other end was soft, sultry, a voice from the shadowy past. "Are you alone?"

"Gwen? I'll buzz you in."

He quickly switched on the entry hall light and checked himself in the mirror. His cotton pullover was a little wrinkled, but there wasn't time to change. When he opened the door and saw her standing there, he felt as if the clock had been turned back years. He had forgotten just how beautiful Gwen Lawson could be out of uniform. Her dark brown hair, freed from its restrictive bun on the back of her neck, fell softly to her shoulders. Also gone were the dark rimmed glasses. She had changed to contacts. Her make-up was artfully applied although the lipstick had long since faded.

"Are you going to leave me standing out here?" she asked.

He held the door open and followed her into the living room. Gwen laid her leather clutch on the coffee table and sat after handing Matt her short woolen coat. She wore a smart straight skirt and a tailored white silk blouse that clung to the soft swell of her breasts.

"What can I get you?" he asked.

"You know what I like."

He took the coat to the hall closet before fixing drinks. The scent of her Tea Roses cologne hung suspended in the air. Matt had almost forgotten its spell. She had cast it on him years ago. Now it brought back memories of long days and nights spent, at first, on patrol and then, later, in intimate moments snatched away from work and the eyes of supervisors or fellow cops.

While he busied himself at the wet bar between the living room and the dining area, Gwen looked over the immediate area from where she sat. It wasn't the typical bachelor's pad, but it was definitely a man's apartment. Matt now had the disposable income to indulge his taste in good solid pieces of furniture and expensive audio-visual components set in a custom built unit that took up one wall of the living room. The tables and trim on the chairs and sofa matched the wood of the entertainment center. She had debated about intruding into Matt's space, but she needed a comfort zone, something old and familiar. She watched him move and felt a hint of desire course through her body, her nipples hardened with excitement. Maybe coming to Matt's hadn't been such a good idea after all.

Before handing Gwen her drink, Matt reached for the remote and muted the game. She took a sip and sat her glass down.

"You still buy the good stuff." She smiled.

"Why not? I can afford it." He pulled a chair over to the sofa. "How did you get away?"

"Ed and Robert had a meeting with some old money tonight, and I certainly didn't want to spend it with 'the mouth'"

"You'd better get used to it. Beth's moved down. They've already sold the Fresno house."

Gwen frowned and took a stiff slug from her Scotch before turning her attention back to Matt. "We've missed you. The boys miss you. Ed doesn't have much time anymore." Her voice was almost beseeching.

"They don't miss me. They just miss having their dad around, but I guess any man is better than none." He scrutinized her face and her body language for a reaction before picking up both of their glasses and going for refills.

"Are you trying to get me drunk", she laughed, "so you can have your way with me?"

"It never worked before."

She looked at the glass he handed back to her, avoiding his gaze. "The getting me drunk part."

"If I remember correctly, you could out-drink all of us. How many times did you have to put me to bed?"

When she looked into his eyes, her levity was gone. "Would you tell me if Ed's fooling around?" she asked.

Matt couldn't meet her gaze. "Ed doesn't, wouldn't jeopardize his position, not now. Why, do you suspect something? Have you caught him?"

"No, but I think I would suspect something." There was a iciness in her voice that hadn't been there before.

"Thought the wife was the last..."

Gwen interrupted. "If she's a cop, she would see the signs. It's more than female intuition."

"How, in bed?"

"He's still a good lover. I guess, when he has time. It's been a while. I just have this feeling of distrust, especially now."

"You didn't trust me, so what else is new?"

"I wasn't in love with you."

Matt's smile faded.

"Ours was different", she continued, "the passion of the moment. We were partners. It's hard to be that close, under that kind of stress, and not have it happen. And..." She reached over and touched his hand. "We're still friends."

"So you come all the way over here to tell me how much you love Ed, and you want me to spy on him?"

"No, I came over to talk to a friend. Things are going too fast. I just resigned from the Special Police Task Force. I didn't want to."

"That's the sacrifice you make."

"Why do I have to be the one to make the sacrifices?"

"Because your husband is the one who has ambitions."

"No, because Robert's ambitious, his wife's ambitious."

"Then this is about Robert?"

She drained her glass and sucked on an ice cube. Matt waited. He knew Gwen was doing more than just venting. A flush of pink spread up her neck.

"I don't like Robert, his squeaky cleanness, his moral...." She couldn't think of the word.

"You want a refill?"

"Don't change the subject. I have to drive. I rented a car."

"A few drinks never stopped you before."

"But I don't know any LA cops."

"I do."

She handed him her glass.

Matt called back from the mini-bar. "I can always call you a cab, or...."

"Is Ed as squeaky clean as Robert thinks?"

"Are we still on that?" He could see the intensity in her face as he handed her another drink. "As far as I know."

"You would tell me?"

"Tell you what?" He still stood over her.

"If he cheats."

"What would you do?"

"I'd cash in his family jewels."

"Ouch!"

She sipped, for a second lost in thought. "Where's all this money coming from? You've seen the condo. They're paying you?"

"Yeah, for security and transportation, but Robert's not cutting loose the big bucks, at least not to me."

"So who's paying?"

"Robert has rich friends. And the women, all those rich women seduced by his good looks, his custom suits, his charm."

"Don't forget Beth's big fat trust fund."

"What about Robert's foundation?"

"It's not really his. That's money from her Dad's church. He's just the director. If he's skimming from.... I just don't trust him."

"He's a changed man." Matt smiled. "He's got religion."

"That makes it worse. I don't like the change. I don't like living down here. I miss the old Ed. I miss the man who could look at someone in trouble and want to help, not someone who wants to be a poster boy for a political campaign. I don't want to worry about how I look or what I say, and I sure as hell don't want to become some carbon copy of Beth."

"Since you're worrying, what if they find out about us?"

"If anyone found out, if the media knew, it would be over for Ed. I'd get him back, but it would be over for us."

"Since I have no control over what info gets out, I feel okay. We were careful. I don't think you need to worry."

"Isn't that your job? Aren't you 'damage control'?" Gwen asked.

"I do my part, but I'm quickly realizing that there's not enough money in damage control."

Gwen moved closer. "Then run for office."

"That's a thought, but I have a few other plans."

SIXTEEN

Stas consulted a Mapquest printout for directions to the Atwood house. When he pulled into the driveway, the house was dark, yet he had that eerie feeling that someone was home. He had just spoken to Mr. Atwood and made an appointment to meet the next morning. After a few minutes, he backed out of the drive, swung the car around the cul-de-sac, and slowly drove out of the neighborhood. This part of the town had literally gone to bed or been snatched by aliens to some distant solar system until the next day, for he didn't encounter another car during the fifteen mile drive back to the Woodwind Hotel where he had deposited Dina.

They went down to dinner in the hotel's empty restaurant and found the food forgettable. A vodka neat helped him wash down a tough, tasteless steak. Dina left most of her overcooked salmon untouched but managed to put away two large hot fudge sundaes. He smiled as he sipped his drink and thought how little he knew about this young woman: her past, her likes and dislikes, her habits? He drained his glass and rose to pay the check. Dina licked the last traces of chocolate from the spoon, grabbed her purse, and followed.

Their room was adequate, and the king size bed that Dina inspected, neatly pulling back the covers, looked comfortable. Stas left her settling in and took a hot shower. Emerging from the bathroom, wrapped in a towel more for her misplaced sense of modesty than his. In the dark she wouldn't have to see what her presence did to him.

Dina was sitting up in bed wearing something green, silky, and clinging. He didn't need much to trigger desire that he was now ready to explore. He fingered the button on the bedside lamp. Tonight, they were on neutral ground. Would the passion be as intense as it had been the first time? He slipped between the lavender scented sheets feeling relaxed and ready. Dina knew how to work magic with her scents and sprays even miles away from home.

"Sleep in tomorrow, babe. See if they have room service. I told Atwood I was here on police business. He sounded kinda old and distant. I hope I didn't scare him."

Dina flicked off the TV and tossed the remote towards the foot of the bed. He heard the whisper of silk slipping to the floor.

"Sleepy?" He pulled her to him.

Her lips trembled as she brushed his neck. "No." Her whisper barely audible,

Stas felt the warmth from a strip of muted sunlight inching through drapes that had been left open the night before. His senses were jolted awake with the movement next to him. A warm hip turned to its side, touching his as Dina stretched and turned towards him. He gazed at her and gently brushed her bare shoulder before slipping out of bed without waking her. It was a well-practiced maneuver.

Staring at himself in the bathroom mirror, he knew he would have to come to grips with this situation: the ease with which his needs were gratified, the latent awakening in Dina, the anger and resentment growing about his own family. He stepped into a cold shower that had seemed to work in the past, but after ten seconds in the icy spray he instinctively knew he'd have to come up with another remedy.

Dina's outstretched hand felt a warm emptiness. She scooted over to the vacant spot and buried her face in his pillow.

As she thought of ways to entice him back to bed, she drifted back into that half-waking sleep when she heard the shower running.

Dina watched him shave. "I use to love to watch my dad. Sometimes he used a straight razor."

Stas stood before the sink, damp and naked, patting after shave on his face. "Where's he now?" He spoke to her reflection.

"On the Southside of Chicago. We don't keep in touch that much, but..." she moved aside as he walked by her to dress. "I can find him if I need to." Her voice trailed off.

He sensed a vulnerability in her tone that he had not noticed before. It made him take a good look at her as he grabbed up his wallet, keys, and change. She stood there, her hair haloed around a sad face and an even sadder smile. He felt the urge to take her in his arms, to comfort her and in doing so, bring some comfort to himself, but he had to leave.

"I'll see you later, babe. Go back to bed. You look tired."

This time her smile was warmer. "I wonder why?"

Stas parked in front of the Atwood house, got out of the car, looked towards the house. He noticed a movement at the front window. Someone was peeping through a raised slat of the blinds. Stas watched for other movement, then walked to the door and rang the bell. It took a few minutes for Atwood to open the door.

In his late forties, Atwood looked like a once robust man on the verge of slowly deflating, his life draining through some minute pin-prick at the base of his soul. His blue eyes looked like washed-out denim, and his sallow complexion sagged as if he hadn't eaten or slept for days.

Atwood barely glanced at Stas's ID.

"I'm Detective Nowak from Los Angeles."

"You're a little off your beat aren't you?"

Stas followed him into the living room that smelled of stale take-out. White boxes of various shapes and sizes were strewn about the floor. Instead of opening the blinds, Atwood switched on a table lamp next to the sofa. He removed a heavy woolen blanket, haphazardly folded it, and placed it on a chair.

"Have a seat."

Stas sat on the sofa's edge, feeling intrusive and unwelcome. After clearing his throat, he waited for Atwood to sit. "I'm looking into the death of a woman whose daughter we've been led to believe you and your wife adopted."

Atwood grimaced, then straightened, making an effort to control the tremor in his voice. "At any other time, I would have been very upset with this intrusion. You wouldn't have made it past the telephone, but under the present circumstances, I don't think it matters anymore." He paused to compose himself. "We adopted Jennifer privately thirteen years ago. We lost her ten days ago."

Stas stared ahead. After a moment, he shifted his weight on the sofa and took his small notebook and pen from his inside jacket pocket.

"Lost her how?"

Atwood's voice quivered. "She was killed in an automobile accident."

"I'm really sorry, my deepest condolences. If you had told me when I called, I wouldn't have disturbed you and your wife." The pen stood poised, but Stas didn't write.

"It doesn't matter. My wife went to spend some time with her sister. She can't function here, too many memories."

"Do you feel like telling me about it?"

"It's still a nightmare, a blur." Atwood blinked back tears. "She was getting wild: smoking, lying to us about where she was going, who she was hanging around with, even sleeping around. Then she started to have trouble at school. June went to see her teachers, thought we could get some counseling or start one of those early intervention programs." He took a deep breath. He seemed relieved to get it out.

"What happened?"

"She said if we didn't get off her back, she'd go to LA and find her mother."

"Then she knew she was adopted?'

Atwood nodded.

"Did she know who her birth mother was?" Stas asked.

"No! She just knew where she lived, the city, I mean. The adoption never seemed to bother her. We loved her so much. Maybe too much. We certainly indulged her, gave her everything." Atwood held his head in his hands.

Stas waited, then asked. "What about the accident?"

"Two weeks ago a bunch of kids went to a party. I think the police called it a rave or something like that. On the way back the driver lost control and hit one of those old oak trees on Mill Road. There were eight kids in the car. Four were thrown out. Three died. We took Jennifer off life support ten days ago. My wife left the day after the funeral." He made no effort to stem the flow of tears. "I don't know if she'll ever come back."

Stas felt a pain jab him deep in his gut.

He pushed his empty plate away and sipped from his drink as he watched Dina polish off her second hot fudge sundae. "You really love those things, don't you?"

Embarrassed, she licked some chocolate sauce from the corners of her mouth. "I love chocolate."

"I'll have to remember that. Anyway, Atwood said he hadn't heard from Sybil since the adoption, and he only knew what Marrs told him about Jennifer's father, that he was white, in his thirties, healthy, and that he worked for the government. They were told that Sybil and the father were not together, and she had to work."

"Did he know what Sybil did?" Dina asked.

"He didn't seem to, and I didn't volunteer any info. He was just told that Sybil didn't want Jennifer raised like she was."

She licked a tiny spot of chocolate off the spoon before pointing it towards a large manila envelope on the table. "What's that?"

"Personal things: copies of the birth certificate, death certificate, school pictures, a copy of a recently written letter Atwood had found in Jennifer's room, addressed to her 'real' mother." He patted the envelope and shoved his unfinished drink to the side. "I had to make several stops. Atwood wasn't about to make it easy for me. I thought I was going to have to promise him my first born before he'd let me take the things to the drug store to make a copies. On my way back here, I stopped at the sheriff's and picked up a copy of the accident report."

"It must be sad growing up and never knowing your real parents." She glanced up at Stas. "Well, I don't know if that's true. I knew my mother, for what it was worth. What about yours?"

"Which one? Irina doesn't count, and Helena, she made me what I am today. Some call it anal retentive." He smiled, remembering. "God, straightening up, picking up, washing up, everything had to be perfect." He started to reach for his drink but left it.

"Did she beat you?"

"Didn't have to. There were other ways of showing her displeasure. It was something I learned to recognize early on. So after the nuns in grade school, the monks in high school, ROTC in college, and the drill sergeant in the Army, there's no turning back; it's spit and polish, order and control and more control."

"Don't forget power. Doesn't all this order give you power, especially when you have a gun?"

Stas's smile faded. "I'm just a cop trying to keep the thugs off the street; I'm not someone with a license to kill." But he had killed before and knew he might have to again.

There was uncertainty in Dina's gaze. "I just don't understand you."

A young waitress set the check down and smiled shyly at Stas, then reached for his glass. "Are you finished?"

"Yeah." He looked over to Dina. "Got to drive."

He paid the front cashier's and held the door for Dina. She paused and turned up her collar to ward off the biting wind.

"Why do you feel you don't understand me?" He opened the car door for her. "You finally got what you wanted, but you don't like discovering that cops are just as warped and damaged as everybody else."

"Cops frighten me."

There was a dynamic, a new energy that neither understood.

"I didn't hear you tell me to stop."

"It's not about sex. It's just that you're the one in control. You have the power to do things not just as a cop but as a man. I'll never have that experience."

He laughed. "You women use your power differently. You know it, and I know it. But right now, it's not about who has the power, it's about who has the answers. A lot of shit has happened, and we end up with more questions and even fewer answers." He removed his leather jacket and handed it to Dina.

"I guess I'm in for a wild ride." She threw the jacket over her shoulders when she got in the car and slightly reclined her seat.

As he pulled out of the parking lot, a wispy fog like strings of cotton candy floated across the evening sky.

The late start and the heavy meal wasn't conducive to conversation. Stas had changed the CDs in the player intermixing Miles Davis, Bonnie James, Marvin Gay, and Chopin before starting. The double dose of chocolate on the hot fudge sundae had put Dina in a quasi-comatose state when she settled down in her seat.

"Go to sleep, babe. I'll wake you when we stop."

She nodded and snuggled under the additional warmth of his jacket.

Within an hour most of the night fog was behind them though spotty patches of ghost-like mist clung to the hillsides and threatened to move onto the interstate.

Eighteen wheelers had begun to dominate the right traffic lanes. Stas stayed to his left, passing the behemoth rigs with little effort. The soft music had relaxed him and lulled Dina into a deep sleep. She had thrown her head back and punctuated the music with her own snorts and snores.

He let himself enjoy the easy handling of the high performance Mercedes. It wasn't often that he got to put it through its paces, blow it out. He pushed the car close to a hundred and realized that this was what he wanted for a vacation, a road trip on nearly deserted ribbons of interstates where he could push the car to the max.

Brief stretches of moonlight almost mesmerized him. A pickup, pulling out to pass a semi, broke Stas's dreamlike concentration. He blinked, taking his eyes off the road for a second and looked down at the speedometer: one hundred and ten. It felt like sixty.

He glanced over at Dina. She had turned towards him, her chin resting on her chest. He smiled, remembering Townsend's advice about having someone with him on his trip. *Good old Ralph.*

He lowered the window an inch, welcoming the icy air that whistled across his face. His eyes watered from the bite of the cold. When Stas raised the window, he instinctively looked into the side-view mirror sensing movement in the blackness behind him, but there were no following headlights.

He slowed to ninety and peered into the rearview mirror. It was impossible to see the car, without its headlights, yet Stas felt the fine hairs rise on the base of his neck. It wasn't necessary to see the danger; his body had long been conditioned to sense predatory threats.

What had first been imagined, materialized as a spectral shape that lightly touched the rear bumper of the Mercedes. The two cars ran in tandem for a split second. Stas had felt the slight impact, and he knew it wasn't the wind.

"What the fuck!"

The loud explicative awakened Dina with a start. Saliva caught in her throat, stifling a cry.

He jammed the gas, shooting forward into the darkness.

Dina grabbed for the dash. "Dammit! What going on?" She peered into the blackness when he did not answer.

In the next instant high beams illuminated the interior of the Mercedes. Stas punched his high beams to see the curve and pull ahead. The chase car, a GMC Cyclone, kept pace until both vehicles were enveloped in a bank of fog that dissipated as quickly as it had appeared.

When both cars emerged into the clear night, Stas barely maneuvered around an eighteen-wheeler. The Cyclone followed, easily overtaking the semi.

The Mercedes accelerated into another curtain of fog hanging like a ghostly pall. Stas decelerated into the menacing whiteness that also muted the headlights of the pursuing car.

Dina gasped and looked around again. "What's happening?"

He leaned over the steering wheel to focus into the cloudy mist, then suddenly turned on the wipers. The wheels churned up gravel. He was running on the shoulder. "Shit!"

The high beams bounced off another solid bank of fog. He blinked adjusting to the reflected whiteness. The new patch of fog left him with just a few yards of visibility. A rush of adrenaline roared in his ears.

Think, dammit, think. Then he remembered. He fumbled, feeling for the fog light button, careful not to turn on the rear lights. *Don't give them anything to follow.*

Though he couldn't see the other car, he sensed it gaining as the smokey-white veil suddenly lifted. He didn't know what the occupants of the other car wanted, but he didn't plan to find out. Since his gun was in the trunk, the car and the interstate would have to be his weapon.

With the fog dissipating, Stas floored the Mercedes again. It effortlessly accelerated, shooting around another eighteen-wheeler just missing its left front wheel.

The Cyclone's headlights, like halogen orbs, appeared in the Mercedes' rear view mirror, their brightness intensifying as they closed the distance.

A warning blast from one of the truck's air horns punctuated the night's stillness. Stas didn't want to tangle with a semi.

Dina stared ahead, only to see their headlights reflected off the silvery rear doors of a big truck as Stas entered another misty fog bank. Shrouded red eyes like some mechanical demon moved before them around another curve.

Stas down shifted gaining all the power he could muster to overtake another semi. He glanced into his rear view mirror. *How close*? In that split second the truck he intended to pass was now two semis running side by side, with one slightly accelerating to overtake the other. There was no room on the left. The shoulder on the right was barely visible. He veered to the right, straddling the section of asphalt and the rough shoulder. He slowed to gain maximum control and gage the distance to overtake the semi, pass it, and not collide with the other truck returning to the right lane.

Dina's intake of breath matched his own as he felt the rough gravel under the right tires. He slowed even more, running along side the semi until he saw its headlights illuminating the highway ahead. He could also see the lights of the other semi in the left lane. It still didn't have enough room to move back to the right lane, but the road was clear ahead. Stas gaged his distance then returned to smooth pavement.

With the highway clear, Stas accelerated. The semi's headlights diminished, and the rear view mirror went black.

Dina looked back, straining to see into the darkness. "What happened?"

His voice was raw. "We lost it!"

"Lost it where?"

"Hell if I know!"

"Were they after us?"

Stas breathed deeply. "That's my impression."

"Don't you need to check?"

"Check what? I can't see. I don't know what happened." He sighed. "Right now, I don't care what happened."

"But you're a cop. Aren't you going to stop?"

"Not until I get to LA."

The Cyclone had attempted the same maneuver as the Mercedes by trying to pass the semi on the right shoulder. The SUV's right wheels threw up a fine spray of dust and rocks as it ran in a graveled rut off the asphalt. The truck's horn blasted when the Cyclone tried to cut in front.

The swing to the left seemed effortless, but the Cyclone's driver misjudged the distance and was clipped by one of the semi's big wheels, sending the car back onto the shoulder and into an even deeper rut, flipping it over its front end. It was tossed onto its side where it rolled, coming to rest on its top in a shallow ravine, its headlights illuminating shadowy trees and ominous boulders. And in the distance, waves breaking on the other side of the ridge punctuated the deadly silence.

Dina did not speak for the rest of the drive to LA, but he knew she hadn't slept. True to his word, Stas did not stop until he pulled into his garage. He parked in his usual spot, got out of the car, opened the trunk, and took out his maglight. He trained the beam on the rear bumper of the Mercedes. There was no damage. She waited for him by the elevator while he got the bags. They rode to his floor in silence.

In the apartment, he dropped their things on the floor by the closet and took his jacket from Dina, putting it on the back of his desk chair. When he reached for her coat, she moved away, wrapping it tightly around her and collapsing on the sofa.

"I need a drink." Stas announced and disappeared into the kitchen, returning with two glasses and a bottle tucked under his arm. He sat next to Dina, poured, and handed one to her.

She recoiled, retreating into the corner of the sofa, refusing his offer. He recognized terror in her eyes. He sat the glass on the coffee table and started to reach for her trembling hand.

"What's happening to me?" It was a cry of desperation.

Before he could respond, tears spilled down her cheeks.

She clasped her hands together to stop their shaking. "I came to you for help, and now I feel like I'm in some horror movie. I'm afraid to go home, and I'm...."

Stas started to touch her, held back.

Dina lashed out from her corner. "You lied to me. You've been lying to me all along. You knew Sybil. You knew her when you were in Vice." A sob caught in her throat. She coughed and continued. "You're the right age."

Surprised, Stas stared. "For what?"

"To be Jennifer's father."

The words stung. "If I fucked Sybil."

"You must have. How did she go free? Nothing, nothing ever happened to her." Dina screamed out the words.

He backed off. "Somebody higher up.... Oh, what the hell!"

"What do I know about you, you wife, your... your mothers?" She shook her head. "It's a nightmare. Lisa warned me."

He snapped to attention. "When did you talk to Lisa?"

"Yesterday, I called her yesterday."

He rose. The discussion was over. The strain of the night, the drive, the questions had taken their toll. His gray eyes were almost colorless, as if the life had drained away in the foggy night. He rubbed his hand over bearded stubble and looked down at an exhausted Dina.

"I'm so tired and confused. I can't think straight." Her voice was hollow and strained.

"Go to bed, babe, we'll talk tomorrow."

Dina staggered to the bedroom. Stas took the glasses to the kitchen and poured the liquor down the drain. He returned to the living room and flopped in his recliner to think, to figure out what went down on the interstate. It was a no-brainer. Someone had known their movements.

When he finally got up, he had resolved nothing. He undressed and dropped his clothes by the sofa. In the bedroom, he flicked on the light and got a blanket from the closet. Dina, resembling one of Picasso's distorted nudes, lay in a heap, asleep. She turned and continued to snore even when he pulled the comforter over her and grabbed the other pillow.

But sleep didn't come. He tossed and punched the pillow releasing her scent, as if she moved under him, moved with him. He wondered if they would ever recapture that first night again. The sofa was uncomfortable. This new nocturnal fantasy was not soft and open to him, but hard and accusing. He'd known that body, that reaction to his touch, to his desire, and it hadn't been Dina. It was an image he kept repressed. The pillow was thrown to the floor. Still, he found no release. Finally, fitful sleep came as streaks of muted sunlight streamed into the living room.

The sound of pounding surf awakened him, but there was no beach, no water, just a throbbing headache, a dry cotton mouth, grainy eyes, and a full bladder. Stas stretched his full length on the sofa before throwing off the blanket and hitting the floor.

He glanced at Dina on his way to the bathroom. She still slept soundly, having thrown her arm over to the other side of the bed, as if inviting an absent lover to awaken her with his slow fluid movements of early morning lovemaking. Then he remembered her accusations and wondered if she would be as receptive to him if he joined her in the throes of her own sleep-induced fantasies.

Instead Stas showered and shaved, but as he dressed, he was torn between tossing off his clothes and reassuring Dina that he was one of the good guys or interview Sybil's lover. The choice wasn't easy. He wanted to see Dr. Meiers after getting his number from Marrs. He'd made an appointment before leaving to go up north so he took his shoes out to the living room and put them on.

He'd have that talk with Dina later. The thought of making up brought some life back to his slate gray eyes.

The traffic to Thousand Oaks was fairly light after he'd passed the 405, but it wasn't a pleasant drive. His car was dirty; all sorts of miniscule interstate road kill clung to his once immaculate finish. Stas would need to have the car detailed and soon.

He had no trouble finding the pink and gray building of the Ran-Dale Research Complex that stretched out into a well-manicured park-like setting. His ID was in his hand as he rolled down the window and pulled up to the security booth.

The guard looked over the car and ignored the ID. "May I help you?"

Stas still held out his card. "I'm Detective Nowak, LAPD. I have an appointment with Dr. Meiers."

Still ignoring the ID, the guard handed Stas a clip-on VISITOR'S tag with bright orange lettering on a white background and a parking placard in the same color scheme. Leaning out towards the detective, he pointed off across the drive.

"Second building on your left. Make sure you park in a VISITOR spot or you might get towed." He laughed as he stepped back into his booth and closed the window.

Stas drove around to his left until he saw the parking spaces. *They'll have hell to pay if they hook any of that towing shit to my car.* He was feeling defiant, but looked for a visitor's space anyway and stuck the placard in his window. When he got out of the car, he clipped the badge onto his jacket pocket.

The receptionist's counter was just inside the double glass door entrance of the building and was staffed by a bespectacled older woman with a short, stylish haircut.

She carefully scrutinized the badge and Stas. "Dr. Meiers is expecting you." She pointed to a door on her left. "Just go on in."

There was a certain no-nonsense air about her. *They need to put her on the front gate.*

He walked the few feet to the office and entered without knocking. The man sitting behind the desk did not rise. It was difficult to determine his age; he looked somewhere between his mid-forties and mid-fifties. His complexion was pale, his light brown hair was starting to gray at the temples and thinning on top, but what struck the detective were the eyes, a deep, azure blue, alert and intelligent. Stas was positive they missed little. Here was a man whose whole existence revolved around the most microscopic details.

"I was wondering when someone would get around to paying me a visit." The voice was a deep, clear baritone.

"This is unofficial, off the record." Stas extended his hand over the desk. "I'm Detective Stas Nowak."

"Hans Meiers."

Meiers's shake was strong and firm. His hand was smooth with well-trimmed nails. It was evident that he spent most of his time indoors yet worked out the upper part of his body. Stas instinctively liked Meiers. He felt he could trust what Meiers would have to say.

"I know you're a busy man, and I must admit, I feel a bit intimidated. I don't know many scientists, unless you count the forensic guys."

Meiers smiled warmly. "I could say the same. I don't know any detectives. So now we both can add one to his list of acquaintances."

Stas nodded. He liked the sentiment. "I was at the reading of the will," he lied. "Sybil left you money." He waited for a reaction, but he sensed only pain lurking behind those intelligent eyes.

After a few seconds, Meiers finally spoke. "Yes, and it's quite ironic, this wind-fall, how might you put it, of her ill-gotten gains being used for research. Are you investigating her death?"

"Officially, there's nothing to investigate since it was ruled a suicide."

"I'll believe that when my legs can run the LA Marathon." His cynical smile faded then returned tinged with bitterness. "I'm sorry, have a seat."

Stas pulled up a chair to face the desk. "Thanks, I don't want to take too much of your time. I just want to get a handle on Sybil ... and you."

"What's there to say? I feel the loss more than you or anyone can imagine." Meiers spoke with detached passion as if he spoke of a love from some far distant and exotic land. "She was a wonderful woman, caring and compassionate. If she felt sorry for me, I never knew it."

"You were one of her clients?"

"No. I met her at a book signing for a colleague's wife. She'd gotten a romance published. I had no interest in the book. I just went to give her support. After the talk, there were refreshments. This beautiful lady offered to get me a glass of wine since there was a line at the drink's table. The wine was awful, so I invited her out for something better. We had drinks, dinner. One thing led to another. The long shot of it was that we became lovers."

Stas glanced over to a wheelchair by the desk.

Meiers continued. "I injured my spine in a diving accident. I have some mobility, but the wheelchair has made me lazy." He paused, as if sensing what any man might be thinking about his condition. "In case you're wondering, there's no erectile dysfunction. My problem wasn't having an erection, it was finding a willing partner, one who saw beyond my handicap. Sybil was the woman who offered me the glass of wine and much, much more. I fell in love with her before I found out what she was, and I continued to love her to this day." He paused. "I want someone to get the fucking bastards."

Stas nodded. "That's what I'm trying to do, find out who killed her so we can, at least, reopen the case. That's why I'm here."

"I know you guys always look for motive. Well, I don't need Sybil's money. Recently I sold a patent. It made me rich. She went with me to Germany to sign the contracts. We had a wonderful time. Ten days of paradise. I wanted more, didn't want it to end." He paused. "But, you know, sometimes we aren't sure what we feel. Lots of times it depends on what we need."

Stas nodded in understanding.

"She was all woman, one who had been betrayed by society and a man she thought loved her. In a sense, we were both damaged, a hooker and a cripple." He waved the empty air as if fanning the painful memory into the past. "Sounds like the title of a play."

Stas edged closer. "If, just if, Sybil was murdered, can you think of anyone who might have had a motive?"

Meiers's gave Stas a hard look. "Aren't there the obvious? But if I had wanted her money.... In research you never have enough. I'm sure there are some men who wouldn't have wanted Sybil to reveal any of their deep, dark secrets. I guess, you could line us all up and take your pick."

His stare made Stas feel uneasy. "Did Sybil keep a little black book?"

"She didn't need one. She had an incredible memory and a computer. That's where she kept the records, the important ones, at least."

"She had a PDA."

"Yes, I bought it for her, showed her how to use it. She was a natural... with technology."

"You wouldn't happen to have helped her with her password?"

"I said we were lovers not... she wouldn't trust anyone with that."

"Then, I'm at an impasse. I have some of her memory sticks but no password. The computer at her office mysteriously crashed, so that trail's cold."

Meiers leaned back in his chair. "Maybe not. We were watching TV one night. This guy was running for something, going on and on about the decline in morals. He was on some crusade against gay marriages, prostitution, dope dealers, baby mommas. Wanted them all in jail. Sybil was livid. I'd never seen her so animated. She screamed at the TV, 'bastards, hypocrites'. I got the feeling she knew this guy but not as a client."

"By any chance did you catch his name?"

Meiers shook his head. "Never seen him before. It was a couple of months ago. That old Liz Taylor movie, *Butterfield 8,* was on, then the news. The spot was brief, but it was enough to send her off."

"Did she say anything else?"

"Just that she had some calls to make."

"Did she make them while you were there?"

"No, but knowing Sybil, if she had calls to make, she made them."

Stas gave him a card after printing his cell number on the back. "Call me any time, twenty-four seven. I'm on vacation, so don't call the office." He rose and extended his hand to Meiers.

"I want you to get the sons-of bitches. Count on me if you need anything."

SEVENTEEN

Brown was stopped in traffic for a good fifteen minutes when his cell phone rang. He looked around, before picking up. "Yeah? Brown here." His voice was curt.

She felt like hanging up. "I'm sorry to bother you, Mr. Brown, Matt."

"Who is this?"

"May West, I worked for Sybil, remember?"

"What's up, May?" His tone softened.

"I have a little problem. Well, it's not really my problem. It's just, that maybe it could be a problem if the police get it." She tried to control her nervousness. "Not a problem for me, you know, but a problem for some other people if the police get it, and they been around, you know."

"You're talking in riddles, May." Brown looked out at the stopped cars around him. He wasn't interested in hearing some cleaning woman's problems, especially if she wanted to hit him up for money. "Just what do you have that's a problem?"

"Well, I found this little thing that belonged to Sybil, and I don't know who to give it to."

A pause.

"Hello, you still there?" she asked.

"Yeah, go on." She had his attention.

"She don't have no family, nobody to make it worth my while. You know, like a little reward or something, since I can't work for Sybil, since she killed herself, and I lost income." Her voice grew stronger now, more confident. She was almost ready to hit him with the price tag, but she waited. She didn't want to seem too anxious.

Brown started to get impatient, but with the traffic at a standstill, he wasn't going anywhere. "Describe this thing to me."

"Well, it's little like a pack of cigarettes or a compact. You open it up, and its got tiny little letters and a little screen like a teeny TV, but I can't see...."

He cut her off. "Where are you?"

"I'm at work, but I don't have it with me. I put it in a safe place. I don't want the cops tearing my house up looking for something that might get me in trouble. I can't afford that. You know them. And I need to get something for it like, you know, a finder's fee." She waited. She wanted the part about the fee to sink in.

There was some static on the line. "Listen, May, if we get cut off, call me back or call me later. We need to get together. I'm sure we can work something out. Just how much were you thinking about?"

Another pause. "Ten thousand." Her voice cracked, then went soft. "Ten thousand dollars."

"Shit, that's a hefty finder's fee, but we'll talk. Let's set up a time. I need to see the item."

"You can see it. You can even have it. I ain't got no use for it, but you need to bring the money. I don't know where else to go." Then she thought of Raven. *God, she's loaded.* "I got to go."

"Don't do anything foolish. Call me tonight. I'll get the money together. Don't do anything until we talk." The line went dead, and the traffic began to move.

Brown needed some money, some big money. Now where could he get some quick, easy cash? He smiled as he thought of his one sure source. After all, politicians weren't the only ones feeding at the trough. If May had what he thought she had, he'd be on easy street for a long time.

EIGHTEEN

The Los Angeles Police Department Video Retrieval Center at Parker Center recorded every channel in the Los Angeles area that carried news programs. The data were then stored in an archival room for future reference and retrieval.

It was there that Stas spent the better part of two hours tracking down news reports of a candidate's speech about declining morality in Los Angeles. *So what else was new? What about the declining morality of politicians, business tycoons, and religious leaders?*

He found the clip, taken at a so-called town hall meeting where the locals were invited for atmosphere but weren't allowed to ask questions. Instead, they sat in the back and watched invited guests listen to the candidate make his pitch, then they were allowed to participate in the scripted question and answer session afterwards.

Stas watched Edward Lawson, a primary candidate for the 39th Congressional District. He was handsome, well dressed, and impeccably groomed with a clear, forceful voice that projected a dynamic personality as he was being televised for an interview with a local TV anchor.

"We must clean up our cities and then the country. We shall return this great state to the good, decent people who work hard and pay taxes. Taxes that, by the way, are much too high. And we wouldn't be in this fiscal mess if it weren't for those tax and spend liberals." He paused for effect, then continued. "You, the overtaxed citizens, are the people we have sworn to serve. The lawless and those without a sense of what is morally right have to go." He was smooth and articulate.

Stas was familiar with this new-age politician with the right cut to his suit, the right hairstyle, the right backers. He took notes, jotting down the name of Lawson before replaying it. On his second viewing he concentrated on those in Lawson's immediate party standing behind him on the podium.

A man stood out like a sore thumb; he was the only black in the entourage, and if he wasn't Matt Brown then Brown had an identical twin working for Lawson.

Stas had to replay the spot again to discern those curly clear plastic wires leading from the black guy's ear into his jacket. If this was Brown, then he must have been providing security for the town hall meeting. Stas wondered if Lawson knew of Brown's other, not so savory, enterprises.

He'd have to check into Brown's licenses and background. Dina said he'd been a cop in Fresno.

Stas decided to go see Detective Chris Marlowe. He had telephoned Chris when he first watched Lawson. In the squad room he found Marlowe alone at the coffee maker. One hand rested on his large, hand-tooled leather belt, the other hand stirred sugar into his coffee mug. He turned when Stas came in. Marlowe was at least six feet three and gained another two inches in his handmade ostrich cowboy boots. He loved all things Western, having participated in the black rodeo circuit for years. He even kept a horse in Altadena where he lived. Cowboy garb and lore were not an affectation but the real deal with the black detective.

He smiled at Stas. "I never believed that 'goin fishin' bullshit. I know you seeing some action." Marlowe feigned a punch to the torso. "You look a helleva lot better than that guy in the Viagra commercial. Who needs vacations? You just needed to lay a little pipe."

Stas laughed at Marlowe's crudeness, but maybe he was right. Most of the guys in the division had been married once or twice. Marlowe had tried and failed three times. In general, wives didn't understand the life, the drill. There were no regular hours, no regular weekends, and many missed dates and appointments. So you did what you needed to do to maintain your sanity even if it meant sex with your female partner, a willing witness, or an available hooker. You did whatever was needed to take the edge off.

"This chick slipped me a Viagra one night. Man, I thought I'd died and gone to heaven," Marlowe continued. "I even asked her to marry me."

"You sure that's what she gave you?" Stas straddled a chair and motioned him back to reality. "Yeah, yeah, c'mon, Marlowe. Did you find out anything on Lawson?"

"Whoa! Damn, you just called. You think I'm some kind of walking search engine?" Marlowe returned to his desk and rummaged through a scattering of papers, before grabbing a sheet off the top. "Your boy's been busy, but he's squeaky clean. Left Fresno PD, did some lawyering a while, then on to the Assembly."

Stas reached for the printout and read it. "So he's moving up the food chain."

"Yep, running for Congress. Says he going to clean up... shit, clean up what? He must've broke out some meth from Fresno's property. Somebody needs to see what he's been smoking." Marlowe inhaled imaginary fumes before he continued.

"I'm impressed."

"He's got a fancy web-site. One of his biggest backers is the Coalition of Moral Renewal. That's some serious shit."

Stas rose, put the chair back, and folded the paper. "Did you get the other report?"

Marlowe looked under some notes by his computer. He pulled out a coffee-stained pad and ripped off the top sheet. "There was an accident, a black GMC Cyclone rolled off the 101 up near Pismo Beach. Two males, one Hispanic, one white, fake IDs, stolen credit cards, enough fire power to make North Hollywood look like a friendly Saturday night bar-b-cue."

Stas sat on the edge of a desk. "Any idea where they were from?"

"The Hispanic had an ATM receipt from a machine in Fresno. The other one had a used book of matches from a bar in Henderson, Tennessee. Who gives out matches anymore? Hell, I can't find any to light my fancy candles when I have company." He broke into a broad grin.

"Candles? You?"

"Yeah, I need to display my warm, sensitive side. Works every time. You should try it sometime."

"I'm fine." Stas looked at the stained paper again.

"There any connection with something we're doing?"

"Not that I know of."

"So what's this all about?"

"I don't know yet. Just something in the rumor mill about some heavy artillery moving this way, and I heard there was an accident. So,...I guess we don't need to worry."

"You goin' home?"

"Yeah, why?"

"Man, do I know her?"

Stas shook his head.

Marlowe turned back to a report. "Be careful, man. You know vacations can get messy."

"I think it already has."

As Stas headed for the stairs, he spotted Townsend, looking around, desperately in need of a cigarette.

"Hey, Stas, I know you guys must have a little closet to grab a smoke around here?"

"Ralph, you know: outside."

"I can't go downstairs right now. I'm waiting for your captain."

"What's up?"

"That's what I'm trying to get details on. Now he's shut up tighter than...." Townsend didn't complete his analogy.

An official-looking clerk darted quickly into the captain's office.

"What do you know about some kind of joint action?" Townsend asked.

"Nothing, I'm still on vacation." But he moved closer, his curiosity getting the better of him. "What kind of action?"

"Someone leaked that a big call girl-drug bust is going down."

"When?"

"Soon, real soon. Maybe even tonight."

"Where?"

"Trend, Tran..."

"You mean the Trendal Building near Little Tokyo. There's nothing much there: offices, some lofts. That's strange." Stas had that gut feeling that something bad was about to happen.

"You know, when I hear 'leaks', the hair rises on the back of my neck." Townsend lowered his voice almost to a whisper. "I think: who wants press coverage at a bust, who needs a photo op? Sounds political to me."

"Did the Captain confirm?"

"Not exactly, said something about it being a DEA show, but I guess some of you guys will be there, you know, standing in the wings. At least it's not the FBI. They're a little too trigger happy for me." Townsend headed for the elevator. "Enjoy the rest of your vacation."

"What vacation?"

"I knew you weren't going fishing."

Stas called after him as he headed towards the stairs. "Call me if you hear something definite."

"Even if it's the FBI?"

NINETEEN

Lisa Bane stood in the doorway of Stas's apartment as if awaiting a royal invitation to enter. Her high-heeled boots allowed her to peer over Dina's head and see into the living room. "So this is your little love nest?"

When Dina stepped back into the apartment, Lisa followed and perched on the edge of the sofa. She slipped out of a soft black leather swing coat trimmed in shirred mink and folded it on the cushion next to her, then reached in her bag and pulled out a gold cigarette case.

"Where's an ashtray?"

Dina shook her head. "He doesn't smoke?" She was wearing a pair of Stas's old sweats, her hair pulled up in a ponytail, her face scrubbed clean. She looked at Lisa, torn between sitting and listening to her proposal or asking her to leave. She didn't want Stas to find Lisa relaxing on the sofa or lounging in his recliner going through his CDs. Lisa was that kind of woman, intrusive to a fault.

"When you coming back to work?"

Dina wrinkled her nose. Lisa had on too much makeup, and her heady perfume had left a vapor trail from the door. "I don't know, I...."

"Listen, this is very prime, very hush-hush. They just want some company: no sex and definitely no drugs."

Dina started to sit in the recliner. "They always say that until someone starts playing grab ass. Who are these sexually dysfunctional businessmen who don't want to get laid?"

"They're Australians."

Dina laughed. "You must be crazy. They're the worst."

"I swear," Lisa waved her unlit cigarette in Dina's direction to make a salient point. "It's a party, for God's sake, not to mention a grand a girl. That's not too hard to take, is it? If someone wants her own arrangements afterwards, well, that's up to her. You can be back with your man, have your own after-party with a grand in your pocket, and no one's the wiser. C'mon, what'd ya say?"

Dina looked down at the gray sweats, her bare feet, and ran her hand up to her ponytail, releasing the band, and shaking her hair loose. "I don't have anything here to wear."

She gave Lisa's outfit an appraising glance: a short lavender suede skirt, matching halter, lavender suede boots completed the look. She wondered how much the suede and leather had set her back.

Lisa finally gave up on smoking and put the cigarette back in the case. "We can drop by your place. I got my new car."

Dina reluctantly nodded. Business must be good. Lisa had wrecked her last car and was forever taking taxis or having someone give her a lift. Now she had new wheels.

In the bathroom, Dina gathered some make-up and brushes. She reached for the perfume then remembered she was going to her own apartment. After dropping her stuff in a small black tote, she took some tissue and wiped off her side of the counter. She checked out the bedroom. Everything was in order. The bed was made, and Stas's LAPD T-shirt was neatly folded on the chair. She grabbed a pen and small notepad by the phone and scribbled a note.

Where should I put this so he'll see it? Maybe I should let him miss me. Maybe he'll even worry.

When she looked up, Lisa was standing in the bedroom's doorway putting on her jacket. "You ready?"

Dina followed Lisa's eyes to the bed and took her arm.

"C'mon, I need to get my coat."

"Is it always this quiet around here?"

Dina slipped into her jacket and held the door open for Lisa. "Always, I'm beginning to go stir crazy."

Lisa's new navy blue BMW was parked around the corner.

"When'd you get this?" Dina asked.

Lisa tweaked the alarm button on her key chain and smiled. "It was a gift."

"Must have been backbreaking work."

"Well, you should talk. I've known plenty of cops in my day, but none ever took me home."

"It's not like that."

"But he has fucked you."

The remark jolted Dina back to reality. She felt blood rush to her neck and reached to finger the scar. She wanted to say something equally coarse but could think of nothing.

"He's that good then?" Lisa asked.

Dina tried another tactic: the truth. "I can't explain the feeling. I know it's not love ... it's just, for once, being satisfied without working for it or even thinking about it. It's like the shoe's on the other foot."

"If he's so good then pass him around for the rest of us to sample."

Dina didn't respond. What could she say? The thought of sharing Stas wasn't an option.

Lisa showed off her CD player and Dolby surround sound. The drive back to the Hollywood area was filled with loud hip-hop music. Lisa tapped her long scarlet nails in a little dance on the steering wheel.

When they exited the freeway, Dina turned down the volume. She had to confide in someone. Even Lisa was a warm body with a willing ear. "He frightens me."

Lisa glanced over at Dina. "Did he hurt you?"

"No, he's not violent. He's just intense. There's no pretending I'm not caught up in all this, but there's also his anger, not on the surface, like violent outbursts, but somewhere beneath, deep down where no one can reach it." Dina took a deep breath. "The sex is great. It sure beats some flabby-assed john who can barely get himself off and does nothing for me." She sighed as she looked out the window. "If you ever experience it, you won't want to give it up."

Before Lisa could comment, she pulled into a parking space in front of Dina's apartment complex. It felt strange entering her own building from the street. Since she rarely used the front entrance, she was surprised to see Livia's fake foliage, an abundance of vibrant silk in full bloom. She looked down the hall. Livia was nowhere in sight. Dina didn't feel like explaining her LAPD sweats, especially if they elicited questions from Livia about Stas.

Lisa hummed a hip-hop tune as they rode up on the elevator. Dina was glad that Lisa hadn't responded to her confession. She felt she had said too much.

Although she'd been away for a little over a week, Dina found the apartment eerily cold and silent. The living room was devoid of the little things that were her signature. There were no fresh flowers, no relaxing music, no scent of lavender or frankincense that she always burned in a small crystal bowl on the end table. Lisa finally lit up, adding ash from her cigarette to the gray residue that had been left by the last burned incense.

"Where's your phone? I'll call and tell them we're on our way." She waved Dina toward her bedroom. "Go on, get dressed."

Dina pointed to the phone on a small antique desk and headed to the bathroom. She took a quick shower and half-toweled herself, dripping her way to the closet.

She hated dressing in a rush. Grabbing a black dress, she draped the towel over her shoulders to ward off the chill, but the combination of no heat, a wet body, and a damp towel made her hurry.

Reaching into the second drawer of her lingerie chest, she felt something cold and hard in a nest of silk. She drew her hand back, then she slowly pushed aside several thongs to discover a device like the one Stas had recently bought. Fear gripped her. She picked up the PDA and perched on the edge of the bed to examine it.

How did this get here? Why didn't I see it when I got clothes to go up north? Then she remembered: she'd grabbed underwear from the very top, and she'd been in a rush.

As she sat there, holding the PDA in her hand, the glaring question remained unanswered: who had been in her apartment? She realized Stas was right, and she shouldn't be there without him. Now the party sounded like a very bad idea.

Her hands shook. A chill coursed through her naked body as she searched for a purse that would hold the little computer, her cell phone, and her make-up. Damn the make-up. She tucked her cell phone and the PDA in a small lizard clutch, stepped into a black thong, and slipped into the dress.

The make-up took about a minute, her hair even less. She did it up in a quick French twist with wispy curls that fell around her temples. It was the best she could do with damp hair. Hose were tossed aside. She'd just have to freeze. I need to get out of here. She grabbed a pair of black four-inch sandals, almost stumbling as she tried to slip them on.

Lisa whistled when she returned to the living room. Dina took a short coat from the hall closet.

"Put out that cigarette." Dina was at the door.

"You look great. They'll love you at the party."

"Let's get this over with."

The key turned effortlessly. "Fuck!" The dead bolt was off Stas knew something was wrong. The knot was there again, growing more painful with each new revelation. His jacket and keys were tossed to the sofa. He surveyed what had once been his ordered world and felt only chaos. "Fuck!"

"Dina?" The empty apartment echoed her name. He didn't need to call again. He knew she wasn't there.

The bedroom was empty and ordered. When he flicked on the light in the bathroom, he saw that some of her things were gone. The toothbrush stood alone, hopefully guaranteeing her return. When he went back into the bedroom, he saw the note.

"I've gone with Lisa to a party downtown. Call my cell. Dina"

The knot tightened its grip on his gut. "Damn!" The phone rang. He rolled over on the bed and reached for the receiver.

"Stas? It's Townsend.

"Where are you?" Stas's voice was tight.

"I'm downtown, and it's show time!"

"It's really happening? Where?"

"I'm at the Trendal Building, between the Parker Center and Little Tokyo."

"Okay, I'll find it. I'm leaving in five minutes, look for me."

Stas went to the bedroom closet and worked the combination to open the safe. He removed a Glock 19 and two fifteen round clips, sliding one into the grip of the automatic and putting the other one on the floor. He unwrapped a small caliber revolver, shook out bullets from a box, then re-secured the safe. The second gun had a short barrel and taped grip. Getting a towel from the bathroom, Stas wiped the bullets, carefully loaded the throw down, and rewrapped it before putting it in his pocket.

Reaching to the back of the top shelf of the closet, he took down a shoulder holster for the Glock and slipped on the addition clip from the floor. In almost one continuous motion, he grabbed his jacket, cell phone, keys, turned off lights, and left the apartment.

Lisa and Dina's arrival at the party, held in a large boardroom on the eighth floor of the Trendal Building had been uneventful. The men milling around hadn't warmed-up yet. The room was too cold, the music too soft, and the booze hadn't flowed long enough to rob the partygoers of their inhibitions. Dina looked around for some place comfortable to sit, but everything looked hard and massive. Several sofas and chairs looked as if they had been brought in from a reception office or storage. All of them looked uncomfortable.

She finally settled on a low sofa near double walnut doors that afforded her a good view of the guests and the exit. She wasn't sure where Lisa got her girls. None of the four other women looked familiar. On their best night they would be hard pressed to make a grand between them. They looked like under-dressed secretaries playing at being whores. The tackiness was there, but the money wasn't. They were loud and nervous as they mingled with the dozen or so men that had gathered around a makeshift bar.

A tall, rather handsome man approached Dina and smiled down at her. "Can I get you a drink?"

Dina returned his smile. "I'll have vodka on the rocks." She looked at his shoes. They needed a shine, his suit needed a hard press, and a slightly frayed cuff peeked from one jacket sleeve. She'd make sure the one drink would last the night if she sipped it slowly.

He returned, handing Dina her drink. "I'm Ted." He sat down heavily next to her.

She sipped but did not introduce herself. "Where are you from?"

Ted gulped what looked like Scotch and hesitated. "Auckland." He put his arm across the back of the sofa and glanced down at Dina's legs.

Before she could respond, her cell phone rang. "Excuse me."

The low sofa made rising difficult and awkward. Ted rose, took her drink in one hand, and helped her up. "You're coming back?"

Dina smiled back and flipped the cover of the cell, then moved to a secluded corner.

"Hello."

"Where the hell are you?" Stas asked.

She hunched slightly over her phone, shielding it from no one in particular. "I'm at a party."

"Where?"

"I'm not sure, somewhere near Chinatown." She tried to sound nonchalant.

"Leave now!"

"Wait a minute, it's just a party."

"Shut up and listen." He spoke slowly, deliberately. "It's a setup. You'll be arrested by the DEA. Babe, if they get you, my hands'll be tied."

"What are you talking about?" She looked around the room.

"You know what a sting is? Well, this is one. May even be for your benefit."

"What about Lisa?"

"Fuck Lisa. If she took you, she's in on it. Don't take the elevator. Don't stay on the main street." His voice faded, interrupted by static, then came back. "I can't think straight right now, but I'll find you. Call me when you get out."

Dina tucked her phone back in her bag and walked back to Ted who still held her drink. He offered it to her, but she looked towards the door.

"Is everything okay?" He asked.

"Oh, yes." She looked around. "I just need to go to the little girls' room." She smiled her most seductive smile, one that reassured and promised.

Ted relaxed and sank back into the low sofa. Dina, although anxious, didn't hurry. *These guys were supposed to be from Australia. None of them sound anything like Russell Crowe. Did he even know where Auckland was? Maybe Stas was right.*

In the hall she opened a heavy door under a red EXIT sign. In the dim stairwell, she slipped off her heels and took the stairs to the first floor. When she opened the metal door to the building's lobby, she recoiled. There, only a few feet away, were two uniformed cops manning the main entrance, and other men wearing DEA windbreakers, and several more men stood by the bank of elevators.

Fear gripped Dina. She had never been arrested, and she sure as hell didn't want to become a police statistic tonight.

She quietly closed the door and started down another flight of stairs to the basement. Dina opened another door to a long, dusty and dimly lit hallway with several red EXIT lights that led back up the stairs. She leaned against the wall to calm her racing heart. She flexed her cold feet and felt the fine grit on the dirty floor, still she couldn't put her four-inch heels on again. *God, please don't let me cut my feet.* She gingerly maneuvered to the nearest door. It was locked. "Shit, shit, damn, damn, damn."

She tried the second door. It groaned as she slowly pulled it open and peered into the inky blackness of the building's bowels. She left it ajar and walked to the last door. If it was locked, she had only two choices: retreat to the first floor and take her chances with the DEA or take the second door.

By now a fine sheen of perspiration beaded on her face and started to envelop her torso. She could feel the silk lining of her jacket sticking to her back. Returning to the unlocked door, Dina took off her jacket and bundled it with her shoes and handbag so she could carry everything with one hand, freeing the other to feel her way. She felt each stair with her toes, inching her way down until she reached the bottom.

Mentally and physically exhausted, Dina rested on the last step, wanting to cry, to curse, to smash something. It took a while for her to gather the strength to move; somehow, the threatening black void sharpened her senses. She started as a faint noise shattered the eerie stillness. She hoped it was only a rat skittering across the floor, but there were other noises, half imagined that made her pause as she stepped onto the cold concrete.

Dear God, please let me get out of here, please let Stas find me.

Townsend stood in the cold shadows of the Trendal Building and watched the media set up for the press conference. News vans intermingled with DEA marked vehicles, patrol cars, and what, he was certain, were unmarked cars. He blew on his hands before shaking out a cigarette from his pack and lighting it with a well-worn BIC.

Security at the site was minimal. Everyone was waiting for the principals to arrive. Townsend shook his head in disbelief as he blew irregular smoke rings into the damp night air. *Well, let's get the show on the road.*

He wondered about the victims of the sting. They had to be deaf and stupid not to have heard the set-up outside.

Stas took a roundabout route to the Trendal Building. He was tempted to leave his car at Parker Center but didn't know how involved LAPD was in this operation, nor did he want to have to explain Dina if he had to bring her back to the car. Instead, he found a spot about six blocks away from headquarters on the fringes of Little Tokyo.

Even though the area was near what looked like new construction, it seemed abandoned. A tall, thin black man who looked to be in his late thirties sat on an upturned plastic bucket marked drywall mud. He was dressed for the cold in a fat down jacket. Next to the bucket were a spray water bottle, some rags, a roll of paper towels, and a squeegee. The only thing missing was a paying customer. He rose as the black Mercedes rolled to a stop.

"Hey, man, you want I should watch your wheels?" The man leaned in toward the partially opened window and walked with the car as the detective parked.

Stas got out and activated the alarm. "That's why I'm parking it here." He flashed his shield. "What's your name?"

"Andy."

"Andy, don't let anyone touch it. If you do, I'll find you and." He handed over a folded twenty-dollar bill.

The bill was quickly pocketed. "I can wash it. You shouldn't let a car like this get so dirty." He drew his finger through the dirt on the hood, leaving a line in the finish. "Is this car stolen or something?"

Stas knew what was coming next.

"You really a cop?"

Stas patted a bulge in his jacket.

"Hell, that don't mean nothing. Half of LA packs, even little old ladies."

"Listen, just sit here and watch it. Don't wash it. Don't let anyone else wash it or touch it. Don't debug it. Just watch it like you would your favorite TV show. If it looks just like this when I get back, there may be a little extra in it for you. Remember, just watch." Stas pocketed his keys and left.

Andy repositioned his white plastic bucket so he could watch the car and the night.

Stas walked to the Trendal and saw Townsend leaning against the building engulfed in swirls of blue smoke, watching the camera crews putting the finishing touches on the equipment for the press conference.

Townsend simultaneously waved him over, cleared his aura of smoke, and ground out the butt. "I didn't think you'd come, what with a vacation and all."

"Something came up."

"You curious? Or was that 'something' compelling?"

"A little of both."

Townsend took out another cigarette and offered the pack to Stas. "You still not smoking?"

"That depends." Stas took the proffered cigarette. "I had a relapse." Lighting up, he inhaled deeply.

"How's my pupil?"

"Dina?"

"You got another one stashed away?"

Stas coughed.

Townsend continued, "She could interrupt my vacation any time."

"I'll tell her that."

"I bet you will." Townsend ushered Stas forward. "Look at this." He waved towards the media congregation. "I counted three satellite vans and four news vans. Can you believe this production?"

"What do you expect? This is Hollywood. Politicians are after the same thing you guys are: audience share. As a matter of fact, audience share equals votes,"

Someone near the makeshift podium with its bank of microphones beckoned to Townsend.

"Got to go in a sec, show time."

Stas watched the news crews continue to set up. It was strange how all the law enforcement officers seemed to be spectators at some strange Greek tragedy waiting for the *Deus ex machina* to descend to the podium and make everything right, if not with the world, at least with LA.

"What made you call?" Stas ground out his butt and looked at Townsend.

"After our conversation I thought...."

Stas turned and walked abruptly to the entrance of the Trendal Building's main lobby.

He showed his shield to an LAPD uniformed officer at a set of double glass doors. "Where's everybody?"

"Some guys from DEA are securing the building."

Stas wanted to laugh. "Securing it from what, some hookers and their johns?"

"From what I saw, they didn't look like ordinary street skanks. Anyway, there's a command post on the third floor. The party was on the eighth. Must've been something. You name it: booze, coke, girls." He smiled broadly. "I'd like to go to one of these parties just once."

"No, you wouldn't. Could be habit forming, and that's bad on this job." He left the young cop dreaming about the party, nonetheless.

Stas took the stairs two at a time to the third floor, keeping his eye out for Dina. He showed his badge again to another uniformed officer at the door of what looked like a command post.

Without entering he could scope out the situation from where he stood. A few uniforms stood off to themselves shooting the breeze, but there were more plain clothes sitting around talking with "the girls." He saw Lisa in a cloud of smoke, waving her cigarette and talking to several officers, but Dina was nowhere in sight. Where were the clients? Or were some of these officers in civilian clothes posing as the out-of-town partygoers?

All of this honey to catch one little fly. So much for a big bust and this phony command post.

He left without speaking to anyone.

On the eighth floor, in what looked like a photo-op, members of a crime unit were being photographed while haphazardly processing evidence. Stas wondered who was going to be prosecuted on what these guys were collecting. The drugs had probably been brought in from a DEA stash or coerced off some street dealer in exchange for a plea to lesser charges. The cops looked like they were setting up for a crap game.

No one bothered to challenge him as he looked into the party room. Stas had seen enough. He took the stairs to the first floor and returned to the news conference that was just getting underway.

Lawson stood behind a bank of microphones talking to the cameras. Bright lights had almost turned night into day. Dishes on the news vans had been raised for the feedback to the stations for the eleven o'clock news.

"...and don't think this is just a one-time operation. If I have anything to do with it, they won't be back tomorrow for business as usual, draining every dime from the people's coffers, double dipping at the pubic trough. And any city official giving aide and comfort or sleeping with the enemy..." He paused for affect, then continued. Lawson's voice was strong and articulate. "you need to submit your resignation, now, tonight, because I'm coming after you."

There was weak applause. Stas smiled. If any city official took Lawson seriously, there would be a flood of resignations on the mayor's desk tomorrow or a fistful of pink slips the day after that. Well, he wasn't worried.

While Lawson rambled on, Stas reentered the building to continue his search for Dina. He wanted to call her cell but didn't want it ringing in the company of the wrong people.

Dina bumped into a large wooden crate a few feet from the bottom of the stairs. Feeling her way around it, she could make out the different shapes of other boxes. *There has to be some source of light.* Then the strong smell of urine and fecal matter assaulted her making her retch. She expelled the foul intake of breath but had to stop and inhale through her mouth, as the vomit rose again. She gagged, keeping it down, leaving only the taste of bile in her throat. Dina continued, her groping foot guiding her until she touched something soft.

Her first reaction was to scream, but she steeled herself and felt further with her toes. She bent to touch, but the smell was so strong at the floor level that she retched and gagged again. Was something dead or dying there?

Then she heard the sound: shallow and ragged, breathing so softly that she had to concentrate, to synchronize her own intake of breath with that of the body lying directly before her. She swallowed hard and tried to think. *Get me out of here.* If someone slept there, maybe he had another way out.

From this vantage point Dina saw a dim, red glow and inhaled the acrid fumes that faintly mixed with the other odors. Someone had a fire down here; someone was living down here. Slowly, ever so slowly, she tried to skirt the pallet to get to the makeshift fire.

Her shriek reverberated off the crates. She was caught. A rough, calloused hand grabbed her ankle. She waited to be jerked down, but she was released as the body rose. Dina couldn't make out his features in the darkness, but she felt certain it was a man. As he rose, an overwhelming stench rose with him, enveloping him like some unholy aura. Dina's hand flew to her mouth restraining another gag.

"How'd you get in?" The voice was raspy and deep.

"The door was open. Please help me." Dina whispered a plea. "Help me get out."

She tried to gage, to get a sense of what he might do. Or worse, what he might do to her. Suddenly, that thought became more frightening than the presence of all the police outside. She didn't want to imagine what was going through his mind. Then she felt his touch as he grabbed her arm and pulled her toward the glowing remnants of what was left of a small fire in a metal bucket about ten feet away. In the dim red glow, she could make out dark clothes, a beard.

"What ya got?" he mumbled

Dina didn't understand at first, and then she realized he wanted something. "I have a watch." She started to slide it off her wrist. "It's gold, real gold, and earrings." It took a second as she nervously removed and offered them.

"What's, what's going on?" He nervously spit out his question. His foul breath pushed Dina back.

"There's a raid."

"What?"

"A police raid." She spoke slowly, desperate for him to understand. "I got to get out."

He moved away from her towards a door.

"Bolt the door!" he whispered.

"Bolt what door?" Dina repeated, confused.

He left her standing by an elevated window or opening, but he didn't return. She could hear loud, angry voices coming from where she had entered the subbasement. Evidently, he hadn't managed to bolt the door in time.

Were the cops checking? Finally, the voices faded as they retreated back into the hallway. *Had they taken him with them? Would he bring them back?* She didn't plan to wait and see.

Dina turned back to the opening in the wall. The filtered light was so faint she wondered if she'd imagined it. She was anxious to get out of this hellhole at any cost. Peering up, she could vaguely make out the latticed pattern of the metal grate about three feet off the floor. She tried to climb into the opening but only scraped her knee and thigh.

Leaving her bundle on the floor, she felt around the area for something to stand on and found a large wooden crate, empty but still heavy. By putting her hip to it, she managed to move it the few feet she gauged she needed. It took every ounce of her strength to push the crate to the exit. When it was situated beneath the opening, she leaned on the crate to catch her breath. Taking her things, she climbed up and opened the steel grate but still couldn't reach the rungs that would give her access to the alley.

Dina returned to the floor of the basement to find another crate, but everything was either too heavy or too large. She slowly retreated to the pallet. It was so putrid that she had to hold her breath while she dragged it toward the exit and rolled it up to get it on the crate. The added height enabled her to reach the first rung, but lost one of her shoes in the process. There was no going back so she let the other one fall in a dull thud onto the pallet. She continued her climb.

When Dina reached a short, dead-end alley, she realized there was only one way to exit. Exhausted, her dress in ruins, her jacket, a filthy mess, she was still afraid of being trapped even though she had escaped the building.

Moving away from the wall of the building, she stepped on a soggy, wet cardboard. Then it started to rain fat, cold drops that promised a heavy winter rainstorm. Turning her head skyward, she was hit with a large splat square on the forehead. If nothing else, she needed to find shelter. Dina had no idea where she was, but now she could try her phone.

Stas picked up on the first ring. "Where are you?"

"I don't know. I just crawled out of the basement in that, that building. I guess I'm behind it in a service alley."

"Babe, get out of the alley, see if there's a street name."

She hobbled to the edge of the alley and peered around the building. The cold penetrated her body to the core, but she made it to the corner.

"I'm on Frank."

"Go back in the alley."

"Why?"

"Because they may still be looking for you.

"Why me?"

"Damn it! Stop with the questions and watch for me."

The cell display read "End Call". Dina slipped her phone into her bag and turned back to the alley and didn't notice a brown private patrol car slowly cruising on the opposite side of the street.

The driver hung a quick U-turn, running onto the curb as he tried to pull along side Dina. He jumped out brandishing a big, black nightstick. "Get over here, bitch."

Dina looked at the menacing figure approaching and started to walk slowly, toward the alley, then stopped, cringing against the side of a building. She was suddenly aware of physical pain. Her feet hurt; her bruises and scrapes hurt. She was freezing, and Stas was nowhere in sight. But she was resolved to put up a fight before getting into the rent-a cop's vehicle.

A plastic name plate on the breast pocket of his gray and brown uniform read "WILLIS". Even with Dina cornered, his movements were hesitant. When he realized she wasn't going to run, he returned to his car, opened the back passenger door, then activated a two-way radio attached to the dash.

"I got her." There was static and a crackle. He glanced at Dina. "Been looking for you."

"Me? You don't know me." She still didn't move. "You'll have to drag me, damn it."

He moved on Dina, grabbing her arm, pulling her to his vehicle. "You goin' downtown."

"You're not a cop," she hissed at him.

He held the back door open but hesitated again and reached for Dina's handbag. She pushed back, catching him off balance. Then she saw a familiar black leather jacket in front of the car. Before Willis could push her into the car she slipped to the car seat. A hand from behind grabbed Willis' arm and pushed him hard against the side of the car.

The Rent-a-cop was too stunned to resist being patted down for a weapon.

"Who the hell are you?" Willis tried to push back but was held against the driver's door.

"I might ask you the same thing," Stas responded.

"I'm a cop. She's under arrest," Willis stammered.

"For what?"

"Prostitution!"

"Did she proposition you?"

"What's it to you? I'm a officer. I got a badge."

Stas laughed. "Well, I'm the real thing, and I've got a real badge and a real gun." He opened his jacket, revealing the Glock, then shoved Willis even harder into the side of the car.

Willis gasped, the air slamming from his lungs.

Stas's response was hard. "I can arrest you for impersonating an officer, harassing women, and just plain pissing me off."

"But, but I got..."

An uneven dark patch slowly spread down the front of Willis's uniform trousers. Stas pushed him again as he gingerly stepped out of a widening puddle.

"Willis?" A crackling voice came over the Motorola. "Willis? Willis?"

Stas opened the door and reached for the two-way radio. "Willis is indisposed." He pushed Willis into the driver's seat, pulled out the connection to the radio, then grabbed cuffs from Willis's utility belt, draped his arms around the steering column, and handcuffed him to the wheel. The movements were so quick and fluid that Willis was momentarily stunned and embarrassed as he squirmed in his dampness.

"What ya doing?" His eyes bugged out.

"Making sure you don't go anywhere."

With Willis secured, Stas reached into the back seat of the car for Dina. She was going to have to walk to his car. He helped her to her feet when another unmarked car pulled up behind Willis'. It was Matt Brown with another rent-a-cop.

Brown's approach was at first confrontational, his jacket hanging open, his hands hanging loose and ready. Then he saw Stas. "I think that woman is in our custody." His voice tightly controlled.

Stas eased Dina back into Willis's car and faced Brown. "You might impress those fuckin' politicians with your security shit, but I don't buy it. I can waste both of you right now and never get a day. And you know that."

Brown backed off and waited. "Okay, Detective NO WACK or whatever your sorry ass Polish name is. You won this round, but tomorrow is another day, and I don't joke. So watch..."

Stas interrupted, "...my back. Do I look like a joke to you? How do you think I've survived? You fucking mercenaries."

He reached for Dina again, supporting her on his arm. She stood, never taking his eyes off Brown, his hands, and his other henchman.

The men returned to the car and pulled to the curb. Stas relaxed his hold on Dina but grabbed her again to keep her from collapsing into his arms. He caught a glimpse of Willis straining to see what was unfolding behind him as he leaned over toward the open window.

Stas walked Dina to the corner and turned away from the direction of the Trendal Building. The police barricades had been removed, and most of the news vans had gone. The press conference was over.

They didn't encounter any more police or DEA officers. Brown's Audi did not follow. The Mercedes and its guardian, sitting on his upturned can, were where Stas had left them. The windows were still grimy, and the bugs were still stuck to the grill. Stas helped Dina into the car, fished a twenty from his pocket, and passed it to Andy.

"Thanks."

"Anytime, man, anytime."

Stas stretched before getting into the car, happy that another rescue had gone off without a hitch. He started the car, wondering how long his luck would hold.

TWENTY

When they entered the apartment, Dina stepped out of her dress, feebly kicked it aside, and almost collapsed with the effort. Stas caught her and helped her to the bathroom, lifting her onto the counter so he could see her injuries. "How did you get these?"

"Climbing out of the fucking basement. A guy lived down there, and I heard rats." She shuddered. "It was horrible."

Stas took a small mason jar filled with green ointment from the medicine cabinet and unscrewed the lid.

Dina drew back, repulsed by yet another foul odor. "You're not putting that stuff on me."

"Hush, babe. It's Polish, a Polish cure-all." He put the jar on the counter.

He turned the shower on full force and pulled the thong down over her hips. When she stepped into the stall, he stripped and climbed in with her, gently lathering her with a body wash that smelled of menthol and burned her eyes when he shampooed her hair. When he finished, he pulled her to him, letting the water cocoon them in its embrace. She screamed when he switched to cold that shocked her system and her psyche. He stepped out, wrapping a towel around his middle, then held a towel for Dina, helping her out of the shower and pulling her towards the counter.

"Let me see." He turned her face towards the light.

There were no marks or bruises on her upper body, but when he examined her legs, he found several deep purple splotches and a long scratch on her upper thigh. He slathered copious amounts of the ointment on the bruises and the scratch. She closed her eyes, hoping that by not seeing the vile substance, she wouldn't have to endure its smell.

"You can look now." Stas chuckled and washed his hands.

She stared into his gray eyes, managing a weak smile. "You enjoyed that didn't you?"

"Damn right. What man wouldn't?"

He went to the bedroom and returned wearing sweat pants and helped her into one of his oversized T-shirts.

After he tucked her in, Dina reached out to him, "Don't leave me. I can't sleep just yet."

Stas got in beside her.

"I thought I was going to have to go back if I hadn't gotten out. I've never been arrested. After my assault, I thought you were going to arrest me, you know, come back for me when I got out of the hospital. I even looked for you when Sybil picked me up."

"Were you disappointed?"

"Yes and, yes, I wanted to see you again."

"Even if it meant being arrested?"

"I thought I could talk you out of it. It usually worked with my father, with most men." She rested her head on his shoulder.

"Your father's in Chicago? You from Chicago?" he asked.

"Milwaukee. I was born in Milwaukee."

"Where's your mother?"

"I don't know. We parted company in Phoenix over eleven-twelve years ago." She was silent for a few minutes. "My dad was a very handsome man: tall, tan, dark curly hair. He worked at the brewery in Milwaukee. That's where they met and ran off. They had my brother and me. Life was okay, I guess. My grandparents lived nearby, but we didn't see them much. My grandfather had married a Thai girl when he was in the Navy. That hadn't gone over well with his German folks. So she ended up going back to Thailand. My mother looked whiter than the other children. She considered herself white, even German, and she liked that, but landing my dad was a coup for her. She told me that all the women at the brewery were after him, but she snared him. My brother was very white, but I was darker, like I was always in the sun. She thought that was the Thai blood. They were happy for a while, until ...until...." Dina shuttered. Stas pulled her closer. "One night, a black woman, not a dark woman, but you could tell she was African American appeared on our porch, said she needed to see my father. His mother was dying. My mother called her a name and said she'd call the police if she didn't get her black ass off our porch. Well, the woman was my father's sister. He had been passing all those years."

"How did that go down with your mother?"

"She was first in shock, then horrified. They had a big fight. He went to Chicago to see his mother, sorta had a mini-reunion with his family, but when he came back, nothing was ever the same between my folks. They divorced the next year. She never forgave me."

"Why you?"

"Because I looked like him and reminded her of his betrayal. I wasn't white enough anymore. She suddenly noticed my color even more. My summer tan was too dark, my hair too curly. Now I was black, and that changed our relationship." She was silent again.

Stas thought she had fallen asleep until he felt her hand caress his hip. He waited for it to move lower, but it just moved lightly on his stomach and remained there. "So what happened after your old man left."

"After that, she used me... like bait to get men. She was still young, still looked good. They'd come over, bring her beer, and she'd parade me like a piece of meat, until it backfired on her. I ran away with one of her boyfriends, Jason. He was a painter and a photographer. That was his scam, but he was just a pimp. I was in my second year of junior college, but I was miserable. My part-time job didn't pay me enough to get away." Dina yawned. "He brought me to LA to model and... other things. I haven't see---" Her voice faded as she drifted off to sleep.

Stas covered her, took the other pillow and went to the sofa in the living room. As he reached to turn off the lamp, he noticed the red light blinking on his answering machine. There was a message from Dr. Hans Meiers. He needed to talk to Stas as soon as possible. It was urgent.

TWENTY-ONE

Gwen uncorked the white wine and let it breathe while she got two wine glasses from the mini-bar. She had prepared a little tray of brie and sliced rounds of a French baguette. The new silk nightgown felt good against her skin. She had showered and slipped into the long, soft print, even laughed at her extravagance, for she wanted the night to be perfect, especially since she had made up her mind to finally resign from Fresno P.D.

Ed had called after his dinner meeting with Aagard and their advisors. Finally, they could spend the rest of the evening relaxing, maybe recapture some of their old magic. His political obligations were over for the evening. Well, the prospect brought a smile to her face.

On her way to the bedroom, she started to hum. She put the tray on the nightstand and went to the bathroom to add a touch of Tea Rose and loosen her hair. There were only two things missing: candles and her favorite music.

Oh, well, I still have a few old tricks to get him in the mood. They've never failed me yet.

Lawson dropped his briefcase at the door and started shedding clothes before he reached the bedroom. "What's wrong with the lights?"

Gwen didn't respond from the bathroom. Her singing had drowned out his question.

He reached under the pillow for silk paisley pajamas and slipped them on.

Gwen picked up trousers and underwear lying across her path from the bathroom.

"Who picks up after you when I'm not around?"

"Don't worry about it. We'll have someone to do it when I'm elected."

He climbed into bed, reached for the remote, and flipped on the TV surfing the late night news channels. Gwen joined him, pulling back the covers on her side of the bed. One strap of her gown slipped off her shoulder revealing the upper portion of a full, firm breast. She made no effort to cover herself but moved closer to her husband.

"I hope you feel like making up for lost time. I've missed you." Her voice was warm and inviting.

Lawson turned and planted a little kiss on her forehead. "I've missed you too."

She stiffened and took the pillow from her back, punching it before putting it behind her again. She sat ramrod straight in icy silence for a moment then turned.

"Ed, I thought..."

"Gwen darling, I've been under a lot of pressure. I really don't feel like it tonight."

"I thought that was the woman's excuse. I didn't fly down here for you to 'Gwen darling' me and turn up your cold ass. Did Robert find you someone down here? One of those little 'Stepford Wives' down at your campaign headquarters?'

"You're crazy if you think I'd touch any of them. Robert would come unglued if I even looked at one of those girls."

"And would Robert 'come unglued' if you touched me?"

"Don't be absurd, you're my wife."

"Thanks for the reminder. So is he preaching abstinence to go along with all of his other high morality sound bites?"

Ed looked back at the TV.

She hit his hand, knocking the remote to the floor. "Look at you, you can't even talk to me, let alone fuck me. You can't believe the bull he's feeding his bank rollers. You can't legislate morality. You should know that."

Ed turned towards her. "Gwen, this is important to me, to us. I thought you wanted this as much as I do. This is just the beginning. You knew there would be sacrifices."

"You know what I want now, and it's not a sacrifice. And, by the way, you didn't tell me I'd be making all of them. Even the boys are beginning to wonder if they still have a father."

Gwen jumped out of bed and went to her suitcase.

He started to get up. "Where are you going?'

"To the bathroom to change into something warm since you're freezing my ass out of our bed and your life." She called back to him. "Robert's too controlling. He loves the power he has over people. Well, this is one bitch he can't sniff and have me cream my pants."

When she emerged, she had changed into a pair of worn flannel pajamas. "You know, sometimes I pray you lose. Let him find another golden boy to take him to Washington.

TWENTY-TWO

Stas Googled directions for Meiers' Burbank address, pocketed the printout, grabbed his jacket, and drove the twenty minutes to the scientist's bungalow. The grey stucco house sat low on the ground amidst green lawn bordered by flowering bushes. A railed ramp led to the wide front entrance.

Meiers opened the door before Stas could ring the bell. "Come on in." He wheeled his racing chair ahead of the detective and led him across the living room to a large, well-lit den.

It was evident that both men had had a bad night. Stas had a five o'clock shadow that was turning into junior stubble. He hadn't gotten much sleep after the sting at the Trendal Building, but Meiers looked even worse. His eyes had sunk into dark cavities in his haggard, unshaven face. It was painfully clear that something besides Sybil's death was taking its toll.

Meiers rolled to his computer console. "Looks like you've been up most of the night too."

Stas flopped into a chair. "I got your message."

Meiers handed over a sheet of paper. "This was faxed to me last night. I was still up, so I called you."

He read quickly. "I'm not surprised." He handed the fax back. "I've been waiting for somebody to make a move. The way they figure it, who's going to the cops, especially if there's been no investigation."

"Damn it, who's doing this?" Meiers waved the fax, his anger growing. "They aren't very bright. The number is on the top."

"You can go anywhere and send a fax. Also, I did some checking and found your politician, Edward Lawson. Ring a bell?"

Meiers shook his head.

"There's another actor on the stage. Name's Matt Brown. He has a security company, runs a bunch of rent-a-cops, limos. Now Brown's doing security for Lawson. He did security for Sybil. I met him at her office when the computer there crashed, and we've run into each other since then."

Meiers looked puzzled.

"Just hang with me, doc. Last night DEA raided an intimate private party near Little Tokyo."

"Why?"

"To bust some girls and their clients."

"But isn't that just a misdemeanor?"

"Not if drugs are involved."

"I see, but what did they really want."

"A couple of Sybil's girls and a political photo op for the Lawson campaign."

"Was that all?"

"There was a high profile press conference for Lawson and a Rev. Dr. Robert Aagard, his religious guru. Now you get a fax demanding half a mil. Somebody's getting greedy."

"I don't give a damn! I'm not paying a dime."

"Suppose someone leaks your sexual activities to the press or your donors."

"I would love it." A smile brightened Meiers' whole demeanor. "Let the world know that cripples love having sex and get it wherever and whenever they can. Do you really think the scientific community gives a shit who I fuck as long as I continue my research? Maybe I'll publish a paper on how we do it. That's what they would really want to know." He looked at Stas and laughed, then reached for a yellow Post-it note stuck on his monitor. "I thought of this after you left the other day. I wasn't sure how important it was. I was going to call."

Stas waited. *Be patient.*

Meiers finally handed Stas the yellow slip of paper. "Sybil was upset about something else. Her security guy wanted in the business. You know, Sybil made lots of money."

Stas nodded. "Brown?"

"Yes, she turned him down, but there had been another person, a woman who was interested in enhancing her business. I got the feeling from Sybil that she wanted a merger."

"Did Sybil seem interested?"

"She told me, 'Over my dead body.' Those were her exact words."

"Do you remember this woman's name?"

"Not really. I was getting ready to go to Germany. I just remember it was something, something sweet like Sugar or Candy, but..." He shook his head.

"How about Honey?"

"Yes, I think that was it."

Stas left thinking about this new development. He needed to make a call. Set up a meet with a woman he had spoken with recently, but he hadn't seen Honey Malone for a while. She wasn't someone that you visited socially. He didn't keep her number in his phone, but it was a number he had committed to memory years ago.

Then he remembered what Raven had said after the reading of the will. If Honey and Raven merged, Honey could come out of semi-retirement and have a flourishing business. How was this going to shake out, and where did Dina fit in the mix?

TWENTY-TWO

Lawson agreed to meet Townsend at a little coffee shop near campaign headquarters. Since there were no cameras, Lawson dressed casually, wearing charcoal gray slacks, a windowpane gray-and-light-blue sports jacket, and a gray merino wool Polo. Townsend was in his signature corduroy jacket with elbow patches, jeans, and crew neck sweater. He wondered who Lawson was trying to impress. This was a print interview. The perky little waitress brought Lawson a steaming pot of herbal tea. He poured a cup of pinkish liquid and added a packet of Nutra Sweet. Townsend drank his coffee hot and black. When he put the half-empty cup down, the waitress was at his elbow to refill it.

"Thanks for meeting me on such short notice. I always marvel how a person can live in an area for forty years and go unnoticed until now." Townsend said.

Lawson sipped his tea. "I'm really not that mysterious. Southern California is my home. As a matter of fact, I used to work for the Long Beach PD, but I'm sure you read that in my bio. That's where I met Aagard. We were partners. We went to a police shooting competition in San Francisco. I met my wife there. We fell in love, I guess the rest is history."

"But it's a little sketchy."

"It's all in my bio."

Townsend unfolded a white sheet of paper, placed it next to his coffee, then took out his reading glasses. "Basically, it says you're married, have two children, were in law enforcement, served two terms in the state legislature, and now you're running for Congress. See? Very sketchy. My readers want to know a little more about you, the man. So you fell in love with someone you met at a shooting competition? See, the romance angle, they love that."

"My wife was with the Fresno PD; I guess you might call it love at first sight. She was my first love." Lawson laughed at his little joke. "I resigned down here, applied there, got hired, got married, and had two wonderful boys. Aagard came up too. He had moved on to the DA's office after getting his law degree. It was pretty easy switching to the prosecutor's office up there."

"But isn't he a preacher?" There was a hint of derisiveness in Townsend's tone.

Lawson sat up straighter. "He's an ordained minister."

"Oh, does he have a church?"

"When he preaches, it's usually at his father-in-law's church in Fresno. Right now he oversees fundraising and serves as my political advisor and spiritual...." He paused.

"Guru?"

"I think 'guru' gives the wrong connotation. We are not linked in any way to any new age religion or cult. We stand for traditional values and morals."

"So that was the basis for your speech the other night?"

"You were there?"

Townsend nodded and wrote something in his notebook. "It was a first for me. I've never been to a combo before."

"'Combo'?"

"Yeah, prostitution, drugs, and a press conference all rolled into one. Think how much the city could save on police security alone." There was a hint of sarcasm that seemed beyond Lawson's grasp.

"Our, my goal is to rid the city, the area, of activities that diminish the sanctity of the individual. We can arrest the common hookers, get them off the street, but it's the madams and the high-class call girls trading their flesh in the boardrooms and courtrooms of America that we need to get rid of. I don't care how much money they make, they are pariahs and need to be wiped out."

A pink blush rose around Lawson's neck and started to move up to his ears. Townsend hoped he wasn't about to have a heart attack.

"I'm just curious. How are you going to link the prostitution industry with the drugs and pornography?"

"We know they're connected. There was a raid on a porno ring in the Valley the other night. I'm speaking with a large group of church leaders in the area in a couple of days. I'll lay down my plans, my policies, and my proof. Come, I'd like to have you there. See for yourself how we're involving the grassroots movement in each neighborhood. We need to show people the connection. When a certain element moves into an area, more than the property values plummet, the moral values fall by the wayside. People are getting involved in reclamation activities. They shouldn't have to continually move away, give up what they've worked years to achieve." Lawson stopped and sipped his cold tea then looked at Townsend.

"Everyone thinks we exclude the liberal press. I'd like your objective point of view. We have nothing to hide."

"Mr. Lawson, you keep speaking of 'we'. You're the one running. Shouldn't I be reporting your views?"

"Yes, of course. When I speak of 'we', I'm speaking of the ground swell of support we... I'm receiving." He reached in his pocket and took out a folded slip of paper, handing it to Townsend. "This is the address. I'll look forward to seeing you." He looked at his watch then rose, ignoring the check the waitress had placed by his cup.

Townsend placed some bills on the table, put his notebook in his pocket, and followed Lawson out.

The doorman gave Stas the once over, let him enter without even a greeting. Inside, the concierge at her desk asked his name and called to see if Ms. Malone was expecting a visitor. She, at least, nodded and pointed to the bank of gleaming elevators.

"Take the one on the left," she offered.

Once inside, he saw that it went straight to the penthouse. There were no numbers, just an UP button and a DOWN button. The elevator was all shiny brass and spotless mirrors. The doors finally opened onto a deeply carpeted hallway. There were four penthouse apartments on that floor. Honey Malone lived in B. Stas gently touched the bell. The door opened before the tone had completed its reverberation.

"Come in." The woman who opened the door wore a long-sleeved black uniform with white collar and cuffs. Marlowe would have described her as "high yellow." Her short dark brown hair was meticulously plastered around her face in a high-tech helmet that drew attention to her hazel eyes and high cheek bones.

"I have an appointment with Ms. Malone."

"I know."

He followed her across a marble entrance into a large, airy, but sparsely furnished living room.

"Have a seat." The maid pointed to one of two floral printed camel-backed sofas and disappeared.

While Stas waited, he looked at the fare on the tall coffee table: several *Nashvilles,* the latest *Ebony,* and two back issues of *Black Enterprise.* And here he was waiting for another woman from the past, Honey Malone. *Who was going to pop-up next?* She had appeared on the scene seeking help but not wishing to file a complaint. He was working Vice, and here was an angry black woman in his face. He had heard about black women from the South with their gleaming straight razors. Well, he wanted to defuse the situation. He listened to her story. An associate had taken off with a large sum of money. Stas never knew the exact amount of the missing funds, but he and his partner believed it was in excess of $100,000.

Well, they got the word out. The young woman had been threatened with having her face cut so badly that the only place she could have worked afterwards would have been in some dark hole that never saw daylight, or any light for that matter. Honey got her money back, the young thief ended up in a brothel in Rio, and the

Vice partners became the benefactors of Honey's largess. Stas looked up when he heard the door close behind him.

Honey Malone. She hadn't changed much since he'd last seen her. Her complexion was still the color of amber honey and despite her seventy-plus years was as smooth as a baby's bottom. Well, Marlowe had commented once when Stas complimented an elderly black woman's beautiful, wrinkle-free skin. "You know, man, black don't crack." Honey wore her hair in a short, curly Afro. It was now all white with a lavender tint.

He stood and extended his hand that she took in a warm shake. Her hands were soft with nails cut short and polished in a natural, pearly shade.

"Detective Nowak, how have you been?" Honey straightened her long purple caftan when she sat on the opposite camel back sofa and angled a cane next to the sofa. "Gout, but I just can't give up the foods I love. My niece just came back from Nashville and brought me some country ham. I've had it with grits and red eye gravy every morning for a week." She shifted her foot. "And now I suffer, but I know you didn't come here to commiserate about Southern cuisine."

"I'm sorry, I've never had the pleasure of visiting the South."

"Well, you'll have to go sometime." She looked at her watch. "Then what *is* your pleasure today?"

"You knew Sybil Jones?"

"Yes, and I was so sorry to hear of her death. And also I'm forgetting my manners." The maid had silently entered the room and placed a tray with silver service, cups and saucers on the coffee table. "Would you like coffee."

Stas moved to the edge of the sofa. "Thanks, black please."

Honey poured from a silver pot into creamy silver rimmed cups and handed cup and saucer to Stas. "Are you working on a case?"

"No, I'm on vacation, but I was curious, did you know Sybil well?"

"We've met, but we did not run..." Honey looked at her foot. "in the same circles. Is that why you're here? Is there an investigation?"

"No. Her death was ruled a suicide, but I was still curious ... for a friend."

Honey took a sip of her coffee. "For one of her girls?"

"I ran into Raven. She told me you asked her to come work for you. Are you expanding?"

"Not really. I just didn't want to see Raven's considerable talents go to waste. When did you speak to her?"

"A few days ago."

"Are you back with Vice?"

"No."

"Then why the interest?"

The question, in a deep, robust baritone, came from the direction of the dining room. Stas turned. The man behind the voice was tall, slender, with a military bearing. He sported a neatly trimmed goatee, a full head of snow-white hair, and piecing blue eyes.

"Detective Nowak, this is my fiancé, Trey Elliott."

Stas stood and extended his hand.

"Nice to finally meet you, Detective Nowak. Is this a police visit?"

Stas caught a slight Southern twang in Elliott's voice. "No."

"He was inquiring about Sybil Jones, for a friend."

"It's always good to have a friend with the police." Elliott smiled.

"You're ex-military or police?"

"Both. I retired from Nashville P.D., former Deputy Chief. But I'm sure you already know that. I would be nice to compare notes some day. I miss the shop talk." He looked over at Honey. "I've got an appointment downtown, and Honey has another appointment in a few minutes."

Stas knew when he was being dismissed. "I've got to be going anyway. I can get back to you later."

"Nothing official I hope." Elliott was at the door.

Honey had risen, taken her cane, and followed Stas. "Everything went well with Alexis?"

"Yes. Why do you ask?"

"She asked that you not be a repeat."

"Why? Did she complain?"

"In a way, she doesn't like uncut men."

"Then she's the one missing out." Stas followed Elliott to the elevator. "How do you like California?"

"I love the weather. Honey's happy. Our situation would have been impossible in Nashville."

They both exited the elevator on the first floor.

The concierge looked up. "Mr. Elliott, your car is here."

A Hispanic driver in a brown uniform held the door for Elliott to get into a black Lincoln Town car. Stas held back and noted the license numbers before leaving.

TWENTY-THREE

On the first ring, May opened one eye and looked at the clock. It was 2:27 a.m. No one ever called her in the middle of the night. She rolled over, folded the pillow around her head, and ignored the ringing. It would stop if she didn't pick up. They would know they had a wrong number, and she could go back to sleep. But it didn't stop. Finally, she picked up, ready to curse out the person on the other end.

"Hello! Who the hell is this?"

"It's Matt, Matt Brown."

Her voice softened. "Matt, I didn't expect a call this late."

"Something came up. I need what you're holding for me this morning. What time can I come over?"

May was fully awake now, almost in a panic. "You can't come here! I don't have it here!" Her heart pounded. She had to think. "I'll have to meet you later. You know Aficionado, the dance club. There's a cafe next door. I can meet you there at two."

"Is it at Sybil's condo?"

"No! No! I'll have it for you."

"You know that place's a dive, but I'll see you there. Make it at one. I have an appointment later."

Her mouth was dry as she asked the question: "You're bringing the money?"

"Don't worry about it. I'll have it. You just make sure you have what you promised. I don't like wasting my time."

"Okay."

"I need one more thing. You have the office number or cell number of the guy she was seeing."

Why did he want the Doc's number? "I think I have it around here somewhere."

"Get it for me. I just have a fax number."

"I can bring it when I meet you."

"I need it now! It's very important."

May turned on the light by her bed and thought. She had taken several cards from Sybil's desk drawer. The Doc's card had been one of them. It was in the tea caddy. "Wait a minute."

She went to her living room, flicked on the ceiling light and dumped the contents of the caddy on the coffee table. It took a few seconds to find the card. There were two for Dr. Meiers. One was a business card. The other was a personal one with his home address and phone number. May took the cards with her to the bedroom and picked up the receiver.

"I have it. Which one do you want, home or office?"

"Give me his home address and phone number. Does he have a cell?"

May read everything off then hung up. She had trouble going back to sleep. Getting the money excited her, but this business with the Doc was disturbing. She didn't want to get him in trouble. He seemed like such a nice guy, and he was a cripple. He had enough problems.

May awoke later and panicked. She hadn't heard the alarm. She was late, so she had to run for the bus if she was going to make her connection in L.A., to get to Dina's place, and meet Matt on time. She didn't have time to make up her eyes. She looked tired, washed out. *Might as well put a bag over my head.*

The bus stop was in front of a bakery. She saw the bus go up Lake, so she had just enough time to run in and get a coffee to go. When the bus came, the driver just looked at her. She knew he hadn't recognized her without her make-up. She pulled her cap down over her forehead, tugged her jacket tightly around her, snuggled into her seat. After drinking the coffee, she took a fitful nap, lulled to sleep by the movement of the bus and the dream of a little car, anything to get her off the Metro.

She'd made good time. Her goal was to get in and out of Dina's place without any interruptions.

Don't leave the key in the door, stupid. You don't have time for a visit from Livia.

Livia wasn't in the foyer.

Good.

Then May saw her when she looked down the hall toward the manager's apartment. Livia just stood there, her hand on her hip, watching.

God, I hate that bitch with all the pictures of her dancing, on the stage, in the movies. You'd think she was Ginger Rogers.

May didn't look back as she took the elevator. There was no one in the hallway, and she made sure to take the key from the lock before closing the door. May went straight to the bedroom, switched on the ceiling light, and checked the drawer in the lingerie chest. She pushed back the panties and thongs. Nothing! She tossed everything. Nothing! The little computer was gone. Her heart seemed to jump to her throat. It had been the third drawer down; she took all the frilly things out and threw them on the bed. Nothing!

Maybe I was drunk or high.

She emptied every drawer. Nothing! Turning her attention to the dresser, she rummaged through each drawer and still found nothing. It was nowhere in the bedroom. On her previous visit, she hadn't gone into any other room, except the kitchen to empty the vases. She ran to the little kitchen and looked in the garbage can. It was empty except for the remains of dead flowers.

May sat on the bed, holding back tears, willing her heart to stop. Death was better than this.

How could I be so stupid? He has it. That cow, Livia told him, and he came and got it, or ...or she took it. I'll tell Matt she has it. She saw me hide it. The door was open. She came in on the QT and saw me put it in the drawer. Matt will take care of her. How she gonna like them apples? May felt better. Her heart rate slowed. She went to the bathroom and took out some of Dina's expensive liner from a cosmetic bag on the counter. She rummaged through finding the right colors, made up her eyes, and left.

Livia was waiting for her near the elevator. "I know you not back so soon cleaning. I'm calling my friend."

May glared at her as she pushed the down button. "You do that." When she got into the elevator, she turned to Livia and smiled. "But you'd better watch it. I got people to call, too."

After leaving Dina's, May had to take another bus to get to Aficionado. Brown was standing outside the club and looked at his watch when he saw her alight from the bus.

"I'm not late." She had rehearsed what she was going to say, how she would accuse Livia. "Why didn't you wait for me inside?"

"I don't think so. I might catch something. The place's a dive."

"I need to sit down. My feet hurt." She started for the entrance.

"C'mon, we can take the car. I told you, I have an appointment."

"But I have to tell you something."

"Tell me what?" He looked past May for a minute "Where is it?"

May stammered out her response. "I, I don't have it. The, the, she, Li, Livia took it. You see, I left the door open, and she saw me hide it. She took it after I left."

Matt threw his hands out and started to turn. "Who the fuck is Livia?"

"Dina's manager." May was confused. "At her, at Dina's building."

"Take me there."

May followed doggedly after Matt. When they reached the car, parked in a half empty lot behind the dance club, he deactivated the alarm and locks.

"Get in."

He watched her struggle, then walked around to the rear of the car, and popped the trunk after May had settled herself inside. The gun at his back fell effortlessly into his hand. It took only a few seconds to make the switch. He placed the gun, legally registered to him, in a special compartment and secured his throw down at his back. It was a Smith and Wesson, hot like the other. He liked both guns and would regret having to get rid of the S and W, but a plan was working though his mind. He would just have to mentally navigate the streets of the city to find a suitable place.

He gently closed the trunk and got in the car. Before starting, he reminded her to fasten her seat belt. Then he activated the "Child Proof" door locks.

"And where's Dina?" He turned to May and smiled.

"With her cop." May was enjoying the big car, inhaling that new-car smell, fingering the soft, supple leather. She'd seldom ridden in such luxury. She was even glad she had put on some makeup.

"When you get the computer, do I still get the money?"

"Let's take care of one obstacle at a time."

She smiled to herself. Livia would be history. May continued to chatter on after giving directions to Dina's apartment. Seduced by Matt's warm smile, the joy of the ride, she never realized until it was too late, that they had taken a detour.

Dina was up nursing her mug when Stas returned.

"You need some coffee?"

He nodded as he sat in his recliner, feeling as if the weight of the world rested on his shoulders, but he needed more than coffee. "Put a little something in it for me, babe."

"Livia called." Dina shouted from the kitchen.

"You takin' my calls?"

Dina returned and handed him his mug. "No, I heard her voice when your machine picked up, so I answered."

"What did she want?"

"To talk to you, what else would she want?"

"I can't imagine. Must be my charming smile or..."

"She's a hot woman. I guess she wants what we all want." She handed him the phone.

He grabbed it, took it over to his chair, and dialed.

"Hey, Livia, this is Detective Nowak."

"I know. How are you?"

"Can't complain." He took a sip from his mug and grimaced. Dina must have put a triple shot in the coffee. "What's up?"

"That woman who cleans for Dina has been hanging around, and she doesn't stay long enough to clean. Anyway, she was back today for a hot minute. I told her I had a friend who's a cop." There was a pause. "She told me I'd better be careful 'cause she had friends too."

"Do you know what she was doing?"

"Not really, like I said, she didn't have time to do any cleaning. She was so fast the other day, that she didn't even shut the door."

"You goin' be home?"

"I don't have anyplace to go."

"Good, then I'll come by. See you later."

Dina had gone back to the kitchen to give him privacy. When he finished, she returned. "What was that all about, an invite to the dance?"

"No, she said May's been hanging around your place."

Dina almost spilled her coffee when she jumped up. "I forgot. Where's my purse?" She looked around the sofa and on the floor. "What did you do with it?"

"I don't remember. It's probably still in the car." He got up, grabbed his keys, and left.

Dina went to the bedroom to search while Stas went to the garage.

When he returned, he handed Dina the purse.

She took out the PDA and gave it to him. "That bastard tried to take my purse."

Stas went over to his desk and got his PDA and the data strip. "Where did you get this?"

"In my underwear drawer."

"And you have no idea how it got there?"

"No, I'd never even seen one 'til you got yours."

"This must be Sybil's. May probably took it. She had access to your place since she knew you were here."

"But I went home yesterday."

He frowned. "How was she to know you'd need your sexy little thong to wear to a party?"

"My thong's not the point. Why couldn't she keep this at her place?"

"I'm sure we're not the only ones looking for it. If there's no pertinent data on that crashed computer at the office, then it means Sybil kept her records on something else. May doesn't have any use for it except to give it to someone who does. She was probably picking it up today."

"But she didn't get it."

"Then May has a serious problem. She's got to tell her contact that someone else has it. Who would she suspect took it?" He smiled at Dina. "You? She doesn't want to send anyone my way. Plus, she doesn't know where I live. But others might suspect you since you and Lisa went back to your place."

"But Lisa's not involved."

"Funny, nobody busted her last night. Think about it. Who took you to that party? Who was hanging out with the cops last night? If you call, I bet she's in the office today." He shook his head. "I just don't trust her."

"Then what about Livia?"

"May might think Livia has it?"

"What would she do with it?

Stas laughed. "Give it to me since I'm her good friend. I'm going to Livia's."

"Am I going with you?"

"No, stay here. I got to change."

"To see Livia?"

"I have to maintain my image." He laughed again. It felt good.

"What about Sybil's computer?"

"Unless she engraved the password on the cover, we're still in the same boat, going nowhere fast."

Livia dusted the leaves of the plants in the foyer while keeping her eye out for Stas. When she saw him at the entrance door, she rushed to open it.

"Are you all right?" he asked.

She nodded nervously as if May still lurked in the shadows ready to pop out from behind some silk foliage and assault them as she spoke. She touched his sleeve and indicated that he follow.

When they reached her apartment, she ushered him in, locked the door, and turned the dead bolt. Stas had that trapped feeling again but shook it off. Lights were on everywhere, but there didn't seem to be any additions to her picture gallery.

"Sit down." She indicated the sofa facing the TV. "I made a fresh pot of coffee."

"Got anything stronger?"

Livia stopped and spun around. It was a classic dance move, fluid and graceful. "I have lots of things. What do you like?"

"Vodka?"

"Chilled, in the freezer."

"You're a woman after my poor Polish heart."

While Livia got the drinks, Stas watched the evening news. A woman's body had been found dumped in brush in the Hollywood Hills. No identification had been made yet. Stas felt his gut wrench but dismissed the sharp pain.

She set a tray on the kidney shaped coffee table. The bottle of Grey Goose was frosted to its neck. The glasses were even chilled. She poured for both of them.

They raised their glasses in a toast.

He paused as he savored the chilled liquid. "Good stuff even if it is French." He settled back in the corner of the sofa, half watching the TV and trying also to focus on Livia's story.

She noticed his distraction and reached for the remote.

"Leave it for a sec."

The news continued but nothing more was reported on the dead woman. He motioned for Livia to switch off the set.

"Now, tell me what happened with May."

She now had his undivided attention. "She usually comes every other week. I see her all the time posing. Well, she came last week. Then she was here twice this week, but I'm sure she wasn't cleaning." She paused and took a few sips of her drink.

Stas rose and walked around. The room was closing in on him. The vodka and some scent Livia was wearing made him feel sleepy. "Continue." He stretched and stifled a yawn. The last thing he wanted was to fall asleep in Livia's apartment.

"The first time she came, when I went up to Dina's apartment, the door was sitting wide open. She didn't bother taking the key out. I mean, anybody could just walk in and rob Dina blind. Then that cow came back today."

"Did she see you?"

"Yeah, she saw me. I was standing in the hall dusting my plants. She kinda looked at me like she was sneaking in." Livia continued. "Something told me to go up and check her out. Whatever she was doing, it wasn't cleaning. She didn't stay long. I stopped her by the elevator and told her I was going to call you. That's when she told me to 'Watch myself'."

Stas sat back down at a close angle to Livia. "I want you to do just that. Can you get away for a few days?"

"I guess I could go to my sister's in Palm Springs."

"I don't know exactly what May was up to, but I think I can guess. She left something here while Dina was away and came back today to get it, but Dina has it. May doesn't know that. She may even think you have it since you saw her when she left it."

"But I didn't see her hide a thing. I just told her I'd call you to scare her. I don't like her anyway. Thinks she can dance."

He rose. "I want to check out Dina's apartment. When I get back, give me your sister's number. Call her and tell her you need a little vacation."

She bounced up and walked him to the door. "Stas, when you first came here, you lied about that witness, didn't you? It was Dina all the time, wasn't it?"

He smiled. "You got me, Livia. I'll be back in a shake."

With Dina's apartment key in hand, he remembered how easy it had been the first time without one. He turned on a lamp by the sofa and picked up the scent of stale cigarette smoke. There was a butt with red lipstick in a little bowl. The smoke must have belonged to Lisa or May.

The light from the hall partially illuminated the mess when he entered the bedroom. When Stas flipped on the bedside lamp, he could see that the drawers of the tall chest had been dumped on the bed. Some of the silk underwear had spilled to the floor. He picked up a tiny black bikini G-string and started to throw it back with the others but put it in his pocket.

In the bathroom, makeup had been left on the counter. A tissue used to blot lipstick had missed the toilet and lay on the floor. May must have been dolling herself up. He guessed she had a meet with someone, someone who'd take the PDA off her hands. He didn't believe she was the type to give it away. She wanted some money.

He went back to the living room and dialed Hollywood Division and asked for Sergeant Torres. He waited for a few minutes before the phone was picked up again.

"Sergeant Torres here."

"Torres, Stas Nowak, we met at Watson's retirement." Stas could hear the faint rhythmic ticks of the machine recording his voice. "I'm looking for his old partner, Joe Turner. Is he there?" He waited as the machine recorded the silence.

Finally Turner answered.

"Stas, what's up?"

"Saw on the news, you picked up a body dumped in the Hills. Did you get an ID yet?"

"The only thing on her was an MTA bus pass and a CD with May West written on it. Don't have a clue what she was doing up there, unless she was trying to catch a fast buck. Instead she caught a bullet. Whoever did it was a good shot. Looked professional, but who'd want to pop some bus riding wannabe named May West. Man, that's Hollywood."

TWENTY-FOUR

After leaving Livia, Stas wanted to swing by Hollywood Station and see Turner or, at least, talk to the Lead Detective, then just as quickly he realized it was a bad idea. What reason could he give for nosing around? After all, he was still on vacation. Did he really want to get personally involved in an investigation, drag Dina into it, and get questioned about their interest?

He would have to reveal the existence of the PDA and most importantly, the data stick. Who knows, maybe somebody in the department wouldn't need a password. Whatever they might find on the hard drive could give somebody in LAPD a lot of shit on a lot of people. The Department had enough experts to break into Sybil's computer. Stas wasn't ready to give up his info just yet.

He also decided to wait before telling Dina about May. There was still time before the police released her name to the press. The remains had to be identified, nearest of kin notified. The ME had to do the cut. He would like to see the slug.

The image of Matt Brown kept surfacing, standing with his hands hanging loose like some twenty-first century gunslinger. Stas imagined May going to Brown about the PDA and his quiet rage when she hadn't produced. Would Brown have been stupid enough or angry enough to use his own gun? Stas shook off the image. Brown, like a lot of cops or ex-cops, would have a throw down locked in his trunk. This was something that Hollywood Division would have to deal with, and he wasn't about to help them out.

When Stas got home, he found Dina curled up on the sofa dozing over a book. He wondered how many she'd read since she'd been with him, or was she just skipping through to the last pages. He realized that he hadn't given much thought to Dina, the woman, somebody's daughter, somebody's sister. Had she ever really been somebody's woman? Ever had a pimp? How had she handled her father's race, his deception, her mother's anger? Why had she become a prostitute? Did she believe there was a difference between a hooker and a call girl? After all, a whore was a whore no matter how much she cost.

She opened her eyes when he removed the book from her hands and sat next to her, slipping an arm around her shoulder.

The question came out of the blue. "Was your mother's boy friend your first?"

Dina dropped her gaze, looking at her fingers before answering. "No, it was someone else."

He lifted her chin to stare into moist hazel eyes. Stas wondered if she was repressing pain rather than holding back tears.

"It's okay, babe."

Her voice was soft. "My mother's cousin was the first. She put him up to it. I think she even watched. Afterwards, when I looked into her eyes, I knew she knew. It was some kind of sick punishment for what my father had done. And she wanted me to know I was being punished so I never told her what Wolff did. But my brother, she never did anything to hurt my brother."

Stas wiped her eyes. He understood others' compulsion to punish. "It's not too late to get out. I told you that before. Let me help."

"Are you offering for me or for yourself, 'cause I need more from you than just your help?"

He leaned back. He wanted to do more than wipe away tears, but taking her in his arms and making some sort of declaration wasn't an option now. They sat in silence. Images that had been deeply buried in his subconscious flooded his mind.

Dina broke into his thoughts. "I can't do what you want. Is that my only option if I have feelings for you?"

"I don't know, babe. I'm being honest. I just don't know."

She pulled away, letting his arm fall. Stas reached for her neck, felt compelled to touch the scar. That raised imperfection was their link, the one thing that had brought them together. He lifted her face and brushed his lip on her neck, touching the scar with his tongue.

Then he got up and went to the kitchen. He started to fix a drink but changed his mind and made a pot of coffee.

Leaning against the counter, Stas felt pangs of guilt for dragging up Dina's pain from whatever deep recesses she had locked it. He understood her feelings, for he, too, had been forced to repress old memories that were now being dredged up by recent revelations. Even thoughts of Elizabeth Nowak, Liz, his ex-wife had surfaced. A mental image of her flooded his senses. The strongest was her scent, Magic Noire, wafting above his coffee, mingling with Peet's Garuda Blend. It was an unpleasant combination that often left a foul taste in his mouth even now. He poured his coffee down the drain.

He hadn't realized the extent of his dormant needs repressed since Liz. And now another woman and a fortieth birthday had brought everything to the surface.

TWENTY-FIVE

A select group had gathered in two adjoining luxury suites at the Beverly Hilton Hotel. The men were well-tailored and well-heeled. Each had on his arm a smartly dressed woman in the uniform of the elite, expensive pearls over St. John knits and Ferragamo pumps.

Flowers were everywhere. In the first suite, several tables, attended by servers in immaculate white jackets and black bow ties, were set up with colorful and delicious finger foods.

The event had been billed as an opportunity to meet the candidate, but the invitation really meant, "Bring your checkbook."

Aagard stood near a small mahogany desk where one of the young ladies from Lawson's campaign headquarters was checking the guest list and handing out literature. Under Aagard's watchful eye, another worker took checks.

His smile broadened when he saw Gwen. "I'm glad you got here early." He took her arm and escorted her to one of the two bars set discretely in the corners of the room under fake silk palms. "What are you drinking?"

"Scotch neat."

He leaned in closer and whispered. "Wouldn't you like a glass of Zinfandel instead?"

Gwen backed off. "Why? You don't want your contributors thinking Ed's wife's a lush?"

The bartender handed her a half-filled wine glass.

Gwen gave it back. "Here, I'm not drinking this. Put my Scotch in a wine glass if you like, but I want Scotch."

Aagard nodded, and the bartender re-poured her drink.

"Thanks." She downed a third and turned to Aagard. "Aren't you going to ask about Ed?"

Before he could respond, two middle-aged matrons appeared at his elbow. He gave each woman a peck on her cheek. Gwen caught a subtle whiff of two very expensive perfumes doing battle in the closed atmosphere of the trio. She stepped back, momentarily ignored by Aagard as he cozied up to old Los Angeles money.

Before Gwen could escape, he grabbed her arm and pulled her into the group.

"This is the candidate's wife, Gwen Lawson."

She could feel their disapproval, as they softly muttered their "hellos".

Each introduced herself, but the names were lost in the atmosphere as soon as he turned from Gwen to give his attention to the ladies.

"I'm going to get something to eat." Gwen walked away, sure that no one heard or cared.

She piled her plate high with vegetable sticks and shrimps. *Is this what I've got to endure for the next three years? I don't know anyone here, and I don't want to.*

Aagard cornered her again rubbing against her arm. Gwen pushed him away.

"What time is your husband planning to get here?"

"He has a cell phone, call him."

Aagard moved on, suggestively caressing the arms of other female guests and glad-handing several of the males.

Gwen had had enough of Aagard's hovering. She needed to escape. Then she saw Beth, lacking her usual effervescence, standing in a corner. Her eyes were rimmed in red as if she'd been crying.

Gwen sat her empty plate down and joined her.

"I used to like these fundraisers, but I don't know any of these people. They're not very friendly. At home, everyone knew me. LA is such a cold place. I hope Washington will be an improvement." Beth bit her lower lip.

Gwen smiled weakly. "I doubt it. I hear the social life is really cut-throat."

Beth frowned and bit her lip again. She looked toward her husband. He was surrounded by a new group of women, a new audience to charm. Gwen was sure, if the power failed, he could have illuminated both suites with his magnetism. Beth watched him, never noticing when Gwen left her side.

A young woman opened the doors to the second suite. Gwen stopped at the bar for a refill before entering. She moved along with some of the men and took a seat in the back row of chairs arranged theatre-style. A podium and microphone faced the red and gilt chairs. She looked around, noticing that none of the women had followed their husbands in. The room slowly started to fill. She felt a hand on her shoulder when she sat.

"Gwen, they need you in the other room." It was Aagard, his hand exerting a gentle pressure on her shoulder.

"Why?

"The women like to visit with the candidate's wife, get to know you."

"Why? I'm not running."

Aagard tried to speak through clenched teeth. He edged closer, stooping down to her eye level. "Gwen."

"Excuse me. Can you move over a couple of seats?" A tall, robust man stood, waiting for Aagard to stand aside. When neither moved, he wedged himself between Gwen and Aagard. "I've got to get off this leg. It's killing me."

Gwen ignored Aagard who finally stood and walked back into the other suite. "Are you all right?"

"Yeah, just a little vain. Left my cane in the car." He turned to watch Aagard's retreat. "Is that the candidate?"

Gwen didn't have to follow his line of vision. "No, he's not here yet. That's his manager."

"I'm Paul Swain. My wife dragged me here. I'm not much into politics."

She offered her hand. "Gwen."

Paul turned again. "That guy sure looks familiar."

"That's Robert Aagard, the Rev. Robert Aagard."

Puzzled, he looked at Gwen. "If he's the guy I think he is, that wasn't his name when I knew him."

Now it was Gwen's turn to be surprised. "What was it?"

"You know, I can't remember now, but he sure as hell wasn't a preacher." He laughed. "This candidate, what's his name?"

"Edward Lawson."

"Eddie, Eddie Lawson?"

Before Gwen could respond, Paul started to rise, holding onto the back of the chair in front of him. "I knew an Eddie Lawson, a cop, an angry bastard. Hated his old man with a passion for what he did to them."

Gwen caught his jacket sleeve. "Them?"

"Yeah, he and his wife."

Now she was on her feet. Looking with Paul into the other suite, hoping to see her husband, to clear up Paul's error.

"Wife?"

"He wanted to quit the force, join the Army, get away from here and his old man."

"Are you sure about this ... about a wife?"

Paul turned quickly to Gwen. "Well, I guess they weren't married long. They got a divorce or annulment, something like that."

"How do you know this?"

There was a coldness in Paul's tone. "I worked with him in Long Beach. I didn't like him then, and if he's the same guy,...." He limped pass Gwen and turned back. "If you're a reporter and print any of this, I'll deny it."

She wanted to follow, to ask more questions but fell back into her seat. She took her cell phone from her purse and dialed.

"Matt, this is Gwen." She struggled to hold back the hot, burning tears.

"Baby, what's up?"

"We need to talk."

TWENTY-SIX

The three cups of coffee that Stas consumed before leaving for Parker Center did little to relieve the knot in his stomach. If this pain continued, he might have to see somebody. The thought of consulting a doctor, whether medical or a shrink made him reflect on his past good fortune and how it had held out for most of his career. Even his move from Vice to RHD had been a positive career advancement, yet he never knew who had pulled the strings to get him such a sweet transfer.

A lot of cops had mentors, someone who showed them the ropes, cut red tape, acted as a sounding board. If he had one, it would have to be Captain Graham Taylor. He had welcomed Stas, happy to have him replace Ivan Ivanov, the "Mad Russian".

Detective Ivanov had gotten a promotion and transfer to Hollywood Division. It was common knowledge that there was no love lost between the Captain and Ivanov. Yet Stas and his predecessor were good cops with a proclivity for order and vodka. As a matter of fact, Taylor hated Ivanov. And Stas's promotion to Robbery/Homicide might have been one of those divisional conveniences to keep the peace amid a department famous for infighting and adverse publicity. And some situations hadn't gotten any better despite the Consent Decree imposed on LAPD by the Department of Justice after the Rampart scandal.

Stas had come with a clean record, no civilian complaints, and no threatened lawsuits. Even though he had the reputation of being a loner, he was the kind of officer who could work well with all sides. He inherited Ivanov's desk and his partner, Sid Edwards, a timid, self-righteous man who worked hard at being a good cop but often came up short, for he lacked those intuitive skills that most street-savvy policemen took for granted. Edwards had happily accepted the change and had hoped that his new partner would be more tolerant and less intimidating, especially since Ivanov weighed in at 250 pounds and stood 6 feet 3 inches in his stocking feet.

Now Stas needed some direction from a superior instead of spinning his wheels around a non-investigation. With May's murder, he felt there was a connection if someone could just make it. He was even considering giving Sybil's PDA's stick to one of the Department's computer techs to have them figure out her password. But he knew that information would jeopardize not only Sybil's girls, but also their clients, who were not the run-of-the-mill husbands who just needed a quick fuck because their wives weren't putting out this month or for those who couldn't get the kinky stuff at home.

The Captain's door stood ajar. He turned from the window when Stas lightly tapped on the glass. "C'mon in, Nowak. How's the vacation?"

"I didn't go anywhere." He tried to withhold the sense of regret in his tone.

"You look like you still need one, now more than ever."

Taylor motioned for Stas to sit in one of his infamous straight, hard-ass wooden chairs facing his desk. It was rumored the Captain picked them up at some yard sale. They were meant to make their occupants uneasy, sort of a modern version of the hot seat. The granite-hard surface was already making Stas uncomfortable. He just wanted to ask his questions, get some answers, and leave. Although he liked his superior, he didn't want to give the Captain time to pontificate or philosophize. If Taylor was in a good mood, Stas could be there an hour or more.

Sensing his detective's discomfort, Taylor settled back in an overstuffed chair, retrieved a pack of cigarettes and gold lighter from his desk, and lit up.

"Close the door," he ordered. Everyone knew the "No Smoking" rules terminated at the Captain's door, and no one had the balls to challenge him on it. "Want a smoke?"

"I quit."

"How? Patch, gum?"

"Cold turkey."

"I congratulate you. I've been trying for years. It takes will power." His tone changed. "But then, you strike me as a man with lots of will power." He flicked ashes into the wastebasket by his chair and blew smoke away from the detective.

Stas wasn't sure if he had just received a compliment or a put-down. He shifted in his seat. Trying to divert the smoke was futile. Its residue had settled like a sticky yellowish film everywhere. If files or reports stayed in the Captain's office long enough, they would later be returned to the detectives discolored with a yellow tint. The lack of proper ventilation and the Captain's chain smoking left a tar-like essence in the atmosphere. And to make matters worse, Taylor smoked cheap cigarettes that smelled like burning hair. No number of plug-ins and sprays could mask the foul odor. While the detectives had given up on doing something about the Captain's secondhand smoke, Gladys Williams, the squad's secretary, still changed the plug-ins from time to time when Taylor had gone for the day.

The Captain broke into Stas's thoughts. "If you're still on vacation, what brings you down here? I can't imagine you miss this place."

"No, I have a situation: a while back, a woman committed suicide, but now there may be some doubt, some questions about it not being self-inflicted. The evidence to the contrary is less than circumstantial. It's really just bits and pieces plus my gut feeling. Putting that together with some recent events makes me believe it was more than coincidence. What would I need to go to the DA?"

"A whole lot more than your damn bits and pieces. Sounds like dog food. You know what she would do with your gut feelings. Sounds like you don't even have enough for a court order to exhume the body."

"She was cremated."

"Then you got nothin'."

"Yeah, nothing but that feeling."

"Maybe you just need a drink or a woman."

"Had a little too much of both already." Stas realized it was time to go. The smoke was getting to him. If he stayed much longer, his suit would have to go to the cleaners. Anyway, he was getting nowhere fast. He didn't want to say too much, to bring down the wrath of someone upstairs, whoever that might be. No need showing his hand until he had read Sybil's data strip.

As he started to rise, the Captain motioned for him to sit again.

"You know I majored in English as an undergraduate?"

Stas shifted his weight again, trying to keep his butt from going numb. The Captain was about to give a lecture.

"I wanted to go to law school. Even did quite well on the LSAT. But my testosterone got the best of me, and I had to get married. So I joined LAPD, had to take care of two babies, one right after the other. Thought I'd go to school later. Well, another kid, a divorce and a second wife, and I'm still here trying to keep up with child support and taking care of ex-wives. I can't even afford a number three. But that's not my point. When I see you younger guys, I think of old Will Shakespeare."

Stas looked puzzled. Taylor had lost him.

The Captain continued: "I love Shakespeare. Read everything he wrote. Here was a man who understood the human condition, unlike most writers today. Sometimes I wonder how Will would see you guys today because you remind me of Macbeth."

Grimacing, the detective shifted his weight again, leaning on the edge of the chair. He needed some air, even the funky air of the men's room. At least it had a fan.

He continued. "You read *Macbeth?*"

Stas nodded. He vaguely remembered the play, but couldn't see where the Captain was going with his analogy.

"Nowak, I'm not talking about Macbeth as a murderer, but before -- when his wife was trying to convince him to kill the king. She told him he had too much milk of human kindness, or something like that, to catch the nearest way! You understand that?"

Stas nodded again and rearranged his butt in the chair, this time leaning toward the Captain, hoping he looked interested enough so that Taylor would hurry up and make his point.

Instead he lit another cigarette with the smoldering butt of the last and continued: "You're a good cop, almost too good. You have keen instincts. You're street-smart and use it without being condescending. And you care about people. That's rare. I've watched you."

Stas was a little surprised but said nothing.

"You're quick, figure things out in your head in a split second while other cops haven't gotten off the dime or are reaching for a gun. Your partner is one of those. That's why I teamed you two. I figured you wouldn't rub his face in the shit the way Ivanov did. But you know what? I don't care how good you are, you won't get promotions because you won't play politics. No one's going to kick you upstairs. After a while, as you watch guys dumber than you, like your partner, tell you what to do and when to do it, you get cynical, you drink a little too much, you may even go off..." He stopped.

Stas rose and flexed his butt muscles. "What if there is another body to connect to the suicide?"

"Listen, I know I've been preaching, and I know what they call me. If you get something that we can take to the DA-- well, we'll see."

Stas stretched his lower back as he walked to the door. When he opened it, he welcomed a rush of fresh air. He took a deep breath and secretly wished for a cigarette, even a cheap one.

When Dina awakened and looked at the clock, it was almost noon. She hadn't heard Stas leave but vaguely remembered a glass of juice handed to her as she tried to will herself to open her eyes.

They argued briefly about her going to her apartment when he told her he had an appointment. They compromised. He left, and she'd fallen back on the pillow and slept.

Will I ever get used to his hours or his ways?

When she threw her legs over the side of the bed, she felt a crook in her hip. Her muscles felt tight. She picked up the phone and dialed.

The voice on the other end was heavily accented. "Yah?"

"Inger?"

"Yah?"

"It's Dina."

"Where you been? You okay?"

"I'm fine now. I'm staying with a friend, and I need your magic. My poor back is killing me."

"But you missed your appointment."

"Please, you must have some time."

"Maybe I give you half hour."

Dina gave Inger directions and went to the bathroom for a quick shower.

When Inger arrived forty-five minutes later, Dina helped set up the massage table while the masseuse lit a candle and slipped a CD into Stas's system. She fiddled with knobs and dials until soft, relaxing strings floated from the speakers.

"Your friend, she gone away?"

Dina smiled. "It's a he. He's a detective."

"Oh, oh!" Inger frowned. "You in trouble?"

"It's a long story."

Inger busied herself arranging the sheets on the table, holding up the top one so that Dina could slip in as she dropped her robe. On her stomach any further conversation was difficult.

Before Stas could get his key in the door, he could hear the music and knew it wasn't anything he owned. When he walked into the apartment, he had to adjust to the drawn blinds and the aroma of citrus and lavender. The massage table took up the space between the coffee table and entertainment center. A big, strong, Nordic looking woman in her late fifties was working her magical fingers on Dina. He stood and watched, fascinated with the way the masseuse kneaded her shoulders.

The woman stopped briefly in her ministration to introduce herself, wiping an oily hand on one corner of the sheet.

"I'm Inger Ford." Her shake was powerful, her grip like iron.

For a moment, he could feel her drain his strength. "Stas, Stas Nowak."

Inger sized him up. "You got nice body, but you look tense. You need a massage." She smiled. "You not afraid to get naked for me, are you?"

He was already feeling stripped to his core. "I think I'll go change."

"You know, I do a lot of men. They don't excite me, but then again." She checked his back as he retreated into the bedroom.

With her distraction gone, she turned back to putting the finishing touches on Dina, massaging the scalp, running her fingers like little rivulets over her face, working on her ears. Dina moaned, her eyelids fluttering as she briefly drifted off to sleep.

Inger finished and sat quietly, meditating, giving Dina a few more moments to relax before removing the headrest and placing it in a niche inside the table and packing her gear. Dina stirred when Inger turned off the CD player and ejected her CD.

"Okay, honey, you get up. I got another appointment."

Dina sat up and wrapped the top sheet around her. Inger dampened two fingers and pinched out the flame of the candle sending a spiral of lemon-scented smoke into the air.

"You know, my mother warned me about men with gray eyes."

"Why?" Dina slipped into her robe and handed Inger the sheet.

"They're cold. You never know what's going on behind that steel glare."

Dina was about to respond when Stas returned and stood by his desk.

"When could you fit him in?" Dina asked laughing at his discomfort.

He shook his head and waved the idea off. Inger grabbed her day-planner looking at her calendar.

"It would be nice to have him mellow ... for tonight."

"What's going on tonight?" he asked.

"That's my surprise. Inger has magic hands. She's been doing everybody in Hollywood for years."

He looked puzzled. "Doing what?"

She continued. "Giving massages."

"Did you do Sybil?"

A sadness clouded Inger's face. "She and her girls, some of my best clients." She folded her table and the bottom sheet.

Dina went into the bedroom leaving Stas with Inger as she continued breaking down the table and packing her things in the oversized tote bag.

"How long did you know her?"

"Sybil? About thirty years."

Not quite comprehending, he asked. "You did eight year olds?"

"No, first the Mom, then her."

Stas felt a surge of excitement. This was the first family connection besides Jennifer. "Her Mom?"

"Ya, Mimi."

He started for his desk for the photo but stopped abruptly. "Is she still living."

"Long Beach last I hear, ya, Long Beach."

"Do you know where in Long Beach?"

Dina emerged from the bedroom, looking relaxed dressed in navy slacks and a white cashmere turtleneck sweater. "Who's in Long Beach?" She looked to Stas for enlightenment.

"Mimi."

"Mimi? Who's Mimi?" She grabbed Inger as she zipped up her bag. "Wait! What? I'm missing something. Was Mimi Sybil's mother?"

Inger ignored the questions and returned to her bag. She removed the folded sheet covering a very worn, very fat Day Planner. She started to flip the fragile pages.

"I use to have the number, but it's old." She looked at Dina. "What's the last name? I don't remember."

"That was before my time." Dina looked from one to the other.

Inger sat on the edge of the recliner, wet her finger, and slowly went through the book again. "Candy, Cake, something sweet, S-W-E-E-T, Mimi Sweet." She looked around for something to write with.

The question blurted out. "Did she trick?" He avoided Dina's gaze.

"No, no she raise 'dem."

"What do you mean?" he asked.

Inger busied herself with a stubby yellow pen and slip of paper that she pulled from the back of her planner. "Here." She shoved the paper at Stas. "You call me, Dina. Have your man call me. I give him a discount."

"He's not..." Dina retreated to the sofa.

Throwing the straps of her bag over her shoulders, Inger grabbed the broad handles of the folded message table. "I'm late." She looked from Stas to Dina. "She can explain."

"Explain what?"

Inger was at the door when he realized she had carried the table as easily as she would a baby. He opened it and helped her out.

It seemed like an eternity before he got back, eager to hear Dina's explanation. He stood over her not realizing at first how menacing his stance could be. "So tell me, babe?" He sat down, making an effort to ease the tension.

She shifted, turning to look into his steel gray eyes and spoke slowly. "Sometimes there're pregnancies. We don't all have abortions. Some quit, others give their babies up for adoption, and some sorta farm the kid out, you know, pay a woman to take care of the child while she worked." She paused. "When she could, she'd visit."

He needed to know. "You had a kid?"

Dina looked away, the question catching her off guard. "No."

"How noble, you girls sending your kids to some nice old nanny."

She turned on him, the anger flushing her neck and ears. "We're not girls. Stop, stop calling us that. I'm thirty."

He wanted to back off but couldn't resist baiting her. "Isn't that a bit old."

"Was I too old for you or your newspaper buddy." She had turned the tables. "Oh, nothing happened, but he wanted me, in your bed, on your floor, on your sofa. Was he too old? So don't talk that age shit to me." The words rushed out. "I know what you want ...want to know, if I had an abortion or if I have some baby stowed away. I've never been pregnant. I don't even know if I can have children." The tears came, burning her eyes, her cheeks.

"Listen, I'm sorry. It's just that things aren't falling into place, only bits and pieces with nothing to tie anything together. This is stupid. It's not a real investigation, I can't ask for help, go through normal channels."

Dina wiped her cheeks. "What do you want?"

"To see Mimi. Let's hope she hasn't met with some tragic accident." He got up and took the cordless phone and dialed the number that Inger had given him.

"The number dialed cannot be reached in your area." The voice was metallic.

Stas slammed the receiver down. "Damn it, what's the area code for Long Beach?"

Before leaving for Long Beach, they had another argument. It was inevitable. It seemed the closer they got to something, anything, that came close to touching feelings, a wrench was thrown into the works. Stas had Sybil's PDA, but now May was dead.

He handed Dina her jacket. "Whatever plans you had for tonight, put them on hold. We'll grab something from Billy's on our way."

"On our way where?" Dina's anger and resentment began to surface.

"Long Beach."

"I don't need to go with you." She put the jacket on the arm of the sofa. "As a matter of fact, I think I'll go home."

"That's not a good idea."

"You calling your newspaper babysitter again?" She smirked at the thought.

"No, it's not a good idea because May's dead."

"Dead?" A hand to her mouth, Dina dropped to the sofa. "How?" Her tone was a desperate plea for a logical, natural reason.

He knew he had waited too long in telling her, and his reluctance had only given her more reason to distrust him. "They found her body dumped in the Hollywood Hills. She had been shot in the head."

Dina couldn't weep. She sat there, shocked, hugging herself, rocking in disbelief. "Why? May was harmless. Why?"

"Because she had the PDA and lost it." It was a clinical assessment, devoid of any feeling. He took the jacket off the sofa's arm and held it for her to slip on. "Let's go."

Dina followed, trancelike, as they exited the apartment. They rode in silence. Only a Chopin's "Polonaise" intruded on their thoughts.

"We need to get something to eat. I don't want you getting sick on me."

Dina smiled weakly but said nothing.

Stas picked up corn beef sandwiches at Billy's Deli. They ate in strained silence in the parking garage before getting back on the freeway.

Traffic on the 5 was just beginning to show signs of congestion. On the transition from the 5 to the 704, a dirty white extended-cab pickup with road-warrior mentality elicited a loud expletive from Stas when it cut him off, almost forcing him onto the shoulder.

"Bastard, fucking bastard!" Stas accelerated to merge into traffic.

The freeway seemed to take on a life of its own with a hierarchy and pecking order, ruled by eighteen wheelers with their muscle and the pickups with their attitude. On any other occasion he would have been less aggressive, but somehow May's murder and finding Mimi took precedence.

After exiting the freeway, he pulled over and consulted a computer-generated map. It took about ten minutes to find Mimi's apartment building. No one had answered the phone when he called earlier, and there was no answering machine.

Dina stayed in the car while Stas entered a well-kept apartment building. He returned a few minutes later accompanied by an attractive middle-aged woman wearing a pair of men's cords and a Laker sweatshirt. They stopped briefly on the sidewalk. She pointed down the street, then turned and walked in the opposite direction.

"Did you find Mimi?" Dina asked when he got behind the wheel and started the car.

"That was her niece. Mimi's living at a senior place over on Third."

Stas drove in the direction where the niece had pointed. He parked at a convenience store and ran in. When he returned, he tossed a carton of cigarettes behind the seat.

Dina looked at him. "I thought you'd given up smoking."

"These are for Mimi. I called her from her niece's place."

The building was a typical senior residence. The wide hallways were equipped with metal railings, and the wide doorways accommodated wheelchairs and walkers. Stas found the apartment on the second floor and knocked. Mimi must have been waiting for them or the promised carton of cigarettes. She opened the door and ushered them into an apartment tightly filled with old faded furniture that had once fit in a much larger place.

Mimi was in her late sixties or early seventies. Her purple velveteen sweats hung loosely on her thin frame. If Stas missed his cigarettes, just the act of breathing instantly filled his lungs with the stale smoke that permeated the confined space. She waved him to a shabby gold velvet sofa and took the carton in one smooth motion. Fine beads of perspiration formed on the bridge of his nose as he watched Mimi extinguish an unfiltered cigarette that looked like she rolled herself, then took out a pack from her new stash, quickly removed a cigarette, and lit up. They were soon engulfed in a smoky haze that seemed to generate a heat of its own.

Dina moved a kitchen chair close to glass doors off a miniature balcony. They had been opened a few inches to allow some outside air into the apartment.

"I don't get many calls these days, especially from the police." Mimi pulled up a chair to face the detective.

"I won't keep you long." Stas took out his notebook and pen.

"I don't get many visitors either."

"I was told that you used to keep a girl named Sybil Hansen? Do you remember her?"

Mimi stared off past Stas, then brought her gaze back.

"The Sybil I took care of was a Jones. Sybil Jones, a pretty little girl, bright as a whip. She shoulda turned out to be something." There was an air of nervous anticipation in her voice. "I didn't keep her long. Her mom got married, got out of the business. What's happened to her?"

Dina broke in, speaking softly, reverentially. "She's dead."

Mimi looked down at her gnarled hands, deformed with arthritis. "Oh, my God, Lord Jesus. Dead." She looked at Stas for confirmation. "Is there going to be any trouble?"

"No, we're just trying to locate any family. We were led to believe you were her mother."

He could sense Mimi's uneasiness as she lit another cigarette while the other still burned in the overflowing ashtray.

"Not suppose to smoke in here." She waved the newly lit cigarette towards Dina. "That's why I keep the door cracked."

He was tempted to open the door wider, flood the apartment with fresh air, but he handed her a photo instead. It was the one found in Sybil's apartment. "Do you remember this?" he asked.

Mimi's eyes filled with tears. "Her mother took this. She was another looker: blond, beautiful skin, lovely eyes. Men couldn't...."

Stas interrupted. "Was she a hooker?"

"Not on the street. No, never. She was too high-class for that. Made good money. Paid me damn good." She sighed. "Didn't last, though."

"What didn't last?"

"Her quitting the business."

"Why?" Stas asked.

Mimi fanned smoke. Dina coughed, barely able to breathe.

"She got married." Mimi looked up, smiled and put out the old smoldering butt. "Married a cop, took Sybil but the cousin stayed."

"Cousin?"

Mimi took another long drag on her cigarette. "May."

"May West?" Stas asked.

When Mimi exhaled, a deep, hacking cough racked her small frame. "Yeah, yeah."

"I don't understand? Sybil's mom and May's mom were sisters?"

"I think it was the other way around. Sybil's dad and May's mom were brother and sister." Another coughing fit.

Dina had gotten up to get Mimi water from the small kitchenette.

Mimi forgot Stas for the moment and watched Dina's movements. "Use the glass on the sink." She waited for the water and drank slowly before answering. "Sybil's dad was May's uncle."

It was Stas's turn to be surprised. "Was this cop Sybil's father?

"I don't know. Could have been. She called him dad. But you know how that is. No one ever told me one way or the other. He was such a nice guy. They took Sybil and moved, I don't know where."

"What happened to May? Was her mother a call girl?"

"Heavens no, she didn't have the looks or the body, but she could con the underwear off you without even disturbing your suit. She was a piece of work. I kept May until her mother got out of jail."

"What was Sybil's mother's name?"

"Jones, René Jones."

"Do you ever hear from her or anyone who knew her?"

"She's dead, a while back, got sick and went east."

"Her husband, was he LAPD or sheriffs?"

"I don't remember, but no use looking for him. He got shot. Somebody killed him a few years after they got married."

As Stas rose, he took a slim leather case from his jacket and gave a business card to Mimi. "If you remember anything about Sybil and René, give me a call."

Mimi squinted at the card, put it in her pocket, and lit another cigarette. As they left, Stas wondered how long the carton would last.

Before he could start the car, the cell phone rang. He looked at the display. It wasn't a number he recognized, but he pushed the "OK" button and recognized Livia's excited voice.

"Stas, Stas."

"Livia, what's wrong?"

"Mrs. Levi just called me. The police are at the building." The words rushed out in a torrent.

"Hey, hey, slow down." He heard the intake of breath.

"Some asshole broke into the building, even my apartment, then beat up the Willards. Pulled the gun on them in the entrance, made 'um let them in their apartment. Hit old Mrs. Levi in the shoulder. Scared the shit out of her."

Dina had come to life when she heard him call Livia's name.

"Where are you?" he asked.

"Palm Springs. I'm leaving now, but it'll take me two hours."

"We're in Long Beach. I'll see you there." He hung up.

"What's happened?"

"Someone broke into Livia's apartment and also a couple named the Willards. Who's Mrs. Levi?"

Dina ignored his question. "My place?"

"She didn't say, but your place...."

"What about my place?"

"It's been trashed." He wanted to turn and look at Dina, but he had to keep his eyes on the road. "It was done before, probably by May, looking for Sybil's PDA that I'm sure she hid there, since she knew you were gone. What better place? If someone else found it, she was in the clear. They'd think you stole it."

"Me?"

"It's like tag, babe. You'd be it." He let the idea sink in before he told her more bad news. "She did a number on your bedroom, got into stuff in your bathroom."

"Oh, shit." Dina sank back in her seat.

It took over an hour for the drive to Dina's apartment building. He still had the remote to open the garage gate. Instead of parking first, he let Dina out at the elevator.

"You go on up to your apartment. I'll come up after I talk to the police, if they're still here. If anyone stops you, don't volunteer anything. They may send a uniform to talk to everyone, see if they saw anything. You didn't. You weren't here."

She took her keys and asked, "Are you leaving?"

"I'm parking on the street and going through the front. Remember, Livia called me."

Dina was at the elevator when he lowered the passenger window and called after her.

"I'll come up when I finish at Livia's."

Stas showed his badge and ID to the uniformed officer at the door. Cleo Miller was the lead. He didn't see her partner, Winston Owens.

Miller looked up at the intrusion, then smiled. "You slumming?"

"A friend called. She's out in the desert. I feel badly, since I recommended the little R 'n R."

Miller looked over the trashed apartment. "The way this place looks, she should be happy she listened to you. Somebody could have been killed." She picked a framed photo off the floor. It was a picture of Livia in one of her skimpy dance costumes. "What does she do?"

"Dance ...not now. Livia used to dance professionally."

"You seem to know a lot about her, so is there something I should know?"

"We're just friends." Stas interjected. "What happened?"

"Two assailants entered through the front, accosted a couple going out, took them up to their apartment, duct taped them. Took money, jewelry, but that robbery didn't seem to have been their goal. Their apartment doesn't look anything like this, then, apparently for no reason, they beat the old man before they left. This was their last stop."

Miller walked to the door and showed him the shattered lock. The knob hung at an awkward angle; the wood around the opening was splintered.

Stas frowned. "They really wanted in."

They walked back to the living room, where cushions were ripped, foam strewn all over the carpet. In the kitchen, canisters of sugar and flour had been emptied onto the floor. The freezer door had been left open, and containers had been turned around with some thrown on the floor, where they lay, melting. Stas looked at the mess and hoped they hadn't made it to Dina's place.

In the bedroom, drawers had been turned out; the mattress and box springs flipped on their sides, and the contents of a jewelry box had been emptied onto the surface of the dresser.

Miller pointed to some rings and bracelets with her pen. "These look like some decent pieces. They could've gotten fair prices even on the street, yet they left them."

"You think they were interrupted?" Stas asked.

She shook her head. "If they had enough time to do all this, they had enough time to dump this in a pocket. No, they were looking for something, something small, compact. Robbing the Willards was a red herring. I don't buy it."

The bathroom was a repeat of the bedroom. As they moved down the hallway, back to the living room, Stas stopped to straighten the picture he had hung. The tech team wrapped up and was leaving when Livia bounded into the apartment. Her ever-present exuberance vanished when she saw the condition of her living room.

Stas took Livia's arm, helping her to the sofa.

"Livia, this is Detective Miller. She's the one investigating the robbery."

Livia held onto Stas's hand a little too tightly and a little too long as she surveyed the damage. "Thanks for coming." She nodded at Miller, then looked up at Stas. "You're not going to investigate?"

"No, Livia, this is out of my area, and I'm still on vacation. You'll need to let Detective Miller know what's missing."

"Now?"

"No, she'll give you some time to go through your things, and I'm going to get out of her hair. She needs to asks you some questions."

Miller walked him to the door.

Stas smiled and waved good-bye to Livia. "Keep me posted if you find anything interesting."

Miller looked back at Livia. "And you keep me posted if there's more to this relationship."

When he left the apartment, he took the elevator to Dina's.

Dina opened the door. Incense was burning in its ceramic bowl; the heat had been turned on, and the place was beginning to feel like it was lived in. Stas followed her to the bedroom where she had returned the drawers to the chest and was in the process of folding and replacing her underwear.

"You're lucky, they tore Livia's place apart."

"If it's worse than this, then I don't want to see it."

He sat on the edge of the bed while she busied herself with her dresser.

"Why do you think they broke into Livia's apartment?"

"When May didn't find the PDA, she made one of two assumptions. Either you had it, but she didn't know you'd been back, or Livia had it. She'd been up here. The door was open. May had no way of knowing what she saw. Then, to top it off, Livia threatened her. If she was meeting someone to give him the PDA, she had to sell someone out. Livia was convenient."

"Him? Who? You think Matt was behind this?"

"Mrs. Levi said the two men were wearing black oxfords, white socks, and brown uniform pants. Sound like anyone we know?"

"Matt's security guards." Dina joined him on the foot of the bed. "So, what do we do now?"

"Go back to my place and take another look at Sybil's stuff. Did you check the bathroom?"

"It wasn't as bad as this. She used my makeup. A lot of good it did her."

"She wanted to look good for someone. She wouldn't make the effort for another woman, but she would for a man, the one she had promised the PDA to," Stas mused.

"Matt?"

Stas nodded. "Get your gear, babe."

"Can't I stay just one night? Can't we?"

He smiled. "We could if the stuff was here. C'mom, I'll buy you a drink, better yet, I'll buy a hot fudge sundae."

It had started to rain as they left Dina's place and drove back to Glendale. Stas exited the freeway at Brand and drove to Mary Ann's Coffee Shop on Colorado. He pulled into the lot and parked in a handicapped space near the entrance.

"Won't you get a ticket?"

Stas reached over and popped the glove compartment, pulling out a blue and white handicapped placard which he hung on the arm of the rearview mirror.

"Be sure to limp when you go in." He reached for her arm. "Watch the puddle."

She managed to run for the entrance without getting soaked. He was still laughing when the waiter seated them. "I always wondered why they always seat you in the back when they're not busy."

"Maybe we look suspicious," Dina added.

Dina handed her damp jacket to Stas which he hung with his on the backs of a couple of empty chairs near them.

"Does your hair always do that when it rains?

"Does what?" She touched the springy curls at her temple. "Yes, and they turn to icicles when it snows."

They ordered and waited in silence.

Within minutes, the waitress brought them two cups of muddy coffee.

"You sure you don't want something stronger?" he asked.

"Coffee's fine. Anyway, you drink too much."

"It's an occupational hazard, but that's okay. When I get home ... we'll go through Sybil's things one more time. I would give anything to see May's phone records, see who she called in the last couple days."

"Can you do that? Isn't it illegal?"

"Not if the records belong to someone who's dead, and we're conducting an investigation. Or sometimes if they're not dead." he laughed.

"I don't know if I want to know more about what you guys can do, just when I was beginning to.... Do all of you carry handicapped signs?" She sipped her coffee.

The ring of Stas's cell phone interrupted their conversation. "Nowak."

"Stas, this is your mother... this is Helena."

"I know who it is."

"You came to my house and went through my things. You are not the KGB. If you want her belongings, come and get them in the morning and don't ever touch my things again."

"Suppose I have something to do tomorrow morning?"

"Come tomorrow morning." She hung up.

Dina looked concerned as the call had changed Stas's demeanor.

"Who was that?"

"Helena."

"Your mother?"

Stas cut her a look.

"I'm sorry. You know who I mean." Dina continued. "What do you call her now?"

"I hadn't thought of that. She's my aunt. She wants me to pick up Irina's things."

TWENTY-SEVEN

Both Robert Aagard and Ed Lawson had rented elegantly furnished executive apartments off Wilshire near Westwood. Lawson had purchased a house in Hollywood and was planning to move his family there as soon as escrow closed. Gwen commuted from Fresno to Los Angeles at least twice a week and would eventually move down after resigning her post with the Fresno Police Commission.

Lawson sat in one of a pair of richly upholstered wing chairs next to a fireplace. He was nursing a glass of mineral water with a twist of lemon. The rain outside could be heard even through the double-paned windows. Lawson closed his eyes, soothed by the downpours' steady rhythm.

Robert Aagard returned from the kitchen with a can of beer. Even in casual clothes, Aagard was impeccably groomed in black slacks and heather gray long-sleeved cashmere sweater. "The press conference was great. Hunter made a DVD that we need to review. If you're going to use parts of the speech again, you need to polish it." Aagard drank from the can, then turned it around to read the label. "This is a good pilsner. I usually don't like German beer." He turned back to Lawson almost as an after thought. "Hunter also recorded the highlights on the 10 and 11 o'clock news. He wants to have it edited so he can present it to several campaign strategists he wants us to consider."

"Were there any negatives?" Lawson asked.

"None, so far, from the commentators or the press."

"Can we trust this Hunter fellow?"

"Hunter Blackstone comes with impeccable credentials. We need information. He gets it. We need something done. He does it."

"Well, I'm anxious to hear what he thinks. God, what a high. The lights, reporters, cops. I love it. I love the theme. People love to hear you're cleaning up their shit. Promise you're going to lower taxes, reform local government, then the state, they love that. Then take on the nation. It can be a powerful platform. Next to crime, they want you to bring back good solid American morality." Lawson laughed. "I feel a revolution coming on."

"Don't get carried away. You mustn't lose sight of our goals. You still have to win the primary. Your opposition hasn't even gotten in gear. Some may try to link you with the mess in Sacramento and the past administration. That's why we're paying Hunter. We can't have anyone or anything tarnish your image. You have great potential and with that comes the power. Our backers see it. What we have to do now is make the people see that they need a different change."

"I think we've covered every angle."

Both men turned from their conversation when Matt Brown entered. He pulled a straight-back chair to the unlit fireplace. "Why don't you have a fire in this thing. It's cold enough outside. Add a little atmosphere."

"It's just gas." Lawson added.

Brown looked for the key that started the logs.

"So we're all set with the fundraiser tomorrow night?" Aagard asked.

"Yeah, Hunter had the schedule." Brown looked around for a drink. "I can't believe you, sitting here like you're having drinks at your fucking country club when we still have our little problem."

"What do you mean? I thought she was taken care of the other night? The raid was the primary reason for the press conference." The color was draining from Lawson's face. "I had to call in some favors to pull it off. I could need those chits later."

"My man had her, but she walked," Matt said.

"How, how? Where were *you*?" Lawson's tone was nervous, agitated.

Aagard just looked on calmly and drank his beer.

"That cop is becoming a real thorn in your side, our sides." Lawson added.

Aagard rose to take the empty can to the kitchen. "Perhaps we can take care of the cop and his whore when he goes back to work. She's got to go back to *work* too. He can't afford to keep her."

Brown stared into the fireplace. "I got the Doc's number."

Aagard barked back. "Dammit, I told you to leave it 'til later."

Brown defiantly turned on both men. "Why the hell do I have to wait 'til later. We're sitting on a gold mine." He looked directly at Lawson. "If you get elected, you're made. I haven't seen a dime from the foundation. I have expenses. All I do is front, when do I see real money?"

"Who's going to believe the hard drive crashed if clients start getting collection letters?" Lawson asked.

"Who's going to ask?" Brown sat back in his chair. "There's nothing on the hard drive. Anyway, it's too late. I contacted the Doc. He's got five days to cough it up."

Aagard stood in the doorway. "You are a dammed fool. Suppose he goes to the cops."

Brown shook his head and smiled at the suggestion. "Would you? He's an award winning scientist who just sold his invention for millions. He's in the news. He's a credible voice that people at the top listen to. He can't afford to go to the cops. He doesn't want people to know he's fucking a whore."

Aagard frowned. "Don't underestimate cripples. Just because his legs have atrophied doesn't mean his brain has."

"He'll pay up." Brown rose. "We got him by his little hairy balls. I'm not worried." He straightened his leather jacket and headed for the door. "Tell Hunter to call me on my cell to reconfirm the time of your pickup." He smiled, but it was an angry, venomous smile.

When Brown left, Aagard returned to his wing chair still holding the empty beer can which he crushed and tossed in the fireplace.

"You think he's a problem?" Lawson nervously asked.

"Potentially! You know, Sybil wouldn't play his game. He never could jump in and out of her bed like he does with some of the others. Matt has made a serious miscalculation."

"With the money?" Lawson looked concerned.

"With our patience. I'll have to make some inquiries."

When Lawson entered the condo, he stumbled over a large brown Bloomingdale's shopping bag. Several others littered the living room floor. Gwen had crashed on the sofa, a tall, half-finished drink stood on the coffee table. Her suitcase had fallen to the floor near the dining table.

"When did you get in?"

Gwen opened her eyes to peer at her husband, then glanced at her watch. "A little while ago."

Ed looked around the room as if calculating the cost of the parcels and bags. "You lugged all this around with you?'

"We took taxis."

"We?"

"Beth and I. Robert suggested that we have a day out, have lunch, shop, get our nails done." She flashed her nails. "I took his advice and let Beth take me shopping so I could present the proper image for a candidate's wife." She forced a smile as she sat up and reached for her drink.

Ed wandered over to her suitcase and stood it upright, then picked up the airline ticket receipt.

"I'll get that!" But it was too late.

He waved the paper at her. "This says you flew down last night." It was a cold, hard fact, spoken without emotion.

"I stayed at a hotel."

"Why in hell would you stay in a hotel when you have a fucking condo. Just tell me why would you stay in a god-damn hotel?"

"Because I didn't want to sleep here with you."

She rose and walked over, trying to snatch, with her free hand, the ticket receipt. Ed jerked back, giving Gwen a violent shove across her luggage. Caught off-balance, she tried to steady herself and catch the glass falling from her hand, but everything seemed to move in slow motion. The drink slipped from her grasp, spilling its contents onto the white carpet. As if in a daze, she watched the irregular stain spread before the back of her head hit the credenza.

"You bastard!" She spat the words out like venom through clenched teeth and growing pain. Before she even felt the back of her head, she could feel the swelling and a rivulet of warm blood trickling through her hair and down her neck.

Ed made no effort to help Gwen up but stared at her sitting on the floor.

"You know, if you had an accident, I would get thousands of sympathy votes. The poor, widowed candidate left with two young boys to raise."

TWENTY-NINE

The lawn in front of the Nowaks' house looked even more desolate despite several days of rain. Stas wondered why theirs was the only yard on the block that seemed to will its own demise. He parked in the driveway and glanced over to the neighbors' on the left when he got out of the car. Their roses bloomed in perfusion. Life and death, what a contrast, but then, that's what his work was all about.

Although he had the door key out, he rang the bell. He knew that Vlade would be sitting in his well-worn recliner with his light on reading the *Times*. Helena might be playing a hand of solitaire at a snack tray.

Before he left his apartment, he'd taken a quick shower and put on jeans, black running shoes, gray sweatshirt, and leather jacket. He didn't even remember combing his hair. He stood on the porch waiting for someone to open the door and nervously raked his fingers through his hair and hoped it looked decent. He finally turned the key and entered the house. Vlade was reading his paper. Helena didn't even look up as she played on her solitaire piles. They sat in the morning chill, warmed by their woolen sweaters and heavy woolen socks, gifts sent from a relative in Chicago who liked to spend the long, Midwestern winters knitting in front of the TV. Stas thought of the knitted slippers he liked to wear around the apartment even in California.

Vlade dropped a section of paper to the floor and looked up at Stas before taking up another section. "You on a stake out?"

"No, I'm still on vacation."

Helena glanced up. "You look like you need a bath and a haircut."

Stas could feel the resentment creeping in. "Unshaven, unkempt, slovenly, well, a lifetime of lies will do that to a man." He turned to Helena. "Where are Irina's things?"

"I started to put them in a bag, but then, you already know where they are. Take them and don't ever go through my things again."

She followed him to her bedroom. As usual, everything was in order. A window was open by a chair, letting in a stream of cold. Helena always aired out the house in the early morning, winter or summer. There was a large, empty cardboard box at the foot of the bed. She stood in the doorway. "You can put her things in the box."

Stas couldn't remember the last time he'd heard Helena use Irina's name. He went to the closet, pulled a string to turn on the bare-bulbed light. Parting the first row of Helena's clothes, he took the garment bag from the second row and again pulled the string that broke off in his hand. Reaching up, he tried to unscrew the hot bulb with his bare hand. He looked around for something like a cloth. There, in the right hand corner on a narrow shelf, was a carved wooden box. Forgetting the light, he took the box and opened it by the window. The box contained trinkets, clips, pins. He emptied the contents onto the dresser.

"Where did this box come from?"

Helena moved into the room from her spot at the door. "That box? It came from Poland. Some friend of the family made them for us."

"Us?"

"One for me and…."

"Where's Irina's?"

"How would I know?"

"I want to keep this one for a while."

"Take it." Helena brushed the air, dismissing the box. "I don't want it back. I don't want any of this." She walked over to the window. "What else?"

"Just curious, why did..." He groped for the right words. "Why did everything have to be so difficult, so unloving, so controlled?"

"Control? You ask me about control. I didn't want you to turn out like her." She sank into her chair. "I had to purge you."

"Purge me! What does that mean? Hell! I was a kid."

"Yes, and she was a kid once. You have to start early. Why do you complain? Look at you, a detective."

"A lot of good it does me when I don't have a clue who I am."

He dumped the garment bag in the cardboard container and put the carved box on top. When he got to the door, he turned back. "Why did Irina stop coming over? You even stopped talking about her, like she was dead."

"She was to me. She tried to break our agreement. She wanted you back." Helena dropped her face into her hands and quietly sobbed.

It was the first time in his life that he had ever seen her cry.

Dina had awakened long after Stas had gone. She hadn't realized how tired she was with all of their running around. Even though she didn't particularly like the police, she had gained a new respect for them and the intricacies of their work. After making a pot of coffee, she warmed up some leftover Chinese take-out but had to search most of the drawers for a packet of soy sauce and laughed when she found several in an individual baggy stored with other baggies containing little packets of mustard, catsup, and plum sauce all zipped-locked and placed in a wire basket in the refrigerator. *All this order, I wonder if he'll ever change, get sloppy in his old age?*

While she drank coffee, she remembered back two years when she looked down from her hospital bed and was impressed by his highly polished shoes. Her eyes had risen to take in his well-tailored suit, crisp white shirt, expensive silk tie. She had always wondered if she would ever meet a man like him, a man she found desirable. She remembered feeling warm all over whenever she thought of him. Now, finally, they had connected.

Dina made a call to Bennett West and told him what she wanted. Bennett was the kind of guy who could get his hands on just about anything in the shortest time and at the best price. He even beat the internet, and he delivered. West told her it would take a few days, and he would get back to her. He called twice within an hour. They sealed the deal with a promised price. The hard part would be to confirm the delivery.

She heard the door just as West hung up, but there wasn't the usual call to her. She took the largest butcher knife from the cutlery block and cautiously peered into the living room. Stas was arranging more things on the coffee table.

Dina put the knife on the counter and joined him. "Here's coffee."

He looked up and took the hot mug.

"Haven't we been over all this before?" she asked.

"There's one addition." He pointed to the second carved box.

Dina sat on the sofa.

He got the PDA from his desk and lowered the volume on the stereo. The poignant sax still set the tone for even more unexplored territory. He sat next to her and started to input a new password. R-E-N-E, nothing happened.

"Where did you get this other box?"

"From Helena."

"That's really a coincidence, I mean having two boxes that look so much alike."

Stas frowned. "Yeah, but I don't believe in coincidence?"

"What did Helena tell you about them?"

"They were gifts from somebody when they were children in Poland."

She almost spilled her coffee as she sat the mug on the edge of the table.

He nervously looked at Dina. "Two sisters, two hand carved boxes from Poland, one at home and one at Sybil's."

She inched closer. "If Irina was Sybil's mother that means that Sybil's your half-sister."

He didn't respond.

Dina touched his hand and stared into eyes that were the color of stormy seas. "You know what that means?"

The storm had passed. "What does it mean, babe?"

Dina had no response but watched him punch in another set of letters, I-R-I-N-A. Still nothing.

"What would Irina be in English?" Dina asked.

At first, he didn't understand.

"You know, like Jose is Joseph in English," she added.

"Irene." There was a hint of animation in his voice. "That's where she got René." He tried I-R-E-N-E. Nothing for the third time. He put the PDA back on the coffee table. "If people knew you, knew your history, you'd want a password that they'd never figure out, something from your mother's past or your father's, if you knew him." He picked up the PDA again and tried the maiden name of the two sisters.

"But wouldn't Irina's maiden name appear on something. You know, a birth certificate or marriage license?"

Stas's body language registered disappointment as he pushed the two boxes aside and snapped shut the tops of the PDAs. He slumped on the sofa flexing his shoulders, trying to relieve the knot in the muscles.

Dina reached over and examined the boxes again, looking intently at the rough-hewn design. "You know they're not exactly alike."

"They weren't meant to be. Some local guy probably carved them to make a few bucks. He didn't try to make them the same, didn't have time for perfection."

"Yeah, I can see that the patterns are different." She pushed the boxes back together and turned her attention to Stas. "You need a massage."

He straightened his back and looked at her. "You calling in Inger the Hulk?"

"No, I'll do it myself, at least I can loosen your shoulders."

She went over to his reading area and tossed the pillow and blanket to the floor. She moved the chair away from the wall. Its back was low enough so that she could reach his neck and shoulders.

"I wish we had some candles and incense."

Stas didn't respond.

"Get over here and take off your sweater." She patted the back of the chair.

He moved over, eased himself down, and leaned backwards towards her outstretched hands. Dina worked his neck with gentle strokes, caressing more than massaging with gliding movements, then continued by strongly kneading the tight muscles in his shoulders before working on his upper back. Her nimble fingers started to have an affect. Stas moaned as he yielded to her artful manipulation. She was doing more than relieving his tension.

Turning slowly, he reached back and grabbed one of Dina's hands pulling her around to face him. She hesitated, before stepping out of her sweats and thong and helping him ease out of his pants and shorts. She kicked the puddle of clothing out of her way and straddled his hips.

Even before she touched him, guided him to her, he felt the urgency course through his body. As she moved on him, his first reaction was to become the aggressor, but he relaxed and let her take control. The awkwardness of their positions intensified his excitement, but he wasn't sure how long he could hold on.

He closed his eyes, trying to slow his breathing, slow his heart rate, delay the inevitable. When he opened his eyes, Dina was damp with sweat. He grabbed her hips, slowing her movements. His mind sought a distraction as he tried to control his release. Images of the past, of dissatisfaction, of regrets, of pleasures, and repressed desires merged with images of women, their faces distorted in passion, as they superimposed themselves one on the other until the vision of Irina shocked him into an agonizing spasm.

"Dina!" He opened his eyes again to face her.

Moist ringlets of hair fell across her forehead as she clenched her muscles anticipating the final paroxysm.

Her cry was one of intense pleasure as she collapsed with a shutter onto his chest. She didn't open her eyes but nuzzled into his neck blowing on his damp skin. When she didn't stir, he strained to reach to the floor and retrieve the blanket to cover their nakedness.

He listened to Dina's shallow breathing, then touched her damp hair, watched her doze, at first with little fits and starts like a infant trying to find just the right position in her nurturer's arms. He was surprised to find himself enjoying this new intimacy. He closed his eyes and rested.

Stas finally had to move his arm to keep it from going numb with Dina's weight. She shifted, slowly opening her eyes. When she rose up and turned from him, he pulled her back, then felt her tense. She was staring at the photos on the opposite wall.

"What are those pictures?" she whispered.

Her question took a second to register. Facing them were six large sepia-toned prints made from photos he'd taken on his last trip to Poland. He had fallen in love with the Highlanders and their beautiful surroundings.

"Zakopane, in Poland. I took them five years ago."

They were staring at the panorama view of the mountains of Zakopane. He then remembered the street vendors selling statues and crucifixes crudely carved right there on the side of the road. He could still smell the warm, damp shavings of the dark wood heaped at the feet of the local artisans.

He eased Dina off his lap and went over to the boxes, holding them up to the prints. The cravings were an awkward rendition of the mountains of Zakopane.

Leaving Dina ignorant of his discovery, Stas returned to Sybil's PDA and typed in the letters, Z-A-K-O-P-A-N-A. The screen opened up, giving him access. "I'm in."

Still wrapped in the blanket, Dina threw him his pants and sweatshirt. She went to shower and dress, leaving him for most of the afternoon with Sybil's little hand-held computer.

He later moved from the coffee table to his desk where he took notes and typed information into his own laptop before copying Sybil's files onto his new PDA.

Dina had busied herself keeping the coffee pot going and ordering pizza for an early supper since there'd been no lunch. Stas drank a lot of the strong, black brew. The caffeine kept him going. However, the coffee was too strong for her so she switched to tea. Around seven she carried the pizza leftovers to the kitchen and cleaned up.

When Stas closed the lid of his laptop, he looked over at Dina. "All the time I worked Vice, I had no idea." He could sense the tension as she tightly gripped the mug.

"No idea about what?"

"About the money and the clients."

"What do you plan to do with it?" She nodded at the data stick that he held in his hand.

"I don't know. In the wrong hands, it could..."

She didn't hear the rest of the sentence as he took the PDA and the data stick to the bedroom.

When he returned, he was dressed in black cords and a gray polo shirt. He carried his shoes and sat down to put them on.

"We're going out, babe."

She looked down at her sweatshirt. There was a red blob of tomato sauce just under the P. "Like this?"

"No, I guess you need to get dressed."

"Where are we going?"

"To the Pasadena Library to read some old newspapers."

"You won't find anything about Sybil in the paper."

"I'm not looking for Sybil. It's Jones."

Stas waited for Dina to change. As they were leaving, Stas grabbed a black leather brief case and put everything from the coffee table and his desk in it. In the garage, he opened the trunk of his car and deposited the case. He grimaced at the collected grime that had built up since their trip up north.

"Got to get you detailed, babe." He spoke lovingly to the car.

Dina turned. "I thought that was a little term of endearment for me."

He closed the trunk. "You and the car, but let a woman in your life, and your wheels go to hell."

"Why Pasadena?

"Because that's where Irina's husband worked. We're looking for him and a cop killing that happened between 1971 and '76. The year might be closer to '73. He was Officer or Detective Jones, may have been working vice. I don't know if he was killed off duty or on."

"Does it make a difference?"

"It could, but for right now we just want to find out when he died."

"Why don't you just call Pasadena Police?"

"I will when we have more details. Remember, babe, we're not official so I have to tread lightly, especially on someone else's turf. I really have no reason to ask them for any info, but the more I can find out, if and when I contact them, the less I'll need to ask them."

"I think I understand."

"The story would have made the headlines, especially in the local paper. There should also be an article, probably on the front page, of the funeral. Look for a photo with a lot of police in uniform or one of his wife at the burial site. Also, check out the obit page."

"Obit?"

"Obituary, death notices."

"Okay. Do I get my junior cadet badge if I do a good job?"

"I'll give you something much better than a badge, babe."

The Pasadena Public Library, Main Branch, was located on Walnut across the street from the Superior Court House and a block away from Pasadena Police Headquarters. He parked in the back and removed the briefcase from the trunk.

The main hall had a classic reading-room ambience with long tables and lamps that looked like those traditional college dining halls of detective movies set in Oxford or Cambridge. At the reference desk, Stas presented his badge and ID to a lovely young lady whose stylish chignon had replaced the dowdy bun of spinster librarians of the past. She introduced herself as Tracy when she came around the high mahogany reference desk and held out her hand to Stas.

"This is my assistant, Ms. Goode."

Tracy smiled at Dina but did not offer her hand. "Nice to meet you."

"I want to look at back issues of the *Star News* and the *Los Angeles Times*."

Tracy escorted them through the periodical room to a stairway that led to the basement. There, she pointed out six large machines and explained that back issues of newspapers were still stored on microfilm. Another attractive young woman sat at a desk in the middle of the room. She stood when they approached and held out her hand when introduced to Stas.

"This is Detective Nowak and his assistant. Jade will help you with anything you need."

Stas caught a light whiff of her perfume and wrinkled his nose slightly. "Jade? What a beautiful name to match your lovely eyes. I don't think I've ever seen eyes so green."

Jade blushed, then escorted them to a wall of tall, gray file cabinets.

"The microfilm's filed here according to paper and date. When you have your microfilm, just take it to a reader."

She helped them find their first spools from *The Star News*. She walked them over to three empty machines next to each other. As Stas was about to sit, Jade touched his arm and directed him to the machine at the end.

"This one is better."

Dina sat next to him and waited while Jade threaded the spool of microfilm into the reader.

"If you want to print, just put your coins in here." She indicated a slot marked "20 cents" and pointed. "The copy will come out here. Let me know if you need any help." Jade returned to her desk where a young man awaited her assistance.

"Does this happen all the time?" Dina asked.

Stas leaned over to set up the reel of microfilm she would be reading. "Does what?"

"Women falling all over themselves to 'help' you out."

"I didn't notice." He smiled as he showed her how to advance the image and scan up and down the page.

"Liar. That badge, you cops use it like some kind of chick magnet. You whip it out, and the women melt in a heap at your feet."

"Gets them every time." He laughed and turned back to his machine.

They worked silently, trying to adjust the speed of the pages as they moved across the grainy images. It was like trying to read copies of old black-and-white movies. Dina started with 1971; he took 1972. The first hour dragged, but they got through their years.

Dina took a break and went to the ladies' room. He repressed the urge to get up and stretch or go look for coffee. When Dina returned, she found 1973 already on her reel.

"Are there people who just sit and read these things all day?"

"I'm sure someone does. Don't worry, I'll find something a little more glamorous for you." He turned back to his machine.

Dina stopped advancing her page when she viewed an artist's rendition of a man's suit that was outlandishly garish. She leaned over to Stas. "Can you see yourself in this? It's called 'the Country Look', but it doesn't say what country." She laughed. "And it only cost $84.90."

He scooted his chair over to take a look. "I wouldn't need the badge with that suit. Women would just throw themselves at me or take my gun and shoot me." As he returned to his machine, he scanned over a full-page ad for vodka. "And I can get a half gallon of Jatta Vodka for $6.66. Can't even get a shot for that today."

"Maybe that's a blessing in disguise."

Stas didn't want to discuss his drinking, so he turned back to his machine. Ten minutes later, Dina took another break.

"Where have you been?"

"I checked out the first floor. This is really a nice library."

"You keep taking breaks, we'll never get through. I'll have Tracy give you the grand tour when we finish."

"I'll pass." Dina rubbed the back of her neck and turned back to reading her screen.

Stas stopped his reel and leaned into the page. "I think I found it."

She stood to his side to read the article. "He's good looking."

"Aren't we all!"

She slapped his shoulder.

"You could be held liable for damaging public property," he said.

"I didn't hit the machine."

"No, me." He stood to get at his wallet and take out some bills. "I'll need some change."

While Stas made change at a machine at the far end of the room, Dina sat in his seat and read. When he returned, he fed the machine some coins and printed several pages, then advanced the reel and printed an article about a downed officer's funeral.

He returned both reels to *The Star-News* cabinet and took out a reel covering the same time period in the *Los Angeles Times*. Loading went quickly, and Stas soon found almost identical material. The printer cranked out several more pages.

Just as he retrieved the pages and put them in the briefcase, a loud male voice came over the intercom: "The library will be closing in fifteen minutes."

"We're out of here, babe." He patted the top of the closed briefcase. "Now I have enough to ask Pasadena PD for help." He returned the reel to the cabinet, helped Dina into her jacket, and grabbed his own. "I'm starved. Let's get something to eat."

As they started for the stairs, he waved at Jade. She smiled coyly and waved back.

Stas suggested they have Italian but settled on a coffee shop on Arroyo Seco. He didn't really care about the food since it wasn't Chinese or Polish. Dina wanted whatever she ate to be followed by a hot-fudge sundae.

The hostess seated them in a large booth near an area usually reserved for groups. It was dark and empty. She smiled at them as if they were lovers until Stas flashed his badge and told her they needed to be away from the other diners so they could talk.

He easily put away two cheeseburgers with fries and slaw while Dina munched her turkey club. What he really wanted was a vodka and a cigarette but could have neither in this coffee-shop setting. Dina left half of her sandwich so she could have room for dessert.

"I'm puzzled." She pointed the chocolate covered spoon in Stas's direction. "You haven't reacted to any of this."

"How should I react?"

"Get angry, cry, drink, hit something."

"I already drink too much, remember? So should I abuse you or kick my dirty car?" He looked away for a moment. "When it all sinks in, I guess it won't be pretty. You may not want to be there."

She scraped the bottom of the bowl. "I guess you've gone into your detective mode. I mean, now I see police work from a different point of view, but it's still like being in the front seat of that careening roller coaster."

He reached over and wiped a dollop of whipped cream from her nose. He smiled but wasn't about to reveal his thoughts as he licked the cream from his finger.

THIRTY

It was one of those typical Southern California winter evenings. The air was crisp and clear. Both Lawson and Aagard wore lightweight topcoats to ward off the bone-chilling cold that was promised. As the remnants of the enthusiastic crowd exiting Lawson's rally still hung on, a black Mercedes and a black Lincoln Towncar were brought to the curb. Others who had been in the audience dispersed, heading for the parking lot or walking to their cars parked on the streets.

Ralph Townsend, dressed in his signature corduroy jacket, pulled his collar up to repel the chill in the night air. Before he could reach the street, an excited and energized Sharon Delfino, Lawson's campaign aide, grabbed Townsend's sleeve.

"Mr. Lawson would like a word with you." She ushered him over to a group standing by a black S Class Mercedes.

"Mr. Townsend, I'd like you to meet my old friend and advisor." Lawson motioned Aagard over. "Robert, this is Ralph Townsend, the *Times* reporter, I told you about."

Both men shook hands. They all moved towards the cars.

"Ralph did a great article." Lawson continued. "I'm sure he'll put a positive spin on this evening's gathering as well."

"I was surprised to see so many of the black clergy here tonight." Townsend commented.

"That's one of the great fallacies in this current political environment. The liberals think the black churches aren't conservative, when those congregations are just as conservative as fundamentalists. Anyway, I'll save that discussion for another night. We're going to have plenty of evenings like this if the positive response tonight is any indication."

Townsend started back towards the street. "I've got to get to my computer if I want to make my deadline. Otherwise, you'll never get my take on this evening."

A black Mercedes sped out of the driveway into the street. Its occupants were invisible behind tinted windows.

"Wasn't that our car?" Aagard asked pointing toward the first car as it disappeared in traffic.

Lawson turned. "Maybe Brown needed it. We're okay. This one's good."

The driver of the second car stood by the back door of an older black Lincoln Towncar, holding it open for Lawson and Aagard as they climbed in. Seeing that they were settled in, he closed the doors and walked to the driver's side. With keys jangling, he was unbuttoning his jacket when Sharon pressed her head to the rear left window. She could see very little through the darkly tinted glass.

The driver reached in and turned on the ignition in order to lower the rear left window.

"Matt left me! And my car's at headquarters. Can I get a ride?" Sharon asked.

Lawson moved over the hump to make room. "Get in."

She climbed in behind the driver, who hit the lights, rolled up the windows, and moved out into traffic.

Lawson sneezed repeatedly and leaned towards Aagard.

"What's wrong?"

"The perfume. Sharon's perfume."

"You want to get in the front?"

"We'll lose the lead car if we stop." Lawson took out his handkerchief and covered his nose.

"The driver can phone."

"Never mind."

The Lincoln accelerated as it moved down the on ramp onto the freeway. With light traffic, the driver effortlessly glided into the second lane.

"I'm sorry Gwen couldn't make it."

"The boys come in tonight, and she's still nursing that fall."

A black Chevy Impala followed, changed lanes, sharply cutting off another car. It kept pace behind the Lincoln.

The driver repeatedly glanced into his rearview mirror. "Damn it!"

Lawson leaned over the front seat. "Is there a problem?"

"I don't know. Some guy behind just cut off a car to get behind us. He's been following."

Aagard took out his cell phone and dialed but got no response. "Get off the freeway!"

The driver accelerated, keeping his eye on his rear-view mirror. The Impala accelerated to maintain the same speed and constant distance until both cars reached a stretch where there was little traffic.

Aagard tried to see out of the rear window. "Are you getting off?"

"Yes, sir! At the next off ramp!"

In the Impala, a black-gloved hand switched off the car's headlights and reached for a white button on the gearshift. The engine revved to a high pitch. The car bolted forward and swung to the left, pulling along side the Lincoln.

The black tinted window on the Impala's rear passenger side effortlessly rolled down, revealing a masked figure who leaned out with a modified AR-15 and sprayed thirty rounds into the car before speeding off into the night.

The Lincoln leapt as if a hammer had been dropped on the gas, veered to the right, and up the embankment leaving a million tiny fragments of glass in its wake when it slammed into a sound wall. The car stalled, as if momentarily caught on a hook, then rolled over and fell back onto the freeway. A rivulet of gasoline from a rupture in its tank flowed under it.

The scream of brakes and the cacophony of horns all added to the chaos. The hood of the Lincoln was peeled back, releasing steam from the radiator. There was no movement from anyone inside.

THIRTY-ONE

The coffee table in Stas's apartment had once again become the "war room" in miniature. The boxes had been pushed to one side. The PDA had been returned to the desk. Printouts from The Pasadena *Star-News* and LA *Times* were spread out over the surface of the table. Stas sat back in his recliner as Dina returned with a mug of coffee and one of tea.

"Now I have a new title: 'Captive goffer'." She handed him his mug.

Stas got up, went to the sofa, and picked up a photo of the funeral.

"Come here, look at this."

She perched on the sofa's arm to get a closer look. The picture was a grainy black-and-white of a woman in black, flanked by two police officers in uniform, narrow black ribbons affixed to their badges.

"This is Irina. The one on the right is his partner, Jack Crowder, and the other officer is...." He hesitated as he read the rest of the caption. "Sgt. Edward Lawson."

She leaned in. "How?"

Stas shook his head in disbelief. "His father?" He turned the paper over hopeful that some answer was to be found on the blank side. "I've got to go back to Pasadena tomorrow, see if Crowder is around."

The phone rang. Stas dropped the articles on the coffee table and reached it on the third ring.

"Nowak."

"This is Townsend. I know you haven't seen the news, but your politician almost got blown away."

"What?"

"Someone tried to kill Lawson."

"When?"

"Maybe an hour or two ago. I was just at Lawson's fundraiser. My editor just called. Told me to forget my story and get on this."

"What happened?"

"They were on the Hollywood Freeway. It looked like a drive-by or a hit. Who knows? Very few witnesses."

"Who's dead?"

"The driver and an aide. Both hit on the driver's side. I remember her, cute." He added, sadly.

"And Lawson?"

"He's in surgery at St. Joe's. They're both at St. Joe's, but I don't know Aagard's condition."

"I'll meet you there in…." Stas looked at his watch. "Thirty minutes. You're sure it wasn't an accident?"

"Not unless they're renting limos riddled with bullets. More like a hit. Looks like someone tried to kill Lawson. They'll probably call it an assassination attempt. That should bump him up in the polls another five, ten points."

"Then he's not critical?" He shrugged.

"Must be serious if he's in surgery."

"I'll see you there." Stas hung up and went to the closet for his jacket as he called to Dina. "I'm going to meet Townsend."

"I don't want to go."

"Didn't plan to take you." He crossed to the door.

"You're leaving me alone, unguarded? I might turn a..." She left the rest unsaid when she saw him scowl.

"Babe, this is serious. I don't know what happened, but they can find me just as easily as Lawson." He had a second thought. "Can you handle a gun?"

She recoiled at the mere suggestion.

"That's okay, babe. Just don't open for anyone."

THIRTY-TWO

Ralph Townsend sat on an empty planter outside the entrance of the ER. He ground out his cigarette when he saw Stas and motioned for the detective to join him.

"God, it's a media circus. I don't know how anyone survived. The driver got his point blank in the head. Never knew what hit him. Car had bullet proof nothing, an old Lincoln." Townsend lit another cigarette and offered the pack to Stas. "Who's the lead on this one?"

"Boyd, big, hungry-looking guy, didn't appreciate being dragged away from his five pound porterhouse especially by some politicians. He hates politicians." Stas lit up and inhaled, letting the smoke fill his lungs. When he exhaled, a stream of white smoke joined Townsend's. "Have you talked to anyone?"

Townsend shook his head. "The head of ER said he would give us an update in a half hour. Doc said the good reverend was giving thanks for the miracle. I can just see him raising his bloody face heavenward with that pronouncement."

"How's Lawson?

"Cuts, abrasions. They're in surgery stitching him up. He'll live and use this assault in his campaign on crime. It couldn't have gone down better if he planned it himself. I take that back. Aagard said it was God's providence."

"How's that?"

"Lawson gave his seat to the aide. She was the one sitting by the door, where he was supposed to be sitting."

Both men stood lost in thought, caught in the aura of smoke and ash, hoping for more answers, especially those not caught up in God's providence.

"They can't say that this was a drug deal gone bad." Stas took another drag on his cigarette then stamped it out, for a second, fascinated by the surrealistic design of gray ash ground into the concrete.

"By the way, did you know that Aagard's foundation owned the Trendal Building and some other choice real estate downtown?"

"Somehow I'm not surprised."

"C'mon, man. I know you're on vacation but give me something. You keep bouncing around these scenes like a damned ping-pong ball ever since you received that call. I know you got something."

Stas shrugged. "There's nothing. You probably know more about them than I do."

"Then what are you digging for? Maybe we should share notes."

"Suicide, drugs, faux raids."

"Is that like *faux pas*?" Townsend asked.

"How the hell should I know? Everywhere these guys show up, something bad happens. Right now nothing seems to fit, but Brown, Aagard, and Lawson are connected. Okay, as the little boy said, 'I showed you mine, now you show me yours.' Let me see what ya got."

"I interviewed Lawson the other day." Townsend cleared his throat, then coughed. "He's bright, ambitious, wants to go further in politics, maybe run for Senate, even throw his hat in the presidential ring at a later date. He's from here, worked for Long Beach PD. Moved up North, married with a couple of kids. Law school, a stint with the DA's office, state office, the usual route."

"What about his wife?"

"He told me he met her at some kind of police shooting competition."

"Who won?"

Townsend smiled. "She did, plus she's advanced through the ranks, just resigned her post to move to LA." He stuck another cigarette between his lips and patted himself down for a lighter. "But who's Brown?"

"One of their old police buddies. He's been doing their security."

"Cops and their little closed society. It's such an incestuous group. What do you do when there're no cops to hang with?"

Stas stared straight ahead. "We cope, or we hit the wall."

"Depressing."

"No more depressing than you guys. You're just a bunch of cannibals. You do anything..."

Townsend interrupted. "So, how's Dina?

"Fine."

"You're not on duty. Why didn't you bring her? I would have kept her company while you do whatever cops do at crime scenes when they're on vacation."

"This isn't a crime scene, and I need a favor."

"What, play cards with Dina?"

Stas was all business. "No, find out if Lawson's father was on the Pasadena PD."

"You can find that out just as quickly as I can."

"Just get me anything on the old man."

"Don't you want to know anything about Lawson's platform?"

"I'll read about it in the paper. What about Aagard?"

"He's his chief advisor and guru, sort of an up and coming Karl Rove." Townsend took out his pack and offered it to Stas, then took one for himself.

"Sounds like another winner. Why don't you light that one?" Stas pointed to the one still dangling from Townsend's mouth.

He returned the pack to his pocket, found his BIC, and lit up. "You going inside?" He blew the smoke out with the words.

"Maybe later. I want to see the car, maybe talk to Boyd, or take a look at the murder book."

"I'll talk to you tomorrow."

Stas looked at his watch. "More like today."

Dina had curled up with a book and dropped it when Stas returned. "What happened?" She frowned picking up the residue of cigarette smoke.

He sat without removing his jacket. "Someone tried to take out Aagard and Lawson, but they survived. Lawson was still in surgery when I left the hospital."

"Did you see Aagard?"

"No, I need to talk to the lead detective at Hollywood Division and see what they have. I also found out that the car that picked up Honey Malone's boyfriend belonged to Brown's fleet. He's playing all sides of the street. I sure as hell would like to know what he's doing."

"He's with Lisa."

"How do you know?"

"Dar Ling called and invited me to a party. I asked about Lisa. She said that Lisa wasn't going. She's been spending a lot of time with Matt, even staying at his place."

"And she's running things now?"

"Not really. She doesn't even come in." There was a little ghetto twist to her head. "Raven took over everything since the reading of the will."

Stas looked doubtful.

"You don't cross Raven, and you don't challenge her." Dina continued. "Matt doesn't know her well, but he will, real soon."

With all of the violence in the streets and those who labored in that market, he knew that Raven had the resources to deal with any interloper.

THIRTY-THREE

Stas was up early and took his horn case from the closet without waking Dina. He sat on the edge of his reading chair and took out his sax, carefully wiping it off with a soft yellow cloth. He assumed the position, sitting on the edge of the chair. He left the horn's mouthpiece in its brass cover and just fingered the notes, humming familiar jazz tunes. At first his fingers were stiff but limbered up as he continued to mimic playing. When he hummed "My Funny Valentine", he eased into the song. He was lost in the soundless exercise and didn't hear Dina open the door.

"Stas!"

His head popped to attention.

"What are you doing?"

"Playing with my horn."

"All I heard was loud humming."

"Yeah, it's an old technique, practicing your fingering." He wiped off the neck and put the sax back into the case, closing it and sliding it in the corner.

"Am I ever going to hear you play?"

"One of these days."

After making coffee and taking a steaming mug to Dina in the living room, he dressed and joined Dina on the sofa while he put on his shoes. "I'm running over to Pasadena to talk with the PR officer at Pasadena PD. She said she'd see me at nine. I should be back in a couple of hours or so."

"What's your friend, Ralph, doing?"

"He's busy. He's writing up the drive-by." Stas paused. "I got a thought. If I get to see Crowder, I'll call."

Dina sipped her coffee, waiting for him to continue.

"I'll come back, get you, and drop you off at The Paseo. You can shop, see a movie. Just don't call any of your girl friends."

The idea brought a smile then a frown to Dina's face. "Suppose someone...."

"I think they have their hands full with what happened last night. Don't worry about it, enjoy yourself."

When Stas met Officer Cathy Cooper at Pasadena Police Headquarters, she was warm, friendly and very efficient. He thought it was too bad the general public didn't see this face of law enforcement very often. Officer Cooper was the person who made sure the connection between one agency worked smoothly with another. If this link wasn't there, or if it were broken, it could mean time consuming delays in an investigation that could cost the lives of civilians or police officers.

She pointed Stas to a seat and pulled a file to her as she sat. "You're lucky we keep very good records. Jack Crowder and Rick Jones were partners on patrol and sometimes worked vice."

She opened the file and looked over some papers and newspaper clippings.

"They were good cops," she said.

Cooper handed a clipping to Stas.

The photo showed two officers standing with the Chief as they received awards for service to the department and Pasadena. Both men were tall, proud, even handsome in their uniforms. If Jones was Sybil's father, he could see why most people wouldn't have thought she was black. He was a light-skinned man, with regular features, nothing too pronounced about his mouth and nose. Stas thought that with a white mother, Sybil would have been fair enough to pass if she had wanted to. He handed the photo back, and Cooper continued.

"Jones was killed down in the Arroyo."

"The Arroyo?".

"You know, down by the Rose Bowl?" she added.

He nodded.

"Well, it sits in a natural gully or canyon. On the north side of Suicide Bridge the Arroyo is much broader, but on the other side, the south side, it's narrower, more natural. People hike, ride. There's even an archery range. He was parked at the range. Someone stood by the driver's side and shot him. The window was down, like they were having a talk."

"Why was he alone?" he asked.

"No one knows. There were no witnesses. No one was ever arrested." She closed the file.

Stas knew the gesture. He knew Cooper had never met Jones, but she felt a sense of loss at the death of a fellow officer especially when his murderer was never apprehended.

She slid a slip of paper across the desk. "Crowder retired about twelve years ago and is still in the area. After his wife died, he moved to a senior apartment complex in Arcadia. Apparently, he likes to be near the ponies." There was a hint of disapproval in her tone.

At first Stas didn't understand.

"The race track at Santa Anita," she added.

He pocketed the paper as Cooper walked him out to Garfield Avenue.

"If you need anything else, just call. I can fax it to you."

The bright winter sun caused Stas to squint as he held out his hand to her. "This is a nice area, compact." He looked across at the Court House and down to City Hall.

"Yeah, makes it convenient for trials. We can just walk."

"Thanks, I'll be in touch."

She turned and walked back inside. The sun burned hot on his face. These were the kind of days that lured people from the East and Midwest to escape subzero winter temperatures. He looked north, up Garfield, which ran from the library, then south to City Hall, through The Paseo, to the Civic Auditorium. It was a nice day to be on vacation.

In the car, he slipped on his sunglasses before calling Crowder. If he liked the ponies, he might not be at home.

"Hello." The voice on the other end was gravelly, punctuated with a cough.

"I'm Detective Nowak with LAPD. Is this Jack Crowder?

"Yes. What's this about?"

"I'd like to talk to you if you could spare me a few minutes. It's about your old partner, Rick Jones."

There was a long pause. Stas knew that old wounds never heal, and the one thing cops hated was to have them reopened.

"I really don't want..."

Stas continued. "I don't want to intrude, but I'm working on a murder investigation." He lied. "The victim was my sister."

He'd said it, although he hadn't wanted to, the words just slipped out followed by old, familiar pain.

"Well, you're in luck. The track is dark today. Come on over."

They set up a meet, giving Stas enough time to go back for Dina, drop her off at The Paseo, and get to Arcadia. He called her and told her to meet him in front of his building. The drive back to Glendale took twenty minutes. He found her waiting at the curb.

"I take it you got in touch with Jack?" Dina asked, settling into the car.

"Yeah, he lives in Arcadia, likes to go to the track."

"Did they tell you anything else about Sybil's father?"

He turned to give Dina a quick look as he merged into traffic on the 134. "I didn't ask. Anyway how would they know who her father was? Remember Sybil was five when Irina married Rick. And she was working before that. Anybody could be the father." His voice faded.

"Then what do you do about how you're feeling?"

"What do you mean?" What could he tell her?

Dina confronted him. "You go to work, drink, read, listen to your music, go back to work. The only friend you seem to have outside of the cops is Ralph. The only woman who's called since I've been at your house is Livia, and you just met her. You're so wrapped up in your work you don't take vacations. You can't even react to what's happening to you."

He didn't know where to start. "Cops are just different."

"I know that. It's just another old boys' club. It's so tribal. Hunt together, drink together. Share your women."

He smiled. "You're being a little hard on me."

"Am I?"

"Yeah. Why the interest?"

"I just want to know more. Where do you meet people?"

"You mean women?"

"Would I have been anywhere to meet you, if I...?" She touched her throat.

"That was a hangout for Vice. Uniforms have their own watering holes. Detectives from different divisions have theirs. We've toned down. It's not like the old 'choir boy' days, but women still know where to find us."

Dina pressed. "And where is that?"

"Ralph and some detectives go to the Second Set. But you know how to get me."

The traffic eastbound on the 134 was light. Stas exited the 210 right after the two freeways merged and took Fair Oaks to Colorado then left to the Paseo, the upscale shopping center that had replaced the old, covered Pasadena Mall. Dina eyes brightened as he drove along Colorado. Before reaching the corner at Los Robles, he pulled over and unlocked the doors.

"I'll call you when I leave Crowder's."

She waved as she hurried to savor her freedom.

Stas got back on the eastbound 210 Freeway and exited at Baldwin. There was the Arboretum on his right, the Santa Anita Racetrack and another large shopping mall on his left. The retired cop had all of the conveniences within walking distance of his senior apartment.

Crowder lived on the fourth floor in the rear of the building. As he slowly opened the door, Stas caught a whiff of a sweet, sage-like scent masked by heavy cigarette smoke, but there was no mistake. Crowder did more than smoke pot, an odor that strong, indicated that he grew it as well.

From the apartment's entrance, Stas could see out through to the double glass doors that led to the little balcony overgrown with foliage of various hues and heights. Crowder wore a v-neck cotton undershirt and poly slacks. Polyester suits had been the detectives uniform back in the seventies. They would throw them in the washer at night, hang them up after taking them out of the dryer, put them on the next morning, and still look like shit when they went to work. No wonder folks on the street could spot cops a mile away. And if they hadn't washed their suits the night before, you could smell them as well.

"C'mon in, Nowak, have a seat." Crowder pointed to a spot on a littered and sour-smelling sofa. "Don't mind my mess. Got to get ready for tomorrow."

Crowder sat in a straight chair at a card table covered with racing forms and yellow legal pads. He was serious about horse racing.

Stas took out his notebook, gold Cross pen, and looked around the small room to get a feel for Crowder. Besides the sofa, card table, and chair, there was an old beat-up desk holding a stack of mail, magazines, and a couple of books.

"Can I get you something?"

Stas wrinkled his nose as if trying to distinguish the various airborne scents. "What do you have?"

He smiled. "You wouldn't bust me, would you?"

Stas shook his head.

"You want a joint?" Crowder asked. "I figured you smelled it." Crowder asked.

"It's kinda hard to miss, especially the fresh stuff. Where do you grow it?"

He nodded towards the bedroom. "In the closet. Sometimes I take it out, give it some fresh air with the herbs. I grow a lot of sage."

"You don't get any complaints?"

"Are you kidding, these old gals think it's fresh herbs. I give a lot of it away."

He noticed Stas's questioning glance.

"Not the pot. But there are a couple of 'em. We smoke together sometimes. One even makes awesome brownies." He slowly rose. "Here, let me show you my set up."

He went into the bedroom and returned with a lacquered teakwood box that he sat on the card table.

Stas drew closer. The vaporizer had a metal rod enclosed inside of a glass rod. There was a switch and dial that controlled the heat to the rods.

Crowder excitedly pointed out the features of his toy. "See I put the weed in the tube. It heats up, and I get pure, unadulterated mist. No bowl, no mess."

Stas recognized Crowder's excitement with his new gadget.

"You sure you don't want to try some. It's good stuff."

"Better not, not this time."

Crowder took the unique paraphernalia back to the bedroom. When he returned, he stopped in the tiny kitchen and took two beers from the fridge. He handed one to Stas before sitting back in his chair.

"My fridge's not working too good, but at least the brew's wet."

Stas fingered the bottle and took a sip. "How long were you and Jones partners?"

"Give or take a couple of years before he got shot." Jack took a long swig on his beer and sighed deeply when he put his bottle down.

"I'm really interested in his family, especially his wife and kid. I'm not investigating his death, but I'd like to know anything that might help reconstruct…." Stas didn't finish. He was sure Jack understood the routine of dredging up a victim's past, putting as many pieces of a life together to see who could have taken it away.

"There's not a lot to tell. He married René, against my advice. Damn, you know how that is. You get caught up with some hot woman.... They had three strikes before they even went to Vegas. He was Negro."

Stas interrupted. "The newspaper photo, he didn't look black."

"Can't go by that." He went to his desk, dug through a drawer and handed over a photo of three men in uniform. "This is Jones. He was just light-skinned. Couldn't have big black burly looking cops pulling over the cream of Pasadena society, giving tickets to the ladies of the Junior League. Scare'em to death. Back in those days...well, black was black. That's when I learned, it was the shade. The city had eased them in. So the first cops were fair, but they were still Negroes. It was the attitude of some white officers. He caught a lot of flack. Then he marries this beautiful white woman, looked like she stepped off some runway in Paris. René was something." Crowder looked at the photo, remembering.

"You knew she was a call girl?"

"I knew. Eddie knew." He pointed to the third man in the photo. "He didn't like it one damn bit."

"That she was a hooker?"

"No, that she was white. He was a mean ass son-of-a-bitch. Every Negro on the west side of Pasadena hated his guts. You'd think he was Bull Connor. But he was our sergeant. After Jones got married, he'd give us the shittiest details, always hustling Negroes and Mexicans."

"Do you remember anything in particular about his death?"

Crowder finished off his beer and sat the bottle on the floor next to his chair. He seemed to need more time to draw out the sorted details from the past.

"He was sitting in the car, in the Arroyo near the archery range. Someone shot him point blank. He must have known who it was, had his window rolled down. His weapon wasn't even drawn. Yeah, I'm sure he knew." Crowder stopped.

Stas said nothing.

"You know, I take that back about his gun. It was on the seat next to him, under a newspaper. I just never figured that one out."

"And the investigation?"

"Nothing, a dead-end. They said he had set-up a meet with some informant. Damn, I was his partner. I didn't know nothing about any informant. We were uniform. We weren't detectives. All these years, and I couldn't do a damn thing about it." He rose. "Want another beer."

Stas had barely touched the one he had. He waved the bottle at Crowder and took another sip. He imagined the taste of luke warm piss, and this was it. "I'm good."

Crowder returned with another bottle and sat down.

"What happened to the wife and kid?" Although he had the notebook and pen poised, Stas had written very little.

"After the funeral, she packed up and went back to Chicago or Cleveland, some city in the Midwest that started with a 'C'."

"Chicago." Stas subconsciously interjected.

Crowder missed it and continued. "She came back when her daughter was in her teens."

"Sybil?"

"Yeah, she was a looker just like her mom. That's when the shit hit the fan."

Stas reacted with a look of surprise that made Jack pause.

"She contacted Eddie, you know, thought he was a friend. Well, when his son saw Sybil, they couldn't keep them apart. Little Eddie was older, should've known better."

Several emotions were working at once. Stas started writing in his notebook more to calm himself than for any record. Jack's words were being etched into his brain.

"Who called Eddie?"

"René. She never knew how he felt about Rick."

"Back-up, what do you mean, they couldn't keep them apart?

"The kids just started running around together. First the movies, then clubs. He got her fake ID. The next thing I heard, they had run off to Vegas."

"Your sergeant's son married Sybil?"

"We called him Little Eddie. I thought his old man was going to have a coronary." He saw the confusion on Stas's face. "I mean the father. Anyway, they got an annulment since she was underage. Then, she got an abortion."

Stas stopped writing. He felt the knot grip his intestines. He willed the taste of bile back down his throat. He couldn't get sick in front of another cop. When he looked up, Jack was still talking.

"...through the grapevine that she went the way of her mother."

"To Chicago?"

"No, the business, became a call girl."

"And Eddie?"

"He took an early retirement, but I heard he's in some kind of hospital, got emphysema. Got it in a bad way. He smoked like a fiend, use to cough his lungs out."

Stas reached for the picture and looked at the three cops. "And the son, is he still around?"

"He was a cop, too, for Long Beach PD. Then he went into politics. Been on the news lately, running for Congress. Boy, you just never know."

Stas rose. "Yeah, I wonder what would have happened if they had just left them alone."

"Probably had a couple more kids, divorced, married someone else. You know the life. I had three, wives that is. Funny, no kids... that I know of."

Jack walked Stas to the elevator where they said good-bye.

So Edward Lawson, the politician, had once been married to Sybil.

Stas felt disoriented. It took a few minutes to focus when he exited the building. The lot was small, but he had to think where he had parked the car, and then he saw her. She was so short that he almost missed her walking away from his car. She was bundled up in a coat that was much too long, cinched with an even longer black leather belt that swung down below her knees. A black knit hat was pulled down over her forehead.

It was the right hand that caught his attention. He could see one yellowed finger blackened at the tip which she quickly withdrew and jammed into her pocket when she walked past, giving him a little bow and a devilish smile. At his car, he saw what she had been up to. Sprawled across the trunk of the Mercedes was "WASH ME" in a ragged script. He smiled and decided it was time to get the car washed. Detailing would have to wait 'til later.

There was a service station on the corner of Santa Anita and Colorado. The cashier gave him directions to a car wash on Santa Anita near the 210 Freeway. While he waited for the car, he called Dina.

"This is Stas."

"I know. Where are you?"

"I'm at a car wash in Arcadia. Can you be in front of Macy's in 30 minutes?"

"Yes. Are you okay?"

"Why?"

"You don't sound like yourself."

"No, I'm okay." He turned the phone off without saying good-bye. *And I'm not okay.*

He didn't watch his car go through the wash. It was like a sacrilege not to have it detailed by his guys in Glendale. Instead, he sat on one of the benches outside and stared into space. He was aware of that dull ache, not in the pit of his stomach this time but in the very depth of his soul. He knew there was no pill, no alcohol, no drug to reach that pain and rip it out.

Dina couldn't understand why he felt nothing when he realized that Sybil was his sister. He had lied and believed his own prevarication, covering his feelings with the myth of professional indifference, that psychological objectification that cops had been trained over the years to present to the public.

He looked out to see one of the attendants waving his blue rag. The car was ready. Stas handed over his receipt with a tip, took his keys, and climbed behind the wheel. At any other time he would have been annoyed by the water dripping from the air vents and the rear tail pipes. He knew when he pulled out onto Santa Anita that he had barely looked at the oncoming traffic and didn't really give a damn if the u-turn he made over the railroad tracks was legal or not. He just wanted to pick up Dina and get home to something stronger than watery beer.

She stood in front of Macy's. Stas pulled over, impervious to several honks as he slowed traffic to get to the curb. Dina had a shopping bag in tow as she got into the car. There wasn't time to pop the trunk, unless he wanted to cause a riot of disgruntled drivers so she tucked the bag between her legs and anxiously turned to him.

"If you haven't eaten, I'll grab some Chinese take-out," Stas offered.

"How did it go with the cop?"

Stas pulled out into traffic and cut into the left lane to turn onto Los Robles. "Nothing new on Jones. The investigation went cold. Either lack of evidence or interest. Now it really doesn't matter."

"Then what about Lawson?"

"Junior or senior? They both seem to be douche bags. I'd bet even money that Ed senior was involved in Jones's killing. He was a racist bastard." Stas's anger was rising. "Junior was another piece of work. He took Sybil to Nevada and married her."

"What?"

"Lawson Senior had it annulled. Ed Lawson and Sybil got married while she was a minor. Someone should have prosecuted his ass for violating the Mann Act, and at the very least, he should have been charged with statutory rape."

"And nothing happened to him?"

"Nada, he walked and joined Long Beach PD. She had an abortion before or after the annulment. I'm not sure." His voice was growing hoarse.

"Then he couldn't have been Jennifer's father?"

"Why not? He just came back for seconds when she was older. If he was her first love..." He gave a quick glance at Dina. "You know how that is?"

"No, that's one experience we didn't have in common. I never had a first love."

THIRTY-FOUR

Stas tossed on the sofa trying to disentangle himself from his dreams when what seemed like a blast from some hellish horn jolted him awake. Reaching for the phone in a state of semi-wakefulness was difficult, but he finally picked up on the fifth ring.

"Nowak."

"Detective Nowak, this is Meiers." The voice was strained and cracked. "I've been given instructions about the money. It's tomorrow."

He bolted upright. "I'm on my way over."

"Come to my home. The door will be unlocked."

Stas hung up, dressed, and was out of the apartment in fifteen minutes.

He parked behind Meiers' van and entered the house.

Meiers sat in his chair nursing a coffee. Stas looked around the living room, noticing several framed photos on the sofa table. One was of a woman, whom he recognized as Sybil. The other was Sybil and Meiers. He wore black tie. She was dressed in a silver and blue gown and smiled down at him, her face full of pride, maybe even love.

Meiers moved from around the coffee table in his sleek, black wheelchair. A large black gym bag was open on a chair near him.

"Is this the money? Stas peered into the bag. "I don't think I've ever been this close to a quarter million."

"It's hard to envision, let alone get it together physically. But you're looking at it. A lot of research..."

The phone rang before he could finish. Meiers picked-up and spoke in hushed tones.

Stas blocked out the conversation and stared at the bundle of bills tightly swathed in clear shrink-wrap. On the street, he had seen what some men would do to uphold a reputation, but he'd never actually seen its value sitting before him in a gym bag. After all, the cemeteries were full of drug dealers and gang bangers who had died for less.

When Meiers hung up, he turned his gaze towards the detective, as if looking for a final nod of approval.

Stas shook his head. "Don't do this alone. Let me talk to my captain. At least put a tracing device in the bag. I want the bastards as much as you do. If we catch them with the money, we'll at least have some proof of their involvement."

"Involvement in what, blackmail? Do you think I give a damn about the money? I'm doing it my way, for Sybil."

"Then let me go with you."

Meiers rolled over to the chair and started to zip the bag. "I don't know yet where they want me to drop it."

"How do they communicate with you?"

"This time they phoned. I expect they'll call again."

"Let me know as soon as you hear something." Stas moved towards the door feeling the futility of the situation.

Most of the Chinese take-out remained in cartons on the coffee table. After a drink, Stas had lost his appetite for food. Dina had eaten little and, lost in thought, munched on a cold egg roll. He had changed into jeans, dark polo sweater and was slipping into his leather jacket. Dina was surprised to see he was wearing his gun.

"I'll call you when I leave the hospital. You want me to see if Ralph is free?" He half-heartedly smiled.

She waved towards the bookcases. "No, I'll manage. I can entertain myself without a baby-sitter tonight."

"I think there'll be some closure one way or the other. Maybe you can go home tomorrow."

Dina smiled and reached for her book.

THIRTY-FIVE

Stas was so used to going through the emergency at St. Joseph's that he had to look for the main entrance after he parked. The main lobby was almost empty except for a few people milling around at the conclusion of visiting hours. He stopped at the receptionist desk and presented his badge.

"I'm Detective Nowak. Can you tell me what rooms Edward Lawson and Robert Aagard are in?"

A young woman in her mid-twenties turned on him so abruptly that Stas stepped back.

"My god, you cops and reporters are all over the place. You know, I have other people who need stuff around here. You got a station on the fifth floor." She turned her head as if speaking to an invisible person behind her. "You'd think those guys were presidents or something, and we don't have work to do...."

He turned from her vitriolic venting before she finished and headed for the elevators. After pushing the UP button, he waited for a few minutes, then glanced at the floor indicator numbers above the door. One number hadn't changed since he'd been standing there, and the other moved so slowly that he wondered if there was some sort of emergency. *Then take the stairs.* He was about to look for the door to the stairwell, when a bell dinged and the double gray doors opened. Stas had to wait while an orderly maneuvered an empty gurney before entering. The elevator took him to the fifth floor without stopping. His only company was Muzak's Yanni playing his latest New Age concert.

A handsome, young LAPD officer, his pecs inflating the short sleeves of his uniform shirt, sat at a desk next to the nurses' station. He watched the comings and goings of staff and the last of the visitors. The fifth floor was reserved for VIP patients, those who could afford large private rooms and suites along with gourmet dining with all of its bells and whistles. Stas stood at the side of the desk as Officer Gage leaned over to check out a pair of shapely legs encased in white stockings moving down the hall. When he looked up, the shield was under his nose.

Gage jerked to attention. "Sorry, I didn't see you there."

"I know. Aren't you supposed to be guarding those ex-cop politicians?" There was a touch of sarcasm.

"I'm not guarding. It's more like directing traffic, reporters, media, aides, friends, job hopefuls. Earlier, it was like Grand Central Station. The only distractions are the nurses. And most of them wear pants. What do you expect? Plus, half of 'um are men."

Stas peered down the hall. "What room are they in?"

Gage tried to stifle a yawn. "Lawson's in 502, and Aagard's in 506."

"Who's in the room between?"

"Nobody, it's a storage room."

He picked up the clipboard and looked over the list of visitors. Matt Brown had been there three times in two days. He put the board on the desk, but the officer handed it back.

"You got to sign in, detective."

Stas bent over, signed his name and time, then heard the staccato tap, tap, tap of high heels on the tile flooring. The tapping grew louder. He raised his head when he saw the suede pumps pause. She was what he had expected, a very attractive woman in high heels that brought them eye to eye.

Swathed in an aura of fashionable good taste and money, she reached with manicured and bejeweled fingers for the clipboard and pen that Stas handed her. Her smile revealed expensively capped and whitened teeth. He wondered which one, Lawson or Aagard, she belonged to. He gave her his official LAPD smile.

"You're police? I'm Mrs. Aagard. Tony has been really impressed with all the attention your department has been giving the candidate and him, of course." She spoke without breathing, her words cascading like a waterfall. "Are you here to guard him?"

Stas stared for a second. "Tony?"

She batted heavily mascaraed lashes over her cornflower blue eyes and never missed a beat. "My husband, Rev. Aagard. That's what I call him."

Stas still looked puzzled. "Aagard, who's Tony Aagard?"

She returned the clipboard to the desk, and smiled at Officer Gage before returning her attention to Stas.

He hadn't moved.

"You know, his first name is Anthony."

Stas didn't know, so he renewed his smile, anxious for her to tell him more.

His attentiveness engaged her, and she continued. "So he took the 'A' from his first name and attached it to his last name and used his middle name, Robert, as his first name. Isn't that clever and so aristocratic?" She finally took a deep breath. "His family's was from England, you know. Not now, back maybe a century ago. He started to add it to his last name, hyphenate it, you know, Robert Anthony-Agard like the British do." She looked into those steel gray eyes to see that he understood. "My father thought it was a little too pretentious. My father's Irish." She took another breath. "But that doesn't matter, at home everyone calls him Tony."

"And where is home?"

"Oh, we're from Fresno. My husband was a county prosecutor. He even worked down here a couple of years before we were married. Then he got the call, not right away, of course, he practiced law for a while."

"The call? What's the call?" At this point he wished for a call, victims of a triple shooting down in the ER for starters.

"The Lord, of course, he was called to the ministry. Do you know Tony? Have you heard him preach? He's wonderful, so inspirational. And now he's spreading his message..."

Stas took a breath for her and turned toward the rooms. He wanted to see Aagard.

She moved ahead of him. "He gave up his private practice to do the Foundation's work."

He followed her down the nicely decorated corridor, passed Lawson's room giving it a cursory glance.

"You know it's so much warmer down here, even in winter. And it's not half as dusty. Fresno is just a dust bowl. We have a furnished condo on Wilshire." She turned to see if Stas was still following and listening. "Here we are."

They walked in without knocking, and she tap, tap, tapped over to the bed, kissing her husband on the forehead.

"Darling, isn't it wonderful, they sent this wonderful detective to guard you." She turned to Stas. "Now what did you say your name was?"

"Nowak, Detective Nowak."

Robert Aagard pulled slightly forward without extending his hand. "How do you do, detective?"

His wife patted his hair. "I was going to see Ed first when this nice officer asked where you were so I brought him to you."

Aagard said nothing while his wife fussed with the covers and pillows. Stas watched the ritual.

"Darling, I've had a long day," she said. "I tried to get Gwen. Then I went shopping and saw the decorator. I'm going to the condo. I'll be back, bright and early in the morning. I want to see the doctor about your release." She revisited the forehead with a light tap of her lips. "Anyway, I'm sure you boys can talk shop for hours, but I have things to do." She waved to both men as she left.

Aagard nervously rearranged his covers. "Is this an official visit? I've already spoken to the investigating officers. It's late, and I'm tired, detective."

Time to cut the shit. Stas moved closer to the bed. "Did you know a Sybil Hansen or Sybil Jones?"

"I don't think so."

"You know I have this pain in my gut, and it's talking to me, telling me you're a fucking liar."

Aagard seemed to reflect. "Now I seem to remember something about a whore who killed herself."

The veins in Stas's neck pulsed.

"Does that embarrass you, detective?" His mouth twisted in a cruel smirk. "Was she one of your girls? I think all men, even cops, have that fantasy of screwing a whore, have her do all those forbidden things your wife won't do. Men see it as their birthright. Did she fulfill your fantasies?"

Stas moved even closer to the head of the bed and let his jacket fall open. The Glock was visible in the shoulder holster.

"I'm not impressed with your hardware. Even if I knew her, I hope you don't think I'm foolish enough to say anything about her."

"Are you afraid I'm wearing a wire? That's the least of your worries. Are you brain dead, you stupid prick. If this wasn't a hospital, I'd take you out and shoot you like some rabid dog. But for now, it's not going to happen, and I'm not going to waste our time discussing it. You know this is not official, but it is personal. Sybil was my sister."

Aagard coughed, the color draining from his face as he broke out into a cold sweat.

"You knew Sybil." Stas continued. "She had your kid. You dumped her, then you killed her."

Aagard regarded Stas with a cold stare. "Son of a bitch!" He spat out the words. "You have no proof."

Malevolence crept into Stas's voice. He had to contain his rage. "I don't need proof, you bastard. There are ways. We both know them. And if I set you up, there'll be no questions. It will be clean and final. Now how does that fit into your holy scheme of things, preacher?"

Stas walked towards the door, then turned. "I have some of your mail, Tony, old mail from an old lover."

THIRTY-SIX

A blue-clad orderly wheeled Ed Lawson into Aagard's room. When the door closed, Ed rose from his chair and walked over to the bed. Although Aagard appeared asleep, he slowly opened his eyes. His skin was pale; puffy bags like dark blisters had formed under his watery blue eyes.

"Isn't it a bit early for a conference?" Lawson asked. "What's so urgent that it can't wait until we get out?"

"We're not being released today."

"Whose decision was that?" Lawson pulled a chair to the bedside and dropped into it.

"Mine."

"Why?"

"I think this is the safest place for the time being."

"Safe from what? I thought the police said we got caught in some gang drive-by cross fire." He realized he was beginning to believe his own press releases.

Aagard folded his fingers over his stomach. "If something happens..."

Lawson interrupted. "What do you mean, 'If something happens?' What could happen?"

Aagard ignored the question. "If something else happens, what better place is there than a hospital under their security and police protection. After all, one attempt has been made on your life already."

Lawson rose and reached for the cell phone next to Aagard. "I see you've been making things happen." He angrily threw the phone back.

"The wheels are turning as we speak." Aagard placed the phone on the nightstand.

"What kind of diabolical scheme have you put into motion this early in the morning?" He fell back in his chair and looked around trying to assess the damage to his career. "So what is going on?"

"For starters, Brown is scheduled to pick up a quarter million dollars this morning."

Lawson rocked forward, shocked. "How the hell does he get his hands on that kind of money?"

"He moonlights. But you know the old saying about ill-gotten gains."

"No, and don't enlighten me, but I assume the money is going to, somehow miraculously, fall into our hands?"

Aagard smiled wanly. "I would think you'd have noticed that Matt has been running his own show. We exercise a perfect plan and now bodies are cluttering up the landscape."

"And you want to make me party to this, this scheme?"

"I would think you'd be eager to be rid of Brown, especially since he's been screwing your wife."

Lawson looked away and said nothing.

"Where do you think she was the other night?" Aagard smiled coldly and turned to a sheaf of papers on his nightstand. "I've prepared a statement for you to read when the press comes again." He handed Lawson a single sheet of paper off the top. "Then, because of some complications you ... we will not be available for the media for at least two, three days. The hospital administration and the cops will see that we're not disturbed."

Lawson folded the paper and slipped it into his robe pocket. "This is insane."

"And next on the agenda is that meddling cop and his whore." Aagard added.

Lisa stood in the doorway of Matt's bedroom as he slept. She went to the den and slipped a key into his inside jacket pocket.

She'd gone out for fresh Danish and had the key duplicated. In the kitchen she made coffee and poured herself an orange juice. While the coffee brewed, she leaned on the counter and read the paper. Soft, muted sunlight began to filter through the half opened blinds. It was going to be a beautiful day.

When the coffee was ready, she poured a cup and carried it to the little green bistro table. She sat and sipped the hot brew before taking out her cell phone and punching in numbers.

"It's done. He should be leaving soon. I'll see you later."

Lisa stretched languorously. *This is going to be a long day.*

She finished her coffee, poured another mug, and carried it to the bedroom.

Matt opened one eye when she brushed his bare shoulder with a kiss.

"I brought you coffee."

"You spoil me."

"That's what I'm paid to do."

"Well, after today..."

Hunter Blackstone sat in a nondescript beige sedan near Matt Brown's apartment. From his location on the street he could see anyone leaving the building from the main entrance or a car leaving the underground parking structure. He chain smoked and sipped from a large takeout coffee as he waited. Startled by the ring of the cell phone, he dropped ashes on his jeans trying to balance the three and not burn holes in his suede jacket.

"Hello!"

"Are you in place?"

"Yeah, I'm sitting down the street. He's not going anywhere."

"Call me when it's over. And wait for Lisa. She has the key and the location."

Hunter flipped the phone's lid shut and put it on the seat next to him.

He watched several cars exit the parking structure and checked his watch with the clock on dash. Then an ear-shattering explosion rocked the building and street.

A car was departing through the opening gate when the blast shot hot metal and debris with such force that the car rocked backwards, sending shattered glass everywhere. The driver collapsed on the wheel bleeding from the face and head.

Hunter watched with excited amazement. Smoke poured from the underground cavern. Somehow, he had expected a fireball, something a little more dramatic, but if it got the job done, that was all that mattered. What he hadn't expected was the noise, the noise of the explosion, the echoing noise of the car alarms, and now the noise of emergency vehicles. In what seemed like minutes, they seemed to converge on the area from all directions. He felt a rush, a need to get out of the car and join the onlookers who had started to gather on the street across from Brown's building.

He'd never been that close to an explosion. The black smoke, the damage, the cacophony of sounds, even the ringing in his ears was mesmerizing. He had a macabre desire to see the twisted wreckage, the mangled bodies, the blood. He stepped out of the car and inhaled deeply, trying to breath in the smoke, to smell the gasoline, the burnt flesh. *Is this like napalm or C-4?*

"Get your ass in the car," Lisa barked.

She slapped his arm knocking his cigarette to the ground.

"What the fuck you think this is, some spectator sport. This ain't no Laker game." Lisa opened the door, got in, and slammed it before Hunter could start the car.

"You know they'll be looking for witnesses. You want to have a little private one-on-one with the cops?"

Hunter shook his head.

"I didn't think so. Can we get out of here?"

"Was Matt in that?" Hunter thumbed in the direction of the explosion and just missed a black and white unit as he pulled out into the street.

She turned to him and hissed, the words seeping through her partially closed mouth. "See, you just missed the cops. They're going to seal all this shit off. I don't know what you were thinking."

"I was waiting for you."

"Yeah, sure. C'mon, we've got something to pick up."

"You telling me where we're going?"

"When we get out of here."

Hunter made a raspy sound that caught in his throat when he tried to force it back. "Will you tell me?"

"Tell you what, Hunter?"

"Tell me how it felt to fuck a guy then see his body blown to bits?"

THIRTY-SEVEN

The Executive Athletic Club was an exclusive affair for members and their guests. Whether a member or not, all one needed was a special code and key card that allowed access to the men's or women's locker rooms.

Hunter drove into a private parking structure across the street. When the car stopped, Lisa stepped out of her sweat pants revealing bright red, hip-hugger shorts. When she removed her sweat jacket, her white sports bra did little to contain her swelling breasts. Even Hunter was distracted as he fumbled with the radio dials. In that outfit, Lisa could distract the guards at Fort Knox.

She rushed across the street, swinging the jacket over her shoulders more for effect than to ward off the chill.

The driver of a black van braked when she ran into the street. Hanging out of his window, he shouted, "Hey, hot mama!"

Lisa flipped him off and entered the club. Inside she waved her card at the young woman manning the reception's desk and dashed toward the women's locker room. When Lisa looked back, the receptionist had turned to her work. *Good, she doesn't give a damn about me.*

Lisa quickly moved over to the door of the Men's Locker room and inserted the key card into the slot, waited for the green light, and opened the door when she heard the click.

An older man sat naked on a bench facing a bank of blue lockers. When he saw Lisa, he started to say something, but she smiled, raised her finger to her lips, and jumped over his outstretched legs. She continued down the row of lockers, scanning the numbers until she found the right one. She took out a key from a pocket on her shorts and unlocked a lower locker. She extracted a zippered gym bag and kicked the door shut with her foot. Another naked man, this one much younger and better endowed then the first, just missed running into her when she skirted the lockers and headed for the door. "Excuse me!"

He reached for his towel, tried to cover himself, and watch Lisa at the same time. But she was gone.

As the heavy door clanged shut behind her, she had to control herself from breaking into a run. Hunter had kept the motor running. When he saw Lisa, he started to back out of his space. She seemed oblivious to the chill in the air, having flung her jacket across the gym bag.

"Get the door for me, damn it." There was a quiver in her voice, goose bumps formed on her bare arms.

Hunter reached across the passenger seat and opened the door. Before getting in Lisa struggled into her sweat pants and jumped in, holding the bag on her lap.

At the cashier's window, he handed the attendant a twenty and the ticket then drummed his fingers on the wheel, waiting for the gate to rise. Change fell to the pavement as Hunter sped out of the garage.

The cashier's "You need a receipt, sir?" fell on deaf and departing ears.

Once in traffic, Lisa turned to him. "You know the way to the hospital?"

"Yeah, I've been there a couple of times."

"My, my, you really get around."

"I'd like to get around to you sometime."

Lisa turned and scrutinized Hunter realizing that unless he had recently become one of the chosen few, he definitely couldn't afford her prices.

She smiled and licked her lower lip. "That might be great, but I'm not cheap."

THIRTY-EIGHT

Dina placed a colorful shopping bag by the hall closet. Stas looked up and frowned. It had been an early morning for both of them. She had been occupied with getting her things together, anticipating with mixed emotions leaving his condo and going home. He had been just as anxious waiting for a call from Meiers.

She jumped when the phone rang, but Stas didn't move to pick up until the third ring.

"Nowak here."

"It's Townsend."

"I know who it is. I can't talk now. I'm expecting an important...."

Townsend interrupted. "Did you know that somebody in Matt Brown's building got blown away?"

This got Stas's attention. "When did it happen?"

"About an hour ago."

"Man, you don't miss a trick." Stas rose. Instinctively, he knew the wheels were now in motion, and he hadn't heard from Meiers.

"I'll never get the Pulitzer sitting on my ass."

"Have they made a positive ID?"

"Got to put the body back together first."

"They blow the whole building?" Stas asked.

"Just the garage. It's swarming with bomb and arson folks as I speak."

"You think Brown was the target?"

"With everything else going on, don't you?"

Stas reached for his jacket on the arm of the sofa. "I got to go. I'll fill you in on what I can. Meet me at St. Joe's." He hung up, slipped on his jacket, and grabbed his keys.

"Aren't you waiting for Meiers's call?" Dina asked.

"He's not calling."

"How do you know?"

"I know."

THIRTY-NINE

Hunter drove around St. Joe's looking for parking. He slowly edged towards the far end of the lot, where he thought he spied a couple of spaces.

"Stop! Let me out! You'll be here all day trying to find a place." When the car slowed, Lisa jumped out dragging the bag after her, almost losing her balance. She ignored the open door and headed towards the hospital's main entrance.

"Where you going?" Hunter called after her as he tried to reach the door.

"You know damn well where I'm going." She shouted after him. "Meet me upstairs."

"Hey, wait!" Hunter leaned towards the passenger side, but his words were lost on Lisa's retreating back.

She continued on, her mind racing elsewhere. She jumped, almost dropping the bag when a black Mercedes 500 honked for her to get out of the middle of the parking lane.

"Bastard!" she shouted.

Inside the hospital he clutched the bag with both hands, watching the floor indicators over both doors of the elevators. It seemed to take forever for one to arrive. When the doors finally opened, she pushed her way into the elevator and pressed the button for her floor before people could exit. She was met with the grumbles of people pushing past. Lisa waited pursing her lips in impatience, then pressed the CLOSE DOORS indicator, and ascended alone.

When she arrived on the fifth floor, she noticed the absence of the police guard near the nurses' station. That was a good sign, but he must still be around. His clipboard was still on the desk.

I'm not signing your little guest list today, sweetie. Lisa hurried down the hall.

Hunter, breathless, finally caught up with her. "Why didn't you wait? I don't want to miss anything."

Lisa glared. "Were you invited to this party?"

"Damn right, gave Aagard my RSVP." He smiled broadly, hardly able to contain his exuberance.

Lisa slowed her pace. His cockiness was beginning to get on her nerves. At the door to 506, neither bothered to knock. When they stepped into the room, Aagard was smoothing the covers on the bed. Lawson stood by the window looking out into the sunny morning. He turned but didn't move to help Lisa put the bag on the bed while Hunter hovered.

"Get off me." Lisa shoved Hunter back.

"Any problems?" Aagard asked.

"Piece of cake." Hunter replied.

Aagard pushed Lisa away from the bed. "Lock the door!"

Hunter moved quickly and turned the dead bolt. When he returned to the bed, Aagard was unzipping the bag. Lawson finally turned from the window and moved closer. All eyes peered into the bag, but their smiles faded when they saw that the large packet of bills was tightly wrapped in plastic.

"What the hell is this?" Aagard's hand visibly shook as he tried to rip the transparent covering. He looked around for something sharp. "Damn it, cut it!"

Hunter produced a Swiss Army knife and pulled out one of the blades. Aagard snatched the knife away almost cutting himself with the effort. He rubbed his finger, examining it for blood, then turned back to the package. He cut the tightly bound plastic around an edge so as not to damage the money.

The first deep incision brought a loud hiss like gas escaping. Wisps of a yellowish vapor curled around, its wavering mist rising and undulating. Lisa looked to the ceiling, her face a mask of gray fear.

Gasps, coughs, then panic. There was no escaping the lethal fumes. In seconds the gas, smelling like burnt orange slowed their breathing.

Aagard fell, as his eyes bulged in disbelief. He clutched a hand full of worthless newsprint bundled with real bills on the tops and bottoms.

Hunter grabbed the edge of the covers to stop his fall. He stared blindly watching pieces of bill-sized paper fluttering in surreal, slow motion around him.

Lawson reached for the phone but crumpled to the floor, his hands slipping off the receiver. Unable to form a word, he blinked in desperation at the sound of the dial tone.

Lisa, the farthest away from the bed, slowly slumped against the door.

After knocking repeatedly and then trying the knob, the LVN on duty turned towards the nurses' station when Nurse Fell approached.

"What's wrong?"

"The door's locked."

"Are you sure?" Nurse Fell brushed the aide aside and tried the knob.

"I know someone's in there. I saw 'em go in a few minutes ago."

Nurse Fell produced a ring of keys, nervously inserted one into the lock, turned it before gently pushing. The door did not yield. Both women shouldered the resistant door in an effort to open it wide enough for Fell to stick her head inside.

She screamed, recoiling in shock at the sight of the death scene. One hand flew to her nose, the other quickly pulled the door shut.

"Call Haz Mat and security." Her voice was hoarse, almost inaudible.

It took only a second for alarm to register, but curiosity prevailed as the LVN reached for the doorknob again. Fell blocked her hand, roughly pushing her further into the hall.

"Damn it, quick, call Haz Mat and get the police. We've got to evacuate."

The LVN turned and ran to the Nurses' Station while Fell stood guard at the door of Room 506.

FORTY

As he searched for a parking space, Stas thought he recognized Lisa hurrying toward the hospital entrance. Although she reacted to his horn, she had not looked at him. In that split second, he remembered the bag she carried resembling the one he had seen in Meiers's living room.

So they have the money.

After parking, Stas found Townsend about twenty feet from the hospital entrance engaging in his favorite activity, lighting up.

"Why are you way out here?"

Townsend pointed to a sign. "No smoking within twenty feet."

"Can't you save it for later?"

"Okay." Ralph stepped on the pinched off smoldering edge of the cigarette and put it in his jacket pocket.

When they entered the building, both men knew that something was seriously wrong. Hospital security was moving people away from the elevators and escorting them towards the exit.

"You can't go up!" A guard blocked Townsend and Stas.

Stas produced his badge. "What's going on?"

The guard moved aside, allowing Stas enough room to pass. "There's some kind of problem on the fifth floor. Haz Mat is on the way."

"I'm going up. Wait for me outside."

Townsend headed for the exit. Before he reached the door, he had his bent cigarette out, and had started to light it. No one seemed to care as the first swirl of smoke curled around his face.

Stas took the stairs two at a time until he reached the third floor. He stopped to catch his breath then continued. When he opened the door to the fifth floor, near pandemonium had broken out. Aides and nurses were moving patients towards the opposite end of the hall to another stairwell. A stream of wheelchairs and gurneys, some with IV's attached were being moved with the flow of foot traffic. Dodging the exodus as best he could, Stas made his way to Officer Ryan's desk.

"What happened?" He joined Ryan against the wall.

"A gas leak in 506? I'm not sure, but you'd better get back downstairs. Hospital security's taking over."

"Is anyone dead?"

He shook his head. "I didn't see anyone come out."

Stas took the stairs back to the lobby and went out to meet Townsend, hunched over still another cigarette.

"Man, can you stop with the smokes. You want to blow us all away? There's gas leaking somewhere."

The reporter stepped on his butt and grabbed his notebook and pen.

By now, security was busy moving people away from the entrance. Emergency vehicles and one marked CORONER were using the ER entrance. That area had been completely sealed off.

"What's going on?" Townsend asked.

"There's been an accident up on the fifth floor, probably with fatalities." Stas looked around to see if he recognized any of the police arriving on the scene. "Lawson and Aagard are on the fifth floor."

"No shit." Townsend's cigarette fell to the pavement trailed by a thin tail of smoke.

Stas ground out the butt.

The reporter's instinct kicked in as he reached for his notepad and pen and started back inside.

Another uniformed security guard waved him away. Despite their credentials, neither Townsend nor Stas could now get past the first floor entrance. All visitors and non-patients had been dispersed during the first hour. No one was being allowed inside. Stas pulled Townsend aside.

"I got to get in. I can't get a story standing out here."

"Let's just wait."

Townsend nervously lit another cigarette, the last in his pack. Even when detectives from Hollywood Division arrived, no one tossed him a bone. Officer Ryan came out and handed Stas a cup of lukewarm coffee.

"Thanks."

"That's the best I could do." Ryan joined them. "You'd think we had the president in there."

"Did the coroner go up yet?" Stas knew no one collected anything until the Medical Examiner finished with his preliminary investigation.

"Nurse told me they're going to post the bodies here."

"Bodies?" Both men spoke in unison.

"Yeah, four, three men and a woman. I do know that much."

At that moment, a police SUV, used for ferrying around VIPs, arrived at the entrance. A uniformed officer jumped out and opened the back door. A woman, dressed in a dark blue business suit, stepped out. She could have been dressed in a uniform so evident was her police aura. The officer rushed around to the other rear door, but the Captain was already coming around to take the woman's arm.

Officer Ryan whispered. "That's his wife."

"Whose wife?" Stas asked.

"The candidate, Lawson," Ryan added.

"Was Aagard's wife in the room?" Townsend was starting to take notes.

"I don't know. I didn't see who went in."

Stas shot him a questioning look.

"I went to the john." Ryan seemed embarrassed.

It was Captain Taylor who nodded to Stas as he escorted Gwen Lawson into the building.

"That's it. I'm going home. They're not going to tell me anything. They'll probably want to know what I'm even doing here when I'm supposed to be on vacation."

"Then read about it in the paper." Townsend laughed. "I'm not leaving 'til I get a story. By the way, where's Dina?"

Stas glared at Townsend but didn't reply.

"How is she?" .

"Dina's fine." Stas replied.

"Can I get her number?"

"No, Ralph, she doesn't like smokers. That's why I gave them up." Stas started to walk toward the parking lot.

Townsend smiled at the obvious lie and peered into the empty pack, hoping against hope to find one last cigarette. He crumpled the pack. "Maybe I'll give them up someday," he paused and blew imaginary smoke in Stas's direction, "for a good woman."

FORTY-ONE

Stas had gone out early for bagels, cream cheese, and chocolate croissants for Dina, but the grocery bag still stood by the door. He had spread out the *Times* and the *Star News* on the coffee table. One headline read, "Gas Leak Takes Four Lives" and the other, "Gas Leak Kills Congressional Hopeful."

What gas leak?

Both papers ran pictures of Edward Lawson on the campaign trail, but it was the photo of Captain Taylor and Gwen Lawson that grabbed Stas's immediate attention. They both looked solemn, yet confident. Both displayed police-spokespersons' faces, the ones they gave to the public when tragedy struck.

Gwen knew the drill. She'd done it often enough in Fresno. The caption beneath the photo introduced the widow to the Los Angeles public. The article announced that she was going to take her husband's place in the primary.

Way to go, Stas thought, get those sympathy votes before your tears dry up.

He turned his attention to Townsend's story. It had made the first page. Stas could almost smell the nicotine whirling around in the details. It was an article written with smoke and mirrors. Any first year detective could have seen through most of it. It seems Lawson, Aagard and two aides had been overcome by gas that had been kept in a maintenance room between 506 and 502. The gas had seeped into Aagard's room through a vent.

Bullshit! Is that the best you can do?

Hospital staff and the LAPD were conducting a full investigation with Captain Taylor coordinating the task force. Stas remembered their earlier conversation. Someone was indeed, "catching the nearest way." Surveillance cameras had recorded a heating and air conditioning tech entering and leaving the area. This was being investigated.

Turning the pages to finish Townsend's article, Stas saw another interesting story, with a picture of a familiar face. Dr. Hans Meiers was handing over a check to a biotech research team headed by Dr. William Meyer.

Before he could finish both pieces, Dina came in with her tote bag. Now all of her things were collected by the door. Then he saw the brown bag. He jumped up and took it to the kitchen.

"I forgot breakfast. Read the *Times* article. Townsend put a great spin on the official story. Marlowe called to see if I'd be back at work Monday and told me that one of the guys from the chase up north was from Tennessee, had recently been released from prison. Last name was Brown. You think that's a coincidence?"

"Unless he was related to Matt."

"Or worked for Honey? Also, they're looking hard for those guys involved in drive-by. I bet I'll be working that when I get back." He smiled, "Might mean some overtime."

Dina did not comment but sat a small box wrapped in silver paper and tied with turquoise ribbon next to the newspaper and turned back to the first page. Stas returned with two mugs of coffee and went back to the kitchen for the bagels and croissants.

Dina looked up. "Thanks." She turned back to the paper after taking a sip. "Do you believe this?"

"The public has to. What I believe doesn't matter. What I care doesn't matter. But...." He turned to the photo of Meiers. "this speaks volumes."

Dina moved closer. "Isn't this the guy being blackmailed? Didn't he give them a bag of money?"

"Quarter million. I saw it, --- or thought I saw it. He told me it was a quarter million. It was in a blue gym bag, the same kind Lisa carried into the hospital." Stas reread the caption under the photo again. "He donated $250,000 to Trans-Global Bio-Chem

Labs. You can make some real special gas with that kind of money."

"You know..." she looked at the caption again, "the other doctor would be Wilhelm Meiers in German. I wonder if they're related? Hmmm, another coincidence?"

Stas sat back and drank his coffee. He felt a pang of satisfaction that the short arm of vengeance could outreach the long arm of the law, and he smiled.

Dina put her mug down and handed him a box as she stood.

"What's this?"

"A little thank-you gift." She started towards the bedroom.

He threw the wrapping and ribbon onto the newspaper and flipped open the hinged lid. The box was empty. He looked up, puzzled. "So what is it?"

"I guess you'll have to strip search me to find it."

Stas rose and followed. "No problem. You know our motto, 'to serve and...'"

Later he emerged from the bedroom still damp from a shower, a towel wrapped around his midsection. He headed for his desk and searched several drawers before noticing the red message light blinking on the phone. The first voice was Ralph Townsend.

"Stas, what's wrong with your cell? Listen, we gotta talk. I'm trying to set up an interview with Mrs. Lawson. Hospital's not talking. Call me."

The second voice oozed honey. He could even imagine one of her dance poses as she spoke.

"This is Livia. I just wanted to invite you over one evening for dinner, sort of a little thank you. Call me or come by."

Stas looked at his wrist at the gift from Dina. It was a Tag Heuer, the real thing. Then he remembered. He wanted, needed a cigarette, and there was one that Townsend had given him at the hospital. It was in his jacket pocket, a little beat-up, but smokeable. He was searching for a match and ended up in the kitchen lighting the cigarette from the stove when Dina stuck her head through the door.

"How long before you're ready?"

He looked down at the towel and his damp body. "Give me twenty minutes, no make it an hour. Got to make a few phone calls."

Stas parked next to Dina's Green Saab in her building's garage. He wondered if it would start after sitting idle since they had returned it. He'd give it a try before he left. Dina was out of his car before he could get to her door.

"Look at my poor car."

"It just needs a good wash and wax job. I'll start it up for you later."

He popped his trunk, took out her shopping bags, and carried them to the elevator. She followed with her black tote.

"You take these things up. I'll bring the rest."

Dina pushed the UP button while he went back to the car. The elevator door opened immediately, and Stas was still fumbling in the trunk. As the doors closed, she dreaded going up to a cold, lifeless apartment.

When she stepped from the elevator into the hallway, everything looked the same, even the smells were familiar. When she opened the door to her apartment, she was surprised by the scent of jasmine. The lights were on, and a lovely bouquet of flowers was arranged in a vase on the coffee table. The apartment was warm and inviting. It felt good to be home.

She took her bags to the bedroom. There was another vase of flowers and a little bowl of still smoldering incense. She sat on the edge of the bed trying to control her emotions.

She forced a smile when Stas entered her bedroom with her other bag.

"Did you do all this?" she asked.

"I had a little help."

"I'm afraid to ask what it cost."

"Livia's having me over for dinner."

"Just make sure she's not having you for dessert."

Later, Stas sat relaxed on the sofa in the living room. Dina had put on a Diana Krall CD, and the soft, sensuous ballads relaxed him. She had lit another bowl of incense before going into the kitchen, and he was aware of the faint scent of something earthy soothing his senses.

She brought him coffee and a glass of wine for herself. A fifth of Chopin Vodka also stood on the tray.

"I found this in my freezer."

"I know, I put it there." He smiled, hoping she would understand the significance of the vodka without him needing to explain. It was something he wasn't ready to discuss. She would just have to let it run out his way.

"Do I need to get any special glasses for the vodka?"

"Whatever you have will do." He reached for his coffee. "What's that smell?" he asked.

"It's an incense called angelica. It's good for balancing, keeping you grounded."

"Nice, I guess I could get use to it."

They sat in silence for a moment.

"You know, I never understood about the wine glasses."

He looked puzzled.

"Sybil's glasses. Especially the one May told us about," she added.

"I guess Aagard put flunitrazepan or something like it in her drink. When it knocked her out, the bastard probably couldn't resist one last fuck before he killed her. He washed his glass but put it in the wrong place. Nobody tested it because nobody suspected. The glass at her bedside had only a residue of wine."

He drained his coffee and put the cup on the table. "I guess the only other thing that wasn't found was the suicide note that vanished."

"I can't believe it's all over." Dina was finding it difficult controlling her emotions. "And us?"

"I don't know. We'll have to see. I have some issues to work through, and the most pressing is your 'job'."

"We've had this discussion before. I don't want to give it up, not yet."

"Don't do it for me, babe. Do it for yourself."

"I like my..."

He interrupted. "You're lying to yourself and to me. If what we have is just physical, then I guess it doesn't matter, but if there's something to start to build on... I just can't share you with other men." He rose and put on his jacket. "I'll call you when I get back?"

"From where?"

"I'm taking the redeye to Chicago. I go back to work Monday."

"Will I have to wait another two years?"

"No, this time I'll call, I promise."

Stas walked over to her little antique desk. He opened the top drawers and took out one of the carved boxes handing it to Dina.

"I wanted you to have this one."

She rubbed her hand over the surface but said nothing.

"Look inside." he added.

Dina raised the lid. She took out the PDA and held it up to him. "What's this?"

"I could give it to Vice, but... I'd have a lot of explaining to do. You can give it to Raven or keep it. This little baby should give you some leverage. Kick you up to management."

Dina put the PDA back in the box and turned as if to speak.

"I've got to go, babe." He planted a light kiss on her lips. "By the way, I love... my watch."

FORTY-TWO

He left his Mercedes at an airport car park with instructions to detail it while he was gone. The redeye from LAX to Chicago deposited Stas at O'Hare at 6:35 a. m. When he stepped out of the airport, the icy wind cut through his lightweight coat like scissors cutting through tissue. Even protected by the overhang on the ground level, he had to retreat back into the glass enclosure to look out for the taxi stop. He waited until he saw one pull up before he rushed out.

After getting into the taxi, he settled in for the ride into the city. There wasn't much to see. The expressway flanked the city's downtown to the west, but he marveled at the towering skyline dominated by the Sears Tower. He wanted to see Lake Michigan, but his cousin lived on the west side of the city, near Oak Park. The lake would have to wait.

His cousin, Josephine Svec, had married a Czech, much to the family's dismay and disapproval. She was now a widow and found herself once again welcomed into the loving arms of her family. She lived with her widowed sister-in-law who was a Hungarian and had also been forgiven for marrying one of the Svec brothers. Both women lived in one of those brown brick bungalows that seem to have been the signature middle-class dwellings of early 20th century Chicago.

When Stas got out of the cab, he had to step gingerly over patches of melting snow. Josephine stood behind the storm door and waited for him to get close enough to whisk him inside without giving up any of the house's precious heat. When he entered, he understood why she guarded the door, for a blast of hot, stale air hit him once he stepped into the little dark entryway.

Josephine had been pretty in her youth, but years of hard work, a drinking, abusive husband, and an unsympathetic family had taken its toll. She took his tote and coat.

"Come on in the kitchen. I got coffee on."

"That sounds good." He followed her through a cozy living room. The dining room looked like his parents' in California, used only for holidays. It was a room that he always considered a waste.

The kitchen was warm and cozy. She had made coffee in an old, metal percolator. It smelled rich and strong. She let him savor the taste and warm his insides before she asked any questions. Josephine asked about family and friends still living in Los Angeles. They both knew it was the small talk leading up to the reason for his visit. They would get around to Irina and Sybil soon enough.

She made breakfast of kielbasa, fried onions, and eggs. There was also a warm poppy-seed coffee cake the likes of which Stas hadn't tasted in years. When he finally pushed his empty plate away, he patted his stomach, and wished for a smoke.

"Thanks, that was great." He looked at his watch. "I didn't have time to book a hotel. Is there something around here?"

"That's nonsense. We got an extra room. You stay right here."

Stas didn't argue. "It's only for one night. I have to be back at work Monday."

"You were on vacation?" Josephine asked.

Stas smiled. "I guess you might call it that."

She brought the coffee pot to the table and refilled his cup. "You look a lot like Irina."

He slowly sipped and waited for her to go on.

"She grieved a lot over you, wanting to have you with her, but it just wasn't to be."

"Irina talked about me?"

"All the time."

"And Sybil? Did she ever ask about me?"

"That was different. She knew she had a brother, but there was never any discussion. I don't think she knew anything about you. After she went to LA, she came back only once, for the funeral. She never liked Chicago. She never fit in. She didn't like being Polish."

"I want to visit the cemetery."

Josephine got up from the table. "I have some things to show you. I had hoped that one day you and Sybil would have come back for a visit."

After taking a shower and a little rest, Stas took a drive with his cousin around Oak Park. She was especially excited to point out some of Frank Lloyd Wright's creations. The chill finally got to him so they stopped to buy an all-weather coat with a zip-out wool lining and a pair of black cashmere-lined kid gloves. Josephine tried to talk him into buying a cap, but he convinced her he still had enough hair to keep his head warm.

In their walk, they passed a small jewelry store with a window display of enamel animals, replicas of some of the residents of the Brookfield Zoo. Stas told Josephine he'd meet her back at the car and hurried in. He bought a black and white panda, dropping the little package into his coat pocket so he wouldn't have to explain it to his cousin.

On his way back to the car, he bought a dozen long stem white roses at a florist and waited while the clerk slipped the end of each stem into little water filled glass vials. She assured him that they would keep beautifully for at least a week.

Sunday morning dawned cold and crisp. WGN had forecast snow. Stas stood in the driveway breathing out misty vapors, enjoying the sensation like a child anticipating his first winter sleigh ride. The Yellow Taxi arrived and honked. Josephine and Vera came out on the porch on their way to mass.

There were hugs and promises of future visits as he cradled the wrapped roses in one arm and threw his bag onto the back seat of the cab.

Josephine handed him a faded blue envelope. "She left this for me to give you, when you found out. Read it later." She wiped away tears and waved good-bye.

The cab took Stas to the cemetery. His cousin had given him a folded map to the gravesite. He wandered around for a few minutes and found it on a raised mound of barren earth covered with remnants of dry, brown grass. As he approached, he looked up. Clouds were breaking up, revealing pale blue sky and bright mellow sunshine.

When Stas unwrapped the roses from their cellophane, they gave off a faint, subtle fragrance that reminded him of Irina. He breathed deeply, from his gut. This time there was no pain, only a bittersweet release. He stood in silence after placing the white roses on the dead, gray stone. It was a stark reminder of the life they never shared. At least Sybil had had Irina for a while. He had only the stolen moments, the secret fantasies.

He bent to read the simple granite marker:

IRINA BAIKOWSKI JONES
1934-1989
NIECH SPOCZYWA W POKOJU
(REST IN PEACE)

When he turned to go, a strong gust of wind blew, picking up several of the delicate white flowers, scattering some of their petals to neighboring graves. Stas watched a few remnants of dead leaves blow before him when he walked to the waiting cab. As it drove slowly down the winding, cemetery roadway towards the east, the skyline of downtown Chicago came into view.

ABOUT THE AUTHOR

B. K. De Paolis, an assistant professor of English at Pasadena City College, has lived and taught in Italy, and now lives in the Pasadena, CA area. This book is the first in a mystery series featuring LAPD's detective, Stas Nowak.

www.ingramcontent.com/pod-product-compliance
Lightning Source LLC
LaVergne TN
LVHW091020080826
845145LV00002B/311

* 9 7 8 0 6 1 5 8 8 0 4 2 6 *